'Amanda Jennings is a writer on the ascendant and *The Storm* is her best novel yet. This twisty, malevolent and gripping story is virtually impossible to put down'
Lisa Jewell

'Beautifully written, chilling and absorbing'
Adele Parks

'Amanda Jennings is a fantastic storyteller and she's at her very best here: warm-hearted, darkly atmospheric, and wholly addictive'
Lucy Atkins

'Suspenseful, beautifully written, and utterly compelling'
Alice Feeney

'A brilliant book. Gripping, intelligent, and beautifully written'
Cass Green

'Vivid and evocative, the beautifully drawn characters and Cornish setting will linger in your mind long after you've turned the final page'
Lucy Dawson

'*The Storm* is both beautifully crafted and chilling. A compelling tale you won't want to put down'
Colette McBeth

'A claustrophobic, brooding, atmospheric novel. No one writes complicated, conflicted characters like Amanda Jennings'
Tammy Cohen

'A chilling, atmospheric and addictive tale'
Roz Watkins

'I was blown away by its brilliance. I loved it!'
Michelle Davies

Amanda Jennings lives in Oxfordshire with her husband, three daughters, and a menagerie of animals. She studied History of Art at Cambridge and before writing her first book, was a researcher at the BBC. With a deep fascination for the far-reaching effects of trauma, her books focus on the different ways people find to cope with loss, as well as the moral struggles her protagonists face. When she isn't writing she can usually be found walking the dog. Her favourite place to be is up a mountain or beside the sea.

Also by Amanda Jennings

The Cliff House
In Her Wake
The Judas Scar
Sworn Secret

The Storm

Amanda Jennings

ONE PLACE. MANY STORIES

This novel is entirely a work of fiction. The names, characters and incidents portrayed in it are the work of the author's imagination. Any resemblance to actual persons, living or dead, events or localities is entirely coincidental.

HQ
An imprint of HarperCollins*Publishers* Ltd
1 London Bridge Street
London SE1 9GF

www.harpercollins.co.uk

HarperCollins*Publishers*
1st Floor, Watermarque Building, Ringsend Road
Dublin 4, Ireland

This edition 2021

1

First published in Great Britain by
HQ, an imprint of HarperCollins*Publishers* Ltd 2020

Copyright © Amanda Jennings 2020

Amanda Jennings asserts the moral right to be
identified as the author of this work.
A catalogue record for this book is
available from the British Library.

ISBN: 978-0-00-848780-5

MIX
Paper from
responsible sources
FSC™ C007454

This book is produced from independently certified FSC™ paper
to ensure responsible forest management.

For more information visit: www.harpercollins.co.uk/green

This book is set in Sabon

Printed and Bound in Spain using 100% Renewable Electricity at
CPI Blackprint (Barcelona)

All rights reserved. No part of this publication may be reproduced,
stored in a retrieval system, or transmitted, in any form or by any means,
electronic, mechanical, photocopying, recording or otherwise,
without the prior permission of the publishers.

This book is sold subject to the condition that it shall not, by way of trade
or otherwise, be lent, re-sold, hired out or otherwise circulated without
the publisher's prior consent in any form of binding or cover other than
that in which it is published and without a similar condition including this
condition being imposed on the subsequent purchaser.

To Chris. My one and only.

Ever has it been that love knows not its own depth until the hour of separation.

KAHLIL GIBRAN

PROLOGUE

The chill December wind blows in gusts, turning drizzle to slivers of glass and scoring the sea with angry white slashes. A boat emerges through the dawn mist like a ghostly galleon. The man at the helm is still and rigid. He cuts the engine and the small vessel drifts into dock. He moves to the side of the boat and bends for a coiled rope, which he throws over a bollard with ease. He pulls the rope tight and secures it at the cleat. His movements are sure, his features set in sombre concentration. The man reaches down and takes hold of the boat's hose and, grim-faced, he washes the deck down. All the surfaces and edges and crevices. He takes great care.

He climbs out of the boat and begins to walk up the jetty. But he stops halfway and his head and shoulders slump forward like a marionette with snapped strings. For a few moments he is motionless, spent, his arms hanging limp at his sides, but then he rallies, straightens his back, forces himself along the gangway past the discarded fishing nets and stacked crates patched with algae and salt stains. Each step is heavy with the air of a condemned man approaching the gallows.

He thinks the port is deserted. He thinks he's alone with only the waking seagulls and the echo of his laboured footsteps for company. But he's wrong.

He isn't alone.

There is somebody watching.

CHAPTER ONE

Hannah

In the early days, when memories of that night ambushed me at every opportunity, routine was my lifeline. Routine gave me a set of stepping stones over the quicksand. It got me through my days without thinking. Thinking wasn't good for me. Thinking was where the madness lay.

These days, fifteen years on, I rely less on routine. I've let go of the smaller things. I no longer wear navy on a Monday, for example, or pull my hair – twisted clockwise, using seven pins – into a tight bun on a Thursday. The bigger jobs, the weekly chores, still have their set days, more, I think, because I find it comforting rather than necessary. Today is a Tuesday, so after I've walked the dog, I'll catch the 10.07 bus into Penzance to meet Vicky, spend an hour with her, shop for what I need that day, then catch the 14.13 home, and make our supper. I cook from scratch every day. On a Tuesday I make something with lamb. For ease, I rotate three of Nathan's favourites: shepherd's pie, Lancashire hotpot, moussaka.

Today it's shepherd's pie.

'Come on then,' I say to the dog.

Cass enjoys routine as much as I do and has been waiting at the back door, her eyes bolted to me, since Alex left for school.

When I lift her lead from the hook she jumps up and spins excited circles around me. I swear this dog smiles proper smiles. Her face breaks in two, white teeth on show, eyes crinkled with joyful anticipation.

'Silly dog,' I whisper, as she bounds out of the back door and along the gravel path which folds around the house. When she gets to the gate she stops and glances back at me, jogging on the spot with impatience.

Cass is a tricoloured collie-cross from the animal rescue in Truro. She has odd eyes, one brown, the other – a wall eye – the colour of glacier ice, the pale blue accentuated by the pirate's patch of black fur which surrounds it. When we aren't walking, she spends her time curled up in her basket in the kitchen or stretched out on the front doorstep, paws neatly crossed, watching the world with her dewy mismatched eyes. Nathan took some convincing. I begged for years. A home isn't a home without a dog, I'd said. Thankfully he was swayed by the 'a large country house needs a dog' argument I pushed. I'm not exaggerating when I say that before Cass arrived to keep me company, the never-ending hours spent in this suffocating place were torture. Nathan has never taken to her, but she's clever and keeps herself inconspicuous when he's around.

The gate clicks shut behind us and I breathe in deeply, relishing, as I do every day, the immediate sense of freedom. I loathe the house. Disquiet ferments in its shadows and the air inside is heavy as if each molecule is formed from lead. To the outside world Trevose House is impressive, huge and undeniably beautiful, a grand building which passersby take note of. I watch them sometimes, from the window on the first floor landing, concealed from sight behind the musty damask

4

curtains. Walkers on the lane who slow down to take a better look, occasionally stop and lean casually over the wall to point out features and nod with appreciation. Some take photographs on their phone. Perhaps for Instagram. Hashtag *housegoals*. Sometimes, if I'm outside, hanging the laundry or pinning back raspberry canes, they might catch sight of me and blush, ashamed of their snooping, hastily informing me how lovely my home is as if this will excuse their intrusion. A curt nod and no attempt to engage invariably sends them scurrying away and I become no more than an easily dismissed entry etched into the diary of their day, *the dour owner of that beautiful house we walked past.*

Trevose House, near New Mill, with iron gates which close with a clang and lock with a large key more at home on the belt of a gaoler. Two stone pillars stand guard either side. The granite walls are studded with a line of sash windows and three wide steps lead up to a grand doorway beside which the date of construction – 1753 – is carved into the seal-grey stone. The house was the principal dwelling on land profitably run by the Cardew family for generations. That was, until Nathan's father got involved. Charles Cardew was a poker-loving drunk who, between inheriting the estate in his mid-thirties and killing himself at fifty-two, sold most of it off in chunks to pay gambling debts. Three hundred acres or so, four farm workers' cottages, and a number of characterful barns which, as Nathan often tells me bitterly, could have been converted into lucrative holiday rentals.

Nathan has no fond memories of his father and rarely mentions him with anything other than contempt in his voice. According to my mother, Charles was a *drog-polat* – a rascal – with a twinkle in his eye. He spent most of his time in the pubs of Penzance and Newlyn, buying drinks for the locals and losing his money to anybody willing to sit down and play cards with him. He shot himself in the face in the study at Trevose House on Nathan's thirteenth birthday. Nathan and his sister, Kerensa, who was seventeen, found him. It turned out the debts he'd run up were far worse than he'd let on and, after she'd replaced the carpet in the study, it fell to Nathan's mother to clear up the financial mess he'd left behind. Sylvia Cardew had, in her own words, *no time for fools, gluttons, the idle or weak*, and slowly but surely she managed to sort out the chaos. Kerensa ran away from home soon after Charles killed himself and – if *sotto voce* local rumours were to be believed – died from a heroin overdose in a squalid bedsit in Hastings eight months later. Though Nathan doesn't talk about his sister, there's a photograph of her in a silver frame on his desk, taken when she was about fifteen or sixteen. She sits in the garden of Trevose, holding a blade of grass, smiling at something, or someone, unseen beyond the camera. Her hair is plaited into a loose braid and she's dressed in a long flowery skirt and muslin shirt. Bare feet. A silver ring on her middle toe. She wears no make-up and her face is dusted with freckles, her eyes shining with joyful abandon. I think I would have liked her.

Sylvia Cardew didn't stay in Cornwall. She once told me, lips pursed, nose wrinkled as if smelling something vile, that she'd never got on with the county – *too parochial, too backward* – but I'm certain it was scandal and snide whispers that drove her away. Whatever the reason, the curtains at Trevose House were drawn and the furniture sheeted, and she and Nathan, aged fifteen, moved to a mews house with neat window boxes in Kensington. When Nathan and I married, she bequeathed him their holiday home as a wedding gift. It was riddled with ghosts she wanted nothing more to do with, so instead gave them to me.

'Live in it. Sell it. Burn it to the godforsaken ground for all I care.'

My mother-in-law is the type of woman who chills the air when she enters a room. God knows what it must have been like having her as a mother. Thankfully she refuses to see me. On our first meeting, over tea served from a paper-thin china teapot decorated with gold patterning, she smiled and said lightly, 'I would have expected Nathan to choose someone quite different. More bookish. Brighter. With a degree in a modern language, perhaps, or the history of art. Still,' she went on, sipping her tea, 'one can never know what happens behind a closed bedroom door. I am sure you are *excellent* at what you do. It's just a shame my son wasn't more careful. Shotgun weddings lack class.'

On the rare occasions Nathan needs to see her, he makes the journey to London alone, but never stays more than an hour or two. Serves her right. She's a stuck-up cow. The only thing I wish is she'd taken her husband's ghost with her. He's there wherever I go in the house. As I walk from room to room I can feel him watching me, his face blown apart, an unidentifiable mush leering at me from every corner. I pleaded with Nathan to sell up, but he wouldn't hear of it. What man wants to live in the house where his father committed suicide?

It's not all bad. The inside of the house might give me the shivers but I adore the garden. The plot is enclosed by a drystone wall that plays host to an array of colourful flowers between

May and October. Beyond the boundary we're surrounded by farmland and in the summer months, when the cows are on the pasture, I lean on the wall and watch them, content and languid as they graze, flicking their tails at the flies which irritate their gentle eyes. The air hangs with their scent, but occasionally, if I'm lucky, an onshore breeze will bring up the smell of the sea and with it the heady memories of my childhood.

There's a substantial lawn which takes over two hours to mow. I do it on a Friday because Nathan likes it nice for the weekend. Huge flowerbeds brim over with rhododendrons, camellias, azaleas and agapanthus, and in the far corner is a regimented vegetable patch, put in by Nathan and covered over with netting to keep off the birds. He restored the Victorian greenhouse a number of years ago and now spends his time nurturing his tomatoes and cucumbers, red peppers and courgettes, protecting them from thieving rodents and brushing their skins clean of greenfly and dust. He digs powdered ox blood into the compost and repots the delicate seedlings, handling each one as if made of glass.

Mum and Dad made their first trip to the house soon after we arrived back from our honeymoon in the Dordogne. Mum had dressed Dad in a tie I didn't know he owned which he apparently kept for *funerals and the like*. The two of them sat on the edge of the sofa, hands clasped in their laps, spines starched rigid, shifting in their seats like fidgeting children in church. Mum cleared her throat constantly, which made me want to scream, whilst Dad tapped out some sort of SOS in Morse code with his freshly polished shoe, knowing full well the funeral tie was fooling nobody. Despite their discomfort a mantle of pride hung over them both. At one point Mum lost

8

control and a beaming smile erupted on her face as she nudged Dad's knee and exclaimed in her broad Cornish accent, 'Oh, Harry, can you believe it? Our *melder*, lady of the manor!'

I remember being dazed and confused, as if waking from an operation, anaesthesia clogging my veins. Where the hell was I? How on earth had I got there? *Stop it*, I wanted to shriek at them. *Stop being so impressed. You've nothing to be impressed by.* It was as if I were no longer their daughter, but had emerged altered from a cocoon, an unrecognisable stranger sitting opposite them.

A few weeks later I'd mentioned this to Mum. Her smile, warm and kind, made my heart ache. 'That's normal, *melder*.' Her voice was silky with love. 'You *are* a different person now. You're Mrs Nathan Cardew.' Then she glanced at my stomach, which had begun to swell against the cotton of my skirt refusing to stay concealed any longer. 'And you've got the *babi* to think about now.'

After our walk, I change quickly, drag a brush through my hair, and kiss Cass before walking briskly down to wait for the bus. The bus stop is no more sophisticated than a laminated timetable nailed to a telegraph pole, riddled with woodworm, on the overgrown verge. It's about a quarter of a mile from the house. I always leave plenty of time to walk down and, as usual, am ten minutes early. I lean back against the telegraph pole and tip my face into the warmth of the sun. For a moment I allow my mind to drift to where it's desperate to be.

With you.

We are on the beach at Godrevy. The sky is the colour of cornflowers, the wind cold and fresh, the mid-October sunshine is bright. Your hand is warm and holds mine tightly as if you're worried I might blow away. I'm talking too much. About everything and nothing. Suddenly self-conscious, I stop myself and look up at you.

You smile. *Carry on,* you say.

I'm not boring you?

Boring me? You laugh and it sounds like music. *How could you ever bore me?*

It's low tide. The beach is deserted but for a man sweeping a metal detector like a metronome over the ribbed sand. I can smell the mussel-cloaked rocks. The sea. Drying seaweed. You unpack the picnic you made. Thin squares of electric pink ham on sliced white, spread with margarine.

Mum would call you a criminal for not using butter.

Your sheepish smile melts my heart. Your body is hard and muscular. Not an ounce of fat. The feel of it excites me as I lean against you.

I'm sorry, you say.

It's delicious, I whisper. *Best sandwich I ever tasted.*

We talk. Drink Fosters. Smoke roll-ups and kiss. We don't notice the tide coming in until the sea skims our toes. We're trapped. We laugh. Jump up. Hold hands and wade through the icy water to reach the path. I stumble, giddy from the lager and kissing, and you catch my elbow.

Saved you, you say.

I miss you.

I had no idea how important these moments would become. At the time it was just a picnic on the beach. With a boy I was falling in love with. Something fun to do at the weekend. We had no idea how fleeting our happiness would be. We took love for granted. We imagined we'd always be free. But now the memory of that picnic on Godrevy is a scrap of precious fabric I cling to like a child with their blanket, comforting and safe, ragged with overuse. I remember the heat of him. I can taste the cigarettes on his breath. As I let his lips linger on mine, my pulse quickens. I recall the smell of him. The feel of his skin against mine. The sound of his voice as he whispered in my ear.

It only takes a moment for grief to take over. My stomach pitches with loss and the image of him dissolves, leaving the space where he was desolate and empty. Regret seeps into every nook of me.

If only I could replay that night. Do things differently. Alter our course.

If only.

I hear the bus wending its way along the lane and push myself off the telegraph pole. It draws to a halt and the door opens with a hydraulic sigh. The driver, who's been driving this route for years, greets me like a friend. I count my fare out. I no longer apologise for the coppers. He waits patiently as I drop them into the dish and thanks me when I'm done.

I don't know his name and the only words we've exchanged are the occasional comment on the weather and a 'Happy Christmas' or 'Happy New Year' when seasonally appropriate. I always sit close enough to watch his face in the rearview mirror. He wears his happiness like a medal of honour. Right there, on show, unashamedly proud of it. He is one of those people who whistles a tune. Sometimes he'll spontaneously smile and when he does, it makes me glow as I imagine he's recalling something funny or touching. Perhaps he's thinking of his wife and children clamouring around him when he gets home from shuttling backwards and forwards between Land's End and Penzance. I imagine he has a simple life. An allotment. A comfortable, threadbare armchair he'll never throw out. I find imagining this man in a life of contentment comforting. My Tuesday bus journey is something I look forward to. On the rare Tuesdays when there's an unknown at the wheel, I can become inexplicably agitated, as if my world has tipped and I'm sliding towards the edge.

Like I said, routine helps.

CHAPTER TWO

Hannah

'Please. *God*. Tell me you're joking.'

Vicky and I are sitting opposite each other at one of the six tables in the café we meet at every week. It's on a back street in Penzance. The walls are light blue, in need of a touch-up, and there are paintings of birds and huge Cornish skies done by local artists. When it's warm enough, the door is wedged open and the small space floods with natural light, sea air and the cry of gulls. It's cheap and basic, the type of place Nathan wouldn't be seen dead in. Which is, of course, why we meet here.

Vicky shakes her head in disbelief. 'But *why*?'

Her blonde hair is tied back in a scruffy bun, and even without a scrap of make-up and four-year-old twins who never sleep, she is as pretty as she always was. Her skin is smooth, religiously moisturised, and the lines around her hazel eyes so delicate it's as if they've been painted on with the finest of brushes.

The waitress places our pot of tea on the table, with a slice of coffee cake for Vicky, and toast and jam for me.

'Guess that means you won't be coming along to cheer for him?' I lift the lid of the teapot to see if it's brewed enough then pour two cups.

'No, I bloody won't. I mean... *really*? An *award*? Why would the council give a lawyer an award?'

'I told you. Citizen of the Year.'

She groans and mutters something under her breath.

Vicky makes no effort to hide her dislike of my husband. When I told her Cam and I were finished and I was with Nathan she was having none of it. We'd known each other since nursery. Our mums were friends and we played together for happy hours while they gossiped and drank tea. From primary school through secondary school we were inseparable. We went to our first gig together, got drunk together, smoked our first cigarette together – stealthily swiped from her mother's pack of Benson & Hedges – and went to as many parties as we could, invited and uninvited. Vicky knows me better than anybody else and there was no way she would ever believe I'd fallen head over heels for Nathan Cardew in only a matter of days. All she did was shake her head.

'No,' she'd said, refusing to believe it. 'No. There's something you're not telling me.'

She also wouldn't accept Cam had just upped and gone in the night without even a goodbye. Her interrogations were exhausting. I'd struggled to keep strong, because all I really wanted to do was curl myself into her arms and tell her the truth. All of it. Every last, filthy detail.

Would things have turned out better if I had? Could she have helped me? Sitting in front of her now, I have yet another overwhelming urge to confide in her. But I can't risk it. The fallout would be devastating. I've kept the truth buried for long enough. I'm not going to unearth it now.

When I found out I was pregnant things got even harder.

'You *have* to tell Cam. He'll come back. Of course he will!'

This was when the real lies began.

'Don't you see?' I said, sobbing into my hands. 'I *did* tell him. That's why he left. He wants nothing to do with me. Nothing to do with the baby. He's moved on and says he's never coming back to Cornwall. He told me he never loved me. I didn't tell you because I was scared. Of the baby. Being pregnant. I hoped it would… go away. But… it didn't.'

Lies, lies, lies.

Lying to Vicky made me feel sick. But though the idea of the baby was terrifying, it finally gave me the perfect excuse for Cam's sudden disappearance. I dropped my head, unable to meet her eyes.

'Bastard,' she breathed. 'The fucking *bastard.*'

I didn't correct her.

'Does Nathan know?'

I nodded. 'He wants to get married.'

'And he'll accept Cam's baby? Just like that?'

I glanced at her but didn't reply.

'*No.* Surely no?' Judgement and shock in her whispered words. 'Hannah, you can't… '

Then I straightened my shoulders and took a bolstering breath. 'Women have done it since forever.'

'But it's not—'

'I don't want to have a baby on my own,' I said resolutely, stumbling unwittingly into the truth. 'What kind of life is that for either of us? I owe my child more than a bedsit and benefits. Nathan can give us a decent life.'

Her disapproval physically hurt.

I took her hand in mine as tears spilled down my cheeks.

'Please don't tell anybody. *Please*, Vicky. I don't want to be alone. I don't want my baby to grow up without a father.'

She went with it reluctantly, but when Nathan started to push my friends and family away, when he began to isolate me, her dislike of him grew into hatred, almost as strong as the hatred she has for Cam, the man who, as far as she is aware, abandoned her pregnant friend without a backward glance.

I unwrap one of the small packets of butter and spread some thinly on one of the triangles of toast.

'What does Citizen of the Year even mean?'

'He does a lot for the community. You know that. Apparently it was the first time in eighteen years that a nominee was universally voted through.'

She scoffs. 'And, what? You have to go and stand at his side and play the dutiful wife?' She breaks off a piece of cake and puts it in her mouth.

'Of course. I want to be there.' My attention is caught by a group of girls on the street outside, fourteen or so, dressed in school uniform, skirts rolled up to mid-thigh, giggling and pointing at something on one of their phones, the case decorated in pink diamante which catches the sunlight, fingernails painted in colours I'm certain their head teacher would disapprove of, eye make-up heavy, lips shiny with cheap pink gloss. Bunking off. These are the kids for whom school is a dull inconvenience and life outside its gates so much more enticing. Nostalgia prods at me like an annoying child. I tear my eyes off them and look back at Vicky. 'Apparently, some VIP from the council is going to do a speech.'

Another groan. 'Don't tell me they're giving him a bloody trophy.'

'A brass plaque in the town hall.' We exchange wry smiles and she laughs with another shake of her head.

The waitress clears our empty plates and asks if we'd like anything else. She's a striking girl with dreadlocks tied back in a floral scarf, a nose ring, and a puffy-eyed tiredness from partying. She reminds me of myself at the same age, smiling through a hangover whilst dropping pasties into bags for sunburnt tourists and beer money.

'How's your mum?' Vicky asks then.

I smile. 'She's OK. Sleeps a lot but seems fine.'

'And Alex?'

I press my finger on to some toast crumbs on the wipe-clean tablecloth and brush them on to my plate.

'He's fine. He's—' I stop myself.

'What?'

'Nothing.'

'Tell me.'

I take a breath. 'He's growing up, that's all. Getting argumentative.' I hesitate. 'With Nathan.'

'Good for him.' She lowers her eyes, perhaps aware that her comment could be taken as a criticism of me for not standing up for myself.

'It's nothing serious.' I continue picking up the scattered crumbs with my finger. 'Teenage stuff. He won't be the first boy in the world to have a tricky relationship with his dad. It's normal, isn't it?'

It surprises me how much the deterioration of Nathan and Alex's relationship still upsets me. It wasn't always the same. When Alex was younger Nathan was a good father, engaged and interested most of the time, albeit uptight and unaffectionate. But when Alex was around seven or eight he seemed to draw away from us. He became colder, more distant, as if somebody had flicked a switch off inside him. His temper was short. He was impatient and moody, too quick with caustic asides. It was around this time he had his first affair. Maybe he just got bored of us.

Vicky notices my anxiety and takes my hand. 'Yes, of course it's normal. God, do you remember the fights I had with my parents? I was convinced I was adopted.'

I smile.

'He's a good boy,' she says then. 'He reminds me of you when you were that age.'

Her words unleash snippets of memory from back then. The biting cold and crashing waves. The fear that grabbed hold of me. The dawning realisation that everything was altered.

'Change of subject.' Vicky's voice wrenches me back. 'Did you talk to him about our night away?'

Her face splits with sudden excitement and my insides cave a little as I recall Nathan's stony face and the definitive way he said *no*. There was no question mark, no room for debate, no way he'd let me go. Vicky was a bad influence. A flirt. Common. She'd poison me against him. The more I begged, the more rigid he became. What about Alex? he'd asked, his voice edged with glass. And the dog? You can't just walk out on them. You have responsibilities, Hannah. Responsibilities.

I give Vicky what I hope is a sheepish smile. 'Not yet.' Another lie. 'But I will. Promise. We'll get the award ceremony out of the way, then I'll ask him.'

'You'll *ask* him?' Her eyes close in an indignant blink.

18

'Hannah. He can't stop you, you know? You're not a kid. Don't *ask* him. *Tell* him. I mean, for God's sake, what's his problem?'

'He worries I won't come back. After last time—'

She rolls her eyes. 'That was *years* ago. And you're not the first woman to get postnatal depression and flip out. He's punished you enough, for God's sake.' She shakes her head and looks up at the ceiling. 'Jesus,' she whispers. 'He's such a bloody *child*.'

I have a vivid recollection of the stillness of the dark, deserted platform. The way I stood there, staring up at the train timetable. No trains. Too late. My head all over the place. I didn't have a clue what I was doing there and no idea where I was going. All I could think about was getting away. Then the next thing I knew he was in front of me, eyes burning with seething anger, hands reaching to rip my baby away from me. Words coming in a torrent. Terrifying words. Telling me if I did anything like that again he'd sue for custody. I'd lose my son forever.

Later, when Alex was asleep in his Moses basket, Nathan came into the bedroom, laid his head on my stomach, and sobbed.

'You have no idea how much you scared me,' he whispered. 'You endangered our son. I can't trust you with him while you're so unstable.'

The next day he took my bank card and passport.

'He's over protective,' I say to Vicky.

'Over protective? You mean *nuts*. Honestly, Han, I don't know how you put up with him.'

My cheeks flush with warmth as I stare fixedly down at my knotting fingers.

She sighs and when she next speaks her tone has softened. 'It's just one night.'

I nod and force a feeble smile. 'I'll talk to him.' I look out of the window and see two seagulls. One is young – new feathers pushing through his brown down – and holds a crust of bread in his beak. The other is older and is intent on stealing the crust. The two birds hop about on the pavement, fluttering and spinning around each other as if dancing and, for a few moments, I'm mesmerised.

'I just want you there with me, that's all.'

One night away, the two of us, to celebrate her fortieth birthday. It's a present from Phil. When he phoned to tell me, I protested. Told him I couldn't possibly accept such a gift. He insisted. I was part of the present. There was no way Nathan would allow me to have a night away and he certainly wouldn't let another man pay for me, so I told Phil he should take Vicky and the two of them could have a relaxing night away from the twins. But he said it was already decided. Vicky missed me, he said. This would be the best birthday present she could wish for. And before I could stop the words coming out of my mouth I'd said yes. The thought of it was thrilling. Eventually I'll have to make my excuses. Phil will end up taking my place. But I can't face telling her yet.

'I can't wait,' I say with a smile.

'Booze, fags, no kids, no husbands. It'll be like the old days.'

The old days.

Before that night. Before the horror of it all. Back to a time so far removed from now I wonder if it was ever even real. Who was that young woman? I remember her vaguely, like one might remember a character in a childhood book, carefree, surrounded by lightness and laughter. Popular and confident. Filled up with joy like an over-inflated balloon, shifting from party to party, pub to beach, living in the moment, working the week with the weekend in sight. Then in the blink of an eye she was gone. The lightness turned dark. The laughter became no more than a distant echo. That young woman, a version of me, trapped in the past like a stranded time traveller.

A new version of me was born that night but not completed. Then, as I followed Nathan numbly into St John's Hall registry, the transformation continued. My husband took over my deconstruction. One by one he took aim at my friends – *unworthy, boring, ill-educated, uncultured* – until gradually they were weeded out. I should have fought it but I didn't. What was the point? It was only a matter of time before they tired of the anaesthetised husk of the girl they once knew. What kind of friend could I be? I was broken. So I let him tell me I needed a fresh start. That it was better to cut ties with my old life. That I deserved more. He spoke with such authority as he pointed out their flaws and failings, I'd find myself agreeing with him. Why was I so dreadful at choosing friends? How had I gravitated to such people? Was it any wonder everything had gone so horribly wrong? It would be convenient to blame my isolation on Nathan but I am complicit. I let this happen. I walked into this life, into this version of me, willingly, and have nobody to blame but myself.

Thank God Vicky was too strong for us. Nathan detested her from the first moment he met her in the pub that night. She was everything he loathed: dressed wrong, loud, uncouth. In the early years of our marriage, we used to meet up as a four, Nathan and I with Vicky and Phil. After an evening out, he would spend hours criticising her, pointing out how crass she was, how opinionated, how her voice cut through him like nails down a blackboard. It was exhausting listening to him go on and on and on. I couldn't bear it so Vicky and I began to meet in secret. Once a week, on a Tuesday, at this tiny café in Penzance. It's clandestine and rebellious and for an hour each week I feel free. Like those girls bunking off school. Like I felt in *the old days*.

I check the clock on the wall.

'I should get to the shops.'

'Yes. And I,' she says with purpose, 'must get back to make two World Book Day costumes for tomorrow morning. Any idea what I can make with some bin bags, a newspaper and about half an hour?'

She takes her bag off the back of the chair and reaches in for her purse and a packet of Marlboro Lights. She tucks a ten-pound note under the salt cellar and puts the cigarettes on the table in front of me. Visiting time is over.

'See you next week and, in the meantime, enjoy being the proud wife of the *award-winning* citizen.'

I drop the cigarettes into my bag and we give each other a hug. 'Thank you,' I say.'

Outside I notice the young gull has lost his crust of bread and is huddling, rather sorrowfully, in the doorway of the shop next door.

CHAPTER THREE

Hannah

Even after all these years, the effort of keeping the bad stuff at bay can overwhelm me, and when it gets too much I'll retreat for a short while to the built-in cupboard in our bedroom. It's a habit, and I should stop it, but the small dark space feels safe, as if I could hide there forever and nobody would find me. Vicky mentioning *the old days* brought it all crashing down around me. I'm taken by a sudden panic. I leave the shopping bags and run upstairs. My breath is coming in shorts gasps. I wrench open the cupboard door, slide the clothes along the rail and crawl in, careful not to catch myself on the exposed carpet gripper, left when we removed the old carpet to reveal the floorboards. I pull the door closed until only a blade of light slices the darkness. There's a vague scent of long-since removed mothballs. The washing powder I use. A hint of dampness in the floorboards.

The recollections come at me in toxic flashes like fragments of a hateful photograph torn into pieces.

The burn of vodka on the back of my throat.

Cam's simmering anger. The incomprehension in Nathan's eyes. Vicky's laugh.

A shot of sambuca lit with a green plastic lighter. The heat on my hand as I extinguish the flame. Swill the glass. Breathe in hot fumes. Drink. Drink.

Drink.

Don't blister your mouth!

Who said that?

Another shot. A new song on the jukebox. Blur. 'Girls and Boys'. Vicky dancing, eyes closed, hands above her head.

Where are you?

So many people. Faces blurred. Names forgotten. Pushing through their sweating bodies. The sting of freezing drizzle. Empty streets.

Where are you?

Footsteps.

Muffled voices. Distant music from the pub. Disembodied laughter.

Then come his eyes. Staring. Their shocked glassiness burrowing through the softest parts of me. The unspoken words.

Everything is changed now.

I see him in the water. His hair sways in the quiet like seaweed. Skin ashen. Mouth stretched wide in a frozen cry…

Nausea spirals through me and I shake my head to dislodge the image, but it holds firm. I hit my hand against the floor and a sharp pain shoots up my arm. The nails on the gripper have torn into my skin. I stifle a cry and lift my hand to my mouth. The taste of blood creeps over my tongue.

In the bathroom I hold my finger beneath the tap until the blood stops streaking the water. I turn the tap off then dry the cut and take a plaster from the cabinet. I apply it too tightly and my finger throbs angrily beneath. Back in the bedroom, I close the cupboard door, straighten the bedcovers and plump the pillows, and scour the room for anything out of place. The air is hot and stuffy up here. I'd love to throw up the sash windows but they are sealed shut with decades of repainting.

Downstairs I set about making our supper. Our kitchen is straight from the pages of a farmhouse-style feature in an interiors magazine, with worn flagstones, a leather armchair with a tartan wool blanket draped over it. A collection of copper pans in different sizes hang over the oak baker's table. They get a polish every other week. On a Wednesday. Nathan likes things to look beautiful. He likes me to look beautiful. He tells me I'm beautiful often.

'You,' he says, fixing his gaze on me, 'are a *beautiful thing*.'

He enjoys it when other men notice me. If he catches sight of a man giving me a second look, his chest puffs out, and he takes hold of my hand. I own her, his body language says. She is mine. He particularly likes it if the man looking is someone he views as beneath him. Like the Spanish beach attendant on holiday who appeared like an obedient dog to the click of my husband's fingers. When his gaze lingered on my breasts, a scornful smile grazed Nathan's face.

'An umbrella for my wife.'

'Of course. This will be ten euro, *señor*.'

'For an umbrella? Ha! You lot are bold as brass.'

The man gave a curt nod and smiled as he slipped Nathan's money into the pocket of his snow-white shorts. I watched him twisting the stake of the parasol into the sand and imagined – for one moment – he was driving it into my husband's head, straight through his eye, rotating it one way then the next until Nathan stopped moving and his blood ran in rivulets into the sand.

When the man finished putting up the parasol, I thanked him.

He smiled. '*De nada, bella señora.*'

The kitchen is the type of quiet that hums. I listen hard for footsteps or the sound of the study door creaking open. The unrest which seeps out of Nathan's study taints everything. Sometimes I wish his father would get on with appearing. I'm sick of him threatening to. Though if he did I'd be screwed. I could scream as loud as my lungs would let me in this house and nobody would hear. I miss neighbours. My mother used to chat to ours over the wall in the back yard. A pot of wooden pegs on the brick wall, a basket of washing waiting to go out on the retractable line which spanned the sunlit concrete space. I fondly remember the peals of laughter and exclamations and snippets of gossip which would drift in through the open doors and windows. I think it's the deadened silence in this house that gets to me the most.

Cass raises her head as I retrieve a copper pan from the hook. I heat some olive oil and soften chopped onions, carrots, a stick of celery, before turning up the heat and browning some lamb mince. I add tomato puree, a splash of Worcestershire sauce, and some beef stock. While it's simmering, I make the mashed potatoes. I take my time. It needs to be free from even the tiniest lump. I transfer the mince into the Le Creuset dish Nathan gave me for our first anniversary and spoon on an even layer of mash. I bend down so I'm at eye level with the dish and then methodically run a fork over the surface to etch perfect parallel lines into the fluffy potato. My eyes water with concentration.

I place the pie on the side, ready to go into the oven, then I set the table

Three places.

I imagine they are for me, Alex and you, Cam. I know, it's a silly, girlish fantasy, but I don't care. It warms me from the inside. I imagine you will come in through the back door, tall and rugged, and smelling of fish and engine oil and cigarettes. I'll raise my fingers to the back of your head and weave them into your gypsy black curls that brush your collar. Your lips are rough against mine when we kiss. Your hands chilled from the winter air.

It's always cold when I remember you.

I put out three glasses and three plates, the bottle of Worcestershire sauce in front of the plate at the head of the table, then I consult the clock. This is a game I play. I like to set the final item – the salt cellar – as the clock strikes five. Today I'm a little early so I hover above the table, hand poised, eyes fixed on the face of the clock. When the minute hand hits the twelve, I set the salt cellar down and step away. I cast a triumphant smile at Cass, but she remains unimpressed and sighs heavily, whilst making herself more comfortable in her basket.

Alex plays football on a Tuesday night and won't be home until half past seven, and Nathan arrives home at six. I have one hour until he walks in. I climb the stairs slowly, my limbs feel heavy and stiff. In our bathroom, I close the door and run a bath. There's a twinge in my lower back when I bend to put the plug in. Age has crept up on me, inched its way into my bones and fibres, thinned my hair, and stolen the rosy hue from my skin. I turn the taps on: the hot on full and a trickle from the cold. I undress and climb in whilst it's still running. The heat stings, but I force myself to lie back, inhaling against the burn as I submerge my body to the chin. I take the flannel and rub soap vigorously on to it then scrub every inch of my body, face, back of my neck, between my legs, around my breasts and throat. I rinse and scrub again. Soon my skin is tingling and pink. I rub soap on to my legs and shave from ankle to knee, under my arms and along my bikini line. When I'm done I place the razor back in the pot on the side of the bath and climb out and dry myself thoroughly.

At my dressing table, which is antique and ugly, with dark wood, carved detailing, and an array of tiny drawers with faceted glass knobs, I slowly remove my hairpins and drop them one by one into a shallow china dish. I unwind my bun and brush from root to tip in long sweeping strokes. My hair hangs to the middle of my back. It's been this way since forever. I often fantasise about hacking it off, cutting away chunks of it until it's short and boyish. Nathan would be devastated and the thought of his reaction gives me a thrill.

I apply concealer to the dark circles beneath my eyes and a blemish on my jawline. Then foundation, a lick of brown mascara, and a hint of soft pink blusher. Nothing too much. Nothing unnatural. I dress in his favourite cashmere sweater, the colour of sea-glass, and my mid-length taupe skirt. Navy ballet pumps. No tights. The string of pearls he gave me for Christmas three years ago. The last thing I do is position the black velvet Alice band he likes then smooth my hands over my hair to tame the flyaway strands. As I do, I hear the front door open and close. Perfect timing. I congratulate myself.

I wait, hands clasped in front of me, facing the bedroom door. I picture him placing his bag down, hanging up his coat, dropping his car keys into the bowl on the hall table. I listen as his footsteps move through to the kitchen. The tap goes on. I see him filling a glass and drinking. I hear the glass on the drainer as he upends it after rinsing. There is quiet as he dries his hands on the freshly washed tea towel I hung over the edge of the sink less than six hours ago.

Then his footsteps on the stairs.

Across the landing.

The door opens and I smile. 'Hello, darling. How was your day?'

He kisses my cheek and walks into the room, undoing the knot of his tie. 'Good,' he says. 'Glad to be home though. You look lovely; a sight for sore eyes.'

Nathan has become better looking with age. He has a full head of dark hair speckled with only a handful of fine grey strands. His skin is clear and even and any wrinkles he has are delicate creases rather than deep furrows. His teeth are straight and, although he'd deny it, were whitened by a London dentist a few years ago. He is slim and attractive in a traditionally English way, with good posture, confidence incubated by his private education, and sharply tailored clothes. He has always dressed well. It was one of the first things I noticed when I met him, how clean he appeared, how crisp his shirt was, how neatly trimmed his nails were, and, of course, how soft his hands were compared to the weather-beaten skin I was familiar with. People describe him as handsome now. It's not something we would have called him back then. In *the old days*. Back then he had an awkward manner and no swagger. Back then, in the old days, we liked boys with a swagger.

I unzip my skirt and step out of it, remove my sweater

and lay it over the arm of the chair. I slip my Alice band off and rest it on the bedside table then unhook my bra and take my underwear off while he drapes his tie over the chair and unbuttons his collar. When I'm naked he lies me back on the bed. The sheets are soft and fresh, changed yesterday, a Monday job. He kisses me from head to toe. His lips linger softly, softly, and make my skin crawl. He moves between my legs. My thighs. My waist. His hand strokes rhythmically. I breathe slowly and focus on relaxing my body. I used to try and think of Cam, but it wasn't enough to make it anywhere near enjoyable. I am one of those women for whom sex is a chore not a pleasure. But I'm good at pretending. I've had years of practice. I detach myself. Go through the motions. Arch my back. Ease my hips upwards. Moan. But not too loudly. Don't want to be off-putting. He responds to my noises with greater urgency. I twitch and twist. Scrunch my fingers into his hair. Clench and unclench the muscles in my stomach and around my pelvis as I fake a climax.

Nathan moves away from me and smiles, drunk on the false knowledge he pleased me.

'Thank you. That was lovely. I've been desperate for you to come home all day.' As I recite my lines I stare at the shaft of evening light that strikes through the ceiling.

He smiles and leans over to kiss my forehead, before manoeuvring himself to sitting on the edge of the bed. He circles his arm and grips his shoulder, wincing slightly as he manipulates the joint. I get out of bed and dress in the green sweater and taupe skirt then sit back down at my dressing table. I reposition the Alice band then lick my finger and wipe beneath my eyelid to remove a smudge of mascara.

'Supper at seven?' he asks as he stands behind me and rests a hand on my shoulder.

'Yes.' I pat his hand and smile. 'Shepherd's pie tonight.'

'Delicious.' He squeezes my shoulder. 'I love your shepherd's pie.'

CHAPTER FOUR

Nathan

I knew from that first moment that you were the one. My sister was right: when you know, you know.

I was back in Cornwall. At Trevose. A holiday of sorts before I left for Paris. The noise and squabbling politics of the law firm were getting on top of me. Until you've worked in an environment like that you cannot understand how irritating other people are. My colleagues were vacuous and lacked discipline. They were inexplicably convinced of their own self-worth when all they really wanted to do was spend money on cocaine and strip clubs. I needed some space. Needed to escape London and breathe in some unpolluted air. So there I was, in the kitchen I grew up in, and out of the blue I was hit with an overwhelming urge for a crab sandwich. I recalled Newlyn had both a fishmonger and a bakery, and given it was only a short drive away, that's where I headed. I'm not a godly man but, to this day, I believe a greater power was in charge of me, making decisions, leading me to you.

I parked near the Tolcarne Inn and walked down Creeping Lane towards the harbour with a vague recollection of where the bakery was. It was exactly where I remembered. Pleased with myself, I pushed open the door and the bell jingled lightly.

As I walked in, you looked up and smiled. It was in that instant I knew.

It makes me cringe to recall how I stood there, mute, my mind blank, a shameful pink blush inching up from my collar to cover my cheeks. You were exquisite, long hair plaited loosely, blemish-free skin which glowed, a neat pixie nose, petite but well proportioned. You reminded me of a sun-kissed china doll.

'Hi,' you said.

One word. Like a note of music.

Hi.

Was I supposed to reply? Say *hi*? Or *hello* or *good morning*? I opened my mouth, but my tongue was tangled in humiliating knots.

'What can I get for you?'

A smile that sent shivers through me. I had to speak but still there was nothing. If I wasn't rooted to the spot I'd have turned and bolted. I prepared myself for laughter or a disdainful sneer, but instead your brow creased with gentle concern.

'Are you OK?'

The gentleness in your voice relaxed me. 'Bread,' I managed to say. 'A loaf of bread. Please.'

Another smile. 'Lovely. White or brown? Or we've got a nice one with seeds in?'

You hovered your hand, sheathed in blue, near the rows of loaves neatly lined up in red plastic trays. You glanced back at me, over your shoulder, waiting for my reply.

'It's for a sandwich. Crab.'

What an idiotic thing to say. Again I expected ridicule. Again I was wrong.

'Oh, delicious! You'll definitely be wanting wholemeal then.'

You dropped a loaf into a paper bag and gifted me another smile. 'Wholemeal makes the *best* crab sandwiches. Slice the bread thick, spread both slices with a little mayo and some butter – *not* marg – pile on the crab meat, white and brown, then give it a squeeze of lemon and a bit of salt and pepper. Oh, it's making my mouth water just thinking about it! Are you going next door for the crab? You should. They sell the best in Cornwall. Fresh and sweet.'

The words fell out of your mouth like a waterfall. When you handed me the loaf our fingers brushed.

Did you do that on purpose?

'God, I tell you what, I *love* a crab sandwich.'

Then you smiled again.

My fingers fumbled hopelessly when it was time to pay and, stupidly, I managed to drop a handful of coins which scattered on the floor like pieces of a broken vase. I swore under my breath. My ineptitude was embarrassing. As I hastily tried to pick up the money, I was aware of you coming out from behind the counter, bending to help, your delicate fingers closing around the copper coins. I stared at your hands. Tanned skin. Softened with moisturiser. Slender fingers, nails free of tarty polish, natural, healthy and clean, filed into even arcs, a half-moon of white at their base.

You held out the coins you'd gathered and for a split second our gazes locked.

'I'm sorry,' I said. 'Butter fingers.'

'Don't be silly! Honestly, I'm the clumsiest person you'll ever meet.'

And that was you, Hannah. Sweet and kind, wholesome, teetering along the fine line between girl and woman.

When you know, you *know*.

I sat on the low wall opposite the bakery and watched you through the window as you worked. It was a beautiful afternoon, mid-September, still warm – an Indian summer – and you were mesmerising. When it finally came to closing, you untied your apron and hung it up, put on your jacket and waved at someone unseen out back. You pushed the door open. Without your apron I could see you wore white cut-off shorts and a shapeless checked shirt, one made for men, I think, and a denim jacket that was a size too big. I imagined taking you shopping for expensive, well-cut clothes in the boutiques in Chelsea. The thought of spoiling you excited me.

My heart hammered as I called out. You turned and squinted through the early evening sunshine as you took a second or two to place me. Then you raised your hand and waved enthusiastically. I waved back and couldn't help laughing. All the years I'd been searching for someone and you were right here, a few miles from Trevose all along.

'Enjoy your sandwich!'

'Thank you!'

Every fibre of my being screamed at me to follow you. But I had to be patient. Women are easily put off. I had to take my time. As I watched you walk away it physically hurt.

I would stay in Cornwall for another week. It meant a call to work. I explained I'd developed a bad case of shingles and asked them to delay my flight to Paris. They weren't happy, but what else could I do? Shingles is nasty.

Over the days that followed I indulged a newfound appetite for iced buns. Every day I made the drive to Newlyn and wandered into the bakery, nonchalant, playing it cool.

'Iced bun?' you asked with a knowing smile.

'They're the best I've ever tasted and I know my iced buns!'

'I'll tell my dad. It's his own recipe. I'd give it to you, but then I'd have to kill you, so...' You shrugged and it was such a charming gesture I laughed.

'I'll have to do without for a while.'

'Oh?'

'I'm a lawyer. I have to go to Paris, to head office. I'll be there for a while, I think. A few months at least. They need me to sort some things out for them. I should be flattered, I suppose.'

The stint in Paris was actually part of my training, but the small white lie was worth it to see your expression change to one of awe. 'Wow, you must be clever.'

I lowered my gaze to affect humility.

'I didn't even do A levels. I love reading though, and quite enjoyed history and English, but school was wasted on me. I was too naughty.'

'I don't believe that for a second.'

You laughed. 'Well, not naughty, as such. But I was definitely lazy when it came to doing my homework and stuff.' You shrugged. 'Guess that's why I'm here in my dad's bakery and not a hotshot lawyer off to France.'

The bell above the door rang and another customer walked in. I wished I could tell her to go away, to come back later and let us finish talking, but of course I couldn't.

'I'll be back in England for Christmas though.'

'I'll have your iced bun ready and waiting.' You winked at me and turned to the lady. 'What can I get for you?'

As I reached for the door handle, something stopped me. My sister's words.

When you know, you know.

'Will you have dinner with me?'

You looked surprised, shocked even, and an immediate panic took hold of me.

'It's, well, I don't have many friends down here, and I've been at home alone for a few weeks. Climbing the walls. And I've enjoyed our daily chats.'

You hesitated.

'But if you can't think of anything worse, I understand.'

The woman in the shop glanced at her watch and huffed quietly. 'Look, can you serve me first then sort this out? I'm in a hurry to pick up my daughter from nursery. They get cross if we're late.'

'Yes,' you said to her, before turning back to me. 'Can you—'

'Just dinner. That's all.'

Then you smiled. 'Yes. Sure. Dinner. It sounds lovely.'

I took you to the most expensive restaurant in Cornwall. The chef had trained at *Le Manoir aux Quat'Saisons*. You hadn't heard of it, which was disappointing as I'd hoped you'd be impressed, but then again your lack of sophistication was beguiling. I'd be Professor Higgins to your Eliza. I'd show you the museums of London and Amsterdam, the canals of Venice and the Statue of Liberty. I imagined us wandering through the narrow backstreets of Rome, eating in romantic trattorias, and making wishes at the Trevi Fountain. My pulse quickened.

Chez Laurent wasn't what I'd expected. It was, if I'm brutally honest, pretentious. You ordered the fish, do you remember? It came with three cubes of something we decided was probably swede. The fillet of John Dory was the size of a deck of cards and undercooked. My heart sank as you examined the translucent grey flesh with the tip of your knife. I tried not to notice you scrape away the orange balls of salmon roe over its surface whilst eyeing the puree of mushroom warily.

'It's nice here,' you whispered. 'But it's posh, isn't it? I don't think I fit in.'

'You don't,' I said. 'You are far too beautiful.'

You blushed and lowered your gaze.

'I'm sorry about your food.'

'It was lovely. I've never got on with mushrooms and I wasn't sure if the orange stuff was for eating. The fish was tasty though.'

You were so desperate to make me happy. I'd have married you then and there, no word of a lie.

Dessert was more successful, pots of chocolate mousse scattered with flakes of edible gold and cherries dipped in white chocolate. You ate half the mousse and I had another surge of warmth towards you. You're right. A woman *should* care about her figure.

Coffee came with sweets arranged on a white saucer.

'They're called *petits fours*.'

You repeated the words under your breath as you reached for a sphere of sugar-dusted apricot jelly and nibbled the edge.

Emboldened by wine I rested my hand on yours. It was electric.

'I'd love to see you again.'

'What about Paris?'

'I'll be back before you know it.'

'You must have loads of girls you like up in London. I bet you have to fight them off with a stick.'

I toyed with the idea of making someone up to make you

jealous. A colleague in the law firm. Emily or Arabella. But playing games wasn't called for.

'The girl I like is right here.' I was pleased with this comment; it came out smoothly. 'Can we have dinner again?'

'You should come to The Packhorse with me and my friends when you get back. Meet some other people.'

I drove you back to your tiny cottage on the outskirts of Newlyn and walked you to your door. The air had chilled and there was the distant sound of a fishing trawler coming into port. A movement from an upstairs window caught my eye. I glanced up to see your mother watching us. The curtain fell back immediately. I smiled at you and you thanked me for dinner.

I thought you might kiss me. But, of course, you weren't that type of girl.

When you know, you *know*.

CHAPTER FIVE

Hannah

The kitchen is silent but for the ticking clock and my own shallow breathing. I check the time again. Seven minutes to eight. Nathan sits at the table, unmoving, fists loosely balled and resting either side of his empty plate. He watches the clock like a hawk on a field mouse.

I check the shepherd's pie again. The potato is turning from golden to overdone. I take it out of the oven, rest it on the side, and prod the crispy potato with a fork for no reason other than to appear busy.

'You know, I think this has improved with the extra time in the oven.' My tone is designed to appease Nathan's mood. 'He won't be long. He probably missed the bus or—'

My sentence is interrupted by footsteps on the gravel path outside. Moments later, Alex pushes through the kitchen door and relief floods me. He dumps his kit bag on the floor and kicks off his football boots. His face is smeared with dirt and teenage indifference, and his white shorts are covered in a camouflage of stains from the football pitch. He bends down to ruffle the dog's neck and whispers into her fur, and she responds with a vigorous beating of her tail on the flagstones.

'Sorry I'm late.' He appears anything but apologetic as he walks to the sink and turns on the tap to wash his hands.

'And why are you?' Nathan is glowering, staring at the wall in front of him, mouth moving in silent, tight-lipped mutters.

'Why am I what?'

Nathan turns his head slowly to look at him. '*Late.*'

My stomach twists in anticipation of the inevitable argument and when Alex shrugs I have to bite my tongue to stop from interfering. From experience I know this doesn't make the situation any easier.

Alex dries his hands and throws the tea towel on to the worktop. Nathan glances at the discarded cloth and visibly bristles, his lips pursing tightly.

'Well?'

Alex rolls his eyes theatrically. 'Rob offered me a lift but his mum was late. I was about to catch the bus, then she showed up, so I hung about because I thought going with her would be quicker than the bus, but it wasn't because she got chatting to the other mums and we didn't leave for ages.'

'And you didn't think to call?' Nathan's words are laced with caustic irritation.

'I kept thinking she was nearly done.' Alex gives a dismissive shrug. 'Turns out they had a lot to catch up on.'

I stare at him and will him to apologise. He doesn't need to do this. All he has to do is say sorry and sit down for supper.

'What's the point of having that bloody phone if you can't use it properly?'

Alex heads towards the door.

'Where do you think you're going?'

Alex gestures upstairs. 'Shower.'

'Sit down and let's *eat*.'

'You waited?' Alex's forehead wrinkles with confusion but it's an act. He knows full well Nathan would have insisted on waiting. He's baiting him. 'Why?'

'*Because*,' Nathan says, spitting the words out like sharpened tacks, 'this family eats together like civilised human beings.'

'Yeah, but—'

'Let's just eat, shall we?' Alex looks at me and I hold his gaze for a moment. 'While it's hot, love.'

Nathan reaches for the bottle of red. He pours two glasses. Alex slouches on his chair, legs kicked out in front of him, fingers toying with a fork. If it wasn't for the leaden tension, their matching cartoon scowls might make me laugh. I make two or three attempts at starting a conversation, but the sullen silence from my son and one-word snaps from my husband ensure that very soon the only noise which accompanies our meal is the scrape of cutlery and the relentless ticking clock.

When he's finished, Nathan leans back in his chair and wipes his mouth, leaving a greasy smear of orange on his napkin. He drains the last of his wine then taps his finger on the table. 'I don't think you've given me the receipts yet?'

Nathan smiles and my insides solidify as heat spreads to my cheeks.

'Sorry. I meant to put them on your desk but got sidetracked in the kitchen.'

'Can I have them?'

'My purse is upstairs.'

'No problem. Alex and I will clear while you fetch it.' The lightness in his voice thinly masks an anger which hasn't faded at all. 'Now, if possible?'

My hands have grown clammy. I force a smile at him and imagine – as I often do – what it would be like to lean forward, close to his face, and tell him where he can stick his fucking receipts.

But I don't.

Instead I nod and leave the table. Cass follows on my heel, her claws lightly tapping the stone floor, and waits at the bottom of the stairs as I go up to our bedroom. I lift my handbag from the chair in the corner and rummage for my purse. Humiliation burns my skin. It shouldn't. I should be used to this by now, but it's always hard when he does it in front of Alex. The pity on my son's face sharpens the shame.

'Here you go,' I say brightly, as I walk back into the kitchen and hold out the receipts, one from the supermarket, the other from a cash machine.

Nathan puts down his wine glass and takes the receipts. My heart starts to flutter. I notice that though the table has been cleared of plates, its surface is scattered with crumbs of food. I walk to the sink and run a cloth beneath the tap, wring it out, and return to the table.

'The cash?'

'Sorry?' I lift a glass and wipe beneath it, moving the cloth in steady, rhythmic circles.

'The withdrawal? Why did you need the cash?'

I place the glass back on the table. 'I forgot something at the supermarket, but the queues were horrific. I was worried I'd miss the bus, so rather than go back, I took some money out at the garage cashpoint and bought what I'd forgotten at the Co-op.' The words run out of me in a nervous torrent.

'What did you forget?'

44

I glance at Alex. He is staring intently at his hands, which are clasped on the table in front of him, as his mouth moves silently.

'Sanitary towels.'

Nathan nods and puts the receipts down. 'Why didn't you pay for them with a card?'

'It was only three pounds ninety and they have a minimum spend in the Co-op – five pounds – and, well, we didn't need anything else because I'd just done the shopping at the supermarket.'

This seems to satisfy Nathan. I pick up the wine glasses and bottle and walk back towards the sink.

'And the receipt for the sanitary towels?'

My face reignites. I turn to face him, wrinkling my brow as I gesture at the receipts. 'You've got it.'

Nathan holds up the pieces of paper, one in each hand, as if doing semaphore with tiny white flags. 'Only two. The supermarket shop and the cash withdrawal.'

I feign confusion as I open my purse and make a show of looking for it despite knowing it doesn't exist. 'That's odd,' I say. 'It's not here. Are you sure you haven't got it?'

He tips his head to one side and smiles as if I've said something amusing. 'Yes, Hannah. I'm sure.'

'I don't understand—'

'Get the towels.'

'Sorry?'

Alex swears quietly.

Nathan glares at him whilst talking to me. 'Hannah, please could you get the sanitary towels you bought today?'

'Do you have to do this?' Alex's words catch in his throat.

'I've told you before, Alex.' Nathan's voice has turned calm and flat like a patch of mirrored sea in the eye of a storm. 'It's important to take care of the finances, watch the pennies as well as the pounds, keep a careful record of what's coming in and what's going out.'

He'll mention his father any moment now. Nathan's nothing if not predictable.

'I know what it's like to live with someone irresponsible—'

Ah, yes, here it is. Right on schedule.

'—and I've seen the devastation that goes with it. Believe you me, if you'd seen a person you love with a ruddy great hole where their face should be because they couldn't manage money, you'd understand.'

'I just… I just think you should take Mum's word for it. Why would she lie?'

My son's words make me ache. I want to run to him and hold him tightly. I want to tell him not to worry, that I'm fine, and don't need protecting.

'Alex,' I say. 'This is how it works for us. I look after the house, you and Cass, and your father works and takes care of the money.'

'But it's only sanitary towels, Mum.' The pleading in his whispered voice breaks my heart.

'You know what, Alex?' Nathan's anger is building as Alex taking my side so overtly stokes the flames. '*I* am the one earning all the money. *I* am the one paying all the bills. *I* am the one who buys your football kit, pays for school trips, puts food on your plate. When your mother gets a job, she can take care of her own money or chuck it about like confetti, but while I'm the one bringing it in, I'll be the one keeping track of it.'

It's all I can do to stop myself bursting into hysterical laughter. A job? Ha! No CV. No references. No car. I'm not far off forty with four crappy GCSEs, an unfinished NVQ from Cambourne Tech, and fifteen years out of the workplace. The chances of me getting a job are next to nothing.

'Now, Hannah,' he says, addressing me again. 'Fetch the damn towels.'

Upstairs, in my bathroom, I retrieve the two unopened packets of sanitary towels from the cabinet. Then I undo the small zipped pocket inside of my handbag and fish out the change. I lied to Nathan, of course. I bought the sanitary towels from the pound store. One pound for each pack. In the Co-op they are one pound ninety-five. The exact same brand. A saving for many people, for me it's a strategy. I'm not as bad with money as Nathan thinks I am. I buy brands in the pound store and pretend they're from supermarkets or corner shops. I buy things and show him the receipt, then return them, buy the same thing from the pound shop, and pocket the change. I keep pennies I find down the sofa or in the car. I lose receipts. I play dumb. With the one pound ninety I'd saved today – plus ten pence from my pitiful stash – I bought a replacement lighter for me and a cartridge for the plug-in air freshener in Mum's room at the care home. I tore up the receipt and put it in the bin beside the bus stop. Just in case.

'Here.' I place the towels and a tower of coins on the table in front of him. 'And six pounds ten in change.'

He regards the sanitary towels for a moment or two then nods before reaching for the coins and closing his fist around them. Then he looks at me and smiles.

'Thank you for supper, Hannah.'

As he heads out of the kitchen, I let out a sigh. But it's premature.

'Why do you treat her like this?' My son's voice is flat and level, as if he's just asked Nathan what his favourite colour is. Both Nathan and I open our mouths to speak but he continues. 'You don't let her do *anything*.'

Again Nathan tries to speak but Alex talks over him.

'She does everything for us. For *you*. And you treat her like a prisoner.'

'Stop.' Nathan slams his hand down hard on the table. Cass slinks out of her bed and crawls beneath the chair where she curls up tightly. 'What are you talking about? A prisoner?'

'Yes. A prisoner.'

'Jesus. You're delusional. A *prisoner*? Are the doors bolted? Is she chained up? Do I feed her watered-down *gruel*?'

I reach for Alex's hand, but he yanks it out of my grip and approaches Nathan. 'Why won't you let her go away with Vicky?'

'It's not like that—'

But Alex doesn't let me finish. 'I heard you asking him, Mum.' Alex doesn't lift his stare off Nathan. 'I heard him say *no*. He used me as an excuse. He said you can't leave me. But that's not true. You can leave me. I'm fifteen and he's an adult. We'd be *fine*. You do everything for us and you should be able to have a night away to celebrate your best friend's birthday.' Alex shakes his head and makes a soft scoffing noise. 'I mean, what do you think she's going to do? Run away?'

I swallow and shift uncomfortably. That is exactly what Nathan is worried about. It's why he keeps my passport locked in a safe in his study and why I don't have a bank account in my name. It's why he goes through each receipt with a fine-tooth comb because without money – without a driving licence, without proof of address, with a mobile phone registered to him and not me – I can't go anywhere.

Nathan takes a moment or two to absorb what Alex has said. I can see every part of his body tensing. I step between them. 'Don't rise,' I say. 'He's a teenager. He doesn't understand, that's all.'

Nathan sweeps me aside and steps closer to Alex.

The two of them mirror each other, frozen in time, holding each other's gaze. Alex's body is rigid, muscles quivering. 'Fuck you.' He turns on his heel and strides out of the kitchen towards the stairs.

'Don't you *dare* walk away from me!'

His feet thunder on the stairs as he runs up them.

'Come back *now*!'

Alex's bedroom door closes with a bang that makes the walls shudder.

When I touch Nathan's arm, he pulls sharply away and storms out of the kitchen. A few moments later his study door slams, mimicking Alex, and I picture Charles Cardew's bloodied body jerking awake with shock.

I open the dishwasher and proceed to rinse each plate before stacking it. When the kitchen is cleaned down, I crouch beside Cass, who has resettled in her basket, and play my fingers through her silky fur.

This house *is* a prison.

Alex is right about that. But it wasn't Nathan who imprisoned me. It was me. I walked into it willingly. This house – *this life* – is nothing more than a prison of my own making.

CHAPTER SIX

Nathan

They say absence makes the heart grow fonder, don't they? Well, that was certainly the case when I was away from you. You grew like a cancer inside me, taking over every part of me, corrupting and altering each cell in my body. It was agony being so far away from you. I missed my daily visit to the bakery. Missed sitting in my car on the street outside your house and catching glimpses of you through the windows.

There was a cork board behind my computer in the Paris office and the first thing I did when I arrived was pin up a photograph of you. It was the one I took as you arrived at work one morning. You looked so beautiful with that serious, faraway expression that I decided not to shout a hello. I'd leave you to your thoughts and I'm glad I did. The photograph is perfection. Your hair taken by the wind across your eyes. Your hand reaching up to sweep it away. You lips parted just a fraction. When Jean-Paul asked who you were, I told him you were my girlfriend. He nodded with Gallic enthusiasm, gave me a crass thumbs-up, and said you were sexy. The man was an irritating oafish type, thick both in body and mind, but all the same, his reaction made my chest explode with love and, I'll be honest, desire for you. It wasn't long before I told him

I was going to ask you to marry me. What I'd said was lost in translation, and he clapped me on the back and insisted we celebrate our forthcoming wedding with cigars and cognac. I didn't have the heart to tell him he had the wrong end of the stick and we weren't yet engaged. If truth be told, I enjoyed the misunderstanding.

Every hour that passed, you crept further under my skin and into my veins. There I was, in the most romantic city in the world, its very streets cobbled with love, but I was without you. Finally, I mustered the courage to telephone you. Your mother called you down in her coarse Cornish accent.

'A young man on the phone for you, *melder*!'

Your feet clattered down the stairs at nineteen to the dozen and the excitement in your voice as you thanked her and grabbed the phone made my stomach flip. I should have called you sooner. How stupid of me to be so nervous.

When I said your name you fell quiet. So sweetly shy. You asked about France and work and if I was having a good time.

'It's hard work,' I said. 'Long hours. And, well, I miss you.'

'I bet Paris is amazing though.'

We only talked for a few minutes. Your mother needed help in the kitchen. I said I'd call again.

'OK,' you said.

'I'll be back in a few weeks. When I'm back,' I hesitated, 'can we go out to dinner again?'

'I'm not sure,' you said. 'It was so expensive last time. Don't spend your money on me.'

That made me smile. You didn't care for frittering away money. You weren't extravagant. Not like some of the girls

I came across in London and Paris, girls who were after anything they could get their over-manicured hands on.

'Let's see, shall we? When I'm back we can make a plan.'

'I should go,' you said.

'Oh, Hannah.' I was unable to contain myself. 'You're all I think about.'

You didn't reply.

I kicked myself. I'd come on too strong. Idiot. I needed to take more care.

Females are, I thought as I put the phone down, too easy to startle.

CHAPTER SEVEN

Hannah

Steam fills the shower cubicle and, as I step in, I inhale the wet heat. I wash and dry perfunctorily – it's my second clean of the day, after all – and dry myself briskly, listening for Nathan's footsteps on the stairs.

'I'll be out in a minute,' I call when the bedroom door closes.

I take the black silk camisole from the hook on the back of the bathroom door and slip it over my head. The fabric caresses my skin and my stomach turns over. I brush my hair through with my fingers and spray perfume on my neck and wrists. Before I open the door, I take five deep breaths.

He waits beside the bed and watches me as I walk towards him.

'Are you OK?' I ask.

'I don't want to talk about anything. I just want to look at you.'

I walk closer to him and press my lips against the curve of his neck. His hand falls to my waist and runs down the silk to my hip, then behind to cup my buttock.

'My turn,' he rasps.

This is a play and I am a character in the play. I know my part to perfection. I'm well rehearsed. I never miss a beat or a cue. I know how to kiss him and stroke the back of his head with the tip of my nails. I know how to bite my bottom lip and look at him through lowered lashes as I undress him. I lie him down and beg him to enter me. As he does, I affect pleasure. He kisses me on the mouth and neck, runs his fingers through my hair, groans and grinds. I take myself away and allow my mind to drift. Today I am on the cliffs at Porthcurno. Cass is up ahead of me searching the yellow fireworks of gorse for rabbits. A breeze caresses my skin like a cold hand. Kittiwakes and choughs cry mournfully. The air carries the scent of salt. The sea is dark grey-green with diamonds scattered over its surface. A boat glints in the winter sunlight. You are on the boat. You are sewing nets. Your shirt is off. Your tanned skin is shining with a film of fresh sweat. There's a small tape recorder beside you. I focus hard. What music are you playing? Ahh. I hear it. 'Zombie' by The Cranberries. I smile. I'd forgotten how much you love The Cranberries...

Nathan doesn't last long and, as he pulls himself out of me, I'm catapulted back into the room.

My final Tuesday job complete.

He lies on my chest, heavy, as if made of stone. I stare at the ceiling and notice a spiderweb. How did I miss it? No problem. I'll get rid of it when I dust again next week. I force my hand to stroke his shoulder.

He kisses me. 'I love you.'

This might be the one glimmer of truth in our house of lies. I know he loves me. Or at least he believes he does. In spite of the other women and the money and lack of trust, I often catch him staring at me with the same dewy-eyed wonder he'd had when we first met. Nathan enjoys the machinations of romance.

When we first met he would send me long letters, sometimes up to five or six pages, filled with earnest proclamations of love. Did he truly feel those things he wrote? Was he really so consumed by love for me? Or was it a display, an attempt at seduction, fabricated words that he hoped would lure me? I don't know. But I do believe he somehow convinced himself that what we had – what we still have – is genuine. Even now, he likes to surprise me with romantic gifts – a scented candle, some bath salts, a cashmere scarf – for no reason. The look of smug pleasure on his face when he does is something to behold.

I'm sure it's no coincidence that his need for love and affection stems from a childhood defined by loneliness, tragedy, and neglect. It sounds plausible enough. I mean, if your father blows his face off while you're waiting to open your birthday presents, you're bound to have issues, aren't you? Ever since he was a boy, as he's told me many times, a wife and children was all he wanted. He wanted the opportunity to lavish them with the stability he'd been denied. Nathan had faith in the family unit. Still does. He was devastated when I didn't fall pregnant again. He blamed me of course. Called me a failure. Threw in accusations of mental illness and poor mothering for good measure.

I switch off the bedside light and he turns away from me and settles himself on his pillow.

'Hannah?' His voice is hazy and quiet, caught in that place between wakefulness and sleep.

'Yes?'

'Vicky's birthday.'

I don't reply.

'You can go.'

'Thank you.'

'Don't make me regret it.'

Tears prickle in the darkness. I should feel happiness. Excitement. But what I feel is dread. As if this is a test which I've already failed.

It isn't long before his snoring fills the room. I've considered leaving him. Of course I have. Just like I did all those years ago with my infant son clutched to my chest. I imagine waiting until Nathan leaves for work before hurriedly throwing clothes into a bag. I imagine telling Alex he isn't going to school. Telling him to be quick. Then walking away. It was the threat of losing Alex to Nathan which kept me here back then. But now he's nearly sixteen, the power of that threat is fading, yet I'm still trapped. Because what the hell would I do? Where would I go? I've no passport or bank account or savings. All I have is a few pilfered pennies in a sock in the back of my underwear drawer. Alex and I would be on the streets, another couple of nameless, faceless people to be ignored by passersby.

How could I do that to my son?

I ease out of bed and put my dressing gown on. I'm careful to open the door quietly. I walk down to Alex's room. He's still up. The shadow of him moves through the strip of light beneath the door. Is he old enough to hear the truth? To know why I'm here and why I stay? The lies gnaw inside me. I want to purge myself of them and the only way to do that is to smother them with truth.

I knock lightly. There's a sound of rustling. Papers? A book?

'Hang on.'

The drawer of his desk opens and closes. His feet pad to the door. He opens it a crack and peers out. His face is flushed and he chews at the corner of his mouth, tense and on edge.

'What is it?' He can't seem to look at me. 'Everything OK?' His words are woven with concern.

'I'm fine.' I expect him to open the door to let me in, but he doesn't. 'Alex… ' My voice trails.

'Yes?'

As always something stops me unleashing the truth. I can't risk it. How can I explain what happened that night? No, it's not fair, not *right*, to unburden on a child.

'Mum?'

'I need you to know,' I say instead, 'that I'm not a victim here. I know it looks that way, but I'm not. I chose to marry your father.'

Alex's mouth twitches, opens and closes, as if he is trying to speak but thinking better of it.

'What?' My hand rests on his arm.

'I need to know.' Alex hesitates. 'Does he… Does he hit you?'

I'm taken aback by the question which seems to come out of the blue but is obviously something he's been grappling with. 'Hit me? *No*! No, of *course* not.'

Alex blanches and a wave of sympathy rolls through me.

'No,' I say, more softly this time. 'He doesn't hit me. He never would.'

I can tell by the fleeting look which crosses his face that, like my mother and Vicky, he doesn't believe me. It's the truth though. Nathan has never hit me and he's never threatened to. It's not that I don't think he's capable of it. Because I'm sure he is. After all, anybody is capable of violence.

'And what if he hit me?'

'He wouldn't.'

Alex scoffs.

'Listen to me, Alex. He would *never* hurt you.'

'But what if he *did*?' As the belligerence and rebellion abandon him, he appears childlike and vulnerable again.

'If he hurt you?'

Alex nods.

I lift my hand to stroke his cheek. 'Then I'd fucking kill him,' I say softly.

Later, when I'm sure Nathan is deeply asleep I go downstairs, careful to avoid the treads which creak like old bones, and retrieve my cigarettes from behind the washing powder in the utility room. I open the back door and Cass trots out in front of me.

It's a beautiful night. Still and warm. The moon is full and bathes the fields in milky light. I climb the stone stile and follow the footpath over the grass and up to the brow of the hill and the neat copse of trees which stand like a group of sentinels. The ground beneath the trees is trodden up by the cows who use it to shelter from heavy rain or blazing sunshine. There's a log at the base of one of the trees and this is where I smoke, hidden in the copse, crouching on a rotting log with my cigarette cupped in my hand like a convict to shield it from the unlikely appearance of Nathan. Vicky gives me a pack every other week. I usually smoke one a day and spread the remaining six over the two weeks, smoking a second back to back when I need it the most. For the minutes it takes to smoke them I am the closest I ever get to feeling like the old me. The me I was before that night. In the copse I am free. The air is light and the space feels expansive. It's an act of rebellion, a secret I keep from Nathan which empowers me.

Beneath the log I keep hidden a battered metal tin, inside

which are some gardening gloves, a woollen hat, a packet of mints, and some lavender spray. When I've tucked my hair into the hat and lit the cigarette, I slip on the gloves then draw the smoke into my lungs. Though I try to focus on the sounds around me, a distant owl, the clicks and scrapes of insects, it's impossible to block the sound of the accusatory whispers from the leaves above.

It's your fault, they whisper.

It's your fault. You deserve it all.

'I know I do,' I whisper back.

I take one last drag then tread the cigarette end into the earth, and reach for the lavender spray.

CHAPTER EIGHT

Cam, 1998

The unrelenting storms had kept most of Newlyn's fishing fleet in dock. One or two of the larger trawlers had managed to get out for a day or two here and there, but the smaller boats had been tied up for weeks. The mood in The Packhorse was sour. The men had given up searching for a crack of blue sky in the ashen grey or a glimpse of the horizon through driving sheets of rain. The storms seemed never-ending, as if the colossal waves would batter the coastline until the land was washed away.

The port was deserted, its familiar bustle replaced by wind-whipped piers and iron chains creaking as they swayed. Tarpaulins flapped like angry tethered birds and nets lay abandoned in heaps on the boats, their loose ends tanning the decks. Beyond the harbour, monstrous waves crashed against the concrete walls sending explosions of spray fifty feet into the air.

The fishermen had grown irascible with inactivity and empty wallets. Three of the crew of *The Annamae* sat at a corner table beneath the dartboard. The table was littered with empty crisp packets, sodden beer mats, and an overflowing ashtray. Davy Garnett was turning his glass in quarter revolutions, a cigarette held loosely between his lips, watching the surface of his beer waver. When it stilled he turned it again. Cam sat with half an eye on the clock above the bar. Each maddening minute passed like an hour. Geren sat between them, muttering and fidgeting, tapping his feet and drumming his fingers manically like he used to do in detention, a cigarette wedged between his knuckles.

'Fuck this,' he said suddenly and jabbed his cigarette into the ashtray. 'I've got eight fucking quid left. *Eight*.' He crossed his arms and kicked out at the table leg. 'Fuck sitting here like a bunch of cunts.'

Davy didn't look up from his glass but sniggered softly. He was medium height but strong; sinewy rather than muscular. His dark hair was shaved, grade two, a hangover from his days in the army. Cam knew he kept it that way because it made him look hard. He had an earring, a small gold hoop, which he'd got after Geren pierced his ear with a fishing hook on a twelve-hour bender. At twenty-three he was two years younger than Cam. Their dads had been best friends who'd fished together for over twenty years until Cam's dad drowned when their trawler went down. Cam wouldn't have had much to do with Davy Garnett if circumstance hadn't intervened, but when Cam's mother met an insurance sales-man from Leeds who promised her a three-bed new-build with a neat garden and no late night calls from the lifeguard, she turned her back on Cornwall, and with it her sixteen-year-old son who wasn't welcome in Leeds. Martin and his wife Sheila had taken Cam in and he found himself sharing a room with Davy who, it turned out, wasn't particularly happy about the arrangement. The boys had sparred, which was unsurprising. Davy couldn't help but be jealous. Cam was

64

gentle and helped around the house, didn't expect anything, and tried his best not to get on the wrong sides of Martin and Sheila who, it seemed to Davy, gave him special treatment. Davy on the other hand was prone to mood swings and never seemed content, always wanting *more*. More friends, more popularity, more attention. He left home at seventeen in a pique of rage when Martin asked if he wanted a job on the trawler.

'Fuck that,' he'd said, shortly before packing his bags. 'I'm not wasting my life on fish.'

He joined the army, but returned two and a half years later. It was obvious there'd been some sort of dismissal. He wouldn't talk about it, certainly not with Cam, and if Martin and Sheila knew what happened they didn't let on. A few weeks after he got back, Martin persuaded Slim to give Davy a chance on *The Annamae*.

'Cam!' Geren kicked the table leg again. 'Did you hear me? I'm sick of us sitting here like useless cunts.'

'I heard.'

'Well?'

Cam smiled. 'What do you want me to say?'

'I want you to say,' Geren said pointedly, 'fuck this too.'

'Fine.' Cam reached for his drink. 'Fuck this too.'

Geren muttered and kicked the table a third time, hard enough to cause the glasses to rattle against each other as they wobbled.

Cam drained what was left in his glass and looked at his friend. 'You know you're being a dick, right?' Cam put the empty glass back on the table. 'Anyway, shouldn't you be home with Gemma?'

'She sent me here. Told me to get out of the house because I was irritating the shit out of her.'

'Really? I find that hard to believe.'

'Yup. Her exact words.' Geren groaned with frustration. 'I need to get out there. The baby's coming in March. Have you seen how much their crap costs?'

Cam laughed. 'I imagine you'll be waist-deep in it for free, mate.'

He glanced at the clock again. It had hardly changed. Three thirty-four. He was meeting her at five and time had never moved so slowly. His head was full of her, her laugh, the softness of her hair, her perfume mixed with the smell of warm bread which hung on her after work, the way she looked at him when he spoke, as if burrowing right into him to make a nest. As he thought about her, his body twitched involuntarily. He didn't understand what he was feeling. She consumed every part of him. It unnerved him.

'Jesus *fuck,* Cam. What's with the clock?'

Cam reached for his pouch of tobacco from the detritus on the table.

'Oh, for fuck's sake.' Geren stifled a laugh. 'Don't tell me. It's your bird, isn't it? You're waiting to get your end away!'

'Piss off.'

Geren laughed. 'Pool?' He gestured at the table which had just come free.

Cam checked the time again – an hour to go – and nodded.

'I reckon you don't give a shit if we don't get out to sea.' Geren bent for the triangle and started to fill it with balls from the pockets. 'I mean, who'd work when you've got a new bit of skirt to lift?'

Davy sniggered.

Cam took hold of a cue and chalked the end. 'And when was the last time you got laid, Davy Garnett?'

Geren laughed.

Davy shot Cam a glare. 'Fuck you,' he said. 'Your bird isn't all that.'

Cam raised his eyebrows and smiled. 'As if a girl like her would ever look at a little git like you.'

'You reckon? I heard she'll drop her knickers for any bastard.'

'Whatever,' Cam said under his breath. He turned his back on him and placed the cue ball on the worn-through spot on the faded baize. Davy could be a proper dickhead when he wanted to be, but Cam didn't give a shit what he thought, and had learnt to ignore his bleating years ago.

'Sounding a bit jealous there, Davy lad.' Geren lit a cigarette and squinted as the smoke rose. 'Don't worry, sweetheart. You won't be a virgin forever.'

Davy turned puce. 'I'm not a—'

But his protestations were drowned out by laughter from Geren, Cam, and a number of men nearby. Davy slouched back on his chair, face cloudy, arms folded like a sulky child.

Cam signalled for his friend to play first.

Geren took a drag on his cigarette and placed it on the ashtray before bending and looking down the cue to line up his shot. He drew his arm back and played his shot. 'Anyway, this little bird only has eyes for our Cameron Stewart. True love for sure.' He tilted his head and winked at Cam in a rare moment of warmth.

Geren could be a dick – he wasn't everybody's cup of

tea – but he was the best friend Cam had. When Cam's dad drowned, Geren had been there in a way nobody else had and Cam would never forget that. Beneath the bullshit he was loyal and honest, and the best fishermen Cam knew, a natural who lived and breathed for the sea and had no fear of it. Unlike Cam, he fished because he loved it. Cam had never thought to do anything else. Like most of those from local families, fishing was in Cam's blood so he never questioned it. He always knew he'd be a fisherman like the generations before him. The Stewarts originated from Scotland. It was Cam's great-grandfather who brought them to Cornwall, when he'd returned from the war-ravaged battlefields of France and found the fishing industry in Peterhead in decline. The Cornish were desperate for crew to keep up with a thriving pilchard industry, so he packed his bags and headed south, found a spot on a boat, met a girl from Penzance, and stayed.

'Did you know she used to go out with that Cardew prick?' Geren struck the cue ball hard to send the others ricocheting off in all directions, sinking two balls. He grinned.

'Who told you that?' Cam was taken aback by the violent jealousy which stabbed him in the gut.

'Her mate. Vicky, isn't it? She was telling Gem all about it. How he took Hannah for a meal at this poncy place up near Truro. Said it cost over a hundred quid.' He shook his head. 'A hundred fucking quid? I said to Gem, don't you get any fucking ideas, girl. Jesus, that guy's always been a little prick.' Geren walked around the table, assessing his options, and puffing on his cigarette.

Nathan Cardew had been at primary school with them, same year, before his parents decided mixing with the likes of Geren and Cam wasn't good enough for their precious boy. He had a tough time because of his habit of telling tales. Cam never understood why kids like Nathan made life so hard for themselves. Who wants to be a grass? Why choose to give the name of the boy who'd drawn cocks on the toilet walls rather than just keep your mouth shut? Was it worth the grief? But Cam didn't care then and he didn't care now. Geren was right, he was a prick. Cam should ignore him, but the thought of him with Hannah was enough to drive him insane. He needed to get out and fish. Needed money to take her out, somewhere nice, somewhere the waiters wore ties and lit candles and called them sir and madam when they brought out their steaks.

Geren potted the black and celebrated his win by giving Cam a dead arm. There was too much pent-up energy there. He needed a vent. Geren lived for the moment and was single-minded in his hunt for adrenalin, whether that was at sea or driving his bike too fast, filling his body with drugs and drink, or squaring up for a *scat* at the slightest provocation. At school he'd been in and out of the headmaster's office for anything and everything, from smoking on the roof to swearing in class to drawing cocks on the toilet walls. Geren was finally expelled a few months before CSEs and left with an insolent shrug and a fist through a window. Predictable unpredictability ran through Geren like a vein of quartz.

They played another game of pool and at ten to five Cam finally said his goodbyes amid a barrage of good-natured jeering. He smothered a grin and nodded, before zipping his jacket and thrusting his hands into his pockets and pushing out of the door.

The rain had stopped but the wind still whipped the streets as he walked down towards the bakery. He thought of his father and the night he died. Weather like this. Stormy and dark. What must it have been like for him out there? He'd been in the engine room below deck when the trawler capsized. No way out. Martin had been on deck and was thrown into the sea and had somehow managed to claw his way onto the exposed hull where he'd lain in the pitch black, exhausted and shivering, listening to Scotty calling for help and banging on the metal which separated them. Martin once told him, after too many drinks, how the sound of his father's desperate banging would haunt him for the rest of his life. There wasn't a man or woman in Newlyn who hadn't lost a loved one to the sea. And all for a bit of haddock? It was a mug's game, but then again, what else was he good for?

Cam arrived at the bakery and pressed his nose against the window. He was a few minutes early. With previous girlfriends he would never have wanted to appear too keen, but with Hannah he no longer cared. He wanted her to know how serious he was. He wanted her to know that he'd never been keener on, or more serious about, anything before in his life. He had developed a ravenous appetite for her. The more of her he consumed, the less full he felt. Sometimes he wanted to swallow her whole so she'd be there inside him forever.

Despite the biting chill a warmth spread through his body from the pit of his stomach as he looked in on the brightly lit shop and watched her stacking empty crates and chattering nineteen to the dozen to someone unseen out back. He thought about the softness of her and the feel of her breath on the skin of his neck. He tapped on the glass. She looked up and beamed at him. Then she turned and leaned through the door which led through to the back of the shop, saying goodbye, Cam presumed, to her dad. She smiled at Cam again, then lifted her apron over her head, hung it up and buttoned her coat. She burst out of the shop and jumped into his arms, kissing him over and over as if she might never stop.

'I've missed you, I've missed you, I've *missed* you,' she said between kisses, her breath smelling faintly of mint.

Her joy enveloped him and his whole body stirred. 'I've missed you too.'

They walked down to the harbour hand in hand and she told him all about her day. Every now and then she'd skip as she walked, her fingers stroking his, looking up at him with that smile of hers, something akin to wonder in her eyes. Hannah was made of goodness. She was uncontaminated, as if nothing bad had ever happened to her and this stroke of good fortune had rendered her pure, and her pureness was a salve which made him stronger.

They walked down the jetty to where his boat was docked. The boat was where they went when they wanted to be alone to kiss and talk and enjoy each other's company away from the Garnetts. He'd bought it a few years ago, when he was drunk, for a hundred pounds from a guy in the pub who was drunker. It took him eighteen months to get it seaworthy, and there was still much to do – a repaint, a cracked window to replace, some brand new seat covers would be nice – and he loved it. The boat was his own space to retreat to when he needed to be alone. Or when he needed to be with Hannah.

He'd been down that morning and hosed the deck down,

washing the dirt and fish bits out of the scuppers and making it all as clean as he could. He'd put some beers in the cool box, and grabbed a couple of blankets and a sleeping bag, and packed them all in the chest on board.

When they reached the boat, he climbed on and held out his hand.

'Be careful,' he said, 'the rain's made it slippery.'

They kissed as soon as they were both on board. Sheltering in the tiny wheelhouse and leaning back against its flimsy wall.

'You know,' she whispered into his ear, 'I haven't been able to stop thinking about you. All day. I was wrapping saffron buns earlier and all I could think about was sex!'

'When you were wrapping saffron buns?' He bent to kiss the curve of her neck.

She tilted her head to let him. 'It's true! And once I'd thought it I couldn't *un*think it. So basically I've been thinking about sex *all* day. Literally. Didn't matter what I was doing, I was thinking about sex.' She drew back and looked at him seriously for a moment. 'Is that what they mean when they say men think about it twenty-four seven? Like you actually *do*? I never really believed them.'

He laughed. 'Who's *them*?'

'You know. *Them*. People who say things.' She shook her head. 'Honestly, though, it must be *knackering* for you all. Poor sods. I had to have a sit down with an emergency doughnut at two just to get through the afternoon.'

'It is exactly that,' he said with a laugh. 'Knackering.'

'And to think we let you operate heavy machinery and fly planes.'

Her attention was grabbed by something behind him. She

reached over his shoulder, the soft skin of her upper arm brushing his cheek. He turned his head to kiss it.

'You know,' she said, 'I keep looking at this and wondering what it is.'

He looked at what had caught her eye and saw she was holding the screw top jar that he kept on a small shelf to the side of the wheel. It was filled with clear liquid in which opaque crystals hung suspended in a gently shifting amorphous mass.

'It's a storm glass. My dad gave it to me.'

'What's it for?'

'It predicts the weather.'

She stared at it, tipping it upside down and watching the crystals tumble like snowflakes.

'It's got a mix of different chemicals in it, ethanol and others I don't know. Some guy a hundred years ago made them for the fishing folk who kept being lost in storms they didn't know were coming. There was a fancy one, made of wood and brass, in the pub until about ten years ago when someone nicked it. My dad made this one when I was lad. It's old but I keep it with me because it reminds me of him.'

'Does it work?'

He smiled. 'I don't think so. If it's clear it means it'll be fine, if the crystals hang in threads there'll be a gale. These,' he said, gesturing at the jar, 'all clumped together like that, mean a storm's coming. But they don't ever change that much, if I'm honest. Seems there's always been a storm coming, right from when he gave it to me.'

Hannah placed the storm glass back on the ledge.

'They were like that the night my dad drowned.' Cam thought about that night. Recalled sitting on his bed staring

73

at the crystals thick in the jar, the wind and rain lashing against his bedroom window, his stomach turning over and over as he thought of his dad out at sea.

'I'm sorry,' she whispered. 'That must have been awful.'

He shrugged. 'Fishermen drown.'

She stood up on tiptoes and kissed him, wrapping her fingers into the hair at the back of his neck and pulling him to her. He felt tears on her cheeks and drew back and saw silver tracks glinting in the harbour light.

'Hey, what's wrong?'

'Nothing can happen to you, OK? You have to stay safe. Promise me.'

He gently dried her tears then kissed her again, but this time harder, as if it was the most important thing he would ever do. His father, the storm glass, the biting cold, the lads going stir-crazy in the pub, all of it was forgotten. She took hold of his hand and placed it on her breast. He moaned and leant close until their faces were only millimetres apart, their breathing in time, her breath hot and sweet on his skin.

'We're going to freeze,' she whispered.

He grinned and walked over to the back of the boat where he lifted the lid on the built-in chest. He pulled out two life jackets and passed them to her. 'Pillows,' he said, as he grabbed the blanket and tarpaulin, two cans of lager, and a heavy musty-smelling sleeping bag.

The air hummed with distant sounds of people arriving at the pub after work, and as he spread out the tarpaulin on the deck and laid the blanket on top, she unzipped the sleeping bag.

'We're going to die of actual hypothermia,' she said, as she shimmied out of her jeans and slipped beneath the sleeping bag. 'We should have got together in the summer.'

He lay beside her and pulled up the sleeping bag so everything was covered but their heads. 'If I die of hypothermia tonight, I'll die a happy man.'

They kissed, losing themselves in it, bodies warm where they touched. Cam concentrated on every detail, committing it all to memory, stored with perfect clarity so it would be there like an easily accessible photograph for the lonely hours back at sea. He wanted it all, the sweat, his bristling body, the sound of the waves, the smell of musty sleeping bag mixed with the unique smell of her – pungent body spray, her shampoo, a hint of the bakery – which tunnelled into him.

'*My a'th kar,*' she said softly, her voice breaking into his thoughts.

'What?'

'You don't speak Cornish?'

He laughed. 'Do you?'

'A few words. Mum taught me.'

'Say what you said again.'

'*My a'th kar.*'

'What does it mean?'

She smiled. 'I love you.'

The words shot through him like an electric shock and he stiffened.

She flushed pink and began to chew on her lower lip. 'I'm sorry. I didn't mean—'

'No, no. It's… ' His chest had tightened so much he couldn't breathe. 'God. I mean… Really? You feel that?'

'Yes. Of course. But if it's going to mean you won't have sex with me I can unsay it.'

'No. Don't unsay it,' he whispered. 'I love you too. I do, Hannah. I mean it. I love you so much.'

Then she kissed him. He slipped his hand beneath her sweater and stroked her skin which was peppered with goosebumps. She lifted his sweater and pressed her warm lips against his aching body. He groaned softly.

His desire was momentarily interrupted by the dread in his stomach.

He swore.

'What?'

He swore again. 'Fuck. *Fuck.* I haven't got a condom. I meant to go to the chemist but I forgot. Jesus. I'm sorry.'

'Oh.' Her voice was thick with disappointment. 'So we can't do it?'

He hit the deck of the boat with his fist.

'Let's do it anyway. Just... ' She hesitated. 'Come out. Before you... you know.'

He didn't reply for a moment or two. They couldn't. It wasn't worth the risk. But then her hand went to his crotch and she stroked him gently as she ran the tip of her tongue over his lips.

'Yes,' he rasped. 'Yes. OK.'

CHAPTER NINE

Hannah

I'd woken early, so slipped out to walk Cass while Nathan and Alex were still sleeping. On my return I can hear them shouting at each other from across the fields. I glance at my watch. It's not even seven-thirty and yet here they are, already at each other's throats. There's a crash and I swear under my breath as I break into a half-jog and cross the lawn to the back door. When I walk in they glance at me briefly before returning their attention to each other. Nathan's mouth is set in a tight, thin-lipped grimace. Alex is red-faced, nose flaring, chest heaving up and down. I scan the kitchen for what might have caused the crashing noise, but can't see anything out of place.

'What's going on?' I ask when neither offers any explanation for their fight.

Nathan's face contorts into a grotesque snarl. He is about to speak but Alex blurts his words out first.

'He wants to take my phone.'

Jesus. *Really?* This is about a phone? I purse my lips and take a breath in an effort to conceal my exasperation, which will only infuriate Nathan and make Alex more defensive, and certainly won't help de-escalate the argument.

Nathan's fist clenches. 'For God's *sake*! I'm not taking his phone. He—'

'You *are* though! You just said it.'

'This is ludicrous. I didn't say I was going to take it; I said I didn't want to see him on it at the awards ceremony this evening. And then he exploded and now here we are. If he'd been reasonable to start with then we wouldn't have got to this. He completely overreacted, and was incredibly rude and aggressive, and he has to understand there are consequences. Now he loses his phone and that's his own lookout.' Nathan stares hard at Alex with unveiled challenge. 'Are you seriously trying to tell your mother I walked up to you and tried to confiscate your phone just like that?'

Alex's brow furrows as he retraces the steps of their argument. His confusion is familiar. It's impossible to argue with Nathan who is as slippery as wet soap and will twist and manipulate every word uttered, then add questions, an incredulous tone, wrap it all up in lawyer-speak, and blind you with a rewritten version of what you clearly remember, leaving you speechless with self-doubt.

'That's not true,' Alex tries, 'you said I wasn't allowed to take it tonight and I asked why, and then the next thing you said was you'd *confiscate* it. I said no and you said I couldn't have it back.'

'That's not how it went, Alex. You know that full well. As if I would take your phone because you asked for simple clarification. You've not only misremembered but I find it hurtful you'd think I would do something like that. You spoke to me rudely and without respect. You didn't look me in the eye. You snapped. You showed absolutely no interest in what is, I'll be honest, a very important evening for me. But all that's irrelevant now. The fact you've got so worked up, that you've managed to get yourself into this hysterical state, supersedes the original grievance. You've proven how addicted you are to that damn contraption and, well, I'm afraid I can't trust you not to look at it tonight. The last thing I want is my son at the town hall, in front of the mayor no less, glued to a screen like a dysfunctional zombie.'

Alex's mouth moves silently as his fists open and close at his sides like a pair of beating hearts.

I step towards Nathan. 'I'm sure Alex wouldn't have looked at his phone during the—'

Nathan interrupts me with a scornful snort.

Alex juts his chin forward, eyes narrowing to slits beneath his heavy brow. 'It's *my* phone.'

'You paid for it, did you? And it's you who pays for the monthly line rental?'

Alex hesitates and glances at me, but all I can do is lower my gaze.

'It was a birthday present,' he says quietly, his voice wavering.

'You know, I think—'

'Be *quiet*, Hannah. This has nothing to do with you. I told you we shouldn't get him a phone and I was right. A whole generation of children are unable to have conversations or look people in the eye. They have no attention span, no opinion that isn't force-fed to them. I can't risk him sitting in the corner staring at his phone at the ceremony. How would that look? How would that reflect on me?' He reminds me of a politician giving a stirring address at a rally, with neat, disorienting soundbites, an assertive thumb, and bulldozing arrogance. 'I want him to be a young man we are proud of. Not just another entitled, disengaged snowflake who believes life owes him everything on a polished silver platter.'

'Nathan, please. Stop now,' I say wearily. 'Alex needs to get to school.'

'*Stop now*? You have a problem – *Hannah* – with how I'm parenting him? You think I don't have the right to discipline him in my own home? Is there any reason why I shouldn't?'

There's something buried in his words. An accusation. I straighten myself and face him, about to speak, about to placate him, but he silences me with a raised hand like a policeman directing traffic, then holds his other hand out towards Alex. 'Give it to me.'

'No!'

'Give me your phone or I'll—'

'You'll what?'

'Alex,' I say calmly. 'Give him the phone. You can have it back tonight.'

'He'll have it—'

'He'll have it back tonight, Nathan.'

Alex's hand twitches. He looks from me to Nathan and back at me. I give him a nod of encouragement and a small, almost undetectable, smile. He hesitates, then looking as if he might kill both of us, he pulls his phone from his back pocket and thrusts it into Nathan's outstretched hand.

Nathan smiles with undisguised triumph. 'Thank you. Now get yourself to—'

'*I hate you.*'

80

I watch in horror as Nathan is possessed by a scorching anger which distorts his features and turns him ugly.

'What did you say?'

'You heard.'

'You *hate* me?' breathes Nathan. 'For *what*? For providing you with a beautiful home? Food? Money for things you want? Giving you a phone and paying the bill each month? You hate me for caring what you do with your life?'

'Please. Both of you. Enough.' Though my voice is firm, I can't disguise its tremor. I walk to Alex and rest my hand on his arm, and as I do I'm filled with self-loathing. I should be taking his side, defending him, but I know from years of experience there's no point. You cannot win against Nathan. He's too good. Too well practised. So instead of standing up for my son, I tell him to apologise.

'What? Why? He's—'

'You need to say sorry.' I drill my words into him. 'You cannot speak to your father like that.'

'But—'

'*Now!*'

The sudden shout makes Alex flinch and I immediately regret it. I can't remember the last time I raised my voice to him. The shock on his face is clear but fleeting, as he rapidly regathers himself and turns back to Nathan.

They stare at each other for a moment or two, tomcats sizing each other up, both wound tight and waiting to see who'll pounce first. But then Alex appears to relax. His fists unclench. He gives a half-smile and shakes his head. 'No,' he says. 'I'm not going to apologise.'

He picks up his school bag and slings it over his shoulder

before reaching for the kitchen door. I say his name, but he ignores me. Then the door closes behind him and he's gone.

I move to follow him, but Nathan grabs me. His fingers dig into my arm.

'Leave him. You said he needs to get to school. Well, he can get himself to school this morning.'

'He doesn't have bus money.'

Nathan smiles. 'Then he'll have to walk, won't he?'

Tears threaten and I breathe deeply to stem them.

'I have to say, that wasn't the start to the day I needed. Maybe if you'd been here when he woke up this morning, rather than out having a jolly walk, he might not have lost his temper like that.' Nathan tugs on the cuffs of his shirt, puts his suit jacket on, and brushes himself down. 'He's been difficult for a while, but his behaviour is definitely getting worse. Do you have any idea what's got into him?'

The look he gives me is loaded, a knowing glint, something he's withholding. It's a trap.

I have no idea what's wrong – if anything – with Alex and don't answer.

'So? Do you? Any clue at all?'

Nathan is staring at me, waiting for me to speak, but I know better. Anything I say will be taken as ammunition, perhaps not for now, but certainly at some stage.

'Nothing to say? Nothing at all?'

I shake my head and his face slowly assumes a smile. He leans forward to kiss my cheek.

'We need to be ready to leave at six tonight. I've laid your clothes out. Why don't you wear your hair loose?'

The outfit is laid out on the bed as if a woman was lying there, fully dressed, and combusted to nothing, leaving only the clothes. He has chosen my navy skirt, patterned with tiny white birds, a white blouse with three buttons on each cuff and a scalloped collar. A pair of navy patent leather court shoes rest neatly on the floor beneath the skirt, obediently waiting side by side. He has even put out a matching set of underwear, white with a delicate lace trim, finishing off the Sunday school teacher look he's gone for, virginal and pure, buttoned-up. But the instruction – not a question – to keep my hair down means he wants a touch of sexiness. He wants his wife to look chaste but desirable, the perfect woman for a man of Nathan Cardew's standing. I stare at the outfit and fantasise about leaving it there, laid out on the bed, and going to the town hall in jeans and a sweater, hair in a scruffy ponytail, wellington boots, and getting so drunk on cheap wine my speech slurs and my make-up runs down my face in grubby black smears.

To the casual observer it might seem that allowing him to choose my clothes is a pitiful relinquishing of my identity. Honestly though? It doesn't bother me. I've no interest in clothes and it's a battle I have no intention of fighting. Nathan cares about *aesthetics*, as he calls it. He likes expensive watches and sharp suits and shoes with genuine leather soles. I don't give a toss. I grew up in a chaotic, untidy house, filled with laughter, dog hair, and clutter on every available surface. I wore things we could afford, hand-me-downs, coats and skirts from charity shops. Mum always said what mattered was people, not things. Nathan would disagree. He has disdain for most people but loves beautiful things. Most of the gifts he gives me for my birthdays or Christmas – a piece of art, a first edition book, or an ornament, maybe – are actually bought for himself. He gave me a painting a few years ago. He said it was expensive. It depicts a hunting scene, a group of men in caps and tweed, faithful beagles at their feet, gathered around the bloodied body of a stag, its dead eyes open, tongue lolling. After a lot of holding it up here and there around the house, going through the motions of deciding on the perfect spot for it, he told me it looked best in his study. I agreed. It's an awful painting and I'm glad I don't have to look at it, glad it hangs in his study with the photograph of his dead sister and the ghost of his *drog-polat* father.

Not caring is another form of self-protection as well, like the small rebellions I use to claw back some control. These seemingly insignificant acts are my oxygen. Like, every Sunday, while I cook the roast dinner and Nathan reads in the sitting room, I pour a large glass of the red wine he's decanted to breathe. It might be a St Emilion or a Châteauneuf-du-Pape, something expensive, bought with care and deliberation from the *by appointment only* wine merchant in Padstow with whom he's on first name terms. Then I top up the decanter with cheap cooking wine and tip the glass of expensive stuff into the gravy pan. Later, when we're sitting at the table, I'll watch him ceremoniously pouring the wine from the decanter, smelling it, rolling it around the glass, sipping it then announcing how delicious it is. Sometimes I buy reduced economy lamb mince as well as the butcher's best he likes. I'll use the cheap stuff for the shepherd's pie and cook the good stuff for Cass. It means juggling the receipts or paying for the cheap mince with coins I've squirrelled away, but I'm an expert at that. Then of course there's the smoking. God, he hates smokers. It's absurd how angry he becomes when people smoke near him, huffing and puffing as if he was a twenty a day smoker himself. When we got married one of the first things he said was *and you won't be smoking anymore?* The question mark was a red herring. It wasn't a question. It was another instruction. Part of our marriage contract. I picture his reaction if he found out about the packet of Marlboro Lights hidden in the utility room in a tin behind the washing powder and smile.

CHAPTER TEN

Hannah

The ornate room is rumbling with voices. There must be at least a hundred and fifty people gathered to celebrate Nathan. He floats effortlessly through the crowd, greeting people warmly, shaking hands, lowering bashful eyes in faux-humility.

'You must be *so* proud of him.'

The woman's voice is as soft as her cashmere sweater. She is gazing across the room at Nathan, her fingers fiddling with the delicate silver chain which encircles the loose folds of skin on her neck. 'He is such a *wonderful* man. You're very lucky.'

The woman fawning over my husband has dull brown hair, greying at the roots, cut into a sharp and practical bob, and an upcountry accent. She's an incomer, an escapee from whatever grey, uninspiring suburb she'd been miserable in before scurrying down here for a 'life by the sea'. I imagine she lives in a tastefully updated granite farmhouse with a distant sea view and *just adores it* when the grandchildren come to visit for two weeks over the summer.

She glances at me expectantly, eyebrows raised, waiting for a reply.

I remain quiet and sip my wine which has turned acidic in the heat of my hand.

What is there to say?

Yes, he is wonderful, isn't he? Award-winningly wonderful. I'm proud. I'm lucky. Who wouldn't be in my position? The wife of a solvent, handsome lawyer in a tailored suit who gives so much back to the community. I turn my head to seek him out and see he is entertaining a small group of people, gathered around him, hanging on his every word like dutiful dogs waiting for a treat. A sudden wave of hatred barrels through me. It happens every now and then, not often, but when it does, like now, it can be breathtakingly fierce. I watch him gesticulating with his hands as he entertains them. Those hands. Fuck. I hate how soft his hands are. Delicate hands, moisturised, with clean nails filed into perfect curves that turn my stomach.

As I stare at him, I picture him jerking as if electrocuted. He clutches his chest. His face drains of colour and his eye widen in fear. When he collapses, the crowd in the room silence, turn to watch, impassively, then return to their animated conversations as he lies there twitching…

The woman in the cashmere sweater smiles. She's given up waiting for a response.

'He's an *amazing* man,' she says, her attention drawn back to him like a magnet. 'So clever. I hear he does pro bono work as well. And, of course, the fundraising! We're so grateful to have him on the board of governors. He was *instrumental* in raising the money we needed for the new gymnasium. On top of all that I just found out he ran the London marathon last year. And for Great Ormond Street, too. What a kind, compassionate man.'

'Three years ago.' I place the rancid wine on the trestle table behind me.

'Sorry?'

'The London marathon. He ran it three years ago. Not last year.'

'Oh, but a *marathon*!' Her exclamation causes a number of people to cast looks in our direction. 'John can't even make it to the fridge without needing a week's rest.'

She guffaws sharply – the noise not unlike a braying hyena – before patting my arm and congratulating herself on her joke. When I give her a tight rather waspish smile instead of laughing, her face falls and her eyes narrow as she decides she dislikes me. It was bound to happen. I suspect I'm rather easy to dislike. It wasn't always this way. I used to be likeable. I made friends easily and enthusiastically. I was easy-going and loved a good time. I didn't have a care in the world. I had no idea how lucky I was. Stupid me for taking something so precious for granted.

The woman drifts away and I'm left alone, stranded on an island in an ocean of people celebrating the virtues of my husband. I want to walk up on stage. Take the microphone. Tell them all how naive they are to be taken in by him.

'This man doesn't do good things for other people,' I want to shout, 'he does them only for himself.'

The messianic smugness painted on to his face as he wanders among his disciples like Saint fucking Nathan of Cornwall is nauseating. Am I being a bitch? Is Nathan a truly good man with a truly good heart? Has my opinion of him become warped? After all, he did run a marathon for Great Ormond Street. Even if it was three years ago and he walked half of it.

I turn my back on Nathan and check the entrance again. Where is he? Nathan is fuming. Alex was supposed to come home from school, grab a sandwich, then travel in the car with us so we could arrive together, Alex and I either side of Nathan, doting wife and beloved son.

The perfect family.

Of course, I made excuses for Alex's no-show. I fabricated a convoluted story about me not remembering he'd told me he had an after-school revision session that he was reluctant to miss. He was very sorry. He would meet us at the town hall. You know me, I'd said. Always forgetting things. But Alex still isn't here and, as the minutes tick by, I'm filled with a growing suspicion he isn't going to show. This will send Nathan into a rage-induced sulk for days, the thought of which is exhausting. I could throttle my son; a few poxy hours was all he needed to give me.

Nathan is working the room adeptly and has moved on to a different crowd of people and already treated them to an apparently hilarious anecdote. If he's aware of Alex's absence he isn't allowing it to interfere with his performance. A woman marches up to me, her mouth forming an exaggerated and insincere oh-how-lovely-to-meet-you shape. She is grey-haired, thin and spidery, and has an unpleasantly limp handshake. After a short silence which seems to bother her more than it bothers me, she says, 'We don't see you at many of the events your husband attends. The talk he gave at the library on the vagaries of the English legal system was fascinating. I had so many questions for him and he knew the answer to every single one.'

'I have a son.'

She waits for me to say more, to perhaps explain why having a son might prevent me from coming to hear my husband bore on about law. But I stay quiet. I don't mind if she thinks this is an unsatisfactory excuse. The truth is Nathan doesn't want me there. He likes me at home to welcome him with a hot meal and a clean house, and he needs me to listen sympathetically when he tells me at length what a dull time he had answering dull questions from dull people.

You, I think, as I give her a tight smile, bore my husband rigid.

Nathan looks over in my direction and cranes his head to see who I'm talking to. A subtle look of distaste passes over his face when he recognises the spidery woman. Most people wouldn't pick up on these fleeting expressions, but I can read him like a book. I smile at her more warmly. It's sad, really, that her admiration is repaid with such thinly veiled contempt.

Nathan says something to the group of people he is with, gestures over at me, then laughs and pats a man's back. The group smile and nod. The man he patted turns to acknowledge me with a raised hand. Nathan leaves them and walks over to us.

'Sorry, darling. I didn't mean to get separated from you.' He gives the woman a larger than life smile. 'Emily. How lovely to see you again.'

The woman beams and places a spidery hand on his arm. 'I was telling your wife what a marvellous talk you gave at the library a while back. Honestly, one of the most fascinating evenings I've spent in a long time.' She pauses theatrically. Leans in conspiratorially. 'You know, you're *wasted* in Cornwall.'

I dig my fingernails into my palm.

'You're too kind, Emily. I wouldn't live anywhere else. I was away from Cornwall for a while in my twenties... '

I allow his voice to slip into the background. It's a skill I've developed over the years. Sometimes I can do it when it's just the two of us. I phase the sound of him out so his mouth moves but there's no noise, as if muting the television. Selective hearing. Another life-raft.

'Hannah?'

I click the sound back on and smile.

'Sorry. I drifted off for a moment.' I pinch the fabric of my blouse and flap it. 'It's hot in here, isn't it?'

Nathan beckons to one of the waiting staff, a boy who looks no older than Alex and who, by the glum expression on his face, would prefer to be anywhere else but here.

'Could you open a window? It's rather stuffy in here and my wife is too warm.'

'So considerate,' croons Emily. 'You know, there was a question I didn't ask—'.

Nathan smiles at Emily as he takes my elbow. 'Would you excuse us?'

She swallows her disappointment with a rapid flick of her hand, as if shooing him away. 'Of course, of course. I mustn't hog you. You're the star of the show and everybody wants to talk to you. It's like a wedding!'

'Hannah,' Nathan hisses, close to my ear. 'Where is he? The journalist wants a family shot.'

I debate lying. I could tell him Alex has been and gone. That he showed up white as a sheet. Poorly. That I sent him home rather than infect everybody. But then what will I do if he then arrives, not ill, but fine? My brain won't work fast enough and I'm forced to tell the truth.

'I don't think he's here yet but I know he wouldn't miss

it. He'll have been delayed at school. Maybe the maths study group ran over?'

'Christ,' he breathes angrily. 'After this morning you'd think he wouldn't dare step out of line. What will people think? Doesn't he know how important it is to be seen supporting me?'

'I don't think anybody cares about Alex, Nathan. We're here to celebrate you and your marvellous achievements. Don't let him get to you.' I smile and make my voice light. 'What time are you on?'

'The marketing girl from the tourist board said around fifteen minutes,' he says, his annoyance still obvious. 'That was ten minutes ago. I should go.' He smiles tightly. 'Can I suggest you circulate a bit more?'

I nod.

'And, Hannah, do try and smile. You look much prettier when you smile.'

I circulate over to a chair near the entrance to wait for Alex. There are banners either side of the double doors with the logo of the sponsors, the Cornish Tourist Board, emblazoned on them proudly. I've no idea how providing the warm wine at an awards ceremony for a local lawyer who ran a marathon three years ago will promote holidays to the West Country, but then again what do I know about anything?

The room quietens at the sound of a knife clinking a wine glass. A man in an ill-fitting suit clears his throat and begins to talk. His voice is monotonous and his attempt at a joke sends a muted ripple of uncertain laughter through the crowd, so when he finally introduces my husband, the audience clap with both enthusiasm and relief. Nathan walks on to the stage with the confidence of a rock star. Watching him is surreal, this attractive, suave character, oozing charisma, is a world away from the awkward, socially inept man I first knew.

I scan the room and see a doll-like blonde with toned arms and perfect figure standing a little way away from me. She is dressed in a knee-length maroon jersey dress, with dewy skin, barely-there make-up, and doe-like eyes that drink him in. Around her neck is a gold chain carrying a solid gold heart. There's a sadness in the way she holds her wine glass, close to her chest as if for comfort, and I know, instinctively, she's screwed my husband. He's had plenty of sex with other women. I can smell them on him sometimes. Once I found a receipt for a Premier Inn in his jacket pocket. I checked the date in our diary. He'd been at home that night. Grubby daytime sex, Nathan? Classy. Was it this blonde china doll who'd spent a few hours with him in that hotel on the outskirts of Hayle? Did she cry when he told her they wouldn't be having sex again? Because that's what he'd have done. An affair is beneath him. One-off sex? Justifiable in Nathan's head. She means nothing, I can hear him say. She pursued me. If you think about it, I'm the victim. Men are, after all, at the mercy of women's sexuality. But I finished it. Immediately. I'd never have an affair. I love you too much.

And now Nathan's acceptance speech is drawing to a close.

'You're all too kind,' he says, glancing down at the typed-out pages on the lectern in front of him. 'I feel, in many ways, unworthy of this award. What I do is not done for thanks or recognition, but because this place is where my heart lies. In Cornwall. I've been away. I've studied and worked in London. I've lived and worked in Paris. But my heart was always here, where I grew up, where my family are. My *home.*'

I watch him search the crowd for me. When he finds me he smiles, but it's a surface smile that doesn't crease his eyes. My cheeks burn hot as people turn to see who he's looking at. The scrutiny makes me want to curl up and die.

'I'd like to share this award,' he continues, 'with each and every one of you who goes above and beyond to support the community we all love so dearly.'

The room erupts into rapturous applause.

After the ceremony I wait near the entrance, smiling and nodding as people leave, but avoiding conversation. I'm tired and Nathan is on a warpath for Alex.

'Any sign of him?' Nathan demands as he appears at my side.

I shake my head.

'He should have phoned.'

'You took his phone.'

Nathan's eyes narrow.

'Shall I call the school?'

'For God's sake, school closed hours ago. He's not at school. He never was at school. He's missed this on purpose and you can't even imagine the amount of trouble he's in.'

The glint in his eye is unmistakable. And is that the hint of a smile? Are you relishing the prospect of punishing him, Nathan?

Before I have a chance to respond, he's turned his back on me, and is talking to Annie, who is gushing about his speech.

'Honestly, you were brilliant, Nathan. You didn't put a foot wrong. I'm incredibly proud of you.' The words drip off her glistening plum-coloured lips as unctuous as double cream. 'But now, I'm *famished*. Shall we eat?'

Supper with friends. His friends. Annie, a colleague of his, and her husband Steve, who works in data analytics at an accountancy firm based in Plymouth. Steve's only conversation consists of blow-by-blow stories of commuting hell, including complaints directed at rail companies and road maintenance departments, both national and local, with special interest in idle workmen, pot holes, and traffic jams, which he'd expect in London, but not in the West Country for God's sake.

Annie is in love with Nathan, well maybe not love, but she one hundred per cent wants to sleep with him. She hasn't a chance though. She goes heavy on the make-up and favours chunky costume jewellery in gaudy colours. One day I might give her a couple of tips on how to tempt him. Ditch the femme fatale. Channel the ingénue. Incredibly, Steve is oblivious to her flirting. I assume this is either because he's having an affair himself or is so consumed by his commuting traumas he hasn't noticed, both of which, I suppose, would explain why she's so desperate to screw my husband.

'It'll be more fun just the four of us,' Annie purrs when Nathan vents about Alex's inability to show up. 'Having a child around makes everybody more boring, don't you think, Hannah?'

I briefly imagine slapping her face, but instead give an insipid smile and nod. It strikes me then how much insipid smiling and nodding I do.

The blonde woman who I suspect, unlike Annie, has already slept with Nathan, walks quietly up to him and touches his elbow.

He registers alarm, but manages to reaffix his mask quickly. 'Hilary,' he says, as he gives her hand a decorous pat. 'So sweet of you to make time to come tonight. I'm afraid we're dashing out to dinner. See you in the office tomorrow?'

As he guides me out of the hall, I glance back. She remains standing in the emptying hall, hands clasped loosely, isolated from the bustle around her, sad and alone. Her hair has a straight-from-the-salon sheen to it. She had it done especially. Poor cow.

Nathan drives us to Mousehole. There's a new gastropub there which he wants to try. At the table I can't concentrate. Annie and Nathan are talking animatedly. Her grating, girlish laughter cuts right through me and makes it harder for me to tune their voices out. I'm vaguely aware of her pouring his wine, resting a hand on his arm, speaking to him in whispers from behind her raised menu while Steve talks to me about a proposed train strike.

'Don't they realise some people actually need to *work*.'

Every few minutes I glance at my phone which I'm holding as surreptitiously as possible beneath the table in the hope Alex might text me from a friend's phone. At various points in the meal I get up and go to the toilet where I lock myself in a cubicle to call our home number. Each time the phone rings and rings. I imagine it reverberating around the empty house and stirring a disgruntled Charles Cardew. Unease creeps deeper into me. My mother's intuition knows something is wrong.

It occurs to me suddenly, while Steve is ordering another bottle of red wine, that if Alex wanted to hide somewhere to avoid the award ceremony, with no risk of being forced to go, he could have gone to Vicky's. How stupid of me not to think of this earlier. I excuse myself again, and ignoring Nathan's irritation and Annie's evident amusement, hurry through the restaurant.

'Is Alex there?' I ask, when she picks up the call.

'No. Should he be?'

My heart sinks and the niggling fear I felt earlier returns tenfold.

'I thought you both had to go and play happy families with your award-winning husband?'

'He didn't bloody turn up, the pest.' I force myself to sound annoyed and unpanicked. 'Nathan's fuming.'

Vicky tuts. 'He only has to blame himself. He shouldn't be such a controlling arsehole.'

I don't reply.

'Hey, don't worry,' she says then. 'Alex is a bright kid with his head screwed on. He'll be fine. He's probably staying over with a friend.'

'But what if he's not? What if he's hurt? What if he's lying in a ditch?'

'He's fine, sweetheart. I promise. He's probably met some gorgeous girl and they've run off for a night of crazy sex away from the prying eyes of Adolf. Genes will out, after all.'

I stifle a laugh through fresh tears as I picture the look of horror on Nathan's face hearing Vicky call him Adolf. We say goodbye and I promise her at least five times I will call – whatever the time – with any updates.

I hang up and spend a few moments breathing deeply to stop myself from crying. Alex should have made contact by now. It's late. My heart hammers as I stare at the reflection of my face in the dead black of my phone. He has to be with a friend. I dial the first name which springs to mind.

'Caroline? It's Hannah Cardew. Alex's mum?'

'Oh, hi. Everything OK?' She sounds understandably surprised. We have only ever communicated very briefly and always via text or the class WhatsApp group.

'I don't suppose Ben is out with Alex? He—' I pause to exhale to keep my voice from wavering. 'He forgot to take his phone today and, well, I'm out and I need to get hold of him.'

'No, sorry, love. Ben's back now. A group of them went to the park after school and played football. He only got back about an hour ago. Little sod. He had cold fish and chips for supper.' She laughs. 'I imagine Alex was with them. He's no doubt home by now. Have you tried calling him there?'

I have to bite my tongue to stop myself saying something sarcastic. 'I have. Yes.'

'I bet you he's lying on his bed with his headphones on and can't hear the telephone.'

'Would you mind asking Ben if Alex was with them and if he knows whether he went on anywhere?'

'These kids will be the death of us, won't they?'

I force a tight laugh.

'Hang on a moment.'

I picture her turning her face away from the phone, holding her hand over the receiver to muffle her voice as she yells up the stairs.

'Ben!'

A pause.

'*Ben!* Was Alex at the park earlier?'

Another pause.

'Alex. Cardew!'

I strain to hear her son's reply. 'Well, try to remember, for Christ's sake. I've got his mum on the line and the daft boy doesn't have his phone. She sounds worried.'

Another pause before she comes back on the line.

'He says he's not a hundred per cent but doesn't think so.

Honestly,' she says with a tut, 'these boys don't have a clue, do they?' She titters gaily. 'My daughter would have known exactly who was there, who everybody spoke to, what time they all left, and who was going where. But I don't suppose that's much help to you.'

Not much help to me, no, Caroline.

'Thanks, Caroline. I'm sure he's fine.'

CHAPTER ELEVEN

Hannah

Cass is waiting at the door when we walk in, her tail wagging frantically. I drop my hand to stroke her head whilst checking the kitchen for Alex's schoolbag. It's not here. It's not in the hall either. Or the living room.

Panic rips through me with the intensity of forest fire. 'He's not home, Nathan.'

'He's in so much trouble.'

'No,' I say. 'I mean, he's not *home*. It's eleven-thirty and he's not here. Where is he?'

I don't wait for a reply and take the stairs two at a time.

His room is a tip and eerily quiet, the bed unmade, the floor littered with schoolbooks, his pencil case and calculator, muddled in with assorted balled tissues, ink cartridges, a browned apple core, as if his bag has been upended.

Nathan appears behind me and mutters something ill-tempered about the mess.

'For God's sake,' he says sharply. 'Stop looking so worried. He's rebelling, can't you see? Missing the ceremony? It's his idea of a petty stand against me. He's probably drinking somewhere, thinking he's oh-so-clever and cool.'

I don't say anything but, God, I hope he's drinking

somewhere. I hope he's with a group of friends drinking cheap cider out of two-litre bottles, laughing and flirting. I hope his friends asked him if he should be at that thing his dad's doing and I hope he made a face and said, 'Fuck, no, why would I do that when I can get drunk with you lot?' I hope this because if he's drunk with his friends he isn't lying in a ditch somewhere.

I want him home.

Nathan takes in the mess on the floor. 'That looks like stuff from his bag. He didn't go to school?'

'Yes, he did. I mean, I think so. They'd have called, surely?'

Nathan moves with purpose down the stairs. I follow even though I want to run to our room and cocoon myself beneath the covers of the bed. I am bombarded by horrific scenario after horrific scenario. Each one more terrifying than the one before it. Alex lying, broken-limbed, at the bottom of a mine shaft. Alex unconscious at the foot of a cliff. Alex dead beside the road. Alex at the bottom of the sea, his bloated body leaking blood into the salty water…

I grip the study doorframe to steady myself.

Nathan reaches for the phone on his desk. I stare at the painting on the wall, the hunting scene, those men in their flat caps contemplating the lifeless stag. I try and block out the image of Charles Cardew, sitting in the chair, turning the gun towards his face.

'There's a message,' he says, pointing at the phone on his desk, on which a red light pulses ominously. 'Why didn't you check?'

I don't know what to say. I never check for messages. They are never for me. The only person who ever calls me is Vicky and she never uses the landline in case Nathan picks up and she is forced to talk to him.

Nathan puts the phone on speaker. He taps the keypad. Plays the message.

'Good morning. This is a message for Mr or Mrs Cardew. It's Mrs Foster at William Brownley. I'm calling to ask if you could telephone the office to confirm Alex is off school today. You can register an absence on the school website if you log on to the parent portal and click absences.'

My stomach hits the floor.

Nathan silences the answerphone and picks up the receiver and dials.

'Who are you calling?' My voice, like the rest of me, is weak and shaky.

'I'm calling the bloody police, of course.'

CHAPTER TWELVE

Hannah

I assumed the police would reassure us. Tell us not to worry with breezy nonchalance: Oh, you mustn't worry. Teenagers do this all the time and nothing bad ever happens.

But they don't reassure us.

Nathan places the receiver down and takes a breath. His face is grave, mouth twitching, fingers tapping his thigh with agitation. 'They're sending over two officers.'

I nod and walk out of the study, with its tight, stale air, hideous painting, and lingering stench of death, and pull a chair over to the Aga. It's June but I'm cold. Cass quietly gets out of her basket and lies down at my feet, her body, the warmth of it, is comforting. I sit still and focus on my breathing, on drawing air in and out of my lungs, concentrating on the rise and fall of my ribcage, anything to push back recollections of our argument. Why did I shout at him? Why did I take Nathan's side over his? What's wrong with me? I should have never been a mother.

I'm struck by an overpowering urge to walk out of the door. Leave right now. Run. If something has happened to Alex, if he doesn't come home, there would be no reason to stay. The threat of losing Alex has always loomed large. Nathan's voice in my head – threatening to take me to court if I tried to leave again, assuring me he'd win custody, after all who would choose an unstable woman like me over a solvent, respectable lawyer like him – has been there ever since he snatched Alex from my arms at Penzance Station. I'd asked Vicky about custody cases. She said judges always went with the mother, but I could hear the hesitation in her voice. She didn't trust Nathan or the authorities to do the right thing any more than I did. People like us always lost out to people like them. It was just how it worked. But if he doesn't come back, I know, hand on heart, that I'll be gone in the time it takes to grab Cass's lead.

It takes forever for the police to arrive, but at last there's a car on the lane. It draws to a halt outside the house. Headlights move across the kitchen ceiling. I walk along the hallway and peer through the glazed window beside the front door. The glass is uneven and old, and the two figures appear distorted, eerie alien forms approaching the house. My heartbeat quickens and I feel the phantom bite of metal as their handcuffs close around my wrists.

Nathan moves towards the door, hand on the latch, and glances back at me. 'I'll do the talking,' he says in a low voice.

I nod mutely and retreat back to the kitchen, sit myself down on the chair, fold my hands in my lap and wait.

Two voices introduce themselves.

'My wife is in the kitchen,' Nathan says. 'She's,' he lowers his voice but not enough so I can't hear, 'distressed.'

'Of course,' says one of the men in a gruff Bristol accent.

Both men are big and make our kitchen feel over crowded.

One is tall and lean, the other shorter, more muscular, with a misshaped boxer's nose.

'Would you like a cup of tea?' Nathan asks.

The one with the bent nose says, yes, they would, both with milk, one with no sugar, one with three.

'Hannah?' Nathan says. 'Would you mind?'

I make the tea and listen to the three of them completing a missing persons report. So many questions. As I drop tea bags into the bin, my inner voice screams, 'Bloody hell stop wasting time and find him!' I can't hold my tears in any longer.

'Has he gone missing before?'

'No, it's out of character,' Nathan replies, glancing my way briefly. 'Though he is prone to storming off after an argument.'

'Are there many arguments?'

Nathan smiles, unfazed by any intended or unintended insinuation. 'Not many. He's generally a calm child.'

I hand them their teas. They thank me and I return to the armchair. My hand falls instinctively to Cass's head.

'Might he have been drinking?'

'Possibly.'

'Drugs?'

'He's not that kind of child.'

The policemen exchange a glance. They've heard this response many times before. Parents, shocked, taken aback, offended, everybody believing their child is *not that kind of child*.

'Anxiety disorders? Depression?'

'No,' Nathan said. 'I mean, he can be withdrawn. He struggles in certain social situations.'

I should interrupt. I should tell Nathan he's wrong. Alex

has plenty of friends. I've seen him with them, laughing and joking and playing football, like a normal kid. It's just around Nathan he struggles.

'He's reserved,' Nathan continues. 'An introvert. Good student. Recently, however, well, he has become rather... ' Nathan hesitates and chooses his word carefully, 'volatile.'

Both officers glance up when he says this. 'Volatile when you're arguing?'

'He's a teenager,' I say quietly. 'He can be argumentative, especially with his father, but it's nothing unusual.'

Nathan's eyes burn into me.

I pick at a tag of skin on the edge of my thumb. I want our kitchen back to normal. I want Alex home and these bulky, intimidating men with their dark uniforms and loaded glances and never-ending questions gone.

'Do you know how much money he has with him?'

'Money?' Nathan asks.

'A debit card? Savings account?'

'He doesn't have anything like that.'

'Cash?'

'None.'

'What about money from a job?' Both men are staring at Nathan now. The one with the bent nose is studying him with a furrowed brow.

Nathan speaks carefully, his eyes locked on the man with the bent nose. 'Alex doesn't have a savings book and he doesn't have a job because we want him to concentrate on his exams.'

The tall police officer writes something in his notebook.

'What about an allowance or pocket money?'

I shift awkwardly as heat flares on the back of my neck.

'If he wants something, he comes to us and we discuss it. If we decide it's something he needs we buy it for him.'

His use of the word *we* is infuriating. I've lost count of the times I've brought up the subject of an allowance for Alex. I realise I'm glaring at Nathan too late to stop the officer from noticing. He writes something in his notebook and I avert my eyes quickly.

'Giving children money without monitoring how they spend it is bad parenting,' Nathan says. 'Too many children these days get exactly what they want when they want it.' He pauses and shakes his head. 'Not in my house. I've no interest in raising an entitled child with no regard for where money comes from. Teaching a child how to manage money and, most importantly, be responsible with it, is vital.'

The policeman with the bent nose gives Nathan a tight smile.

'And have you checked to see if any cash has gone from either of you?'

'He wouldn't steal.'

Another glance at each other.

'Mr Cardew, I appreciate your son is very well-behaved, but he's gone missing, which you yourself said is out of character. We need to be realistic about whether or not he has money. He can get much further if he does.'

My stomach turns over as an image of Alex's tin comes at me.

Nathan shakes his head. 'Look,' he snaps. 'I don't keep cash in the house, something I imagine you lot would encourage, and I had my wallet with me, so he can't have taken any from there.'

The policeman turns to me. 'And your purse, Mrs Cardew? Have you noticed money going from it?'

'My wife has no cash in the house either.'

Humiliation overwhelms me and I drop my head.

'What about cash cards? Does he know the PINs to your cards?'

'Of course not,' Nathan says flatly. 'That's illegal, isn't it?'

Any respect the men might have had for Nathan has now evaporated and both are eyeing him with dislike. I admire them for this. It's unusual.

The taller man gestures to the door through to the stairway. 'Do you mind if we have a quick look around his room?'

'I'll take you up,' I say quickly. I need to get them on their own. I have to tell them about the tin.

The policeman smiles. 'Kids have no idea how much we worry,' he says gently.

I nod and pull repeatedly at my sleeve. I think of Alex paying for a train ticket, a bus ticket, counting out coins to buy a burger, walking the streets of London watched by drug dealers and thieves and gangs with knives, and feel sick.

I step to one side and allow the men to walk into his empty room. My heart hammers. Nathan has followed us and has no intention of leaving us alone. I have no choice. I have to tell them.

'Excuse me?' My throat is dry and catches my voice. The two police officers turn and look at me expectantly. I can tell by their expressions they've been waiting for me to speak. 'It's… well… '

'Hannah?'

I glance at Nathan who is staring hard at me.

'It's just… He – Alex – he has money.'

I walk over to his desk and bend down.

'What do you mean?' Nathan says sharply.

I open the bottom drawer and rummage at the back. My fingers find the tin and clasp it. I pull it out and face the three men. 'He keeps it in here.'

'Where did he get it from?'

I hesitate. Give the policemen a weak smile. 'My friend Vicky.'

'*Vicky?*'

I ignore Nathan and continue to talk to the officers. 'She gives Alex money on his birthdays. Christmases, too. Not a lot. But enough to buy himself a few bits. A magazine or sweets. A cinema ticket, sometimes. He bought a penknife last year. He watched something about whittling on the television…' Tears prickle and I have to pause for a moment. 'He doesn't buy much,' I whisper. 'He likes to save it.'

'Jesus,' Nathan breathes.

I remove the lid from the tin. It's empty. I hear Vicky's voice as she hands him his birthday card, 'There's a little something inside, sweetheart. Spend it on something fun and pointless.'

'Do you know how much he had?' asks the policeman with the bent nose as he writes in his notebook.

'I'm not sure,' I say, careful to avoid Nathan's eyes. 'Maybe seventy pounds?'

'*Seventy pounds!*'

It's almost comical to see how livid Nathan is but also how hard he's having to work to contain his anger in front of the policemen and, despite the fear and the worry and the sadness, I have to stifle a laugh. As I do, my gaze falls to Alex's desk, and a piece of paper lying on its surface. It's a page torn out of an exercise book with his handwriting on it. I reach for it and trace the words with my fingertip, the writing so even, so neat. Even when he was tiny. Always such neat writing.

I read it and the words blur in my tears, then I hand it to the officer with the bent nose.

Dear Mum

I'm fine. I'll be back soon. I need a bit of space. Sorry not to tell you first but I didn't want you to stop me.

Love you,
Alex

CHAPTER THIRTEEN

Hannah

I should feel happier. Relieved. He planned to go and if he planned it there's less chance he's been abducted or murdered or left for dead in a hit-and-run. But I don't feel reassured. This is proof that there isn't an easy explanation. He isn't with friends. He hasn't 'just lost track of time'. He has left me on purpose.

The floor dissolves beneath me.

I'm vaguely aware of the police officers reassuring us they are still taking the situation seriously. They mention his status. High to medium risk. They will update the police national computer. Units will be on the lookout for him. They want him home safely. I'm aware of Nathan offering to show them out. Aware of them saying goodbye, of them walking away, their feet crunching on the gravel. The sound of their patrol car ignition jumpstarts me and I run down the stairs and fling myself at the front door, fumbling hopelessly with the catch. I want them to promise me they'll find him. They have to bring my son home. They have to.

Nathan reaches over my shoulder and presses my hand flat against the metal lock which digs into my palm. 'Enough now.'

I try and shake his hand off me, but he presses harder.

'*Enough.*'

His face is devoid of even a scrap of sympathy. 'They have to find him, Nathan.'

He turns his back to me and slides the chain across, bolts the door, top and bottom, then locks the Chubb and drops the key into his pocket. He faces me, his expression glacial. 'Behaving like a lunatic isn't going to bring him home. You need to calm down.'

My body is trembling. He doesn't take his eyes off me. I try to control my breathing. Breathe in, breathe out. Breathe in, breathe out. 'I feel so helpless.'

'He has a lot to answer for.'

'I just want him to be OK.'

For a moment or two he says nothing, only stares, slow-blinking and angry. But then he takes a deep breath through his nose and intensifies his gaze. 'Vicky should never have given him money.'

'It was a present,' I whisper. 'That's all.'

'That's not all, though, is it? Do you see the damage she's done? How far do you think he'd have got without money? If she hadn't given it to him he'd still be here, Hannah. Do you see that? You should never – *never* – have let him accept it. What were you thinking?'

This is a rhetorical question and I make no attempt at an answer.

'If he doesn't come back... '

Nathan's half sentence hangs in the air around me like a poisonous gas. When I look at him I can see the unsaid words in his eyes.

. . . it's your fault.

He walks into his study and closes his door. The hallway

is dark and silent. The walls inch in on me, the ceiling creeps downwards. Claustrophobia takes hold and my chest tightens, my fingers turn numb. Anxiety has made me jittery. I need to get out. I need to breathe fresh air. I need to walk. I think of my cigarettes behind the washing powder and my log in the copse. But I can't leave the house in case Alex or the police call. The helplessness is paralysing. I need to do something. I need to keep myself occupied. I tread the stairs, as quietly as possible, not wanting to alert Nathan to my movements. I want him to leave me alone. I don't need his anger or his judgement or blame. I open the door to Alex's room. I scan the mess and the ache in my stomach throbs violently.

I decided to tidy his room. At least it's something to do. I begin by making his bed. The sheets could do with a change, but I leave them; I don't want to wash away the smell of him. Not yet. Just in case. The musty odour of teenage boy might be all I have left of him. I sweep rubbish from his desk into the waste bin and put three coffee-stained mugs outside the door on the landing next to the pile of dirty clothes I've assembled. I straighten the papers on his desk, tidy his pens away, and return the tin he kept Vicky's money in to the bottom drawer. I stand, hands on hips, and tip my head back and sigh. Cleaning his room was supposed to make me feel useful. I'd hoped it might ease the gnawing fear, but it only intensifies my feelings of inadequacy. As a mother, the only job which matters is keeping your child safe. If I haven't managed that, I've failed. Everything else is meaningless.

I sit heavily on the edge of his bed and grip the duvet either side of me. The empty silence hums in my ears.

'God, Alex,' I whisper. 'Where are you?'

CHAPTER FOURTEEN

Hannah

Exhaustion has crept into the centre of my bones, but there is no way I can sleep. Visions of him out there, God-knows-where, plague me, cold and hungry, huddled in a doorway in a faceless city, miles away from me, fending off predatory advances from tough-lads after Vicky's roll of five-pound notes. I consider taking the car out to search for him, but it's a fleeting thought. Being stopped without a licence in a car I'm not insured to drive or, worse, being involved in an accident, won't help anybody. Plus I have absolutely no idea where he might have gone, so here I sit, impotent and useless in a chair beside the Aga, mobile phone in one hand, landline in the other, watching the door until the sun pushes into the night sky and dilutes the darkness with gauzy light.

At seven-thirty Nathan's footfalls descend the stairs. He goes into his study. Papers rustle. His briefcase clicks open. Clicks closed. He approaches the kitchen and I straighten myself in the chair and instinctively smooth my hands over my hair and pinch the skin of my cheeks to give them some colour.

'You look shattered.' He fills the kettle and takes two teacups from the cupboard. 'You should have slept. Stupid to stay up all night.'

He makes two cups of tea and hands one to me. I take it and refocus on the back door as if this is the only place I will ever look from now on.

'I'm in client meetings most of the day, but if there's any news leave a message with my secretary.'

He drinks his tea, places the mug on the worktop, then kisses me on the head and walks out of the door.

The rest of the morning passes in a blur with acute periods of alternating fear and guilt interspersed with aching tiredness as I stumble through this nightmarish haze. It's my day for doing the laundry but instead I pull the door to the utility room closed and shut away the piles of sheets and clothes waiting patiently in front of the washing machine. As I do, I catch sight of the study door on the other side of the hallway. It's open a crack and I turn away quickly, terrified of glimpsing Charles Cardew lying on the floor, his blood seeped into the threads of the expensive Oriental rug beneath him.

I need to get out.

I phone the police station and am reassured that if there's any news they will call my mobile. I write a note for Alex, hope firing inside me as I form each word, and stick it on the fridge door telling him I'm with my mother and to call me the moment he walks in. I sign it with a kiss and take a moment or two to stem my tears.

Mum's care home was one of the first places I telephoned when Alex went missing. Even though they promised to call immediately if he turned up, I still have a glimmer of hope he'll be there, in Mum's room, sharing a cup of tea and some Bourbons with her.

Moving her into Heamoor was horrendous and broke my

heart, but after she broke her hip and wrist we had no choice. In a split second, the time it took to trip on a step, she went from fit and independent to frail and reliant on help. She could no longer get to the shops and was unable to cook for herself. She found it hard to dress, and getting in and out of the bath was impossible. I begged Nathan to consider letting her come and live with us but he wouldn't even discuss it. As care homes go, it's passable. There are no frills, no luxuries, and the stench of cheap disinfectant lingers in the corridors which are painted beige to match the food. But her room overlooks a small internal rose garden with a birdbath that attracts a variety of wildlife which she loves. Nathan views my mother's health with contempt, as if she is somehow to blame for growing old, for letting her body atrophy and her joints seize up with arthritis, and now, devastatingly, allowing her memory to fade. By contrast his own mother is hugely capable and maintains every bit of her independence and dignity. She is fit, looks years younger than she is – helped by expensive face creams, weekly facials, and, I suspect, a surgeon's knife – plays bridge twice a week, does *The Times* crossword every morning, and plays tennis at a fancy members' club in West London. She holidays in Tuscany for weeks at a time with Phillip, a man she refers to as her *gentleman companion*. She sent Nathan a photograph of the swimming pool at the villa they stayed at last year. Phillip was in the background, sitting in a comfortable chair in the dappled shade, reading a novel with a Panama hat perched on his head and thin white legs poking out of salmon pink shorts. Both Phillip and Sylvia are, Nathan tells me categorically, testament to the importance of taking care of your mind and body. What he means is inferior life choices are to blame for my father's heart attack at fifty-eight and my mother's incapacity. I can't be bothered to explain that choice never came into it. We ate what we could afford, exercise and work were one and the same, and a holiday, well, that was a word other people used.

The sale of my childhood home, the tiny terraced cottage up a steep hill in the backstreets of Newlyn, was never going to be enough to pay for her care for more than a few years, and I was forced to rely on Nathan to top up the meagre council contribution. Nathan views his financial support of my mother as a clear demonstration of his philanthropic nature. He is, by his own admission, a generous and compassionate son-in-law, and takes great pains to point this out at any opportunity. I see it as another reason why I continue to have sex with him.

The staff at Heamoor are pleasant enough despite being overworked, underpaid and often verbally abused by patients and their unreasonably demanding families. I never kick up a fuss. If something hasn't been done for Mum, whether that's emptying the bin or running her dinner tray from the previous night down to Paul in the kitchens or cleaning her toilet, I do it myself in the hope, perhaps misguided, that if I help and don't complain, they'll be kinder to Mum.

Even though I knew Alex wouldn't be there, my heart sinks to see my mother alone, sitting in her chair, looking out of the window. I close the door behind me and, despite feeling hollowed out, this tiny room envelops me with a blanket of calm. The lemon yellow walls might need repainting and the curtains are decades old, but here, with my mother, it feels like a haven. The windows don't open all the way, apparently to stop people climbing out, but enough of a breeze gets through to allow the air to feel fresh and light.

'Hello, *Dama*.'

My mother turns in her chair and smiles at me. 'Hello, *melder*. Oh, goodness, is it Friday already?' Her voice is faint, but retains the sing-song quality I remember from my childhood.

'Thursday,' I say as I drag a chair over to sit beside her. 'I just felt like seeing you, that's all.'

Her hand is soft and light against my cheek. I lean against it and close my eyes.

'Sweetheart. *Melder*. What's wrong? Is Alex OK?'

I nod. 'All OK, *Dama*.' When I've managed to control my tears, I take her featherlight hand in mine. Her papery skin is so soft. She has always taken good care of her skin. There was hand cream in every room in our house, by the sink in the kitchen, the basin in the bathroom, by her bed, and mine. I lean forward and take hold of the pot from the windowsill. I unscrew the lid. I dip my finger into it, leaving a deep groove in the creamy whiteness, and rub it between my palms. I cream her hands one at a time.

She looks down. 'Oh, thank you, *melder*. That's kind. I like to keep my hands soft. They take such a beating with all the family chores.'

Her mind has drifted and she is looking out of the window again. She is watching a blackbird washing in the birdbath, dipping his head into the water, shaking out his wings, using his beak to tease out his glossy feathers.

'Pretty isn't he?' Mum says, her watery eyes fixed on the bird.

'He is.'

My gaze falls to the storm glass on her windowsill. It's

in the form of a bird, about the size of a hen's egg, and was a birthday gift from Alex. Nathan gives him ten pounds every year to choose something for me. Of all the presents I've had in my life it's the most precious. Nathan sneered at it, dismissed it as ugly, dismissed the chemistry behind it, the idea that a mixture of chemicals dissolved in ethanol can predict the weather by forming different configurations of crystals. He was so carping I decided to bring it up here, to Mum's, where she and I could enjoy it, and Alex would know it was appreciated. Mum loves to sit peacefully and stare at the opaque crystals suspended in the clear liquid inside. Alex had been fascinated by the mechanics of the storm glass ever since I told him the story Cam had told me about the nineteenth-century admiral who designed a barometer – a storm glass – to help fishermen in poor areas predict storms at sea. When Alex presented it to me, hopping about with excitement as he thrust the badly wrapped gift into my hands, and I'd opened it, seen this delicate thing, weather crystals formed inside her, I cried. I pick up the bird and stroke the edge of my thumb over the smooth glass, remembering his beautiful beaming face when I told him I loved it, then slip it into the pocket of my cardigan.

There's a soft knock on the door which then opens. It's Patricia, my favourite of Mum's carers, a cheerful, bosomy woman who smells of talcum powder and has unruly brown curls held at bay by an array of brightly coloured hair grips.

'Ah, hello, pet. This is a nice surprise. We don't usually see you on a Thursday. All OK? The girls on the desk told me you'd phoned looking for Alex. Is he back?'

I glance at my mother whose eyes have fluttered closed, a streak of sunlight warming her face, like a cat in a sunbeam.

Part of me wants to open my heart to Patricia, cry and sob, let her hold me and tell me it's all going to be OK, that boys will be boys and teens will be teens and who doesn't know a kid who's played truant from school. But I can't risk Mum overhearing. 'He left a note and said he'd be back later. His room's such a mess, I didn't see it before.'

She chuckles and shakes her head. 'They have no idea how we worry, do they? Tell him we missed him yesterday. Always a pleasure to see his lovely, happy face.'

Alex visits my mother every week after school on a Wednesday. He's done it for the past two years and rarely misses a week. The nurses love him and tell me he brings a breath of fresh air to the place.

I don't reply to her. I can't.

'Last week he was showing me all those lovely photos of yours. I love a bit of—'

'Sorry?' I say, interrupting her sharply.

'What?'

'What photos?'

She furrows her brow and gestures towards Mum's cupboard.

My heart skips a beat.

'You know, the ones you keep here in her wardrobe. The box with the old photos and letters and bits and bobs. Kids love looking at that sort of thing, don't they? He had it all spread out on the bed for the whole time he was here. Bless him. We were looking at the photos. Lovely to see Newlyn back then. Not that's it's changed too much, of course.'

My mind is turning over and over. I open the wardrobe door and look up at the top shelf. It's rammed with those things Mum couldn't bear to throw out when she moved out of her home: a collection of ornaments she'd chosen with Dad, trinkets, her grandmother's lace handkerchief, a tiny tarnished photo frame displaying the dried four-leaf clover she found when she was a girl. Photograph albums. The veil she wore on her wedding day, wrapped carefully in tissue paper and slipped into a plastic bag.

Behind all this is a box which belongs to me which I keep here so it won't be found.

I stand on tiptoes and search with my fingers until I make contact with the box. Why was Alex even looking in Mum's cupboard? Did he stumble on the box by accident or go looking for it? A strange sensation envelops me, as if two separate incompatible parts of me are being forced unnaturally together. I hold the box tightly to my chest as if trying to protect it.

'I loved the photos of you when you were young. You were such a pretty thing, weren't you? I mean,' she adds hurriedly, looking comically worried, 'you still are, of course. I think I mean you must have had a queue of boys at your door. Speaking of which,' she says, 'your husband's quite the looker, isn't he?'

There are no photos of Nathan inside the box.

My heart hammers hard enough to burst through my ribcage. The feeling of exposure makes my knees buckle. It's as if she's stripped my skin away. I want her to stop talking. To wipe her memory and tuck everything from my past back into the box and hide it at the back of the cupboard.

She raises her eyebrows and winks. 'I can see why you held on to him!'

I try to smile, but the thought of Alex looking through my private stuff is paralysing.

'Right, well, I should get on,' Patricia says, suddenly serious, realising, perhaps, her salacious glee isn't finding its audience. 'Shout for me when she wakes and I'll pop along with a cup of tea for you both.'

Patricia leaves me alone and closes the door behind her. I take the box into Mum's tiny shower room with its easy-to-hose-down moulded plastic, a handrail and an alarm on a red cord. I close the toilet seat and sit down. The box is old and battered with flimsy sides and bits of yellowed sticky tape holding three of the edges together. The photo of Cam and me is lying on the top. I feel sick at the thought of Alex unpacking everything, pouring over my personal things, then placing it all back. I stare at the photo and presume this is the one Patricia saw, which made her think that he was my husband. We look so in love – which, of course, we were – leaning against the metal railings on the pier. He's wearing jeans and a thick sweater, a black woollen hat on his head. His beautiful eyes glint as he laughs. I can hear the echo of it, deep and gravelly, and my stomach clenches. In the photo I'm curled into him, my head tilted, so my cheek rests on his chest. My hair has been taken by the wind and both of us are squinting against the early winter sunshine. Sitting in Mum's room, my heart still thumping, I recall the warmth of him, his smell, the taste of him. I'm laughing too. Though I can't remember why. Had we shared a joke? Or were we laughing because laughing for the sake of it was what we did back then? I don't even remember who took the photo. Vicky? Or Geren? Or one of the others whose names I can't remember. I turn the photograph over and read the writing on the back.

My a'th kar.

I stare at the Cornish words I'd taught him. His handwriting is irregular and messy. I trace the shape of each letter with my fingertip as I recall the horrors of that night. What followed. Losing him. Accepting I'd have to live my life without him in it.

I picture Alex holding this photograph. A window into a time before he was born. A version of his mother he doesn't know. I see his face as he studies the rest of the photographs, as he absorbs every detail, assesses the people he doesn't know, the smile he gives when he recognises Vicky, his brain whirring as he tries to piece together this historical jigsaw.

I pick up my diary and leaf through it. Full of teenage angst and exclamation marks, capital letters, hearts, stars and doodles. Paisley scrawls filling the spaces. The bands I loved scrawled in spiky letters. The names of the boys I kissed. Then the pages dedicated to Cam. Embarrassing entries detailing private thoughts and emotional proclamations in the flowery prose of a twenty-two-year-old girl truly in love for the first time. Those passages where I describe what I want to do to him. What I want him to do to me. God.

Did Alex read it?

I turn to the back page of the diary. Drag my fingers lightly over the back sleeve. The edge of the letter tucked into it pokes out. I wish I'd never met him. I wish we hadn't gone to the cinema that night. I should have stayed home. Gone to the pub or watched television or played cards with my dad.

I can see his hand on the armrest. Long, weathered fingers resting on the crushed red velvet.

My finger inches close enough to graze his.

Don't do it!

It's too late. With dread I watch my finger touch his hand

and his thumb move imperceptibly against me. Electricity sparks. A glance. My breath held as he looks at me.

No!

I close the diary. I can't change history, can't change what happened, can't alter the events which followed after our fingers grazed against each other in that darkened cinema.

I pack the letters, photographs, and diary back in the box, and return it to the top shelf of Mum's cupboard. The air seems to have curdled and the smell of disinfectant and baked beans is creeping through the gap beneath the door like gas. There are footsteps in the hall. Voices. The woman in the next room is moaning, as she often does, the paper-thin walls doing nothing to muffle her. She can make these distressed noises for hours, standing beside the suitcase she keeps permanently packed at her door, telling anybody who'll listen that her son is on his way to collect her. I don't have the heart to explain her son is never coming.

Patricia coughs gently and peers around the door. 'I'm going home now, love. Marie is taking over. Give Alex my love when he comes in.'

I sit with Mum for a while longer, but she doesn't wake from her nap. Her face is serene as she sleeps, her lips loose, mouth open a fraction, her breathing easy. Guilt has thickened in my stomach. It seems wrong not to tell her about Alex but knowing her grandson is missing would devastate her, and I have enough of my own worry to deal with without having to cope with hers on top.

Before I go, I kiss her forehead. She stirs a little, but doesn't wake. '*My a'th kar, Dama.*'

I don't usually smoke during the day, but today I sit on the bench outside the care home and have two. As I smoke, I hold the storm glass, my beautiful little bird, up towards the sky. The sunlight passes through her delicate casing. I bring her closer, stare harder, and as I do, I see the crystals trapped inside are now perfect tiny diamonds.

CHAPTER FIFTEEN

Hannah

The horrendous waiting, coupled with helplessness, is driving me insane. I've scratched the inside of my wrist so much the skin is raw. Nathan is calm. Too calm. I don't understand it. I lean against the sink, my foot tapping, desperate for a cigarette and watch him as he sits in the armchair with a book. His reading glasses are perched on the end of his nose, legs crossed, licking a finger and turning each page deliberately and slowly.

His serenity makes me want to run at him and scream in his face.

How can you be calm? Are you made of actual stone?

'There must be something more we can do?' I mutter.

He places his book on his lap and looks up at me. When he speaks his voice is placid and soothing, almost priest-like. 'We have to trust the police to do their job.'

I ball my fists and dig the nails into the heel of my palm. I glance at the door for the thousandth time. 'I can't stop thinking about the argument you had and what—'

'Sorry?' His brow furrows into a quizzical frown. He closes his book, pauses, then makes a soft scoffing sound.

I chew the edge of my lip.

'Hang on a moment,' he laughs. 'You think this is something

to do with *me*?' He smiles and shakes his head incredulously. 'You think this is because of an argument *I* had with him?'

I stare at him. 'When I came back from walking the dog. You were shouting at each other. You took his phone—'

Nathan stands up and walks over to me. His expression now one of manufactured bafflement. It's a look I know well. 'I can't believe you'd think it was because of *me*. He got upset because *you* shouted at him. He's used to me being the one to discipline him. He and I come to blows all the time. He doesn't care if he provokes me. It's water off a duck's back.' His words are coated in honey, but his stare is a red-hot poker. 'How many times in the last month have Alex and I argued?'

The hairs on the back of my neck prickle. 'I know what you're doing.' It's hard to keep the waver out of my whispered words. 'This isn't my fault. You can't—'

'It's a simple question, Hannah.' He moves to the sink and fills a glass of water. Heat has crept over my skin. We are only a few inches from each other. The smell of his coal tar shampoo and sickly sweet aftershave catches in my throat.

'How many times have he and I argued about,' he pauses and thinks theatrically for a beat, 'oh, I don't know, his home-work, let's say. Or the state of his bedroom? His table manners or what he should be studying at university?' He drinks then places the glass down precisely before looking up at me. 'How many times, in fact, have we argued about his mobile phone? I mean, in the last month. Roughly?' He stares at me. 'What do you think?'

I don't reply.

'Hannah?'

I draw in a breath. 'Lots,' I whisper.

'What was that?' he says. 'I didn't hear you.'

I straighten my shoulders and lift my chin with as much defiance as I can muster. '*Lots*,' I repeat, louder this time. 'In the last month, you've argued lots of times.' I try and make my words sharp and pointed, but he counters them with a satisfied smile.

'Exactly. *Lots*. Alex and I have argued many, many times, and not once has he done anything more dramatic than sulk in his bedroom for few hours. But this time? This time *you* weighed in. You didn't need to – I don't need your help when it comes to discipline – but nonetheless you stood right here, in this kitchen, and shouted at him. Can you imagine what it must have been like for him? How hurt he was? His mother turning on him like that? You lost your cool and tipped him over the edge. You gave him nowhere to turn. No safe harbour.'

A lump forms in my throat and I quickly blot the tears which are streaking my cheeks. I revisit the argument. It's hard to recall. Did I really shout like he says? All I can remember is being desperate to stop the argument between them, wanting Alex to hand his phone over so Nathan would get off his back. Another two tears fall and I drop my head as I swipe at them.

'Hey,' he croons, his voice now soft, free of the vindictive needling of moments before. 'Parenting is tough. Especially with teenagers. We all get it wrong sometimes. I know you were trying to do the right thing. Alex was being extremely rude and disrespectful and, yes, he was hurt, and, *yes*, he's overreacted in a way that endangers him, but Hannah… ' He reaches for my arm and strokes it. 'You weren't wrong to reprimand him and even though, in retrospect, I wish you hadn't, I appreciate you meant well.'

I don't know what to say. I'm fully aware of what he's doing, aware of the facts being twisted and contorted and reshaped, but even so, I can hear the truth in it. Guilt and blame flood me. Nathan's right. If I'd have taken Alex's side, if I'd fought my son's corner, he'd never have run away. He'd have been cross with Nathan. He'd have hated him for confiscating his phone. But when I took sides he felt abandoned and had nobody to turn to. All I needed to do was stand up for my son. What's the worst that could have happened? Nathan would have been angry with me. Right now, I hate myself so intensely it's a physical pain. I deserve this.

I deserve it all.

Nathan goes back to the chair and picks up his book. 'I've got a bit of work to do before we turn in. I'll be in my study if you need me. Try to relax. The police are doing all they can. That money won't last forever and, when it's gone, he'll be back.'

I go to Cass's basket and crouch down and take her head between my hands and press my face against her silken fur. Then something startles her. She pulls away from me. Her head turns and her ears prick up. She gets out of her basket and trots out of the kitchen, her claws tapping on the stone tiles in the hallway as she moves down towards the front door. Then I hear a car. Headlights move across the window. I hold my breath. The engine quietens. I jump up and run down the hallway. I can see headlights stopped beside the gate. They switch off and outside turns black again.

'Alex?' I fumble desperately with the lock. 'Oh, please. Alex…'

I reach up to yank down the bolt Nathan insists on using,

but my fingers slip and slide like the damn thing is buttered. I'm aware of Nathan's voice behind me. I ignore him as I fling open the door and run out on to the path. The gravel grazes my bare feet, but I don't care at all because there, in front of me, is my son.

I laugh and cry simultaneously as I run to him. My boy is walking through the gate. When he sees me he drops his bag and sprints to me, arms wide, like he used to do across the playground after nursery. I throw my arms around him and squeeze him, kiss him all over, knowing I will never let go of him and we will stand like this on the path, his body held tight to mine, forever. I breathe him in as if I've been starved of oxygen. His hair needs a wash and his clothes hold the scent of two days' continuous wear and unfamiliar smells. I want to rub the smells off him and make him smell like mine again.

I stroke his cheek and kiss him again and whisper in his ear, 'Don't *ever* do that again. Christ, please, I couldn't live without you.' I stand back from him, hold his face in my hands, and allow the tears of relief and love stream my cheeks. 'Jesus. I thought I might die from worry.'

'I'm sorry,' he says quietly. 'I told you not to.'

Cass barks and jumps up around us, so manic in her joy, I worry she might explode. I laugh and Alex drops down to kiss her, pushes his face into her ruff of fur, and whispers words I can't hear. He smiles up at me, but then his attention is taken, and his happiness melts away. His body stiffens and he stands slowly.

I glance back to see Nathan who is lit from behind by the light from the hallway. His fists are clenched at his sides. It's hard to make out his expression in the shadow cast across his face, but I can tell from his body language he's filled up with rage.

'Don't be angry, Nathan,' I say. 'We have time for that. Let's go inside. Have a cup of tea. All that matters is he's home.'

But Nathan doesn't respond.

Then I realise he isn't looking at Alex. He's fixed on something behind him. I turn and follow the line of his gaze then inhale sharply.

There's a man standing at the gate. In the light from the house I can see he is dressed in jeans and some sort of Parka jacket, hair unkempt. The eyes staring out of his face are as familiar as my own.

'Oh my god,' I breathe. '*Cam?*'

CHAPTER SIXTEEN

Cam, 1998

Cam drew up beside *The Annamae* and squinted through the driving rain. He could see Slim's shadowy figure through the window of the wheelhouse and took his hand out of his pocket, put his fingers in his mouth, and gave a loud whistle. Slim looked up from what he was doing and when he saw Cam he raised a hand in solemn greeting. Even through the rain-obscured window, Cam could tell he was in a grim mood and considered turning on his heel.

Cam climbed up on to the side of the boat and jumped nimbly over the gunwale and on to the deck. Slim kept a tidy ship and everything was in its rightful place, tight coils of rope, heavy rusted chains wound carefully, washed down stacks of yellow plastic boxes ready and waiting to be filled with fresh fish and ice.

As Cam walked into the wheelhouse Slim greeted with him with a nod of the head.

Cam leant against the doorframe. 'The boys,' he said. 'They're keen to get out.'

Slim raised his eyebrows in mild amusement. 'And they've sent you to convince me?'

Cam didn't reply.

Slim's real name was Jim Baker, but everyone knew him as Slim, a nickname he'd been given because of the many things Baker was, slim wasn't one of them. He was a big man, six foot two or three, and heavy-set with a stomach that strained against his clothes. He dressed well, in white collared shirts and neatly pressed trousers. His wife, Betty, had *standards*, and would send him on every trip with a holdall of perfectly ironed clothes, with a fresh shirt for each day. The rest of them wore the same clothes for days at a time, some not even changing to sleep. Slim never set foot on any boat without his scrimshaw knife, a bone-handled penknife engraved with a simple drawing of a clipper ship. The crew of *The Annamae*, like all fishermen, were slaves to superstition. Slim's knife had become their talisman. Who knew what bad luck they'd be hit with if he ever came aboard without it? The knife had belonged to Slim's great, great grandfather who was famed for causing the only recorded injury in the Newlyn fishing riots of 1896 when he clocked a policeman on the head with a fish box. According to Baker family lore, after knocking the man to the ground, he kissed the handle of the knife, disappeared into the melee and escaped.

Slim rubbed his jaw and sighed heavily. 'There's a break coming in the next day or two. But it's short. Maybe not even half a day. Enough to get out but with more gales forecast . . .' He sucked on his teeth. 'The other skippers are staying in. Say it's not worth it.' Slim hesitated. The truth was it could well be worth it. Trawlers had been tied up throughout the country for over two weeks and prices were soaring. There was money to be made for the first boat to take a chance on the forecasts. When he next spoke, Cam was surprised to hear uncertainty in his voice. 'But then again, we're all skint as monks. Christmas is coming. Betty's worrying about presents. Jesus, she's ordered a turkey the size of a car. I owe money on *The Annamae*. The repairs last month cost a small fortune.' He glanced at Cam with an expectant expression.

'You want my opinion?' Cam stifled a laugh.

Slim didn't reply. He never asked for advice. It was his job to make the decisions, Cam's to haul the fish in.

Cam thought of Hannah's arms looped around his neck, her fingers lightly stroking his back as her tongue explored his mouth. The thought of leaving to battle freezing waters, haul nets until his bones ached, and sleep in the bunk room, stacked like sardines next to unwashed fishermen, while she was lying warm in bed, hair fanning the pillow, soft and sweet-smelling, was agonising. But he needed to get paid. Just thinking about that Cardew prick turning her head with fancy meals was enough to make him breathless with jealousy.

'I vote to go,' he said. 'The lads are climbing the walls. Geren's like a caged dog.'

Slim laughed. 'He a madman, that's why.'

'We're all madmen. Have to be to do this job. Look, it's your call, Slim, but you'd not get any argument from us.'

The Annamae set off from Newlyn a shade before two in the morning. There were no stars or moon to soften the darkness, and as she chugged through the ebony water towards the opening in the harbour wall, they could hear the sea raging like a ferocious beast in the dark. The fishing gear was stowed on deck, the heavy chains and nets tucked in beneath the overhanging gunwales, and the cupboards were stacked with supplies for two weeks. There was a palpable sense of excitement in the galley as the crew sat and nursed mugs of thick coffee. The group of men included a youngster – seventeen years old – called Lawrence Mould, or Lawrie, he said, for short. Lawrie Mould had shown up a few days before and begged Slim for a place on his next trip. He arrived on the pier that morning holding a rucksack and looking exactly like a kid on his first day of school. He hadn't spoken a word as they'd loaded the boat with provisions, and all the crew knew about him was what Slim had told them: that the lad came from a nowhere town in the Midlands with a string of jobs he'd stuck at for no more than a day or two behind him.

'For fuck's sake,' scoffed Geren, in a loud enough whisper for the boy to hear, 'just what this trip needs, a lazy kid with no balls.'

Lawrie's cheeks pinked up and he pulled at his sleeve, looking, worryingly, as if he might start crying.

Cam watched Geren and Davy exchange conspiratorial looks. Lawrie would have to take it. It was the way things were. Teasing *deckie learners* was tradition and there was no way this wet-behind-the-ears lad would escape it.

'I'm not lazy,' Lawrie said, unable to meet anybody's eyes. 'I want to work.'

'Well, you see lad, there's work and there's fishing.' Geren was unable to keep the smirk from his voice. 'You might want to work, but I can tell already, there's no way you've got what it takes to fish.'

Lawrie's face grew pinker still.

Davy laughed and muttered 'dickhead' under his breath.

'Right.' Slim interrupted them with a sharp, teacher-like clap.

'When we get to the fishing grounds I want you lot pulling in like crazy men. We're looking for big hauls. The market is dead and people are desperate. We're one of the only boats out and if we fish large we'll rake it in.'

The men started to jest and joke, but he quietened them with a raised hand.

'Like you know, there's weather on the way. I'm going to do all I can to skirt it, but there's a chance it might catch us.'

Cam noticed the knuckles on Slim's calloused hands were white with clenching.

'They said it could hit a force ten.'

Geren whistled through his teeth. 'When?'

'Two days. Thursday evening. Could be Friday.'

'Right, so we haul from when we reach the grounds and don't stop,' Geren said. 'Who needs sleep anyway, right?'

Lawrie started to speak. His lips were stretched thin and pale as milk. 'Should we be out there?'

Geren snapped his head around and scoffed loudly. 'We don't need to hear from you. Shut your mouth and do what you're told.'

Lawrie looked down at the floor and swallowed.

'Get some sleep.' Slim ignored both men. 'We'll be sixteen hours before we shoot away.'

Cam trusted him to avoid the brunt of the storms. It would be rough out there in the freezing Atlantic seas, but nothing they hadn't coped with a hundred times before. The men headed down the hatch into the bunk room. These hours were precious, an opportunity to rest; once they got hauling there'd be little time for sleep and it was gruelling work.

An all too familiar anxiety thrummed in the pit of Cam's

stomach. Heading out to sea always gave him a sense of vulnerability and, when they lost the lights of Newlyn and were surrounded on all sides by blackness and endless water, isolation. Six men, no more than specks of dust on an ocean so powerful and unpredictable, so savage, they could be swallowed up in the blink of a mermaid's eye. Thoughts of his father were never far from his mind. He was fourteen when his dad was lost. Memories of him were murky and undefined. However hard he concentrated, any image of him was no more than a vague shape. But he remembered how excited he used to be whilst waiting for his father to return from sea, and though he had trouble picturing his face, the smell of him was easy, thick with salt and fish, oil and old sweat. There were the stories he used to tell him as well, sitting on his lap beside the wood burner, tales of the sea he recalled word for word. His father would have loved Hannah, Cam was certain of that, and he ached when he thought about the two of them remaining strangers.

'Try and get some shut-eye, lad,' Cam said to Lawrie who hovered at the hatch to the bunk room. 'You'll need your strength.'

Lawrie reluctantly climbed down the ladder, but Cam didn't follow. There was no point trying to sleep. His mind was buzzing. Instead he went up to find Slim in the wheelhouse.

Slim was at the wheel, mouth set, eyes hooded with grim concentration as he looked out of the window into the blackness, then down at the screen, at the green illuminated lines and flickering dots which gave him the information he needed to get where he was taking them.

'Can you smell where the fish are at?' Cam pulled his tobacco pouch from his back pocket.

'Of course.' Slim cast him a fleeting smile. 'But I don't think we'll escape the weather. Like I said, I'll try, but it's not looking great.'

Cam rolled a cigarette and licked the edge to seal it. 'We've done storms before and we'll do them again. You've got your lucky knife. We'll be fine. And, anyway,' he said, grinning, 'a good storm'll sort the deckie learner out, for sure. Lad looked pretty green just now. I sent him to his bunk, but I reckon we've got some puking to look forward to.'

Young Lawrence Mould – as Cam predicted – started throwing up around four in the morning and didn't stop for six solid hours. The others sat around the table in the galley clasping mugs of tea and smoking cigarettes. Each time the boy vomited into the stinking latrine behind the apology for a door, Davy and Geren sniggered. If there was one thing to sort out a cocky lad who thought fishing was an easy wage, it was a dose of seasickness. Even Cam couldn't hold back his smile. Martin was too old to waste energy teasing kids and was seemingly oblivious to the gut-wrenching as he sat reading his paper and eating toast and jam.

Cam was thankful for the distraction, even if that distraction was the sound of Lawrie Mould heaving his guts up. He couldn't get that prick Cardew out of his head. Images of him and Hannah sitting opposite each other – all dressed up, drinking wine, her eyes flickering in the candlelight – bombarded him. Why hadn't she mentioned it? Was she playing around behind his back? Just thinking about that made his body rage. He thought back to their last few hours together. His lips on hers. Moving inside her. The conversation they'd had as she lay in his arms, her thigh resting on his, her fingers toying with the hair on his chest. No. It wasn't possible. There was no way she was sleeping around. And definitely not with that dickhead. Cam would have given everything to be with her rather than stuck on a boat with a puking deckie learner and the prospect of hauling nets for the next thirty-six hours without sleep.

Another bout of violent retching interrupted Cam's thoughts.

'Don't worry, Lawrie,' Geren called through his laughter. 'Only ten days to go!'

'Ten days?' came Lawrie's plaintive moan.

Cam laughed.

'Should have listened to your mummy when she told you to work hard at school,' Geren shouted.

Lawrie was sick again.

'Jesus,' Davy said. 'How much puke can one wanker throw up? If he was in the army we'd have beaten the crap out of him for this.'

The latrine door opened and Lawrie appeared, green as peas, wiping his hand across his mouth.

'Ah, here he is! The seasick fisherboy!' Geren raised his mug in a toast.

Lawrie walked hesitantly into the galley and started to sit at the table.

Geren stretched his arm out to block his way. 'Woah! You're not sitting anywhere near me. What if you puke on my toast?'

Perhaps it was the sickness or perhaps Lawrie was just a crazy motherfucker, but rather than nod and move away, he pushed against Geren's arm and scowled at him. 'I'm not going to be sick, OK?'

Martin looked up in surprise at Lawrie's tone.

Geren blazed. He stood up, both hands on the table, and

leant close to Lawrie's face. 'Can't you hear properly, you twat? I said, *fuck off*, and when you've fucked off, you can fuck off some more. You little pussy.'

The atmosphere in the galley had chilled as the laughs had faded and Geren's anger poisoned the air. Cam was about to tell Geren to take it easy, but Geren predicted it and snapped around to face him. 'You want him sitting next to you, eh, Cam?'

Cam glanced at Lawrie, who had lost his earlier defiance, and was horrified to see tears gathered in his eyes. Cam shook his head almost imperceptibly in the hope of sending a silent plea to this lad who was no more than a child.

Don't do it, Lawrie. For fuck's sake don't cry.

'Sure, he can sit next to me.'

Cam ignored Geren who hissed through his teeth and shifted himself over, reaching for Martin's discarded paper, pausing to wait for permission to borrow it. Martin nodded and stretched, wincing a little as he uncoiled himself. But before Lawrie had a chance to sit down, he clutched his stomach with one hand and put the other over his mouth before tearing back to the latrine. Moments later the noise of retching filled the galley.

Davy collapsed with laughter and Geren gave a derisive shake of his head. 'Jesus, what a fucking *tuss*.'

'Maybe you could give him a break for an hour,' Cam said carefully. The tension in the galley was wearing him down; it was bad enough having to leave Hannah without having to listen to these grown men squabbling like kids.

Geren snorted and knocked back the dregs of his coffee. 'You're joking, right? I'm not letting a little prick like that off the hook. I mean, Jesus. He thinks he's got what it takes to be a fisherman? My Gem would be more use than him and she's seven months pregnant. And, anyway,' he said, with the sullen voice of a tantruming child, 'he came at me. You saw that look he threw me. Who the fuck does he think he is? Snotty little dickhead.'

Cam glanced at Geren. 'I just think you could take it easy for a bit,' he whispered softly, so Lawrie Mould wouldn't hear.

Geren turned on him. '*Take it easy?* What the fuck are you on about? You remember being a deckie learner, Cam? Anybody *take it easy* with you?'

Cam sighed. 'Look. I get it. The lad won't make a fisherman. But he's here now and we've got to live like sardines for the next two weeks and you lot ribbing him all the hours until he cries isn't going to make that any easier.'

Geren and Cam's eyes locked. Cam's body stiffened and his hands instinctively balled on the table. Geren clocked the movement and a questioning look passed over his face like a cloud. 'So you're taking that little *tuss's* side over mine?'

Cam hesitated. There was a furnace burning in Geren and he didn't want a fight with him, not because of some kid who'd likely never step foot on a trawler again. He relaxed his shoulders and shook his head. 'No, I'm not. Just thought you could let him quit throwing up first.'

Geren reached for the pot and topped up his mug. 'Love has turned you soft, mate.'

Cam wondered if it had. He wouldn't usually give a shit about Geren giving a deckie learner a hard time. He was about to smile when Geren added: 'Or is it the sex? I bet that one's a beast in the sack. She's got that look about her.'

Davy smirked and flared Cam's anger.

'You know what, Geren?' Cam slammed his fist down. 'You can be a prize fucking dick sometimes.'

He pushed away from the table and stormed out of the galley and on to the deck. As the boat rocked and pitched he splayed his legs enough to brace himself and rolled a cigarette then cupped his hand against the wind to light it. As he inhaled he caught sight of Lawrie Mould sitting on his haunches against the rail of the gunwale, head bowed, hands clasped around the back of his neck.

Cam drew on his cigarette and regarded the pathetic figure of the crouched boy with disdain. He shouldn't have told Geren to back off him. There was no place at sea for a man who couldn't stand up for himself. Nobody had given Geren or Cam or Slim an easy ride when they started out. The ribbing was a rite of passage. Fishermen had to be brave and tough, have the mettle to survive in the harshest conditions, but they also had to get on with people, know how to fit in and work as a team. It was those same men who gave the new kids hell who taught them all they needed to know to survive the sea. If they wanted to make it as fishermen, the youngsters had to respect the experience of the crew. They had to watch, listen, and learn from them. If they didn't, mistakes would be made, and mistakes could be fatal.

Cam finished his cigarette and threw the end over the side then walked across the deck. He pulled his tobacco out of his back pocket and held it out towards the boy. The lad was no doubt too sick to smoke it, but it was a peace offering of sorts. Lawrie glanced up and they held each other's stare for a moment or two. The boy looked even younger out here. Did his mother have any idea what her son had let himself in for? Perhaps she didn't care.

'You're here to learn, lad. You got that? Slim and Geren. Martin. Davy. Me. We know what we're doing and we're some of the best at sea. If you want to learn you need to start listening. Quit puking and lose the attitude. It's not doing you any favours. You've got a chance to do something with your life. Don't blow it. Understand?'

Lawrie glanced at the tobacco and reached out to take it. Cam held on. Lawrie hesitated then gave a nod and Cam released his grip.

'Thanks,' the boy whispered.

'And don't be a dickhead, OK?'

CHAPTER SEVENTEEN

Hannah

'Get inside the house, Alex.'

Nathan's anger is palpable.

'I *said* get in the house.'

Alex hesitates. He glances back over his shoulder at the man – at Cameron Stewart – who is standing at our gate. My whole body is shuddering and my knees threaten to buckle beneath me as I stare at him, lit by a soft light from the open front door. His skin is craggy, the whites of his eyes are watery – too much drink or too little sleep – he's lost weight, his cheeks are more gaunt, his black hair has thinned and lost its youthful shine. Though unmistakably him, he is haggard and old.

Do I look as aged? As haunted? I suppose I must.

'Did you hear me?' Nathan's bark makes me jump.

'Alex...'

I hear myself whispering my son's name, but it sounds displaced, as if somebody else is speaking from a vantage point a little way away. Nathan steps beside me. The fug of merlot on his breath turns my stomach as he rests a heavy hand on my shoulder. I want to shrug it off, but it's taking all my strength to withstand the barrage of emotions I'm feeling. Relief and happiness my son is home, mixes with panic, confusion, horror and fear. Part of me is desperate to throw my arms around Cam's neck and never let go. Another part wants to scream at him and drive him away.

You can't be here, I want to screech. Why are you here? You promised me. You promised me you'd never come back!

Guilt engulfs me like a mudslide, suffocating me, making each breath torturous. Memories strike like balled fists. Cam standing over the unmoving body. His tears shining in the scant moonlight. The way his hands raked his hair, fingers scraping his scalp, muttering, his voice low and shaky, repeating breathed words over and over.

I can make it OK. I can make it OK. I can make it OK.

Blood pounds my ears as the ground tilts beneath me.

Mum?

Alex's voice comes from somewhere distant.

Mum?

Cam's eyes bore through to my centre. It's as if he's slit me from throat to groin to expose everything inside. Everything else melts away: the house, Nathan, Alex; all of it shrinks to nothing.

There is only me and Cam.

Nathan steps forward. His hand on my shoulder. Pulling me back. 'What the hell is he doing here?'

I can't move or speak. My body has solidified.

Nathan digs his fingers into me and turns me roughly to face him. His mouth moves but the words are scrambled, too hard to decipher, distorted as if we are underwater. He shakes me.

'Hannah?' Finally, his voice comes into focus like a tuned

radio. 'Take Alex indoors. Your son needs you. He's been missing for two days and you need to look after him.'

A movement grabs my attention. Cam has stepped forward. His hands are held up as if surrendering to an invisible gun.

'I'm not staying.' His voice is unaltered, its gravelly texture caressed at the edges by that soft Newlyn accent. 'I just wanted to make sure he got back safe.'

His words flick a switch inside Nathan.

'Why do you have our son?' he shouts.

I flinch and watch Nathan walk up to Cam as if watching a film. He grabs Cam's sweater with both fists, pushes them up to his chin, presses his face close to his. Alex draws in a sharp breath. I should take my son inside. I should make him hot chocolate and butter him some toast. Run him a bath. Call the police to tell them he's home safe and sound.

Why can't I move?

Cam doesn't react to Nathan's assault. He stands, impassive, arms loose at his sides, face tipped back from Nathan's rage.

Alex cries out for Nathan to stop. I should intervene. I should step between them and pacify my husband. Tell Cam to leave.

What's wrong with me?

'The lad came to me. To my place in Reading,' he says then. 'He turned up out of the blue. I got home and he was on the wall outside the block of flats.'

'You expect me to believe that? How the hell did he know where you live?'

I have a sharp image of Alex looking through my box at the care home. Opening my diary. Turning the pages. I see him studying the photograph of me leaning against Cam, the two of us laughing as we squint into the sunlight.

Why can't I remember who took the photo?

'He told me who he was. It was late so I fed him and let him sleep on the sofa.'

'Why didn't you call the police?'

Cam swallows and lowers his gaze.

'Oh yes, I remember. You don't like the police too much, do you?' Nathan scoffs with contempt. He loosens his grip on Cam's sweater, shoving him hard as he releases him. Cam stumbles and catches his fall on the gatepost.

'I had to go to work in the morning,' Cam carries on. There is a vulnerability in him which tugs at my heart. 'He watched TV in my flat. I told him to eat what he wanted and we left as soon as I got home. I stopped to fill up with petrol, but otherwise we drove straight here.'

'You didn't think about how worried we were? You didn't think to telephone?' Nathan appears to be getting stronger as Cam diminishes. I want to shout at him and tell him not to falter.

Don't let him weaken you. Stand tall. Stay strong.

'Well?' Nathan's anger is burning. 'Why didn't you telephone to let us know he was safe?'

'Because I told him I'd called you!' shouts Alex, biting back tears. 'I lied and said I'd told you where I was and that I was on my way home.' My son's visible distress jumpstarts me. I walk over and wrap my arms around him.

'It's OK,' I whisper, rubbing his back. 'It's OK. Don't cry.'

'I should have called you, but I was worried he'd pick up and I didn't want to talk to him.'

Nathan ignores Alex and addresses Cam again. 'Hannah told you she never wanted to see you again. She told you to keep *away*. What bit of that did you not understand?'

Cam glances at me. It's the briefest of looks – a split second – but in that moment I can see a world of pain.

Do my eyes hold as much pain as his?

Unwanted recollections bombard me. People laughing in the distance. Music carried on the biting winter chill. Footsteps in the harbour. The smell of old fish and engine oil and damp nets. The sickening silence. Then Cam's face. The horror. The sound of him throwing up.

I can make it OK.

'Get the hell off my property!' Nathan yells. 'Leave us alone or I'll call the police.'

The threat galvanises me and I snap out of my stupor. I walk towards them, my gaze on Nathan unwavering. 'It's OK,' I say. 'He brought Alex back to us. It's late. They've driven a long way. Let's have a cup of tea and something to eat. We all need to calm down and go indoors.'

Horror blooms on Nathan's face. '*What?* You think I'm letting that man set one foot inside my house?'

'Nathan—'

'It's fine,' Cam says, interrupting me. 'I'm not coming in.'

His voice catapults me back in time and another barrage of memories. Us on the beach. A damp blanket wrapped around our shoulders as we throw stones into the roiling sea. Gulls fighting over the bits of sandwich we've thrown them. Our sandy feet rubbing against each other softly.

'I called the hostel in Penzance. They have a room. I'm staying there—'

'No, Cam—'

'*Hannah*!' Nathan grabs my wrist and pulls me backwards.

Cam turns and walks towards his car. Small and battered. A Volkswagen Golf. Red. The same car? Bile billows up and burns my throat. I'm back there, sitting in the passenger seat, numbly staring through the windscreen at the darkness.

'He's a great kid,' Cam says, as he climbs into the car. 'You should be proud of him.'

He closes the door and the engine fires. He grasps the wheel with both hands and for an instant he seems to hesitate. We stare at each other through the window for a moment before he shifts the car into gear and pulls away.

Panic flares in the pit of my stomach. Without stopping to think, I run out of the gate and shout for him to stop. Nathan calls my name. Cass barks frantically. For a horrible moment I think he isn't going to stop, but then the brake lights flare like two monster eyes in the dark.

But Nathan has appeared at my side. 'Don't you dare.' He grabs my arm.

'Nathan, please. He brought Alex home to us. I have to thank him. *We* have to thank him.'

'The man is a *cold-blooded killer*, Hannah. I don't want him anywhere near any of us.'

'Shush! For goodness' sake,' I say sharply, glancing back to make sure Alex isn't in earshot.

'How did Alex know where to find him?' He leans in, anger drilling into me like a laser. 'Why did he go to him?'

'I have no idea.'

It's not a lie. I know Alex found my box of memories. I know he saw the photos and read my diary. But I don't

152

know why he went to find Cam. I'll talk to Alex later, when we're alone, and I'll ask him the same questions Nathan just asked. 'I promise I don't. But I have to thank him for bringing Alex home to us.'

I wrench free of his grasp and run to the car. Cam has turned off the engine and wound down his window. He turns his head slowly to look at me and I am hit by the weight of our history. There's so much I need to say. So much I want to say. But how do I even begin? Once again, it's as if my tongue has been cut out. Over the last fifteen years I've imagined hundreds of conversations, but standing here now, face to face with him, my mind is blank.

'Thank you,' I say quietly.

His face is devoid of expression. 'No problem.' He puts his hand to the ignition key.

'Wait. I need to talk to you.' I glance back at Nathan whose shadowy figure is silhouetted in the light from the house.

'There's nothing to say.'

My stomach clenches. 'Cam?'

He turns the engine on. 'I'm sorry.'

Tears bite and I swallow them back as I shake my head. 'Are you... OK?'

He blinks slowly. 'Am I *OK*?' His words are laced with bitterness.

'*Hannah*!' Nathan's shout makes me jump. I glance over my shoulder and see him approaching. 'For God's sake!'

Panic mushrooms inside me. No. He can't leave. Not yet. This isn't right. We need to talk.

Nathan draws up behind me and rests his hands on my shoulders and I stiffen.

'Thank you,' he says. His voice is eerily calm and flat, his composure restored. 'For bringing my son home.' He rubs the tops of my arms. 'We're very grateful. Have a safe drive back.'

Cam nods and shifts the gear.

As he drives away the air in my lungs chills to ice.

CHAPTER EIGHTEEN

Hannah

I sit on the edge of Alex's bed and watch him devour the ham sandwich I made for him.

Nathan is downstairs on the phone to the police, his voice coming in breathy snatches with the effort of repressing his anger. When we came back into the house and closed the door, he was visibly trembling, and his skin pale. The only words he spoke, uttered to Alex in a low growling tone, 'Get up to your room and stay there.'

Nathan was always going to be angry with Alex for running away, but knowing he ended up at Cam Stewart's? I can only imagine the corrosive anger eating him from the inside. Somehow I'll need to diffuse him, massage his ego and ease the rage, but not until I've talked to my son.

I let him finish his sandwich without talking. I am so grateful he's safe, and sitting here with him in comfortable silence is bliss after the hours I've spent worrying. But I have so many questions and it isn't long before I have to break the quiet.

'Why did you go to him?'

Alex puts the last of the sandwich into his mouth then leans to one side so he's able to pull a folded sheet of paper from his back pocket. Still chewing, focused on his duvet not me, he holds it out. The note is written in his own neat handwriting. Just a few lines which I recognise immediately; the address Cam sent me in a letter six years ago. The letter which was tucked into the back sleeve of my diary.

I know each word by heart.

Hannah

This will come out of the blue. I'm sorry. I'm moving on to a new place. I know you won't write. I don't expect you to. But disappearing feels wrong. It's been nearly ten years but I still think of you. Do you ever wish we could go back and do things a different way? From next week my new address is Flat 46D, Clare Court, Fosters Lane, Reading. I think I gave you my phone number when I last wrote. It hasn't changed but in case you've lost it: 07555 678456.

I hope life has turned out well.

Cam

I fold the note and wait until Alex raises his head to look at me. 'You shouldn't have read my diary,' I say then, 'and that box is mine, it contains my private things. It wasn't for you to go looking through.'

Alex presses his finger on a tiny sliver of ham and puts it in his mouth. 'I read somewhere that photos can help people who might be developing dementia. Gran's memory. It's going. She keeps drifting away.' He hesitates. 'I was looking for a photo of Granddad for her and one of you when you were a child. I was going to stick them to the wall near her bed. I thought the box was hers.' He sniffs. 'You should have chosen a better hiding place if you didn't want it found.' Alex pauses, chewing on his lip a little, before looking up at me. 'Why didn't you tell me Cam is my father?'

I inhale sharply and my fingers dig into my thigh. 'Because he's not.'

Alex stares back at me and shakes his head. 'You're lying. He—'

'Enough.' I glance nervously back at the door, terrified in case Nathan is standing there. 'He's not your father.'

'Why are you lying—'

'How did you get to Reading?'

My stomach churns at the thought of Alex thinking Cam is his father and Nathan overhearing that. I need to stop him talking about it.

'Tell me why you didn't—'

'Stop it *now*,' I say firmly. 'How did you get to his house?'

He is clearly frustrated by my unwillingness to let him finish, but after a moment or two, he sighs. 'Train to Reading. Then I asked people in the street. It would have been quicker if I'd had my phone,' he said and rolled his eyes, 'but it wasn't too hard. I had to wait ages for him to get back from work. I wasn't sure if he was even coming home. I didn't think about what would happen, if he wasn't in or didn't live there. I didn't have enough money for the train home.'

I don't care about how he got to the flat. I'm not even that concerned he thinks Cam is his father. What I really want to know is what happened when he arrived on Cam's doorstep. How Cam reacted when Alex introduced himself. What they talked about. What television programme they watched. If Cam asked after me.

'Mum?'

He pushes my arm gently and I refocus on him.

'Answer me. Please. Why are you lying about him not being my dad? Your diary has one short entry about Nathan Cardew and some meal out where you ate undercooked fish and cubes of jelly or whatever, but it's full of Cam Stewart. You go on about how much you loved him and then there's that diary entry, the one where you're waiting for him to come back from the fishing trip and then getting excited because you're going out to the pub with him. The date. It's nine and a half months before my birthday. I'm not stupid. I know how long babies take.'

I glance urgently back at the door again. 'We can't talk about this now.'

'But I want to.'

'Alex, *please*.' I take his hand in mine. 'I promise you Cam is not your father. The man downstairs is your father. It's on your birth certificate. I met Nathan around the same time. I'm not proud of it, but I got together with him before Cam and I split up. Cam moved away from Newlyn because I got together with Nathan.' The lie hurts so much and I have to fight to stop my voice cracking. 'But you're right,' I whisper. 'I *did* love Cam—' I pause to let the wave of emotion wash over me. 'I was young. Only a few years older than you are. It didn't even last two months. We were just kids.' I rub his hand and smile softly. 'Alex, whatever you think you discovered, you were wrong to run away like that. You should have come and talked to me. You caused a lot of trouble. The police were involved. People were out looking for you. But more than anything – *God* – I was worried sick. I thought I'd lost you.' My voice cracks and I squeeze his hand. 'I was losing my mind. Your father was worried too—'

Alex scoffs.

'Don't make that face. Of *course* he was worried. It's been a horrible few days for both of us. I don't know what I'd do if something ever happened to you.'

'I'm sorry,' he says, so quietly I can hardly hear him.

I wrap my arms around him and pull him close. 'Don't do anything like that again. Do you understand? You're the only thing that matters in this whole crappy world. Well,' I add, 'Vicky and Cass too, but you the most.'

We hear Nathan on the stairs, and Alex grabs at the duvet, lies down, and turns his back as he pulls the covers over him. Nathan looms darkly in the doorway.

'He's asleep,' I whisper, putting my finger up to my lips. 'He was exhausted. Don't wake him.'

I turn off the bedside lamp and join Nathan at the door. I kiss his cheek. 'Thank God he's home,' I whisper. 'And thank you for being such a tower of strength. I'd have fallen apart without you.'

Though the words are hard to get out, they have the desired effect, and Nathan thaws a little, his body relaxing, eyes losing their steely edge. 'The police need to speak with him,' he says. 'It's standard apparently. They need to run through a set of questions to check he was where he said he was, and that he wasn't coerced,' Nathan pauses, 'or a victim of grooming. They want to talk to him – Cameron Stewart – too.'

'Why?' Fingers of ice patter my skin.

'It's routine and makes sense. We haven't seen this man for years and he suddenly turns up with our son? They want to know how Alex knows him. They have lots of questions. And,' he pauses again, 'so do I.'

I nod and walk past Nathan, taking hold of his hand and pulling him with me as I head towards our room. Nathan stops walking and drops my hand.

'Why did he go to his house, Hannah? How does he know where he lives?'

Of course, I knew this was coming, but nevertheless my stomach tumbles as I search for a plausible reason which doesn't incriminate me. If Nathan finds out about the letter, he won't care about the facts – that it came years ago and I never replied – all he'll care about is Cameron Stewart sending me a letter which I kept hidden. The silence is painful, but I can't think of a decent lie, my brain is a mush, so I tell him the truth. Well, it's a version of the truth.

'He found my old diary.' I talk loud enough for Alex to hear in the hope he'll understand that this is the story I want him to use.

'Your diary?'

'Yes, I wrote a diary when I was young. It was full of non-sense. Poems and cuttings and bits and pieces like that. Teenage girl stuff. You know.'

Nathan's flat expression communicates clearly he definitely doesn't know what 'teenage girl stuff' is.

'I wrote about an evening out I had with Cameron Stewart. I exaggerated. Made it more romantic than it was. The entry was dated in late November and Alex put two and two together.

He made five and got confused and upset. He thought,' I hesitate, 'I mean, he suspected there was a chance Cam might be his real father.' Nathan grimaces. 'He wasn't happy about it. He was angry. Especially with me and wanted to find out the truth. You know how teens are. They don't think clearly. He was acting on impulse.'

'But how did he know the address?'

I hesitate. 'A letter. Cam sent it. It was in the diary—'

'A *letter*?'

'A note, really. With a forwarding address. I've no idea why he sent it. I should have thrown it away but—'

'Give me the letter and the diary.'

'Sorry?'

'Give them to me now.'

'Alex chucked them. In Reading. He was frustrated. Probably a bit embarrassed he'd got it so wrong, you know, when Cam corrected him. You know how Alex overreacts.' It's interesting how much more comfortable I feel when I'm lying. Lies are less exposing than the truth. They form a protective barrier around me. Nathan doesn't look convinced, but I don't let it worry me. 'He shouldn't have taken them, but they mean nothing to me, so it's no matter they're gone. I should have got rid of them years ago. The diary is just a silly thing I held on to from my youth. Anyway,' I say again to drive the point home, 'Cam put him right. Told him, of course, that he isn't his father. And Alex dumped it all in the bin.'

Every fibre in Nathan's body is taut, like guitar strings tightened as far as they'll go.

'Try not to take it personally. He's going through adolescence. It's a difficult time for any child. He's kicking against the rules—' He tries to interrupt me, but I press on. 'He was upset with us – with *me* – and found my stupid diary and his brain went into overdrive. I should have thrown it away. You're always saying how I hoard things. But now I've set him straight. Cam has set him straight. And,' I rest the flat of my hand on his arm, 'most importantly I have no feelings whatsoever for that man. You have to believe me. I love you. It's always been you.'

As I speak I stroke his arm until he softens.

'I won't let him take you.'

His words seem flimsy and desperate, bound together with unappealing vulnerability.

'Nathan,' I cajole. 'I'm married to you. Not him. Cam and I were young, we went on one or two dates, he meant nothing to me. I can barely remember it. But I am *your* wife and we have a home together. A family. I don't want to leave you.'

How easily the lies slither out of me. I know how to get what I want and what I want is to protect my son from Nathan's anger and jealousy. What I want is for Nathan to forget about Cam Stewart.

'Alex is happy to be home. Don't punish him or get so angry you push him away. He *needs* his father.' I run my fingers down his arm and take hold of his hand. 'He needs *you*.' Then I take a breath, lift his hand to my breast, and smile. 'I need you too.'

CHAPTER NINETEEN

Hannah

Nathan Cardew moves in and out of me but my head is filled with Cam. He is real again, sleeping in a bed only a few miles away. In Penzance. Penzance, where we went out, where we bought sweets and cigarettes and cans of cheap cola, where we drank cider and pushed ten pence pieces into the arcade machines on the seafront. I can picture him there without even having to try.

I've lost count of the times I've wished I'd never met Cameron Stewart. But I can't change the past, and as Nathan fucks me, I recall the night it hapened. Vicky and I were supposed to be going to a party on some farmland near Redruth. But she had period pains and wasn't up to dropping pills and dancing until dawn in a churned-up field. So we decided to watch a film instead. We went to Blockbuster to choose a video, but then Vicky saw some friends walk past the window. She dragged me out to say hello. We got chatting. They were going to the cinema to watch *The Crying Game*. We'd heard of the film. Everybody said there was a mind-blowing twist so we tagged along, bought popcorn, and chose our seats. Vicky wanted to go at the back. I wanted to go at the front. We compromised and sat in the middle. As the lights went down, two men sat next to us. Vicky nudged me. Raised her eyebrows. I told her to shush but stole a look at the one beside me. He was gorgeous, breathtaking actually, with strong wrists and tanned skin, his hands weathered and rough and scarred. A fisherman, I guessed. I felt him looking at me and cast him a quick glance. He looked away. Vicky whispered something and we giggled like schoolgirls. I laid my hand on the armrest between me and him. When our fingers touched, a shot flashed up my arm as if he'd electrocuted me. I can't remember the film. I can only remember our fingers grazing. At the end of the film, when the lights went up, my heart was beating fast and shallow like the wings of a hummingbird. The man's friend, I later found out to be Geren, had short-cropped hair and a loud voice, and was making sure we all knew he hated the film because he wasn't a 'fucking nonce'.

'I loved it,' I said, as we followed them out.

The man with the electric fingers looked back over his shoulder and smiled. 'Me too,' he said. He had dark brown eyes, almost black, crinkled skin at the edges, shaggy dark hair which curled at the collar, and a wide mouth with clean, ever so slightly uneven teeth.

Vicky took my arm. Laughed. Pulled me through the people inching towards the exit and he was lost. In the foyer, she began marshalling us all to go on for a drink. As she talked I searched the crowd.

And there he was.

He was alone outside the cinema. Smoking. Leaning against a lamppost and watching the doors as the people spilled out. I left Vicky and her friends and walked out of the cinema and approached him. When he caught sight of me he beamed, wide, honest and open. We chatted about this and that, and it was as if we'd known each other for years. He was relaxed, confident but not cocky, funny and cool and, oh my god, sexy.

Vicky appeared at my shoulder. 'Come on,' she said, eyeing him with a smile. 'I've got us a lift to the pub.'

'Stay,' he said to me.

I laughed as Vicky pulled me with her.

'Where can I find you?'

'The bakery in Newlyn!'

'It's fate! I fish out of Newlyn!'

'Guess I'll be seeing you then!'

And then Vicky and I tripped off, giggling, heads together, Vicky batting me with her hand and teasing me for being such a shameless flirt.

Nathan slumps on top of me. 'I love you.' He kisses my forehead.

An owl hoots some way off. I think of Cam now. How haunted he appears. How sallow and pale his aged skin is. How different we are now to those young people who met at the cinema. How altered. I know without doubt that I have to see him. Alex brought Cam back into my life. I can't let him walk out of it without talking to him.

As Nathan snores softly, I lie there and stare at the ceiling. How much can one person stare at the ceiling? Sleep isn't my friend. Most nights I don't sleep at all, merely drift in and out of consciousness as my thoughts tumble, and the house creaks and rattles and groans. When we were newly married, I was terrified every night, convinced the noises of the cooling timbers were the sounds of Nathan's father pacing blindly about. A cold sweat would creep over me and I'd watch the door, waiting for him to appear, and if it wasn't Charles Cardew it was *him*, the other, with his glassy stare and blood-let pallor, his waterlogged body leaving ghostly pools of seawater. Some nights I still hear his footsteps, on the landing, on the stairs, in the attic above me. Tonight he paces the gravel path below the bedroom window. I hold my breath and strain my ears. Is it him? Yes. It's him. I recall the stab of happiness when I heard those footsteps approaching from the shadows.

Cam? Is that you?

It wasn't.

I'm looking for Cam. Have you seen him?

But he didn't answer. He just kept walking.

CHAPTER TWENTY

Nathan

I'd be a liar if I said I didn't feel a distinct sense of victory when I watched him walk away from you. You were understandably quiet. Perhaps even a little sad. Of course you were. Nobody likes to hurt another person like that. Especially you with your gentle, caring nature. But you made the right decision. The sadness would fade. You'd get over it like a child recovers from a grazed knee. The man is no good. A heinous criminal. Rough and violent. Rotten to the core. And like a rotten apple in a crate he would turn those close to him rotten too. You had no choice and you knew that, didn't you?

Nobody, least of all Cameron Stewart, will ever love you like I do.

We sat in the car. I took your hand. 'You've done the right thing, Hannah.'

You nodded.

'You're free of him now.'

'Thank goodness,' you said as you looked out of the window, pondering, I imagine, your lucky escape.

'Hannah?'

You turned. Your fringe was obscuring your eyes and I brushed it to one side. 'Yes?'

'I'm going to take care of you. Forever.'

And then we kissed. Do you remember how tender that moment was? You were shy, reserved, as if this were your first-ever kiss. Desire knocked the air from me.

'I'd like to see you tonight.'

CHAPTER TWENTY-ONE

Hannah

The floorboards creak as he moves from the bathroom to the bedroom. I can hear the faint and tuneless humming as he dries himself. I imagine him taking a pair of folded trousers from his cupboard, pressed as he likes them, with a single crease down the centre of each leg. He unhooks a shirt, snow-white and starch-collared, from the hanger. He raises his chin as he buttons it. Lifts the collar. Wraps a carefully selected tie around his neck and ties it perfectly, before tugging lightly on each cuff in turn and running his hands over the sides of his head to smooth his hair.

Hurry up and leave.

'Can't I catch the bus today? I don't want to go in the car with him.' Alex bites into his toast and crumbs fall like snowflakes on to the table.

'You'll be fine.'

'He'll shout.'

'You deserve it,' I say with a smile. 'Look, let him shout. Accept what you did was wrong and say sorry.'

'What will I tell people at school?'

I shrug. 'That you wanted to check out the bright lights of

Reading?' I ruffle his hair and he bats my hand away. 'People will move on. As Mum used to say, it's yesterday's chip wrap.'

He groans. 'Oh God, they'll send me to Miss Yardley.'

'Who?'

'The student brain-doctor. She's there to make sure kids don't top themselves between Maths and Biology.' Alex strokes the dog's head and she blinks up at him, nosing his hand for more.

Nathan comes into the kitchen and drinks the cup of coffee I hand him. 'Come on then,' he says to Alex. 'Oh, and the police want to talk to you later so I'll pick you up at the end of school. I've had to cancel an important meeting, which is tedious to say the least.'

Alex swings his school bag on to his shoulder and then they are gone. I watch them through the window, Nathan marching, Alex dragging his feet in sullen silence. I close my eyes and listen to the sound of the car retreating.

It's quarter to eight. I need to leave now. From nowhere, I'm hit by the image of Cam hunched over the body on the boat, shaking, raking his fingers so aggressively against the wooden deck he rubs them raw. I grab the worktop to steady myself and take a few deep breaths. My nerves are ragged. I think back to last night. The torment in his eyes and the past bearing down on him like lead. I've held on to a fantasy version of Cam Stewart – a man I've pictured as tall and broad, young and virile, with an easy, generous laugh – for so long. The haunted version I saw yesterday has shaken me. The need to apologise to him, to make things better, is overwhelming.

Even as I think these things, I realise how pathetic I am, how delusional.

How on earth can I make it better?

The bus drops me a few minutes' walk from the hostel in Penzance. I have no idea if he'll be there or if he's already left. Or if he was ever even here. Maybe he told me the wrong place by mistake? Or on purpose? Perhaps he's in a B&B somewhere else entirely. Or maybe he actually drove back to Reading last night? My anxiety is at an unbearable level, nerves ragged, and stomach churning; I have no idea what I'll say to him.

The hostel is an old Victorian townhouse, its walls now painted a garish yellow, large sash windows and various notices – some years out of date – pinned to a board by the front door which is painted the colour of wine bottles. As I walk up the steps I hit a wall of doubt. I recall the way he looked through me, how flat and cool his voice was as he told me we had nothing to say to each other. What if he doesn't want to see me? What will I do if he shouts, runs at me, tells me to get the hell out of his life? Is he hidden, watching me from an upstairs window, pretending not to be here? Instinctively, I glance upwards, expecting the telltale fall of a curtain, but everything is still.

The door is stiff when I push it open. Inside, the grandeur and colour of the facade is replaced by bland cream and the strong smell of damp and plug-in air freshener. The reception desk is crowded with leaflets, postcards for sale, and various charity boxes. The man at the desk puts down his mug when he hears me and looks up from his newspaper. Middle-aged, with red-rimmed glasses and a green thick-knit cardigan, he looks behind me, perhaps for luggage, then scrutinises me suspiciously. I shift uncomfortably.

'Can I help you?'

His brusqueness throws me. 'I'm… I'm looking for some-one?' I hesitate. 'Cameron Stewart? I think he was here last night?'

The man appears taken aback and regards me as if I've asked something absurd, something mildly offensive. 'I'm afraid I can't possibly give out guest information to all-and-sundry.' His patronising tone spreads my skin with a pink flush.

'It's… it's quite important? You see, he helped me. With my son? He ran away. Cameron… Mr Stewart, well, he brought him home to me. I want to thank him.'

The man looks sceptical and I bite back an overwhelming urge to shout at him. He bends and rummages in a drawer beside him, then slides a pencil and a piece of paper across his desk with a single finger.

'I suggest you leave him a note.'

'So he's here?'

The man is momentarily lost as he realises he's inadvertently broken his confidentiality rule. My tummy fizzes with nerves. Cam slept here. He hasn't left yet.

The man smiles primly. 'Leave a note with your phone number. If he wants to see you, I'm sure he'll—'

'Hannah.'

I turn and there he is, standing not far from me on the other side of the entrance hall. He is wearing the same clothes as last night. They seem more crumpled, as if he has slept in them.

'Why are you here?'

I can only shrug helplessly, the words I was unable to pre-pare even more elusive, it seems.

After a moment or two he says, 'Do you want to get a coffee?'

'Yes please,' I say quietly.

'Can she have a coffee?' he asks the man behind the reception. 'I'll pay for it.'

'Sure,' he says, with a pithy smile, before returning to his newspaper. 'But no breakfast. The breakfast is for my paying guests only.'

There's a lobby off to the side, with three musty-smelling purple sofas, a mismatch of armchairs set around some low tables, and a long trestle at the back which holds a couple of hot water urns, a basket of miniature cereal boxes, a jug of milk, and a glass bowl of green apples and over-ripe bananas. A group of three girls chat animatedly as they lean over an Ordnance Survey map. They are wearing ethnic-style clothes – loose trousers, coloured knits, tasselled scarves – and one has a large metal circle which forms a porthole through her earlobe. They briefly quieten when we walk in, but on finding us of little interest, return to their route planning.

Cam makes a cup of coffee and tips three sachets of sugar into it. My heart aches when I watch him. It's like we've travelled back in time. I hear a faraway me remarking on his sugar habit. It's disconcerting to see this behaviour unchanged, but the essence of him so different. His bright eyes dulled, young skin craggy and lined, his vigour replaced by a battered weariness. So familiar and yet a stranger with the years passed. I don't know him anymore. The Cam Stewart I knew exists only in my head. The sugar is a red herring.

Cam stirs his coffee.

'Is he OK?' He watches the rotating spoon.

'Who? Alex?'

Cam nods.

'Yes. He has to talk to the police later. Nathan says they

173

want to talk to you too. I'm sorry.' I hesitate. 'I'm sorry he came to you.'

He doesn't react but continues to stir his coffee in slow, rhythmic circles.

'Look, Cam, I don't know where to start. I—'

The sound of a mobile phone interrupts me. It takes a few seconds for me to realise the noise and vibrations are coming from my bag. I try to ignore it, willing whoever it is to ring off and leave us in peace, but then I think of Alex. What if it's his school and something's wrong? What if he's run off again? Or got angry or upset and needs me?

'Sorry,' I mumble, as I scramble to find the phone.

I accept the call without registering the number. 'Hello?'

'Mrs Cardew?'

'Yes? Is it Alex?'

'Alex? No. No, this is Heamoor. I'm calling about your mother.'

'Mum?'

There's a brief but heavy pause as the woman on the other end of the line takes a breath. 'I'm afraid it's bad news. She had a stroke in the night—'

Blind panic takes hold of me.

'—we've called an ambulance to take her to Truro. It should be here soon.'

'I'm on my way.' My hands are shaking so much I can hardly switch off the call. 'I have to go,' I say to Cam. 'I'm sorry.' I push the chair back from the table and grab my bag as I run out of the room towards the door.

'Hannah?' Cam calls as he follows me.

'Sorry. It's Mum… ' I fight my tears.

'Do you need me to drive you somewhere?'

'There's a bus. I'm fine. I'm sorry… I'm… I'm sorry.'

He follows me out of the hostel and grabs my arm to stop me. 'Let me drive you.'

His face blurs and I draw my sleeve across my eyes. I have no idea what time the buses run. Perhaps I should walk. How far is it to the bus stop from here? Half an hour? Less? More? I need to get to her.

I stare at him.

He nods earnestly. 'It's no problem to drive you.'

'OK,' I say after a hesitation. 'Yes. Thanks. She's… up at Heamoor.'

I'm not sure if it's anxiety to do with Mum or if it's being back in his car again, but as I clip my seatbelt I'm overwhelmed with nausea. I pull on my sleeve to try and calm myself. The car is full of rubbish and bits are held together with duct tape. There's a rip in his seat out of which spews yellow foam and a cloying smell of junk food hangs in the air. Nathan's car – a silver BMW – smells brand new even though he's had it three years. He watched a YouTube video on how to preserve the smell – compressed air to clean the vents, an air freshener called 'New Car', and a full weekly valet.

When we get near to the care home I point out directions in monosyllables and gestures. He turns into the car park and as soon as he draws to a halt, I throw open the door and rush up the steps and into the reception. The lady on the desk is regretful when she informs me there's been a hold-up with the ambulance, as if its her fault, which of course it's not.

'I'm sure it won't be long,' she says and smiles. 'Would you like a cup of tea?'

My voice cracks when I say no and thank her. When I get to Mum's room, I find Patricia is with her. The concern on the kind woman's face intensifies my fear and when I get close to Mum's bed, my stomach contracts violently. The right side of poor Mum's face has dropped as if the strings holding it up have been sliced through. One eye is closed and peaceful, the other droops open to display the yellow-tinged white, shot through with spidery-red capillaries.

'God. Please. *Please* don't leave me, *Dama*.'

'Hannah.' Patricia's voice is soothing like ointment. She reaches for my hand but I snatch it away. I don't want sympathy. I don't deserve anybody's sympathy. 'She's stable for the time being. When the paramedics get here they'll transfer her to Treliske.'

'Where are they?' I whisper. 'Why aren't they here?'

'I'll go and check. If they're not here I'll call and get an update.'

When she leaves the room, I lean forward and rest my chin on the bed beside Mum, and take her soft hand in mine. 'Oh, *Dama*,' I whisper as the warmth of her seeps into me. 'Please be OK. I need to talk to you. He's back. Cam. And, Christ, everything's a mess.'

Gwenna Whitehead, my mother, with her strong Cornish accent and wolf-grey eyes had always had a soft spot for Cam Stewart. As I sit and stroke her hand, I recall us side by side at the kitchen sink, Mum washing, me drying, when a smile cut her face in two.

'So tell me then, *melder*.'

'Tell you what?'

'About this new man of yours.'

I laughed.

'A looker?'

'Gorgeous.'

Mum handed me the last plate to dry then dropped her hand into the sudsy water to pull the plug. The drain gurgled.

'He's dark – like a gypsy – eyes almost black and hair so thick there's enough for two.'

'Hair's important. I love to stroke your dad's hair.'

'Oh, God, *Dama*!' I said, batting her gently. 'Stop. I do *not* need to hear stuff like that.'

She leant back against the sink and raised her eyebrows. 'Go on then. Him with the nice thick hair and dark eyes. What else?'

'He's a fisherman. On the trawlers. So he's brave and strong.'

'Of course.' She tapped the tip of my nose and beamed. 'And he's making my *melder* sparkle just how she should.'

When I told her I'd split with him to marry Nathan Cardew, my voice tight and quiet in the aftermath of that night, her face had darkened. 'Ah, *melder*, but how can you be marrying a man you've just met? Do you love him? You have to love him. *Rag kerenza*. That's what your gran used to say. *Rag kerenza*. Marry for love. Marriage lasts a long time. Without love you'll not make it.'

'Nathan is a good man.'

But Mum shook her head like a dog shaking off river water.

'Don't look at me like that. Nathan is a good man and I love him. I do.'

A knock at the door startles me. 'Yes?'

Cam's voice comes through the laminate. 'Hannah?'

I tiptoe to the door. My hand hovers above the handle and

I chew on my lip. I glance back at Mum, lying there, ravaged by the stroke, in a tiny institutional room in need of a repaint. I don't want him to see her like this.

Another knock.

My whole body trembles as I open the door.

We face each other either side of the threshold, but neither of us moves. The air between us so thick with hateful memories it's an impassable barrier. Seeing him here, in my mother's room, is difficult. The memories of her, the ones I hold close, when she was fit and well and laughing heartily, belong to a time when this man was my future.

'Can I see her?'

I hesitate, but then step to one side. He sits tentatively down in the chair beside the bed. 'Hello, Gwenna.' His gentleness stabs my heart. 'She looks peaceful.'

I stare down at the lopsided face of my mother, her breathing regular and quiet, hands relaxed and graceful like a ballerina. I know he's saying this to comfort me, but I don't want her peaceful. I want her awake and fighting and ordering death to leave her the fuck alone.

Cam looks up at me then. 'Hannah?'

'Yes?'

'Is he mine? Is Alex my son?'

The question kicks the breath from me. I have a flash of us on the boat, beneath the tarpaulin, chilled faces, warm bodies pressed together. The yearning I'd felt for him. All I'd wanted was to have him inside me.

'No.'

'Are you sure, because the dates—'

The pain in him is raw.

'I'm sure. I got my period while you were at sea. That was after we…'

Cam looks back at my mother. 'I knew he was your son before he even opened his mouth. He looks so like you, but, well… his hair. It's… it's dark.'

Dark like mine, he wants to say.

A knock on the door cuts through the silence which follows. Patricia bustles into the room and I clear my throat, suddenly self-conscious, as if interrupted in a compromising situation. Two paramedics follow. Their radio crackles with static. They lift Mum on to the gurney they've wheeled in, faces serious as they check her and hook her up to wires and monitors.

Mum appears too slight in their busy hands and I bite my tongue to stop myself telling them to be careful with her. One of them, a man with sandy hair and two days' worth of stubble, explains what will happen to her when she gets to Treliske as he wraps a blood pressure gauge around her arm. The other administers a drip, finding one of her old, blue veins and sliding the needle expertly into it. A flash of blood hits the saline like a puff of red smoke.

'Do you need someone to come with you?' asks Patricia, resting a kind hand on my shoulder and rubbing it lightly.

'I'll follow the ambulance,' Cam says, before I can answer. 'I'll be there if you need me.'

I'm about to protest and tell him he's done enough already, but then I think about the hospital and what might unfold there. 'Thank you,' I whisper. 'That's kind of you.'

'By the way, love,' says Patricia. 'You didn't happen to take the little glass bird last time you were up? It's just she noticed it was gone from the windowsill.'

'Oh,' I reply. 'Yes. I didn't think she'd miss it.'

'That's a relief. She was ever so worried. She talks to it, you know.' Patricia smiles warmly. 'She thought it might have flown away.'

My stomach seizes up as I imagine Mum wondering where the little bird had gone. Was that why she had the stroke? Because the bird wasn't there to watch over her?

As I watch them load her into the ambulance. I'm struck with a deep sense of foreboding, remembering the time I stood and watched them put my father into the ambulance. He didn't come out alive. His heart gave out on the journey to the hospital. The attack was unexpected. He was a fit man who swam every day off the beach at Wherrytown. He was happy and relaxed and looked young for his years, but one Wednesday afternoon, he got up from his chair to make a pot of tea, and never made it to the kitchen. Part of Mum died with him too. He was her one and only love, and had been since the day they met aged fourteen.

Cam is waiting on the tarmac when the paramedics open the ambulance doors. 'Do you want me to come in with you?' he asks.

'No. I dont think so.'

'I'll wait here. Drive you back.'

'Don't you have to get home? To work?'

'I said I'd be back on Monday. It's only packing in a warehouse.'

I hestitate, but then imagine calling Nathan and having to put up with him huffing and puffing about coming to get me. I nod. 'Yes, OK. That would be great, thanks.'

Mum is stable, they say, but they are keeping her in for

observation. Machines beep and whirr. A nurse monitors various charts. I follow her out when she leaves the room and talk to her in the corridor.

'I have to get back. My son is off school. He's sick.' I can't look her in the eye. 'Will you call me if there's any change?'

'Of course. Try not to worry. She's a tough old bird, I can tell.'

My lie sits heavily. There's nothing I need to leave for. I could stay at the hospital all day. Alex and Nathan are self-sufficient. Even Cass would be fine. She sleeps when I'm not there; she's not a young dog anymore.

But I want to go back to Cam.

He is leaning against his car smoking a cigarette. When he catches sight of me he raises his hand and as I approach, he retrieves his cigarettes from his jacket pocket. 'Still smoking?'

'When I can.'

He puts a cigarette in his mouth and lights it from his own before handing it to me.

'She'll be OK,' he says gently.

We look at each other and I experience a moment of peace as the painful memories and paralysing regret seem to fall away. Leaning against his old red car, sharing cigarettes, surrounded by calling seagulls and salty air, I'm twenty-two again. I recall how intensely I loved this man. It was as if our souls were magnetised, north and south, pulling our bodies together to fuse them. As if the essence of him had crept out of his body and into mine, throwing out barbs, bonding itself to me. I recall how safe I felt with him. As clichéd as it sounds, when I met him outside that cinema in 1998, it was as if I'd come home. I miss that man. I miss the Cornwall of my youth. I miss the way the air felt light and fresh and how cool the sea was on my skin.

I miss it all so badly.

Something takes hold of me then. It overrides rational thought. I close my eyes and inch my hand over the body of the car to find his. Our skin touches. For a moment we stay like this. Our fingers making the slightest of contacts. But then, without warning, he yanks his hand back and pushes himself off the car and away from me so abruptly I wonder if I physically hurt him.

CHAPTER TWENTY-TWO

Cam, 1998

The sun rose on the second morning and light flooded the sky as if God himself had pulled back the curtains. The sky was layered, a yellow the colour of clotted cream and a soft blue-grey, and the wind had dropped such that the sea was undulating calmly, its navy surface streaked with sunlight like a slick of cooking oil.

'Right, boys,' Slim called. 'Let's go.'

They'd worked hard in rough conditions to shoot the gear in the dark, and though they'd only managed a few hours' sleep, and their cramped bunk room was already beginning to smell of rancid clothes and unwashed skin, waking to sunshine on a flat sea and the prospect of hauling in for the first time in weeks, had put smiles on their faces.

Looking back, Cam would wonder whether the euphoria they'd experienced as they brought in that first haul, bulging, as it was, with sole, monkfish, John Dory and brill, might have been the start of it all. The first link in a chain of events which would end in tragedy. But at the time he was as jubilant as the others and thought of nothing more than the money which would be coming his way.

As the winches turned and the nets followed, the men

expertly guided the gilsons and strops so everything ran smoothly. Each of them knew their job. Lawrie watched from afar. Cam was filled with a peculiar pride as he caught the lad's solemn face studying them intently.

Geren whooped and punched the air when the nets lifted clear of the water. 'This is what I'm talking about, baby!' he cried. 'Can you see them, Cam? Can you see those beautiful fish!'

'I can see them, Geren. Oh, I can see them.'

'All hail the monk! Handsomest fish in the goddam sea!'

They shot the nets again and once shot, Geren, Davy, Lawrie and Cam went below to wash, gut and pack the fish. Lawrie passed the plastic boxes to Geren and Davy, who filled them with gutted fish, which went down to Cam in the ice room. Cam always arranged the fish neatly, in regimented lines, tails facing one way, heads the other. Geren teased him for this, but he didn't care. Cam was sure the buyers paid more for a pretty box of fish, and he'd been doing it this way for so long now it was matter of habit, his hands moving fast, no need to think. He covered them with chipped ice and stacked the boxes, smiling broadly to himself. It had to be said, when the fish came in, when the weather was good, it was the best fucking job in the world.

He finished packing and went up on deck and found Lawrie standing in the hopper, directing the hose into the corners to wash the mud and broken shellfish into the sea, a treat for the seagulls that followed the boat.

'I'll show you how to gut next haul,' Cam said.

Lawrie nodded at him, no smile, no thank you, just a look of concentration.

The next haul was even bigger, rammed with fish, nets heaving and pulsing and bursting at the knots. Cam whistled through his teeth and glanced at Geren who grinned.

'Might be a few Christmas presents after all, eh?'

Geren called up to the wheelhouse. 'I think I love you, Slim!'

Slim laughed. 'I'll break your heart, princess!'

The banter continued as they gutted and washed. Cam was good to his word and found a knife for Lawrie. He showed him how to slice each fish along the length of its belly, pull out the innards, wash them and send them down the shoot.

'Are you sick of fish yet?' Lawrie asked.

'Sick of fish? Are you joking? These fish,' Cam said, as he hefted up a huge monkfish, three feet in length, ugly as a demon with its rows of sharp teeth, flattened head, and bulbous eyes, and held it up cheek to cheek, 'these fucked-up-looking bastards are everything to us. Look closer and you'll see he's made of money, lad. You see it?' He kissed the monster and, for the first time in thirty-six hours, Lawrie cracked a smile as he reached down to grab a shining silver hake and kissed it.

Cam laughed and batted his arm. 'Well, look at that. There might be a fisherman inside you after all.'

'Oi, Lawrie!' It was Davy.

The smile slipped off Lawrie's face.

'You're punching above your weight with that hake. This beauty's more your type, don't you think?'

Davy was holding an octopus, tentacles like Medusa's snakes, and black ink from its burst sack coating its slimy skin. Before Lawrie could respond, Davy had hurled the creature at the lad. Lawrie cried out and jumped backwards, slipping on the floor which was slick with fish grot and water. As he scrambled, desperately swiping at the octopus trying to get it off him, Davy creased up with laughter. Cam smothered a smile as he ran his knife down the centre of a fish. Lawrie picked up the octopus and threw it back at Davy who ducked to the side and dodged it. Lawrie was red-faced, but Cam was pleased to see him get on with the gutting, gloved fingers rooting around to hook out the red mess of guts, and keeping his upset hidden.

They stopped around one in the morning for another draft of sleep. Two or three hours here and there was all they could manage. Cam followed Lawrie through the hatch and down into the bunk room. The boy dragged his feet like the walking dead. It was harder for the youngsters when they first started out. Most had no clue what hard work was and this lad was no exception, but give him his due, he was putting the graft in.

Cam climbed into his bunk and pulled the duvet over him. He drew the privacy curtain and lay his head on the pillow. A moment or two later, Lawrie screamed, high-pitched, panicked. Cam dragged the curtain back and jumped out.

'Jesus, fuck. What's wrong?'

'I hate them.' Lawrie's face was streaked with hot tears. 'I hate those dickheads.'

Cam followed the line of Lawrie's angry stare and there, in the centre of Lawrie's cot, was the octopus. It stank, they'd left it in the sun for most of the day, and his sheet and pillow were stained with foul-smelling gloop.

Davy and Geren climbed down into the bunk room, smirks on their faces.

'Everything OK, sweetheart?' Davy said, as he lay down on his bed. 'We heard a squeal down here.'

Lawrie shot him evils but nodded. 'Yeah. I'm good,' he said, steeling himself to take hold of the creature, 'but your girlfriend seems to fancy me more than you.'

Geren snorted with laughter and climbed into his bunk, ignoring the huffs of Davy who'd had the wind taken out of him. Cam climbed back into his cot and, before he turned off the fluorescent light above his head, he winked at Lawrie, who smiled as he carried the dead octopus out of the bunk room at arm's length.

Two hours later the lights went on and Slim was in their faces, 'Rise and shine, pretty boys!'

By the end of the third day they were dead with exhaustion. They sat in the galley, nursing triple-strength coffees, eyes raw with tiredness.

Martin put a metal tray on the table between them. 'From the missus.'

The men grinned. Pasties. Homemade. Sheila baked some for every trip. Either, she said, to keep up morale when the hauls were poor, or to keep up their energy when they were tiring. There were six of them, baked to golden perfection, each one marked with their initials, except Martin's, which had a pastry heart on it, and one with a horseshoe for the new boy whose name she didn't yet know.

They grabbed the pasties and groaned with delight as the crisp, buttery pastry gave way to the succulent filling of swede, potato, chunks of beef, all liberally flavoured with fresh ground pepper. Nobody made pasties like Sheila Garnett, not even Hannah's dad in the bakery, though his were a close second. It was six happy fisherman who went back on deck to haul the gear in. Bellies full, a break in the weather, and the promise of cold, hard cash before Christmas, was all they needed to keep their spirits high.

Geren and Cam steadied the bag of the net, which was the size of a mini, as Martin lowered it on to the deck. Cam released the cod ends and the haul spewed out of the net and into the hopper. He leant on his hands and looked down at the fish writhing and flapping, the whole hopper filled to the brim and seething with life.

'You beauty!' Geren cried. 'Look at that monster right there. And, Jesus, there must be at least fifteen cuttlefish.'

Cuttlefish. *Black gold*. They were raking it in. Geren whistled tunefully as they hauled the winch. The prospect of money had relaxed them all. Fishing was a bugger of business when it wasn't going well. There were no wages on *The Annamae*, the crew got a share of the haul. No fish meant no pay. Shitty hauls, torn nets, and broken gear could stretch to thousands of pounds. Slim was in debt up to his eyeballs. Geren had a baby on the way. Martin had his mortgage and two daughters to support, who were studying at colleges upcountry. Cam needed to start saving; he wanted to move out of Martin and Sheila's. And he wanted to spoil Hannah. He wanted to take her somewhere nice, somewhere better than where Nathan Cardew had taken her; the Italian restaurant in Port Haven, maybe, with its fancy checked tablecloths and red roses.

Though it wasn't quite the same as Newlyn in the eighties, when fish were bountiful and prices consistently high, the cash they would get, stuffed into each man's envelope, would mean heading straight to The Packhorse where the booze and drugs flowed. Whole days were lost to the hangovers which followed. There were only two rules in the pub: keep the fire burning at all times to dump drugs on if the police showed up and don't cut cocaine on the bar. The landlady didn't like the varnish marked. The party they'd have when they docked would be a good one

The men prepared the fish, working quickly, chatting freely. Geren's mood had lightened and since the octopus he'd backed off Lawrie. At one point he even smiled at him. 'Hey, Lawrie!' he called, as he slid his knife along the line of a cod and hooked out the mess. 'I tell you what, lad, you won't get a trip as good as this for a while.'

Lawrie glanced up, checking to see if Geren was being genuine or if there was a barbed comment to follow. Geren met him with a smile and Lawrie ventured a small one in return, and went back to his fish-washing with vigour.

The skies began to grow heavy that afternoon. Dark grey clouds concealed the sun and the wind picked up, touching the choppy waves with white. Cam glanced up at the wheelhouse and noticed Slim's face, brow furrowed, radio held to his grimly set mouth, gaze fixed on the sea. He went up to the wheelhouse and raised his eyebrows in greeting when Slim turned. The skipper made a gesture to give him a minute.

'... yup. Right. OK, mate. Thanks for that.' He hung the radio up. 'Falmouth,' he said without looking at Cam.

'And?'

'If we stay out we'll be hit by that weather. I've checked the forecast. I've no time to get around it.'

'Big?'

'Falmouth said at least an eight. Could reach a nine.'

Cam took his tobacco papers out and started to roll a cigarette.

'We're netting gold out there. Never seen anything like it. I reckon we could shoot the nets on the hour for the next two months and not see an empty haul.'

'The men are dead on their feet. Do we want to go through a big one when everybody's shattered?' He sighed heavily. They both knew the crew would be reluctant to leave the fish and the prospect of earning the type of money on offer. 'We've done well, but I think we should cut our losses.'

'Did Falmouth say how long until it hits?'

'It's going to pick up from now. We're moving into its path. A five or six in the next few hours and, if they've got it right, tomorrow morning it'll strike hard. If we turn now, there's a chance I'll outrun the worst of it, but if we carry on… ?' He rubbed his face.

Cam stayed quiet. Slim wasn't asking for advice this time. Nobody knew the sea like he did. Jim Baker's veins ran with saltwater, not blood. He'd learnt to fish before he could walk, and Cam knew – they all knew – he wouldn't put their lives at risk unnecessarily.

Geren appeared behind them. 'What's up?'

'Storm coming.'

Geren's face registered no worry. All fishermen were brave, they had to be, but Geren was one of the few who got a kick out of riding huge waves.

'We've still got a quarter of the hold left to fill and the nets keep giving.' He took off his woollen hat and rubbed his hair, which stuck up like a scarecrow's with the grease and grime. 'Man, I'm so skint and with the baby coming… '

Cam watched Slim's brain whirring as he weighed up the risk and reward.

Then he shook his head. 'You're all too worn. Too easy to make a mistake. How about we turn about, drop the nets on the way home for one last haul. By the time we bring the gear in, we'll only be fifty miles from Newlyn, and should beat the worst of the gale.'

Geren started to protest, but Slim silenced him. 'That's my final word on it. It's a mid-ground. Your safety, the safety of the boat, these are my priorities. You know that. It's that or steam home without the final haul.'

Geren returned to deck, grumbling, and smacking his hand against the wall when he was out of sight of Slim. Cam thought about Hannah and glanced up at the sky, which was changing colour like a ripening bruise.

He couldn't wait to get back.

CHAPTER TWENTY-THREE

Hannah

His eyes can't find mine. He is twitching, mouth forming silent words, hands trembling at his sides.

'I have to go back. I'll run you home, then get going.'

I drop the cigarette, cross my arms around my body, and lower my head. I watch the end of the cigarette burning on the tarmac, a thin trail of smoke wending its way upwards, disappearing to nothing.

'Yes. Of course.' Two stray tears sting my cheeks and I turn away so he can't see as I drag my sleeve across my face to dry them.

He fixes his gaze straight ahead as he drives back towards Penzance on the A30. I don't know what to say. Without even being aware of what I was doing, my body moving on autopilot triggered by nostalgia, I've crossed a line and it's clearly shaken him. I could kick myself. Stupid of me. Stupid, stupid, stupid.

'I'm sorry,' he says then. 'It's… I don't know… ' He hesitates. 'What… what happened that night. Fuck. *Jesus*,' he whispers. 'Fuck. I need to get away from here. I shouldn't have come back. I should have put Alex on the train. I don't know what I was thinking.' His words have turned to almost incoherent muttering. The way his body is flinching and twitching is unnerving.

This is my fault.

My fault.

For the last fifteen years I've lived with constant guilt. It runs through my veins with my blood. But what I'm feeling now, the nauseating thickness of it, is suffocating. I can't put any of it right. I can't fix it. Raking over old ground won't do any good. Nor will reminiscing. Nostalgia is an enemy dressed up as a friend.

Sitting in the same car seat I sat in fifteen years ago when I was frozen with shock and chilled to the bones of me, I know there are no words I can say, no apologies or explanations I can give that will make things better.

It's as fucked now as it was back then.

We get to a mini roundabout and Cam flicks the indicator on. The ticking keeps time with my heartbeat. He reaches for his cigarettes, taps the packet and manoeuvres one into his mouth, presses the car lighter and, when it clicks, holds it up to light it. A car horn sounds from behind us. He ignores it, waits until the cigarette is lit, before pushing the car into gear. I catch the angry face of the driver behind as he overtakes on the inside of the roundabout. Cam doesn't seem to notice him. If he does, he doesn't care.

'Help yourself.' He gestures at the packet.

I don't take one; Nathan will be home soon.

Cam winds down the window and rests his arm on the sill of the door. He draws on his cigarette, squinting against the smoke. 'I still see his face everywhere I go,' he says then. 'In my dreams, on the streets, in crowds. Sometimes he's beside me on the sofa or behind me while I brush my teeth.'

The stab to my stomach takes my breath. I see him too.

I hear him. He inhabits my dreams; his body, waterlogged and pale, suspended in a sea that's saturated with blood.

We pull up outside Trevose House and he turns off the engine. His hands don't leave the steering wheel.

'I loved you so much, Hannah. Did you know that?'

My hands knot around each other in my lap. I want to get out of the car. I don't want to be here.

'I thought we'd be together forever.' He laughs bitterly, quietly. 'Jesus… I got it so wrong, didn't I? It broke me when you chose him. After everything we went through? I didn't understand it. But I'm glad you have this good life. This house. Nice things.' He winces and draws in a breath. 'I was never good enough for you.'

I turn my head to look at him. How can he think these things? How can he think I want this house? That I'm interested in *nice things*? 'It wasn't like that,' I say, trying hard to keep from crying. 'I hate this house. I hate it all. It's just… It was too hard. To see your face. To be reminded all the time.' I stop myself talking and remind myself for the thousandth time I chose Nathan for a *reason*. That reason was to protect Cam. 'We couldn't be together after what happened,' I say then. I'm not looking at him now. It's too hard. Instead I keep my eyes fixed on the road ahead and talk as if I'm reading from a script, monotonous and calm. 'You see that, don't you? How could we have stayed together? Please, know—' I pause when my voice cracks. 'Please know how sorry I am. Truly. I fucked it all up and I'm sorry.'

It's all I can say.

I'm sorry.

His face contorts. 'You're sorry? It's me who should be

sorry. Not you. I was an idiot. Got jealous. Angry. I've been over it all a million times in my head. It wasn't your fault, Hannah.'

I'm hit then by an unbidden image of that man, out there in the water, bones picked clean by the fish, crabs scuttling in and out of the hollows where his eyes should be.

Whose fault?

'I wanted you to be happy,' I say. 'I wanted you to get away from Newlyn and make a life for yourself. Away from the shit. I couldn't see you to go to prison.'

'Sometimes I wish I had. When things got harder, I thought prison would be a relief. A warm bed. Three meals a day. Would have been nice. But they'd have come for you too.'

I've lost count of how many times I lay in bed waiting for the knock on the door. Waiting to find the police on the doorstep. Waiting for the metallic bite of their handcuffs.

'Have you been happy?' Would this make it easier? Knowing he'd had a life, and that it was the right choice to drive him away.

'Happy?' He considers it. 'There were moments of happiness.' He pauses. 'I married briefly.'

I should be pleased, but instead I'm hit by an irrational stab of jealousy. The thought of someone else sharing his bed. Touching his body. Talking to him about the things closest to him. Listening to his secrets. His confessions, even. Did she know about me? Did he tell her the truth about why he left Cornwall?

'It didn't last. She was bad for me. Drugs and drink. I was on a road to self-destruction. We both were. And I was having these dark – dark, *dark* – thoughts. You know?'

Yes. I knew.

'She couldn't hack it. Wasn't strong enough herself. I was too much for her to cope with and she met somebody else…'

He sighs. 'When she left I spiralled. Hit rock bottom. Stopped working and missed a couple of rent payments and got evicted. Ended up on the streets for a year or so.'

I inhale. 'Oh Cam…'

'It's all a blur. I guess I'm lucky to be alive.' He smiles. 'In a way you helped me through.'

'What do you mean?'

'I was thinking about everything. What happened. What we did. And then I had this weird feeling that you were watching me, looking at me in the state I was in, dirty, sleeping in a doorway, and hating me—'

'But how could you think that?'

'It's hazy. I can't remember it clearly, but I don't think it was you I was really thinking of. It was me. Me hating myself, thinking I was weak and pathetic, seeing myself with your eyes. Imagining what you'd think of me. I don't know, hearing that out loud sounds strange. It doesn't matter now, what matters is it was enough to get me to a drop-in. They set me up with a counsellor. Helped me kick the drink. The drugs. Put me back on track.'

We fall silent. Both drowning in a sea of regret. For a moment I consider taking his hands in mine and telling him how I really feel, like lead characters in a schmaltzy Hollywood romcom. But it's short lived. This is real life, not celluloid. Real life is messy and complicated. Our relationship comes with too much baggage. Too much risk. How long would it take for our crimes to be unearthed? Nothing has changed. I won't let

Cam go to prison. Not then and not now. And I won't hurt my son. Alex might be too old for Nathan to take away, but he's not too old to hate me.

All these years spent fantasising about a different life with Cameron Stewart. But that's all it was. A fantasy. Trevose House with its ghosts and nightmares is my reality.

Cam opens his mouth as if to speak, but I silence him with a shake of my head. 'No,' I whisper. 'Don't say anything else.' Tears well in my eyes as I open the car door. 'Thank you for bringing Alex home to me.'

When I reach the gate, his car starts, I breathe deeply, fighting every urge I have to turn around and run back to him. His gears grind, the engine revs aggressively, and his car screeches as he drives off at speed.

The front door closes heavily behind me and I collapse against it, hands covering my face, knees so weak I crumple and slide down to the floor. My head is filled with that night. Cam's arms around me as we walked, trembling and trancelike, to his car, where I sat shivering and staring out at the darkness, the coat he'd wrapped around my shoulders doing nothing to repel the biting cold. I had no idea how long he was gone. Time stood still. When he returned, when he opened the door, the car filled momentarily with wind and waves. He climbed in, closed the door, and everything stilled.

I didn't ask what we were doing. I didn't speak. At one point he stopped the car and got out. He walked to the edge of the road, bent over, and vomited. We ended up at Lamorna Cove. The car park overlooking the sea was empty. He explained in monotone we'd be there until morning. We would tell our friends we'd driven there to have sex. People did. It's quiet and romantic with cliffs rising in vertiginous walls providing an illusion of privacy. He leant over me and released the lever to lower my seat. He did the same to his own and we lay in the car, like terrified babes in the woods.

'I'm so sorry,' was the last thing I heard him say.

I'm so sorry.

Neither of us slept. Shortly after eight there was a sharp knock on the window. It was the man who ran the café, his irritated face mouthing words, jabbing angrily towards the sign: *No Overnight Parking*.

'We fell asleep. We're sorry. We'll leave now.'

The man trudged off and we watched him unlock the café. Cam turned to me and rested his hand on my arm. I flinched.

It'll be OK, Hannah.

Ha! What did Cam Stewart know?

It was going to be anything but OK.

CHAPTER TWENTY-FOUR

Hannah

'He went *where*?'

'To Cam's flat. In Reading.' I'm in the far corner of the garden, concealed behind a purple-flowered rhododendron, talking to Vicky on the phone with an eye on the gates to watch for Nathan.

'Why? *How?* Tell me again. But slower.'

I repeat everything I've already told her.

'Jesus,' Vicky breathes. 'That fucking arsehole is back in Newlyn? You actually *saw* him?'

'Yes. I told you. He drove Alex back to the house.'

'And you talked to him?'

'No. He dropped him then drove off.'

Lies, lies, lies. I feel weak with lies.

'Jesus, I'd like to give him a piece of my mind. *Bastard.*' She mutters something I can't make out, then asks, 'Did you tell Alex the truth then? About Cam? Is that why he went?'

'He found my diary. I wrote about Cam in it. The entries were dated and he worked it out.'

'How on earth did he know where to find him?'

Her pitch is getting higher and higher with each question.

'A letter. With his address on.'

'But you told me you hadn't been in touch since he left?'

The lies are thickening the air and my chest feels tight. 'It wasn't worth mentioning. I knew you'd get cross. It was one letter. It said he understood if I didn't want to see him, but gave his address in case I did.'

'But you didn't?'

'No. I couldn't see the point.'

This is a welcome nugget of truth and I take a breath. Lying is second nature, but lying to Vicky is painful.

'How did you explain it to Nathan?'

'I told him Alex had found my old diary and was curious about meeting an old friend from my past. I said he was angry and struggling, and who can tell why teenagers do what they do.'

'He believed that?'

There's a car on the lane. I peer through the rhododendron and see Nathan turning into the driveway. 'Nathan and Alex are back from the police station. I should go. Oh, by the way, it's all good for your birthday. I can definitely come.'

'What? Are you serious? Oh my god. That's great! And he let you? Just like that? How come?'

'Don't know. He just said yes.' I pause. 'Maybe he's relaxing in his old age?'

'And maybe hell's frozen over.'

When Nathan and Alex walk in it's clear they've either argued again or spent their time together in stony silence. Nathan huffs and puffs and stamps around the kitchen like a wounded bull.

'So? How did it go?' I venture, offering the question to either of them.

Nathan picks up the post and leafs through it without acknowledging me.

Alex shrugs. 'Fine. They weren't bothered. They basically wanted to know why I went there and whether he'd made me go and if he'd been chatting to me on the internet. I don't know, maybe they thought he was a paedo or something. They asked loads of other questions I can't remember. I told them I was bored and don't know why I went. They looked like they didn't believe me but then I made up some bullshit about being overwhelmed by school work, which they liked better.'

Nathan glares at him and I drop my head to hide a smile.

'I think they should have done a lot more to let him know what a bloody idiotic thing he did,' snaps Nathan. 'His little stunt was a complete waste of police time and resources and, if it had been me out there looking for him, I'd have been angry it was just a selfish kid on some sort of self-absorbed jolly.'

Alex ignores him. 'They asked if I felt I was getting too much pressure from my parents to do well in my exams. Then they reeled off some statistics about the numbers of kids with mental health issues and said pressure was often the cause.'

Nathan snorted.

'What's for supper?'

I'll say one thing for my son: two nights away from home, a trip to the police station, and a fuming father doesn't seem to faze him. 'Your favourite,' I say with a smile.

'Bolognese? You *legend*!'

'Garlic bread, too. Go fill a jug of water and let's eat.'

I fill a saucepan with water and put it on the hob, resolutely avoiding Nathan's glowering.

'Two plates not three,' he barks, when I walk the plates to the table.

'Oh?'

'I'm out tonight. Remember?'

I shake my head vaguely.

'A supper meeting. I've an important client who lives in Dubai. He's in the UK for a few days. This is the only slot he can make. It's a pain, to be honest.'

It's Nathan's turn to look away. I wonder, Nathan, is it the blonde from the award ceremony who'd touched your arm? Hilary, I seem to recall. Maybe she's getting another outing after all.

'Hannah,' he says impatiently. 'Take that blank look off your face. I told you last week. Standing right here in the kitchen. I said I had an evening meeting. You nodded.'

This used to make me scream with frustration, but I'm used to it now. He'll spring something on me then swear blind we discussed it. He can sometimes regale me with whole conversations he says we had. Sometimes he shouts and blames me for my appalling memory or not concentrating on anything he says (which, to be fair, is true more often than not). I used to stand up for myself, or at least try, but it's exhausting. It's easier to nod and allow him to moan that I never *listen* properly.

'Honestly, Hannah. You never *listen* properly.'

'What time will you be home?'

'Late, I imagine. Don't wait up. The client is travelling down from Heathrow,' he says, as he heads out of the kitchen. 'And then we're meeting for supper.'

'You said,' I say as his footsteps climb the stairs.

'Your Bolognese is the best,' says Alex, either oblivious to, or disinterested in, our conversation. 'I mean, literally the *best*.'

He eats like he hasn't eaten in weeks. Sauce spatters his cheeks and lips, grease from the garlic bread slicks his lips with a sheen of butter.

'What's the best ever food you've eaten, Mum?'

My chest swells with love for him. Fifteen years old, capable of unbearable surliness and mood swings, but right now, belly full, grinning widely, he could be eight years old again.

I press a napkin against the corners of my mouth. 'Best food ever?' I muse. 'Well, your father has taken me to some lovely restaurants, but—'

I lower my voice and glance at the door then back at Alex conspiratorially. This is a dangerous game to play. Nathan would be furious if he overhears, but fuck him and fuck Hilary and their seedy fake supper meeting.

'—the best food I've tasted was when I was going out with Cameron Stewart.' Alex's eyes light up. 'He invited me out on his fishing boat and said he'd be making me tea. I thought it would be a picnic, a sandwich, a chicken salad or something, some beer. I didn't pay much attention when he dropped a fishing line into the sea. We sat and talked for a while, then he leant over and pulled up the line and there were three shiny mackerel caught on it. *Dinner*, he announced.' I furrow my brow and make a face at Alex. 'I wasn't overly impressed. I wasn't that fond of mackerel.' I pause and reach for some bread and break off a small corner. The garlicky butter runs down my finger and I lick it off before popping the morsel into my mouth. 'But he told me I hadn't tried mackerel until I'd tried it his dad's way, the way the Scots cook it. He filleted the fish, fingers moving as fast as quicksilver, then dropped them in some oats which he kept in a battered old tin on the boat. Then he got out a single burner, the type you have when you're camping, an old blackened frying pan from this chest he had on board, then a pat of butter wrapped in foil like you get in a café and a salt cellar from his pocket. And, oh my *god*. It was incredible. Fresh from the sea and covered in crisp buttery salted oats.' As I think about it I can recall exactly how it tasted. 'It was like heaven.' I smile and tear off another corner of garlic bread as Nathan's footsteps come down the stairs. I raise my eyebrows. 'Seriously,' I whisper. 'Best thing I've tasted in all my life.'

'Don't wait up. I've no idea how long this will take,' Nathan calls.

'Hope it goes well.'

And give Hilary my love.

The door closes with a slam and Alex helps himself to another portion of Bolognese. I get up and clear a few things, put my plate on the floor for Cass to lick, and turn the tap on to run a sink of water. A knock on the front door makes me start.

'Must have forgotten his key,' I say to Alex, who is wiping his plate with some garlic bread.

I walk down the hallway and see the bowl on the hall table is empty. Nathan has his keys. I peer through the side window. My heart skips a beat. I glance over my shoulder but there's no sign of Alex, so I open the door.

'Cam?' I whisper. 'Jesus. What are you doing? You can't be here.'

'I saw him leave. I was in my car a little way down the lane.'

'You were watching the house?'

He shrugs.

'How long have you been there?'

He doesn't reply.

'Shit, Cam. You can't come in. Alex is here. It's too complicated. You have to leave.'

He looks up at the sky, shakes his head, and looks back at me. 'Why the fuck did you marry that prick?'

CHAPTER TWENTY-FIVE

Hannah

'I'm taking Cass down to the woods, Alex!' I call back towards the kitchen. 'Load your plate in the dishwasher and leave the rest for me. I'll tidy the kitchen when I get back.'

A mumbled reply comes back, but I'm already through the door with the dog.

I'd told Cam to drive further on and park near the track which runs down to Trevaylor Woods and wait for me there. He had answered with a grim-faced nod.

Cass and I turn off the lane and walk down into the woods. The ancient trees that flank the track form a dense skein of branches overhead, which allows only dappled light to penetrate. The air is cool and damp and scented with mulching leaves. Cass bounds on ahead, rooting through the leaves and undergrowth in search of rabbits. I walk a little way down and lean on the farm gate and wait for him to follow. The fields overlook Mounts Bay in the distance and the last of the evening sun is glistening like fire on the sea. I hear footsteps and turn to see Cam walking towards me, hands shoved into his pockets, shoulders slouched. He is dressed in the same jeans and boots, and has swapped his sweater for a T-shirt, faded khaki and creased. A number of frayed fabric bands encircle his left wrist and his arms are pale, not tanned and weathered as I remember them.

He stops a little way from me as if he's met an invisible barrier and is unable to get any closer, twitching and shifting his weight from side to side awkwardly.

There's a rustling in the hedge and Cass appears, pushing through the undergrowth to run at Cam, tail wagging madly. He crouches and ruffles her with both hands, talking in low whispers as he presses his face to the top of her head.

'She's lovely,' he says as he stands.

I nod.

The sun has set below the horizon now and the sky has turned a deep pink shot through with purple and grey. We walk down the track, through the woods and on towards a small stream which babbles over and around the moss-covered boulders which rest on its bed. Cass leaps over it and disappears into the brambles and ferns on the other side.

'I need to know,' he says again, his voice diamond-tipped. 'Why Nathan Cardew? Why him of all people?'

Has this been playing on his mind all these years?

I stop walking. He does the same and we face each other. I should fabricate something. Another lie to add to the towering pile, but even though lying has become second nature, right now I'm weary of it. Exhausted, in fact. Lying seems easier, a quick fix to hide something more complicated, but it's much more demanding than recalling what actually happened. You have to take more factors into account: credibility, plausibility, consequence, as well as remembering not to give yourself away with any number of tells. You have to act to affect honesty. It's energy sapping. So I decide not to lie.

'He saw you.'

Rather than watch him try and work out what I've said, I turn and walk on down the track.

'Hannah?' He catches up with me and touches my arm.

'That night. He *saw* you. He watched you go out to sea.' I blink slowly and take a breath. 'And he waited and watched you come in. He was there. Hidden behind the buildings.'

Cam's brow furrows as he attempts to process what I'm saying. 'But if he saw me… why didn't he tell the police? It wasn't as if he didn't hate me. He did. Why did he keep quiet?' He shakes his head as if attempting to dislodge something. 'I don't understand.'

I take a deep breath and dredge the next words up from deep inside me. 'He was going to go to the police. I asked him not to. Begged him, in fact. He told me he loved me. Said you were no good and violent and he should do the right thing and turn you in. And… I said… ' I blow air slowly out and wince. This is harder to get out than I ever could have imagined. 'If you love me, you won't.'

My hands tremble as if an electric charge is passing through them. I stop walking and we face each other again. His face is pale. His lips drawn tight.

My stomach somersaults. Why did I tell him? I should have lied. I should have lied, but I didn't and now it's too late. I press on, ignoring the gathering nausea.

'Then… ' I hesitate and shake my head.

'What?'

'Then he asked me if I loved him. And… and I said yes, because I didn't know what else to say, because I didn't want anything to happen to you and my head was clouded up.'

I pause and purse my lips, glance up at the darkening sky. 'He said if I really did love him I'd be with him and not you.'

Cam is silent.

'It was a pact, Cam. A deal. He wouldn't go to the police about what he'd seen if I ended our relationship to be with him.' My throat constricts as memories of that conversation bear down heavily. Dread had curdled my blood as my world caved in. 'It went from there. Things snowballed and gathered pace. It was like I was trapped in a car hurtling towards a cliff. I couldn't think straight. My brain was full of mud. And, God, I was scared. I was so, *so* scared. The thought of the police getting involved? Visions of you and me in prison.' I pause and blink slowly. 'It seemed like my only option. It seemed like the right thing to do.'

Understanding gathers on Cam's face like a squall.

'I couldn't let you go to prison. And,' I sigh heavily, 'I didn't want to go to prison either. I kept thinking about Mum and Dad and how it would destroy them. They would have been so ashamed.'

'You wouldn't have gone to prison,' he whispers.

Dusk has set in and his features are becoming obscured in the murky light.

'I hated him from that moment. We slept together. The night you left.' I pause to wipe the tears away. It hurts to recall it, me lying there rigid and scared, my mind closing down as he kissed me and told me he loved me in hot sticky whispers. 'I thought about calling his bluff. Leaving him and trying find you. I thought we could get on a plane to some-where miles away, like Mexico, like they do in American films, and it wouldn't matter if he told the police.' I rub my face and smile ruefully. 'But then a month or so later I found out I was pregnant and everything changed. I had to stay. Because what else could I do?' I breathe steadily, trying, but failing, to stem my tears. 'How could I be pregnant and go to prison? They would have taken him away from me. Put him into care.'

I bite down on my lip until I taste a trace of blood. His breathing has grown heavier and I'm aware of his body tensing, as if he is about to speak. I press on, worried that if I let him talk now, I won't finish what I need to say.

'When Alex was a few weeks old I ran away. I had no idea where we were going. I was all over the place with postnatal depression. I'm sure I was suffering some sort of PTSD as well. I had nightmares. I'd relive it all over and over again.' I blot my tears with my sleeve. 'Nathan found me at the station. He was furious and threatened everything. The police. Prison. Custody of Alex. He said he couldn't trust me and after that he barely let me out of his sight.'

The air around us is damp with the approaching night and I realise how cold I am, my teeth chattering softly. I wrap my arms around my body.

'I'm sorry,' Cam whispers.

I shake my head. 'Don't be. I love Alex with all my heart and having him gave my life meaning. I haven't told you this because I want your sympathy and I don't want you to worry about me. I just want you to know I didn't choose him because he was a lawyer or because of the big house or the money or the spotless car we aren't allowed to breathe in.' I pause and take a step closer to him. 'Watching you walk away was the hardest thing I've ever had to do and it haunts me every single day.'

Before I know what's happening, he has put his arms around

me. His body is lean and hard. He smells strange and my breath catches. I rest my cheek against his chest and my tears soak into the fabric of his shirt. I can hear his heart beating and it takes me back to when we were young, when I laid my cheek against this same part of him and dreamt of being happy forever.

I can't do this.

'I need to get back.' I push myself away from him. 'This is wrong. Jesus. If Nathan finds out I've seen you, he'll go to the police.'

Cam reaches for my hand but I snatch it away.

'Hannah, listen, he won't go to the police.'

'You don't know him. He will—'

'He won't. He's a lawyer. He knows he can't. If he saw me that night and didn't report it, he's in as much trouble as I am. Keeping quiet makes him complicit. There's no way he's going to let himself go to prison for a fifteen-year-old crime he didn't commit. Think about it.'

His words take shape in my head and leave me breathless. I could kick myself for being so stupid. So naive. How can I not have seen such an obvious thing in all these years? If he goes to the police he'll have to explain why he withheld information. Information which would have shed light on a missing person. Withholding information is a crime. There's no way Nathan will take himself down. Not for a crime he didn't commit. Especially when the crime is murder.

My mind races so fast it trips over itself as I realise he couldn't even prove he wasn't involved himself. It would be his word against ours. Nathan's hold over me is decimated. But is it? Nathan is clever, manipulative too; there's no way to be sure he hasn't planned for this, that he hasn't constructed a means to protect himself, so he could still turn us in but remain safe himself. I'm hit by a vivid image of him and Alex watching from the front doorstep as I'm led away in handcuffs to a police car parked at the gate with its blue light twirling.

'I can't risk it. I couldn't put Alex through it.'

We get to the top of the lane and the canopy of trees thins. It's time to say goodbye but neither of us makes a move to leave. Cam's face is clearer now we're out of the woods and in the light of the moon. I smile, a weak apologetic gesture, which feels insubstantial. Without warning, he bends close to me and hovers in the sliver of air between us before gently touching his lips to mine.

It takes me by surprise and for a moment everything else falls away. It's just me and him. The kiss is tender and soft, free of urgency or lust, but soaked with pain and regret and a longing for things to be different.

What am I doing?

No. No…

No!

I shove him hard away. Shake my head. Step back. I shake my head again and two tears tumble down my cheeks.

'No,' I whisper.

He stares at me, forlorn, uncomprehending, needy of love or affection or forgiveness, or whatever it is he craves. Unexpected anger flares inside me. 'Jesus, Cam, don't look at me like that. What do you *want* me to do? What do you think's going to happen? That we kiss then tear each other's clothes off for old time's sake? Fuck here against the farm gate?'

'What? *No!* Of course not.' His face screws up. 'It's just seeing you again. It's—'

'It's what? Time to put everything behind us and crack on where we left off?' I give a bitter snort of laughter. 'Time to forget what happened and give our tragic story a happy ending?'

His mouth opens then closes and his eyebrows knot, before he drops his head, defeated. I'm hit again by how damaged this new version of Cam is. How his pain infects the air around us. How weakened he is. I cover my face with my hands and breathe the hot air, then stifle an exasperated growl; I can't carry his damage as well as my own.

'I'm sorry you've had such a difficult time,' I say in barely whispered words. 'But it's too late for us. Do you understand? What we had is gone. We can't ever get it back.'

He starts to speak, but I don't let him.

'Nothing has changed. I'm married. I have a *son*. This is what I chose. This is how our story ends. You and I don't get to live happily ever after.'

He is silent.

'You need to leave Cornwall. You need to get away from me and this whole sorry fucked up mess. You don't need this.' I take a weary sigh. 'And, frankly, nor do I, because seeing you again, having you back here,' I say, my voice barely audible now, 'is too hard.'

My words have dried up and I am drained. I give Cass a feeble whistle and she bursts out of the bushes and trots happily to my side, her wet nose finding my hand in the dimness. Without saying anything more, I turn and walk away from him, up to the lane, in the direction of home, and I don't look back.

CHAPTER TWENTY-SIX

Hannah

The first thing I see when I walk through the gate is Nathan's car glinting in the moonlight on the driveway. My heart skips a beat. I tell myself to relax. I've done nothing wrong. I took the dog out. That's all. I take her out every night. It's normal. Breathe. You've done nothing wrong.

Breathe.

I follow the gravel path around the side of the house and take Cass in through the kitchen door. The lights are off. The dishwasher is on and whirring softly. The door closes behind me and the air immediately tightens. As soon as I step into the kitchen the smell hits me, an unpleasant hint of something in the air, sweet and rancid. It catches the back of my throat. I turn the light on and scan the room, searching for the cause of it, but the surfaces are cleared of everything, polished down, spotless. There's no way Alex would have done it and the thought of Nathan cleaning the kitchen so thoroughly gives me the chills.

I walk to the sink and the smell gets stronger. I open the cupboard beneath, where the bin is, and when I do, I pull back and lift my hand to my nose. Whatever is causing the stench is in the bin. I peer in and there, on the top of the rubbish, is a plastic bag. I can see something brown and soft inside it. I flick back the opening of the bag to reveal whatever it is and, when I do, draw back in shock and cover my mouth with my hand. Inside the bag is a collection of rodents curled around each other in a Celtic knot. Their matted fur is wet and putrid, their eyes rotted away, lips pulled back from sharp yellow teeth in macabre grimaces. The smell is hideous. They've been in the bag for some time, which I imagine must have been sealed and somewhere warm.

'Jesus,' I whisper. I breathe through my mouth and keep as far back as I can, while I reach in and pick the bag out.

As I grasp hold of it, Nathan appears at the door. I hold the plastic bag out towards him, my hand still blocking my nose, my heart racing. 'Did you put these mice in the bin?'

'Not mice. Voles. Nasty little voles which were attacking my seedlings so I poisoned them. Did you know they can eat through a whole greenhouse of plants in a matter of hours? I collected them up and put them in the bag, but forgot about them. They stank the greenhouse out spectacularly.'

'Why are they in the house bin?'

'Because they've been poisoned?' he says as if I'm stupid. 'You said I wasn't to throw poisoned animals in the bushes or over the fence in case the dog ate them. Remember?'

'They should be in the wheelie bin. *Outside* not in.'

'I didn't know you were quite so sensitive. I can double-bag them if you'd prefer?' A glint of maliciousness flickers in his eyes.

I stare at him for a moment or two before turning towards the kitchen door and marching the hideous creatures to the black bin inside our gates. When I come back he has taken a bottle of wine from the cupboard and is retrieving a bottle opener from the drawer.

'So how come you're home so early?' I say as casually as I can muster. I turn the tap on and squeeze some hand soap on to my hands to wash them.

'I didn't feel like it in the end.'

The smell of the rotting voles still hangs heavily in the kitchen. I knot the bin bag and as I do he clears his throat and leans back against the worktop.

'I thought I'd spend the evening with you instead. Where were you?' The lightness in his tone masks a direct accusation. I watch him driving the corkscrew into the bottle. He yanks it out easily and it gives a soft pop as it releases. He inspects the cork and holds it up to his nose. 'I didn't know you were going out.'

'Walking Cass.' I open the back door and put the bin bag outside. My knees threaten to buckle.

'Nice walk?'

My heart picks up speed as I bend to retrieve the disinfectant from beneath the sink. 'Yes, thank you. It's a lovely evening.' I reach for a cloth and tip the liquid on to it and begin to wipe the inside of the bin. The chemical pine smell is acrid and almost as unpleasant as the lingering odour of decomposed rodent I'm trying to get rid of. 'I stayed out longer than I expected to because you were out and Alex went up to bed, and, well, I like walking at night. Especially when it's not too cold… ' I stop myself, aware I'm rambling.

'Where did you walk?'

'Across the fields.' The answer is instinctive and I regret it immediately. The thing about a good lie is it should be as close to the truth as possible.

'You seem jumpy. Is everything all right?'

I swallow, but my throat is dry. 'Yes, of course. It's nice you're home. I might join you with a glass of wine.'

He doesn't move immediately, but then takes a second wine glass from the cupboard and pours some red wine. He holds it out to me. For a moment I imagine it's poisoned and I'm going to end up like the voles. I take it and he turns to pick up his own glass.

'Cheers.' He stares at me and raises his wine. 'By the way, if you still want me to take you to visit your mother tomorrow, I want to leave at eight. I need to get to the garden centre for some more poison. I seem to have used it all up on those vermin.'

I watch his face like a hawk but his smile doesn't falter. Something's going on, there's something he's storing up, and he wants me to worry about what it is. My mind jumps back to the woods. To what Cam said to me. How much pleasure, I wonder, would I get from turning myself in and seeing Nathan go to prison for concealing a murder? Cam would be collateral damage. Alex and my mother, too. But would it be worth it?

'We can catch the train if you'd prefer. It's not far to walk from the station.'

'Half an hour.'

'Not far.'

We are dancing around each other, watchfully, as if engaged in the opening bars of a dangerous tango.

'I said I'd drive you and I will.' That smile again.

I nod.

'Hannah?'

His voice has turned flinty and my stomach spasms.

'Are you sure you walked in the fields? Not the woods?'

I remain as passive as I can.

'Only, I drove home through Gulval and Trevaylor tonight.'

He knows.

I sip some wine. 'Yes. Definitely the fields. The woods are too dark at this time of night.'

'There was a car parked on the side of the road. Near the track down to the woods.' He smiles. 'It looked familiar. But, of course, I could be mistaken.'

The tremor in my voice is hard to conceal. 'I was in the fields.'

'It's just the crappy old jalopy parked at the woods was remarkably similar to the one Cameron Stewart drives. Almost identical, in fact.'

'But he's gone back to wherever he lives, hasn't he?'

'I thought so, but, well, it's hard to be in two places at once, isn't it? And if his car is parked at the top of Trevaylor Woods, it's almost impossible for it to also be parked on a street in some shitty part of Reading.'

'Why do you think it was his? It could be anybody's. Lots of people walk there and all those red cars look the same, don't they?'

His exaggerated smile finally slips away. 'You appear to think I was born yesterday.'

I don't react. I am careful. I drink some wine then place the glass down and cross my arms firmly. This bravado is a mask; inside I am jelly.

'You never stopped seeing him, did you?'

'What?'

'You kept in contact. You're still in a relationship. Alex knows him. That's why he went there.' He steps close to me and moves his face so close to mine I can smell the wine on his breath. 'You've been *fucking* him this whole time, haven't you?'

I shake my head and hold back tears.

'Will you visit him in prison?'

'You can't,' I begin, struggling to get the whispered words out. 'You can't prove anything.'

'Excuse me?'

'It's been too long. We'll tell them you're lying. I'll tell them he was with me... in his... car. All night. At Lamorna.' I swallow hard and clench my fists in the hope it gives me strength. 'It'll be our word against yours. I'll say... I'll say you're making it up because... you're jealous... '

'*Jealous?*' He erupts with laughter, dabbing imaginary tears of mirth and shaking his head as if I've told the funniest joke in the world. 'Your word against *mine*? The word of a housewife with depression who can't get a job or manage a bank account? And that of a pathetic drifter? You think they'll believe the two of you over *me*? A respected lawyer and upstanding member of the community?'

Each word stings. I have to dig deep. I think of Alex and the way he stands up to this man and how proud it makes me. When I speak, I do so slowly, pausing between words to steady my nerves.

'But not upstanding enough to go to the police and report a crime.'

The sentence is no more than a whisper, but I see him double-take, a flicker of surprise skims his face.

It emboldens me.

'You watched Cam put a body in his boat and head out to sea with a dinghy tied to that boat. You waited until he returned. Empty-handed. No body. No dinghy. You witnessed him dispose of a body, but never breathed a word. You let a village believe a man had drowned at sea. You withheld evidence.' Adrenalin pumps through my veins like a drug. 'A lawyer withholding evidence that might lead to a conviction for *murder*? What would this do to your reputation?' Hatred fills me like an inflating balloon. 'You know something?' My words drive into him. 'If it wasn't for you, following me around, refusing to leave me alone, none of it would have happened. If you'd just stayed away then Cam and I could have had a chance at being happy. I could have married someone who truly loves me.' I laugh bitterly. 'Jesus. Imagine *that*?'

He stands, open-mouthed, as if I've slapped him.

'I've loved you from the first moment I saw you,' he says, brow furrowed with incredulity. 'You consumed me.' I struggle to keep looking at him under the burning heat of his stare. 'I *saved* you, Hannah. I got you away from that man. I didn't contact the police for *you*. He was no good for you. A *murderer*? Is that the type of man who'd make you happy?' He pauses for a moment or two to study me, searching my face for some sort of reaction. 'I gave you a second chance, a beautiful home and family. I gave you all of this,' he says, as he gestures around him with a dramatic sweep. Then he takes my hand in his. His thumb strokes mine. 'Tell me, who stood by you, Hannah? Him or me?' He raises his hand to my face and trails the backs of his fingers down my cheeks. 'You're misremembering it all. Things happened differently. When

I found you, you were barely functioning. You were a shadow of the girl I knew. And when he abandoned you, I was there for you. If he loved you even half as much as I do, he'd never have left you. He'd have fought for you. Like I did. If it were me back then? I never would have run away from you. I'd have taken you with me. Left in the night. I'd have moved heaven and earth to not be separated from you. And I did. You *asked* me to let him go free. It went against everything I knew was right and I did it only for *you*. And what did he do? This man you think would have made you happy?'

Nathan is speaking softly now, his demeanour gentle and unthreatening. His words are muddling me, as if he's taking a jar of my memories and shaking it until it's silty and unclear.

'He abandoned you, Hannah. I watched him walk away from you. He didn't even look back.'

An image of Cam leaving blindsides me and I'm catapulted back to that afternoon.

My voice telling him to go. Telling him I never wanted to see him again. Him pleading with me. Trying to hold on to me. Both hands against his chest. Pushing. Powered by anger at the staggering injustice of it.

It's over, Cam. I don't love you. Just go.

And that was it. He turned his back on me and didn't look back.

My mind wrestles with everything Nathan said. Is he right? Am I so swept up with the fantasy of Cam that I'm not remembering things correctly? Why didn't Cam fight for me? For us? If he truly loved me, how could he walk away?

CHAPTER TWENTY-SEVEN

Hannah

The body was never recovered. The days and hours which followed his disappearance were hellish. What felt like the whole of Newlyn assembled at the church the following Sunday to pray for his safe return, yet not one member of that congregation believed he was alive. You could see it in the way they carried themselves, broken by sadness, resigned to the loss and trying to process the tragedy. The church buckled beneath the weight of shared grief, the town mourning one of its own, brother, friend, pupil, son, a young man with his whole life ahead of him, exhausted, emotionally traumatised, so drunk he wasn't thinking straight, took a boat out at night in rough seas, and never returned.

I had to lean on my father to keep myself steady during the service. I couldn't look at any of them. Couldn't look at Cam. Whispers swept the church and the bakery, the pub and the post office, street corners, playgrounds, the dock, and the fish market. Children throughout Newlyn and Penzance, Long Rock, as far as Hayle and beyond, were warned – yet again – to respect the sea. Don't be foolish. Don't take risks. Never take the sea for granted, never take your boat out when you've been drinking.

Foolish boy.

Even he, the whispers said, who knew the sea like the back of his hand, who'd grown up with it, who earned his livelihood from it and faced its power every day. Even *he* made mistakes.

His upended dinghy was found stranded on rocks below Penlee Caravan Park, not far from Mousehole.

The current was strong that night, the whispers said. We won't find him. Not now. He'll be halfway to America.

I stumbled through those days in a stupor. The lies started immediately. First I lied to my parents. I told them he was a dear friend of mine, we were close, and his loss hit me hard so I needed time to get over it. I went up to my bedroom, closed the door, pulled the curtains shut, and climbed beneath the covers. Every part of me ached as if I'd been beaten with steel bars. My head throbbed so violently the light stung my eyes.

Cam visited. Once. He sat on the chair in my room holding the mug of tea my mother made him. We didn't talk. Instead we sat in silence and stared at nothing, our tentacles of guilt wriggling outwards, knotting together, snarling up the space between us.

On the fourth day, in the morning, after my fifth sleepless night, Nathan came. I could hear his voice at the front door. My mother telling him I was too sick for visitors. But he insisted. He told her he wouldn't be long. She appeared at my door.

'It's Nathan Cardew to see you, *melder*. I told him to come back another time, but he's hard to argue with.'

I can't recall my reply, what I said, if, indeed, I said anything. Moments later he walked into my room. Shut the door. Sat on the end of my bed and calmly told me what he'd seen. He appeared victorious in some way, elated, as if he'd won a sports match he was expecting to lose. He seemed to relish telling me in intricate detail about the body of a man in Cameron Stewart's boat. How he'd seen Cam untie a dinghy then drag it out of the harbour on a rope. How he'd waited and seen him return some time later with no dinghy and no body. He peppered the story with dramatic pauses and snide comments on Cam's violent character. He told me how at first he wasn't sure what he'd seen, but the next morning, when he heard a man had drowned at sea the night before, well, he said, it was easy to put two and two together. All the while he spoke he held my hand. I couldn't see straight as spores of panic multiplied like bacteria and spread throughout me.

'Did you know about it? Did you know it was him?'

I didn't answer.

'I see. Well, that explains why you look so pale and drawn. You know I have to go to the police, don't you?'

I shook my head. Tears scorched my cheeks. 'Please don't.'

He made a regretful face. 'It's out of my hands.'

Cam couldn't go to prison. Not for this. If he went to prison there would be no justice in the world. I had to protect him. It was the only thing that mattered.

I squeezed Nathan's hand.

'Don't go to the police.'

'I have to. I love you, and I don't want to upset you, but can't you see? I have no choice.'

I lifted his hand to my face, rested my cheek against it.

'If you love me,' I whispered, 'you won't tell the police.'

He didn't answer immediately. His eyes clouded a little as he stroked my cheek. His fingers played with my hair. He stared at me with such intensity it scared me.

'Do you love me, Hannah?'

I held back my tears. I had no idea what to say, but I knew if I said no, if I told the truth, that Cam would be arrested. My head began to fuzz up. Nathan became indistinct as my vision blurred.

'Because if you really loved me, you'd be with me, not him…'

And there it was, hidden in that hanging sentence, Nathan's deal. Cam's freedom. In exchange for mine.

'I do love you.'

His face broke into a childlike smile. 'Oh, Hannah, you have no idea how happy hearing that makes me. You must tell him. You've been wrong to let him think you're in love with him and not me. Do you understand? Don't be scared of him. I'll protect you. You must tell him now. He needs to know you don't love him and he needs to know you want to be with me. You have to send him away.' He lifted my hand to his lips and kissed it. 'He needs to leave. If I see him here again I'll go to the police. Do you understand, Hannah? Cameron Stewart has to leave Cornwall and must *never* come back.'

CHAPTER TWENTY-EIGHT

Hannah

'I can't drive you this morning.' Nathan opens his wallet and leafs through his money. He selects a five-pound note and holds it out towards me. 'You'll have to catch the bus.'

This doesn't surprise me. He often offers to drive me places – my mother, the shops, the vet, school – but more often than not, something else gets in the way. When I'm in a less generous mood, I can't help but wonder if it's yet another example of him wielding his control. I *could* drive you, but I *choose* not to, and there's nothing you can do about it. This morning, though, I'd hoped he might show a little more compassion given how poorly my mother is.

I'm well practised, however, and force a smile. 'Alex was hoping to come with me. Are you able to give me money for his fare as well?'

Nathan closes his wallet and slips it back into his pocket. 'He can use the money in his tin, can't he? After all, that's what it's for, no? A little *independence*?'

The deliberate way he closed his wallet means his mind is made up but, like the masochist I must be, I press on nonetheless. 'That money is gone. You know that. Please, Nathan. He'd like to visit his grandmother in hospital.'

Nathan beams with grotesque smugness. 'He shouldn't have spent all his money bringing Cameron Stewart back to Cornwall then, should he?' It's clear he's been waiting patiently for the perfect opportunity to use this well-rehearsed line. It wouldn't surprise me if he planned it before he'd even said yes to driving us to Treliske.

Alex is disappointed he can't come with me. I don't tell him Nathan wouldn't give me the bus fare. Instead, I tell him Mum's not up to lots of visitors.

'We don't want to tire her. She needs her strength. She's still asleep, anyway, so won't know if you're there, but I promise we'll go again in a few days.'

'Will you tell her I love her?'

'Of course.'

When Alex was younger, I'd take him to visit the bakery and Mum and Dad would rush out from behind the counter and shower him with kisses. My dad would drop a Chelsea bun into a paper bag and wink as he passed it to his beaming grandson. Alex and I would then walk over the bridge to the shingle beach at Wherrytown where he'd proceed to lick every tiny bit of the icing off. When the icing was gone I'd tear pieces off the bun and pass them to him so he could feed the seagulls. He loved it when one was clever enough to catch it mid-air and would clap madly. On occasion, I've tried to work out what my life might have been like if I hadn't had Alex, but just the thought is unbearable. There were times, like when he and I were feeding those gulls, together, content, his laughter ringing in the air I was breathing, when my marriage made complete sense. Alex and I were safe, with a roof over our heads and food in our stomachs; the difficult stuff seemed a small price to pay.

The insubstantial bunch of flowers rests on my lap as the bus makes its way towards Truro. I asked Nathan for some money for a bouquet. He told me to cut some from the garden, which was fine because that was always my plan. The flower money would have been a welcome addition to my secret stash which is almost empty after buying some new hand cream for Mum. I picked a few roses and some greenery and added some blowsy cow parsley from the verge by the bus stop. Mum loves cut flowers. I hate them. They remind me of the memorial service, of watching Mum carrying the bunch she'd brought to the church, tears coursing her cheeks as God, Jesus, and Mary stared down at me, fingers pointing, anger burning.

'All right, *melder*?' my dad had whispered as he rubbed my knee. 'You're pale as death.'

I'd nodded, clenched my fists, caught sight of Cam a few pews in front, sobbing uncontrollably.

'I need some air.' Excusing myself I squeezed past the mourners in our row, hurried out with my head low, and only just made it to the yew bushes in the corner of the churchyard before I threw up.

The bus wends its way through the country lanes on the way into Truro. I'm glad Nathan wouldn't drive me and I'm glad Alex isn't with me. It's more restful alone. I lean my head against the window and stare at the hedgerows and houses and shops which run alongside the A30. Nathan drains me. The way he twists everything and the mental gymnastics I have to perform in order to keep my head straight is exhausting. It doesn't matter how strong I feel when we begin a conversation, by the end I'm left shattered. I heard a woman talking on the radio a while ago. I was cleaning the fridge so it must have been a Monday. The programme was on Radio 4 and she was talking about a book she'd written. It was called *Power Gamers*. The presenter described it as an *unflinching and often painful account of a toxic marriage*. The author might as well have been talking about my life not hers. The behaviours, the control, the humiliation she encountered on a daily basis, the way her ex-husband eroded her dignity and self-worth, and, of course, the financial control which kept her captive. The woman's sickly sweet voice began to eat into me. It was shame, she said, which kept her from reaching out for the help she needed. She finally found the strength to leave when he smashed her in the face with an iron because of a crease in his shirt. I turned the radio off at that point and focused on cleaning the fridge, tears stinging my cheeks, the self-hatred almost too much to bear.

As I creep through the privacy curtain, the first thing I notice about my mother is how still she is. The rough, greying sheets cover her to her chest. Her arms, made from pipe cleaners and tissue paper, rest alongside her body. She is feather-light, as if all that remains of her is a delicate casing which might dissolve in the slightest breeze.

'*Dama*, it's me. It's Hannah.' There's no vase, so I lay the flowers on the table beside her.

When I take hold of her hand, her eyelids flicker as if a breeze brushed over them.

I fill the air with words and pretend she's talking back, which makes it easier. We discuss the bakery and how we used to take mischievous pleasure in watching unsuspecting tourists walk out of the shop and lose pasties to thieving seagulls. We talk about how we used to swim in the Jubilee Pool and how fancy the recent refurbishments are. I remind her of the play we saw at The Minack where the wind was so strong we couldn't hear a word, and we ate crab sandwiches made with Dad's best bread, and Cadbury's Fruit and Nut, and how cold we'd got, our faces spritzed with mizzle, huddling together with a blanket laid across our knees, as the group of hardy actors tried admirably to bring *A Midsummer Night's Dream* to life.

I'm not sure how long it is before the doctor appears. Long enough for my back to stiffen. The doctor is young and tired and pretty, puffy dark circles beneath her eyes, freckles speckling her nose and cheeks, her auburn hair tied up in a scruffy bun.

'Your mother is out of the woods for now, but I'm afraid the independence she had before the stroke will be compromised. She'll need a period of rehabilitation and some physio. We can't determine how much of her movement will return at this stage. She'll also need input from a speech therapist, and, of course, increased help with feeding, bathing, and dressing.' She smiles over at Mum then back at me. 'She's tough though. You've got some good genes there.'

I manage a smile.

The doctor consults her notes, flicking the pages over her clipboard. 'I see she's currently at Heamoor Residential.'

'Yes,' I say quietly, thinking of her room, its window on to the courtyard, the little storm bird which had kept her company, now in my kitchen.

'She'll need somewhere with round-the-clock care. Have you looked at any places?'

I shake my head.

'We can give you details of a few, but it's worth ringing

around. Perhaps get recommendations from friends and family. There are a few funded by the council, but most are privately run. The quality can vary. Best to visit a selection and make your decision based on what feels right. She'll be here for at least a week so there's a bit of time.'

My stomach churns as I watch the doctor running through her checks, listening to Mum's heart, taking her blood pressure, consulting charts, monitoring the drip, writing notes. There's no way Nathan will pay more for her care. I know how astronomical the private places can be.

'What happens,' I ask, 'if people can't afford this type of care for their parents?'

Her face softens with sympathy. 'It's hard, isn't it? I suppose most opt to have loved ones at home if they have the space. Getting a carer in to share the burden with a son or daughter is probably the most cost-effective way to ensure a decent standard of care. It depends what the patient needs, of course. And if there's enough space and if the relative has a job or other commitments. But for those who can make it work it seems to be a good option.'

For a moment I think about how perfect it would be to have Mum with us, but it's a short-lived fantasy replaced quickly by Nathan's dismissive contempt when he asks if I'm joking.

It's nearly five o'clock by the time I get home. Nathan is in the garden standing in front of the barbecue, vigorously flapping a square of cardboard over the smoke. He smiles when he sees me and I know that, as far as he is concerned, this morning's altercation is over and done with and no more shall be said on the matter.

'I thought we should make the most of this heatwave and

cook outdoors. I knew you'd be tired from seeing your mother so thought I'd take care of supper tonight.'

I kiss his cheek and he smiles again.

'How is she?'

'Stable. The doctor says she won't be able to go back to Heamoor though.'

'Oh? Why?'

'She needs more care.' The sentence hovers unfinished to give him the opportunity to put his arms around me and tell me I have nothing to worry about and that, of course, he'll make sure she gets the best care.

'What does that mean? *More care.*' He bends to rest the cardboard against the base of the barbecue and picks up the poker. When he stokes the coals, orange sparks leap into the air like mini-fireworks.

What does it mean, Nathan? It means exactly what I said. She needs *more care* than Heamoor can provide.

'I don't know exactly.'

Nathan responds better when I appear helpless and in need of his guidance. For all his weaknesses and insecurities he needs to be needed. The dependence of others is like some sort of drug. If I were a psychiatrist, I'd probably deduce that his father blowing his face in half, rather than turning to his mother for help, has something to do with it.

'The doctor mentioned having to monitor her,' I say with a confused shrug.

'What did he mean by *monitor?*'

'She.'

Nathan pokes the coals again.

'She said Mum would need more help with bathing and

feeding, a physio and speech therapist, and somewhere with medical staff on call. Heamoor doesn't offer this kind of care.'

I take a breath. 'I suppose,' I say, as if the idea has just popped into my head as an afterthought, 'she could come here? The doctor said that's what often happens. Care homes are so expensive, as you know, and well, we have the space. I'm here all the time. Alex doesn't need me very much so I could easily take care of her?'

He opens his mouth to speak, but I can see the refusal coming, so add quickly, 'maybe for a short while? A few weeks? I'm worried about moving her. There aren't that many nursing homes close by... ' I pause for a moment as I'm hit by the realisation that at some stage, maybe soon, I'll have to say goodbye to her. 'I worry I don't have long left with her.'

'Not workable.'

'Are you sure? We have so much room and—'

'She can't have the guest room in case we ever have people to stay.'

'But we never have—'

'My mother said she might come for Christmas.'

'But you know she won't.'

'You know my mother. She can be unpredictable and if she did decide to come she would need that room and I don't want the place to feel like a hospital.'

'Could she have one of the smaller bedrooms? Her room at Heamoor is tiny. So she's used to it. Or the playroom down-stairs? The toilet is just down the corridor. Maybe we could put a small shower in there?'

I'm aware of how desperate I'm sounding, my voice risen

in pitch and speed, which he hates. I take a breath and force a smile.

'If she was in a bedroom upstairs she'd have to use Alex's bathroom which isn't appropriate for either of them. The spare bathroom is up three stairs and that's impracticable. The playroom isn't suitable and it would cost a fortune to *put a small shower in.* Plus it's next door to my study and you know how I need to be undisturbed when I'm working. It's impossible. Your mother needs specialised care in a place set up to provide it. Do you honestly want to be taking her back and forth to the loo and trying to wash her on your own? Bathing someone is physically demanding, Hannah.' He places the poker on the ground and picks up the wire grill, which he slides into the runners on the barbecue. 'You're not putting her wellbeing first. Or that of your family. You're thinking about what would be most convenient for you. You're thinking about yourself again.'

He really is spectacular at this.

'Try, for once, putting the needs of other people before your own. Presumably,' he says, 'you won't be going away with Vicky now?'

I stare at him and take a long breath. I can't say this isn't unexpected, but I thought, idiotically, it now transpires, that he might actually let me go.

'Not if she needs me,' I say, looking him directly, 'but if she's still not come round then I can't see the harm—'

I am interrupted by Alex wandering out of the house holding a can of Coke. Coke – along with all fizzy drinks – is something Nathan doesn't allow in the house. I can see him glaring at it and no doubt blaming Vicky all over again for Alex's *independence.*

'Hey, Mum,' he says. 'How's Gran?'

'Stable, which is a relief. She needs to find somewhere else to live, somewhere with more care. I sent her your love.'

'Can't she move in with us?'

Nathan swears under his breath.

'I'm not sure we have the facilities she needs here, my love,' I say. The angrier Nathan becomes, the harder he will dig in his heels, so it makes sense to ease the pressure off.

Alex nods. 'I'm heading out for a bit. Should be home around eight.'

Before I can reply, Nathan is shaking his head and jabbing his finger in the direction of the barbecue. 'Supper first.'

'I'm not hungry.'

The air between them condenses.

'Then you'll sit and watch us eat.'

'*Watch you eat?*' Alex repeats in an amused tone. 'Are you actually joking?' He holds Nathan's stare as he lifts the can and pulls back the seal. It fizzes loudly and he moves it to his mouth to catch the foam.

'I'm certainly not joking,' Nathan says icily.

Alex wipes his mouth with the back of his hand. 'Well, you'll have to eat without an audience because I'm meeting friends in Penzance.'

'If you leave, I'll—'

'You'll what, *Nathan*? Lock me in my room? Take a belt to me?'

I flinch at his tone.

'How dare you speak to me like that in my own house?' Nathan growls. 'I've never taken a belt to you in your life. Though maybe that's where I went wrong.'

Alex smiles as if he has won some sort of battle then turns and saunters casually back into the house.

Nathan's face has turned puce and his hand is clenched so hard the knuckles have turned white. He's about to go after Alex, but I step in front of him and press the flat of my hand against his chest to hold him back. 'Let him go,' I say softly. 'It was such a nice idea to barbecue. Silly to ruin it. And,' I pause, 'we'll have the house to ourselves.' I lift my hand and trail my fingers over his lips. His eyes lose their intensity and his tension ebbs, and I am filled with an unexpected sense of control, as if I've seized a sword and am holding the blade to his neck. Emboldened, I stand on tiptoes and whisper in his ear, allow my warm breath to brush him. 'We could go up now. Before we eat.'

After he's finished I'm acutely aware of my body tingling. This is an unusual feeling. I don't feel dirty or ashamed or disgusted. It's hard to put my finger on exactly what I'm feeling instead, but whatever it is has energised me, as if I've been given a shot of adrenalin and I'm aware of a distinct shift within me. A shaft of evening sunlight falls across me and warms my skin. 'Don't worry about Alex,' I say and rest my hand on his chest to stroke the fuzz of greying hair as if calming an anxious animal. 'He's like I was, always pushing boundaries. It's a phase and he'll grow out of it.'

Nathan turns his head and stares at me. His eyes are watery like limpid pools. I know what's coming and I smile to cover my revulsion as his face contorts and tears gather. As he cries, it strikes me how defenceless and weak he is, like a small child, vulnerable and self-absorbed. Nathan is only ever the victim or hero in his story. There are no other variations.

'All I ever wanted was a family of my own. A wife to love and look after. Children too. All I want is to be a good husband and father.'

'I know.'

'I want to be better than my own father. He was pathetic. And a *coward*.'

I don't say anything. I've learnt over the years it's best not to comment when he talks like this. All I need to do is listen and comfort him. This is the other side of Nathan. The damaged part, the thirteen-year-old boy who saw his *drog-polat* father lying on the floor with half his face missing, blood spattered like berries on the gaudy floral wallpaper.

'I've lost Alex,' he whispers. 'I can't lose you too.'

'You haven't lost Alex.'

His eyes tunnel through me like a burrowing worm. 'I lost him a long time ago.' Unspoken words flicker beneath the surface. 'When I saw that man's car—'

'Don't,' I say. 'I don't want to talk about him.' Not now, not with Nathan, not ever.

'It was like you'd stabbed me in the stomach.' He moves closer, rests his head on my chest, curls into me like a baby. 'Nobody can hurt me like you can. Don't leave me, Hannah,' he says. 'It would send me over the edge.'

There's something in the tone of his whispered words which chills me to the core.

'I love you so much.' He runs his fingertips down my cheek and I try not to recoil.

I'm used to Nathan's emotional vortex, but the speed with which he can move between peaks of explosive rage and troughs of limp vulnerability gives me vertigo. If I had to choose one, though, I'd take the rage any day. The fragility makes me nauseous.

Later we sit down to supper at the table on the terrace and eat lamb steaks, perfectly cooked, caramelised on the outside, pink within, with a crisp green salad and some new potatoes which I prepared while he was tending to the meat. Nathan has opened an expensive – *special occasion* – red wine. He has showered and changed and is talking animatedly, relaxed and charming, attentive as he pours my wine, rests his hand on mine, and tells me about his day at work.

Nathan Cardew: my very own Jekyll and Hyde.

CHAPTER TWENTY-NINE

Hannah

The leaves above me are still. Not even a whisper rustles through the trees. I'm on my log in the copse smoking a second cigarette. I can't sleep, of course, but I don't mind. This time of night is my favourite. Three in the morning. Before dawn, when even the nocturnal creatures are resting and the fields are quiet as death.

Nathan didn't shout at Alex when he arrived home. He didn't shout when Alex abandoned his football boots at the kitchen door. If I hadn't taken Nathan upstairs and given myself to him spontaneously, unscheduled, his mood would have been very different. Until now I hadn't thought about the way I use sex. I was in denial, finding the concept of using it explicitly to get what I want distasteful and demeaning, but it's not either of those things.

It's empowering.

Confronting the fact that I use sex to manipulate and manage my husband should sit awkwardly with me but I'm surprised to discover it doesn't. Am I rotten inside? I don't feel rotten. But perhaps I must be. After all, I used Nathan from the start. I exploited his desire so I could keep Cam out of prison. It's naive to think pleasure is the only permissible reason to have sex. People use sex for myriad reasons and because of this sex is complicated. Especially for women. A *quid pro quo* for a weekend away. A *thank you* for a gold necklace beneath the Christmas tree. Sore knees and a grubby ten-pound note to exchange for a hit of crack. Sex is a commodity; men want it, so women trade it.

I was two weeks off my seventeenth birthday when I had sex for the first time. It was with a boy called Ryan. I never knew his surname. Ryan was best mates with Adam, and Adam wanted to go out with Vicky. Vicky fancied Adam back, but would only go on a date with him if I went too. So Adam brought Ryan. Ryan worked in Halfords on the A30 and, between swigs of Diamond White, he told me proudly it paid the same as shifting cement on a building site, but came with a uniform. He was nice looking and smelt clean, and wasn't awful at kissing, so we ended up having sex in the back of his mum's Cortina. It was quick and uncomfortable and the smell of Royal Pine air freshener jammed up my throat. I'd be lying if I said I'd been desperate to do it, but the smile on Vicky's face when she emerged from the other car, red-faced with a love bite the size of a golf ball on her neck, made me happy, and when she threw me a questioning look, I nodded and gave her an enthusiastic thumbs-up.

There were a couple of others before Cam. Nothing special. Drunken fumbles followed by awkward trips to the pub or cinema. It tended to be with the most persistent boys. I wasn't that bothered by the thought of having sex. If I'd had my way, I'd have been happy to stick to the laughing and drinking and flirting which preceded it. The sex bit was always underwhelming. Until, of course, the first time with Cam, on his boat, in the freezing cold with a musty old tarpaulin pulled over us.

I think of Cam standing at the top of Trevaylor Woods, shoulders slumped forward, beaten by what happened. I recall his lips against mine, tentative, desperate for some sort of reconnection or comfort, perhaps even absolution. But what did I do? I pushed him away. After everything he'd been through? All I had to do was show him I cared, that I hadn't rejected him, that I understood the enormity of what he'd done for me and its effect on his life. Would it have been so dreadful to show him some affection? Nathan is right. All I do is think about myself. I'm a spoilt cow and Cam didn't deserve to be pushed away like that.

I grind my cigarette into the dirt and pull my phone out of my pocket. I press the home button and the screen bursts into life. I press my finger to the message icon and bring up a new text box then type the numbers in, carefully and deliberately, before writing my message and pressing send.

I don't care anymore.

This isn't over.

CHAPTER THIRTY

Cam, 1998

Cam tossed and turned in his bunk. In around an hour, they'd be hauling the nets in and he was so tired he was verging on delirious. He'd had no more than a couple of hours of broken, cramped, uncomfortable sleep, sheets pungent with unwash, in getting on for a week, and on top of that was the worry of the oncoming storm. There was nothing normal about their way of life, wearing the same clothes for days, no baths, no softness, risking your life for someone else's dinner.

From the way *The Annamae* pitched and rolled he knew the building storm was already up to force seven or eight. His curtain was drawn, but the huffing and puffing coming from Davy told him he was also far from sleep. Lawrie was humming softly to himself. Cam recognised the nerves in his tuneless noise and his heart went out to the lad. He'd been at sea for years and these storms still unsettled him. There was always the voice in his ear telling him this time it could be the end. Young Lawrie Mould would be terrified.

Geren, of course, was snoring in the bunk below. Cam suspected he could be neck deep in icy Atlantic waters and, as long as he was tucked up in his sleeping bag, Geren wouldn't stir. Martin had opted to stay up with Slim on the graveyard shift. He hardly slept at all, which he blamed on old age and creaking bones and tiny bunks.

Cam put his hand beneath his pillow and felt for the picture of him and Hannah. It was taken on the dock a few days before they left. He'd paid a pound extra to get the photos back in two days not five. Most of the photos had been useless, with stickers stuck across them, pointing out the obvious: *over-exposed, out of focus, subject too close*. One, however, was perfection. Lying in his bunk, he stared at the photo, the two of them leaning against the wall, him smiling, her looking up at him, laughing, hair taken by the wind. He touched her face and recalled her whispering in his ear as they made love on his boat. He wanted to be back with her, not stuck here on *The Annamae* with a load of men and the prospect of fishing a storm. As the boat moved on the heaving sea, he imagined her beside him, warm and comforting. He imagined kissing every inch of her. Every curve. Every beautiful blemish. Thinking about her turned him on, but he resisted the urge to touch himself. He might have the privacy of a curtain across the bunk, but being thrown about on a grotty trawler in the middle of the Atlantic in a gale-force wind with three unwashed men within spitting distance was no place for that. He'd wait. He'd soon be back with her, buried in her sweet-smelling softness.

Cam must have drifted off because the shout from Davy as he put his head through the bunk-room hatch cut through him like razor wire and he sat up with a start.

'Get up! She's come fast. We need to get watertight. Move your arses!'

Cam was out of the bunk and pulling on his trousers before Davy had even finished shouting.

'I'll seal the engine room hatches.' Now awake, Cam was aware of the boat straining and groaning unnaturally. 'The gear's fast?'

Davy nodded. 'Slim's trying to free it, but the stern is taking water.'

The men ran to put on their oilskins. Nobody spoke. Lawrie was white-faced.

Cam put his hands on the boy's shoulders and spoke firmly. 'Do not do *anything*. Stay here, out of the way. If you go over in this, when we're fast, we can't turn back for you.'

Lawrie swallowed and nodded.

'We'll be OK, lad. But you keep yourself safe, yes? Nobody wants to lose anybody tonight. Not even you.' Cam winked and patted Lawrie's shoulder.

Lawrie nodded again. The boat heaved to the side and Lawrie stumbled, fell backwards, his head cracked against the wall. It would take a number of trips to find his sea legs and in a gale like this he didn't stand a chance of keeping upright. Cam grabbed some rope which hung on a hook, and pushed Lawrie down on to the bench. He looped the rope around his chest and tied it secure, then tied it to the hooks either side. Lawrie started to protest, glancing nervously to Geren and Davy.

'Let him,' Geren said. 'We want you alive. I'll rip into you again when we're sailing home safe.'

Cam smiled at Lawrie. 'Bet you still wish you worked on that building site, eh?'

Lawrie laughed weakly and glanced out towards the deck, flinching when a lump of water the size of a tower block smashed against the side as if trying to bulldoze them.

Davy and Cam secured the hatches. In weather like this,

with the boat held fast on God-knows-what on the seabed, wires pulled so tight *The Annamae* couldn't rise and fall with the swell, the stern could quickly flood and turn them over. They had to free the boat and they could only do this from the deck where they were in huge danger; no man would survive if he went overboard.

Geren opened the door and a rush of driving wind and lashing rain burned their faces. Waves the size of mountains broke as the boat pitched and rattled and strained. There was an ominous grating noise, louder than overhead thunder, followed by a deep shudder through the body of the boat. They didn't have long. If they couldn't free her soon they'd be dragged under.

The rain was coming in hard and horizontal and cut into Cam's skin like arrow tips. The men didn't speak. They knew what they had to do and got on with it as the wind rolled the boat like a cat with a mouse. Cam and Geren moved quickly to the winch control. There was nothing for Davy to do until Slim had managed to work *The Annamae* free and he stood in the doorway, his face serious, hand bracing himself to ride the waves. Slim hung out of the wheelhouse window and yelled instructions down at Cam and Geren. The noise was deafening, the roar of the sea and wind underpinning the ear-splitting noise of the engine and gearbox screaming as Slim pushed the boat forward and astern as he tried to free her.

The men struggled to keep their footing, wedging themselves tight and making sure there was something to grab on to as each relentless wave swept from astern and flooded the deck. Ropes and fish baskets washed this way and that as the boat was buffeted on ravines and crests. They were in the heart of the storm now. Waves were coming again and again, hitting the boat like a thousand tonnes of concrete, causing her to groan and the windows to tremble in the battering.

Slim's face was set in concentration as he continued to manoeuvre the boat to release it from whatever held it like an anchor, whilst simultaneously steering *The Annamae* between the waves so as they hit, she was best positioned to ride them out. Cam's heart thumped. He glanced at Geren as they worked the winch, and saw the thrill of it written over his face. This type of situation gave him a kick, an adrenalin rush as intense as a hit of cocaine.

'Fucking come at us, you bitch!' Geren shouted, his words whipped away as he tilted his face into the brunt of the wind.

They all knew there was every chance they wouldn't make it. Every trip they went on carried that risk. Even when they were lying on deck, heading home, sharing beers beneath a beating sun, they always knew things could turn. Complacency wasn't something trawlermen indulged in.

There was a violent jerk then, which came with a crash so loud Cam wondered whether the hull had been split clean in two. Geren swore and shouted something at Cam, but his words were lost as there was another horrendous crashing. Out of the corner of his eye Cam saw Lawrie emerging from the inside, his oilskin hood obscuring his face, gloved hands grasping the gunwale to balance himself.

'Get your fucking hands off that rail!' Cam screamed. 'You'll lose your fucking fingers. And get the fuck back down below.'

'I want to help!' The boy squinted against the rain and sea spray as another wall of water broke and collapsed over them like a demolished building.

A sudden lurch knocked Cam off his feet. He cracked his

head on the corner of the hopper and a sharp pain stung him. An irrational swell of anger surged inside him. If he hadn't been talking to the lad he'd never have hit his head. Lawrie had no right to put his life in danger. Or those of the others. Cam righted himself and started to shout at Lawrie again, but another dramatic lurch sent *The Annamae* surging forward. There was no doubting it; *The Annamae* was freed. Cam looked up at the wheelhouse and saw Slim punching the air in celebration.

'You fucking beauty!' Davy shouted.

Geren clapped him on the back and shook his shoulder with joy.

'That lad should be down below.'

'We need him,' Davy shouted. 'We need all the men we can get.'

'No, he's too inexperienced—'

'Davy's right,' Geren shouted. 'We need the trawls on board quick. He can help.'

Cam hesitated, glanced at Lawrie, then nodded. He lurched over to the young lad. 'Get up front with Martin. Do what he says. We need to get the trawls up and on deck as quickly as possible. You hear me? Do what Martin says,' he repeated. Lawrie nodded and walked unsteadily up to the front of the boat, bracing as a lump of water broke over the boat.

With Geren and Cam back on the winch and Martin and the lad under shelter at the front, the four men worked to haul both sets of gear to the surface. Next they needed to get the trawls on deck. And fast. The first caused no problem. Lawrie did what he was told. Between waves, they lifted the trawl clear of the water, then lowered it with Martin and Lawrie at the forward end of the beam, Davy steadying the aft, and Cam and Geren working the winch. Slim shouted instructions down from the wheelhouse as he concentrated on keeping the boat as steady as possible. They'd usually take time to land it carefully, allowing each piece of gear to slot into place. But in conditions like these, a storm raging, they had no time to waste. They needed to get the gear on deck as fast as possible then haul in the other trawl.

When it was landed, they didn't stop to breathe, but immediately began working on the second trawl. They were tiring now, digging deep into their energy reserves, wet and cold and struggling to keep balanced as the deck swilled with water. They lifted the trawl and guided it over the deck. And then, with the gear suspended, a lump of water the like of which Cam had never seen, crashed over *The Annamae*. There was a loud crack. Something whipped past his face, so close he could feel the wind of it.

'Fuck!' Cam shouted. 'A wire's gone on the derrick!'

Cam looked up towards Martin and Lawrie and saw they'd lost control of the beam and it was swinging dangerously close to them. They had to secure it. He needed Lawrie out of the way. The kid was going to get himself killed.

Cam tried to shout over the wind, but there was no way he could hear him. He tried again, but he was stopped short by another mountainous wave hitting the stern and sending a cascade of water over them.

Cam swore and turned his back on Lawrie. 'Davy, we need to get the gear secure. It's like Indiana Jones and the fucking Temple of Doom out here!'

The boat nosedived into a trough. Cam held his breath

and grasped the rail. As the boat righted he breathed in, awed as ever by the trawler's ability to ride these waves. How did a hunk of iron and steel stay afloat in conditions like this?

'Physics,' Slim once told him, when Cam remarked on it. 'Don't know the first thing about it myself, but I know it's physics we have to thank.'

The deck was almost impossible to walk, up to their knees in water which was unable to drain before the next wave struck. The men fought hard to try and secure the rogue beam, but they were exhausted.

What happened next was a blur.

A huge wave – thirty, maybe forty, foot – swept from astern, filling the deck with seething water. Cam went down a second time. He was tumbled. Saltwater filled his mouth as he was dragged across the deck as if it were an ice rink. There was a sharp pain to his thigh. Terrified of being swept into the sea, his hands grabbed madly for anything to stop his slide as he hurtled to the side and was winded against the gunwale. As the wave drained from the deck, he scrambled to his feet, and searched for the others. Geren was nearby, holding the rail, a thin trail of blood trickling from his nose. Cam looked forward in time to see the beam careening into the whaleback casing at the front of the boat. There was a god almighty yell. Then Lawrie screamed and Cam watched in horror as he saw Martin pinned between the beam and the casing. Lawrie jumped up and was pushing fruitlessly against the beam. Time slowed. Cam and Geren started to run forward to get to Martin. The boat rolled as another wave hit. Cam unbalanced and fell into the gunwale again. As he got up he saw the beam was swaying away from Martin with the movement of the boat.

'Get up to Martin. That beam's going to swing back,' Cam screamed at Davy. 'We'll get it secure. Get up to him and get him the fuck out of the way.'

As Davy stumbled trying to get up to the forward end, he saw the beam tipping back with the swell. But Lawrie noticed too. Cam watched as he moved, quick and nimble, and threw himself at Martin, grabbing his oilskin and pulling him out of the way, moments before the beam swung back and crashed into the whaleback at the exact spot where Martin had been pinned.

Geren and Cam worked quickly to secure the beam. They could hear Lawrie shouting for Slim. Davy was yelling. Martin was howling like a banshee. Slim got the message. The prop was clutched, the engine humming now, not fighting, and *The Annamae* suddenly became more stable as she rode with the waves rather than against them.

Cam and Geren were able to secure the gear and, when it was done, Cam ran to the front of the boat. Lawrie was panting and white-faced, terrified, as rain ran down his face and oilskin. But it was only when he moved past Davy and Geren and looked down at Martin that the true horror of what had happened became clear.

Martin was lying on the deck, wedged up tight against the whaleback casing, silent now, as shock had set in. His eyes were rolled back in his head, teeth gritted, foamy spittle bubbled at his mouth, his skin as white as a cuttlefish bone.

'Jesus,' Cam whispered.

Martin's arm had been crushed by the beam. The oilskin was torn and blood ran in scarlet rivulets in the creases of the fabric. The top of his arm was flattened, his visible flesh like minced meat, matted with slivers of skin and bone and yellow waterproof.

Slim appeared behind them. A few seconds later, having taken the situation in, he started barking orders at them.

'Geren!' he shouted. 'Get on the radio and get rescue out to us now. Ah, Jesus,' he said, looking down at Martin and grimacing. 'Stay with me. For Christ's sake stay with me.'

'The chopper will struggle in this,' Geren said, his quavering voice lost in the roar.

'If we have to, we'll steam to a lee but let's hope they can make it to us. Just get them on the radio. Tell them if they don't get here, we'll lose Martin Garnett. They'll get to us.'

Slim looked at young Lawrie. 'Lad, get the medical kit. I need to strap his arm.'

Nausea swept through Cam as he knelt by Martin's head and stroked his wet hair off his forehead and rubbed his thumb across the deeply crevassed skin to remove a smear of blood.

Martin opened his eyes. 'The beam… ' he rasped. 'I… didn't… didn't see it. Sheila. I… '

Lawrie appeared, carrying the medical kit against his chest like a float.

'Get the bandage out. And the morphine. I need to tie his arm to his side, then we need to drag him undercover.'

Slim worked fast to strap Martin's arm to his side to secure it. He cut the bandage with his knife, which he handed to Cam, before tightening the knot. Cam held the knife for a moment, felt the roughness of the etching, and wondered if he should throw it into the sea. It clearly wasn't the talisman Slim believed it to be.

The boat tipped as they rode over another huge trough.

Cam and Geren grabbed Martin's legs, Slim grabbed his good arm, and they dragged him under the shelter of the whaleback.

'We'll get you off the boat, Martin. You'll be OK. You'll be lying warm in bed with Sheila in no time.'

Martin's mouth moved in silent prayer.

Moving Martin had clearly caused him immense pain. His lips were ghost-white and he was slipping in and out of consciousness.

'Lawrie, get blankets from the bunk room. Quick as you can, lad.'

Lawrie nodded at Slim and ran below.

Slim prepared a shot of morphine and administered it. 'That'll help, my friend.'

'My arm,' Martin rasped then. 'Can't feel my arm.'

Cam bent down and held Martin's good hand. 'Your arm's fine. It's all fine.'

Davy hovered nearby, terrified eyes fixed on the mess of flesh where Martin's arm used to be.

'Hey. He'll be OK,' Cam said to him then. 'We'll get him to hospital and they'll make him OK.'

Davy slammed his hand against the deck. '*Fuck*!' he shouted. 'Fuck, fuck, *fuck*!'

Lawrie appeared from the wheelhouse with all the blankets he could find and they covered Martin, tucking the blankets around him like a baby in swaddling.

'Helicopter's on its way from Culdrose,' Geren yelled down from the wheelhouse window. Slim shouted up to Geren and told him to put the boat back into gear. They'd need her moving if they had to steam out to meet the helicopter. *The Annamae* roared back to life, immediately bucking and pitching, her engine rumbling loudly.

257

Cam had a flash of sharp fear that *The Annamae* would upend completely and catapult them all into the freezing sea. Martin slid against the wall and his scream split Cam's head, like a fox being torn up by rabid hounds. Martin's hand shot out from the blankets and grabbed for Cam and held on to him tightly. 'Don't leave me, Cam.'

Cam shook his head. 'Not going anywhere, old man.'

Martin moaned and his eyelids flickered open to reveal the whites shot through with broken capillaries.

Cam squeezed Martin's hand as he braved another glance at the arm, at the flesh mashed in with oilskin, bits of bone, fingers twitching as if in the last throes of death. The skin was already turned pale purple, the tips of his fingers white as if they'd been dipped in paint.

The helicopter lights eventually appeared through the angry gloom.

'I'm heading up to take control of her,' Slim said to Cam. 'You stay with Martin and help the rescue team.'

Cam nodded then patted Martin's hand. 'The helicopter's here, Martin. You're home and dry.'

Cam knew the rescue team were going to have trouble landing a man on deck in this weather. He'd been here before. Too unsafe. But they would try. The crew of *The Annamae* stared up through the wind and driving rain at the helicopter. Slim was back in the wheelhouse, keeping her going at slow speed, as steady as possible. She was feeling more stable but beyond the deck lights Cam could see the ominous waves as tall as mountains, black and angry, and he mouthed a silent plea that they got Martin off before something else went wrong.

Cam squinted through the rain and watched as the wire

lowered one of the rescue team down. He carried a stretcher. The wire swayed dangerously. The helicopter was illuminated by the cockpit lights and Cam winced as he saw how hard the pilot was fighting to stay in control as he tried to keep station over *The Annamae*. Geren reached up and tried to grab the ankle of the man on the wire. He missed and stumbled. Righted himself then tried again. Missed and slipped backwards and lost his footing. Lawrie moved forward and jumped then, stretching up with his hand and managing to catch the end of the guide rope. But when the boat lunged to the left he was unable to hold on. The man at the winch in the gaping hole in the side of the helicopter made gestures. Crossed his arms. Slim was doing a fine job of keeping *The Annamae* heading in to the wind with just enough power to keep her as steady as he could. Cam glanced up and saw him talking on the handset held close to his mouth as he communicated with the pilot. Face solemn. A single nod. A glance up.

The helicopter rose into the air, swung away in a wide arc and the pilot repositioned to try again. The man on the wire swung rapidly downwards, a stretcher strapped crossfire across his middle and when he was close enough Lawrie made another grab for it and caught the man's ankle. Cam could tell by the determination on his face that nothing was going to make him let go a second time. He held fast and Geren and Davy joined him to help guide the man and stretcher down.

When the stretcher was ready, the men helped Martin on to it, slipping their arms beneath him and hefting him on to the stretcher, then strapping him securely and trying not to let his moaning get inside them. As the man gave his pilot the thumbs-up, Cam glanced at Geren. Any illogical pleasure he'd been feeling earlier had vanished. Now he looked haggard and distressed. They were all feeling it. Martin could've died. He still could. They all could have died.

When Martin was at last strapped to the stretcher, they stepped back and watched as he was lifted up, skimming the peaks of the waves for a moment before spinning upwards towards the helicopter. Slim was wracked with worry. There were too many lives at risk, not only his crew, but the rescue team too. If anything happened to any of them, Slim would never forgive himself.

Hands appeared at the hatch far above, hauling both the crewman and the stretcher inside, and within moments the helicopter was heading for shore and swallowed by the darkness.

In the galley, clutching mugs of sweet tea, the crew of *The Annamae* sat with their thoughts. On deck they worked on autopilot, no time to think, but now, sitting in the aftermath, the shock had kicked in. Cam noticed Lawrie's hands were trembling almost uncontrollably.

'Hey,' he said, reaching out to rest a hand on his arm. 'You did good out there, lad. You saved Martin's life. You did really, really good.'

Lawrie smiled weakly and sipped his tea, as Davy shoved back from the table and left the room.

CHAPTER THIRTY-ONE

Hannah

Alex laughs at my fussing.

'Don't forget to feed Cass. And make sure she has water.'

'You mean in case she gets… *thirsty?*'

'Yes, of course—' I stop myself when I realise he's joking and he laughs again.

'Don't worry, I'm not going to let her die of thirst or starve or waste away. I might even cuddle her a bit. You're back tomorrow anyway.'

'I know but—'

'I guarantee when you get back we'll both be alive.'

'I've left a fish pie in the fridge. A hundred and eighty for forty minutes. And be nice to your father when he gets back.'

Alex gives an exaggerated eye roll.

'Please. He's worried in case something happens to your gran while I'm gone. Look, please, just don't aggravate him, OK?'

'He doesn't give a shit about Gran.'

'Of course he does. I've told him I'll be back if there's any change in her and the hospital has my number.'

Everything will be fine at home; I've made sure there is nothing for either of them to think about, apart from letting Cass out tonight and Alex walking her first thing, but I'm jittery nonetheless. My hands tremble so much I can't fasten the straps of my bag. I try not to think too hard about what I'm doing. I know it's wrong. How much more guilt can my body take before it finally collapses beneath the weight of it?

'If there's any problem at all—'

'There won't be,' he says.

'Yes, but *if* there's a problem—'

'Call your mobile?' he says with a mocking tone. 'Yeah, yeah. I *think* I've got it.' He loops his arms around my middle. 'Mum. Stop worrying. Go and have some fun with Vicky. You totally deserve it.'

My legs buckle and I hold on to him tightly to stop myself stumbling.

As the train pulls out of Penzance I close my eyes and watch the flicker of orange light dancing on my eyelids. My body thrums with anxiety, and I grip my bag tighter to my chest and rest my cheek on it, turning my head so I can watch the sea. I think about staying on the train. All the way to London. I could disappear. I watch myself step on to the platform at Paddington to be swallowed whole by the ravenous city. It would be easy to run. I could turn my back on everything, draw a line beneath it, start again, live hand to mouth, hour to hour, and have nothing else to think about but keeping warm and fed. I recall Cam telling me about his time living like this and a physical ache tightens like a vice.

'Excuse me?'

I look up. The woman in the seat opposite is staring at me with a soft and sympathetic gaze. She is dressed in a fleece and has a utilitarian rucksack beside her with a just-in-case umbrella tucked into one of its external pockets and a blue metallic water bottle in the other.

'Yes?'

'I just wondered… ' She hesitates. 'Are you OK?'

'I'm fine,' I say as I turn my head away from her and refocus on the view through the window, the sea now replaced with buildings and grey. I know she is staring, but I resolutely don't move, my skin flushing hot as I silently will her to leave me alone.

A few minutes later, the train starts to slow and the announcer tells us we're coming into St Erth. My stomach tumbles as I walk along the carriage using the headrests to steady me. When the train draws to a halt, I lean out of the window to open the door. My hand is sweaty and slips on the handle. I'm the only one to get off. A few people file on, then the doors clang shut and the guard's whistle blows. I watch the train draw away from me as I stand, alone and wracked with doubt, on the empty platform.

With each step towards the station exit, my jangling nerves heighten, tightening around my innards like a noose. I climb the stairs. Cross the footbridge. Turn to go down.

My heart skips.

He is at the bottom of the steps.

Waiting for me.

CHAPTER THIRTY-TWO

Hannah

Don't think for one moment I don't know I'm a bad person. I do. I'm a bad person who's done bad things. Lying to Vicky is the least of it, but even so, as the words tumbled out of my mouth, it felt like the worst thing I'd ever done.

I think she always suspected I was going to bail. I'd called her from my log in the copse after chain-smoking three cigarettes for Dutch courage.

'Jesus. I knew it. I bloody *knew* it.'

I wasn't able to reply. What could I say?

'He's such a fucking arsehole.'

'It's a client who's flown in from Dubai. He was supposed to see him for a meeting one evening last week, but it got cancelled last minute. He has to go to London to meet with him now.'

'Can't Alex stay with a friend?'

'There's the dog... ' It sounded so weak out loud. I lit another cigarette and inhaled, pretending the tobacco was arsenic and soon I'd be dead.

'Shall I speak to Nathan? Or get Phil to? Maybe they could have the meeting next week.'

I'd panicked. '*No!*' Then I'd taken a deep breath. Forced myself to calm. 'I don't think it works like that. Please don't phone him. He won't budge and it'll make things worse for me…' I left the sentence unfinished, added a hint of worry to my tone, left her to insinuate I was a little bit fearful. I was sick with shame.

'Can Phil go with you?'

There was a heavy pause.

I crossed my fingers and took a drag on the cigarette before treading it, half finished, into the ground.

'Yes. I made Mum keep the evening free to look after the girls. I had my suspicions he'd stop you somehow.'

I let out a sigh of relief. 'Thank God. I'm so pleased you can still go.'

'I'd prefer to be with you.'

'I'm sorry.'

'And I hate your husband.'

'I know.'

And now here I am. Standing at the top of the station stairs looking down at Cam. I walk down and we face each other. The awkwardness between us is suffocating. What the hell am I doing? We don't talk as I follow him to his battered red car in the car park. He feels like a stranger, a taxi driver, perhaps, or hotel staff, as he solemnly takes my bag and puts it on the back seat. When the car doors close, my chest tightens even further as the air becomes so dense I can't draw it in. I should get out of the car. Walk away. This is madness. I breathe as calmly as I can and concentrate on slowing my pulse.

'Where do you want to go?' His soft voice cleaves the silence in two.

I shouldn't be here. I should be with Vicky, sitting in the

pub with two huge gin and tonics, giggling over antics from our misspent youths.

'The beach,' he says, answering his own question. 'I've not seen the sea since I left.'

I manage a single nod as I fight back the tears. Not seen the sea? This man who lived and breathed it, who tasted of salt.

He turns the engine on and drives in the direction of Helston. I thought he might take the road to Godrevy, but perhaps his memories of that day, and those electric pink squares of cheap ham between white over-processed bread, are less vivid than mine. Instead, he indicates right at the incongruous Chinese restaurant which has been here forever, and follows the lane down to Perranuthnoe. We park the car and as we walk down towards the sea, though we are still quiet, the tension begins to ease. I haven't been to this beach since Cam left. When I was younger, it was one of my favourites. Top three. His too. It was something we had in common, something we talked about in the pub on our first night out, exaggerated joy when we discovered a shared love for this small and perfectly formed bay, enclosed by low headlands of rock, its golden sand, exposed, like now, when the tide is low, but disappearing completely when the sea comes in.

'Beach or cliffs?'

I smile. 'Cliffs first? The tide is still on the way out. There'll be sand until late this evening.'

He nods and asks me to wait a moment and he jogs over to the small café, a wooden cabin with a well-tended garden, set above the beach, overlooking the sea. It's a beautiful day. Blue skies with wisps of cloud. Warm but not hot. The seagulls so high on the thermals they are no more than dots and a mirror-flat sea of polished platinum in the sun.

Cam returns a few minutes later and we set off along the dusty road towards the coastal path. We join the footpath and walk in single file. Me behind him. Butterflies gather in the pit of my stomach as I go over the words I need to say to him. That I am grateful for what he did and I'm sorry I drove him away and that, back then, before everything was ruined, I loved him very deeply.

'How about walking down to the cove below the castle?' he calls over his shoulder.

'I don't think I know it.' A gentle breeze carries my hair across my face and I tuck it back behind my ear.

'Really? We're definitely going then. It's where we used to go and drink sometimes when we bunked off school. Hope I can find the path. It was always pretty overgrown.'

We round the bend and an ostentatious house with Disney-style turrets looms into sight. A little way on and Cam stops to search the shrub and gorse. He walks on, stops again, and then turns and walks off the path, pushing his way through overgrown vegetation, arms raised clear of the spiky gorse.

'Wait here,' he calls back. 'I'll check we can get through.'

There's a ladybird on one of the bright yellow explosions of gorse flowers near to me. I extend my hand and block her path so she's forced to crawl onto my finger. I hold my finger upright and watch as she climbs to the tip. When she gets there she seems to hesitate for a moment or two before taking flight and lifting into the sky. I watch her until she's no more than a speck in the blue.

'It's not great at the top but gets better,' calls Cam from somewhere further down the path.

I copy Cam and hold my arms above my head and ease

268

myself carefully though the gorse and brambles which snag my clothes and catch my hair. The smell is strong: warm sea air, heavy with salt and drying seaweed. As I breathe it in I feel something close to homesickness.

Cam clambers down the rocks at the base of the path and jumps on to the beach below. He turns back and shouts, 'Be careful, it's slippery.'

The cove is large and empty, mostly made up of flat slices of rock sparsely patched with sand and pebbles. The surrounding cliffs protect it from any breeze, which intensifies the heat of the sun. The rock is dark, almost black, and lies in horizontal slabs, severe and otherworldly, more lunar landscape than cosy beach. The cliffs are formed of layers of clay and rock in sloping stripes. Two birds peck at the soft clay in search of insects, sending stone and earth crumbling to the ground below.

Cam has walked to the water's edge. I watch him as he bends to select a pebble. He draws his arm back and throws it as far out to sea as he can. He watches for the splash, then bends to select another, and repeats. I recall him doing the same when we were younger. Bending, selecting, throwing, watching. His movements are unchanged with time, and the flashbacks, hearing the echo of my laugh, are piercing.

I walk down to join him and we stand side-by-side facing the sea. It feels isolated and remote, as if we've arrived at the furthest edge of the world, with nothing in front of us but never-ending water.

It's breathtaking.

'It hurts how much I miss it.'

It was me who infected him with this stark pain. I want to lance the abscess and drain the poison from him. But I can't and knowing this makes me want to scream. He straightens his shoulders and casts me a glance. His expression has altered, a small smile escapes him. He gestures out to sea with his head. 'Fancy it?'

It takes me a moment to realise what he means. 'A swim?' I start to shake my head – it's far too cold and I don't have a swimming costume or towel with me – but then I follow his gaze over the water, which glints in the sun as if someone has spilt a bag of diamonds across its surface. There are no waves and the water laps at the shore with gentle kisses. I imagine it cool and fresh on my skin, washing away the sweat and dust and melancholy, and smile. 'Yeah. OK. Why not?'

He grins, then points to the right. 'Be careful, though,' he says. 'There's a rip current.'

I look out to where he's indicating and see the telltale ripples on the surface of the sea, as if an unseen stream is flowing out into the ocean. I wonder for a moment what it might feel like to swim into the riptide and be dragged away, powerless to fight it, my only option to give in and let it pull me under.

'If we stay this side we'll be fine,' he says. I glance up at him and he smiles.

I smile back, then kick off my shoes. The sand is cool and damp beneath my feet. I take off my shirt then unbutton my jeans and step out of them. Standing in my underwear, I'm aware of how my body has aged, the silvery stretch marks around my stomach and thighs, the looseness of the skin on my tummy and upper arms, and feel suddenly self-conscious. I hurry down to the water and take three steps before diving in. My lungs constrict with the cold but – *Jesus* – it's incredible.

As I duck beneath the surface, and push through the water, familiar icy fingers caress and calm me.

There's a splash to the side of me. I break the surface and see bubbles where Cam has disappeared beneath the water.

'How fucking good is that?' he cries when he emerges, hair slicked back from his head, water dripping off his nose and eyelashes. He slams his hands down then raises them, pulling up an arc of water. A flash of rainbow forms in the spray.

I dive under again and take two firm strokes, then turn and drift beneath the surface, staring up at the shimmering sun through the water. The silence is perfect. I am like a china doll wrapped in cotton wool, safe and protected, but it's short-lived. As I turn and head back to the shore, pulling myself underwater, my skin numbed and my blood pumping, I see him. He lunges at me. There is a macabre grin on his face. His hands reach out to grab me, skin sliding off them in rotten strands. I tell myself it's not real, but I can't get rid of him, he's right there and refuses to fade. My lungs burn. I need oxygen. I need to swim for the surface, but the sight of him has paralysed me. Still he hangs suspended in front of me. His eyes are black hollows. The flesh which clings to his face is pale and tinged green, and his mouth is stretched wide in a noiseless scream.

My pulse hammers and my vision wavers, and in my frantic clamber to escape the sea I stumble and trip on the pebbles and rocks. I fight the image of him but he won't leave me. He's still there, somewhere behind me, reaching out to pull me down with him.

When I reach my clothes, I snatch up my shirt, but struggle to push my wet arms through the sleeves. I discard it in frustration. This will never go away. It doesn't matter whether I'm walking in the woods or smoking in the copse or swimming in the sea between Perranuthnoe and Prussia Cove, he'll always be there, lurking, waiting for his moment to ambush me.

Cam draws up beside me. 'Are you OK?' The sun has lit his skin and turned it golden. Tiny grains of salt stick to the hairs on his arms where the water's evaporated. Concern has folded itself into his face. 'Hannah? What's wrong? What happened out there?'

I ruined his life. I need to say sorry. I need to thank him for what he did then I need to move on. I stand on tiptoes and put my hands on his cheeks, guiding him towards me so I can press my lips to his. They are cold and salty from the sea. He protests, leans back from me, but I slip my hand around his neck and hold firm. Then his resistance falters. I open my mouth and touch his tongue with mine. He flinches and pulls away, harder, fumbling behind his head to unclasp my fingers.

'What are you doing?' he rasps. 'This doesn't feel right.'

I reach for his hand and bring it to my breast. At first he resists and his brow furrows with confusion, but then I see it, the glazing of his eyes in that telltale way men's eyes do when their minds are hijacked by sex. I lead him to the base of the cliff which encloses the cove where a series of small caves gape like open mouths. I lift his hand to my face and lean my cheek against it. My heart pounds as I turn and kiss his palm. I trace my tongue along the base of his thumb. Finally, he gives in and the tips of his fingers graze my cheek and he kisses me with a desperation which was absent from the chaste, sad moment we shared in the woods. Desire has overridden his damage and the man I remember is revealed, his quiet intensity, the strength which made me feel so safe, the passion which lit a fire inside me back when that was still a possibility. I move the flat of my hand to his crotch and begin to rub.

But then, without warning, he freezes. He pushes me backwards and spins away, crouching down, hands going to either side of his head.

'Cam?'

He searches my face. 'I don't understand. Have you left him?'

The question derails me. 'No. No, I haven't left him. I'm sorry. That's all. About what happened. About everything. I want to do this for you. I want to show you how grateful… '

'What?'

My words are crass and vile, but it's too late now, all I can do is press on. I desperately grab at his hand. 'Let me do this for you. Let me thank you—'

'Thank me? What the fuck?' His face is riven with horror. 'You want to *thank* me?'

Panic billows like an electric surge. He is staring at me as if doesn't know me. His face is contorted, appalled, sickened, even. No. No, cries the voice in my head. This is supposed to help. It's supposed to bring us some sort of closure. I want to ease your pain, not make you hate me. My breath catches. I want him to stop looking at me like this. I want him to fuck me. Drive himself into me. I want him to thrust hard. Again and again and again. I want to hear him shout, feel his teeth sink into me, scratch me so hard it draws blood and scars my skin.

'Let me get this straight? You want to have sex to pay off some sort of twisted debt? What? So you don't feel *guilty*? Is that it? So we're *even*? Jesus,' he whispers. He rakes his fingers against his scalp. '*Fuck*.' He stands and faces me. 'You *planned* this? You messaged me and said you had to see me so you could have *sex* with me and then – what? – your conscience is cleared?'

'No... it's not like... that. It's... ' My words fade because he's right: I did plan it.

He walks away from me, back to his clothes which lie in a pile by the water's edge. I watch him bend to put on his jeans, balancing on one foot then the other as he pulls them on. He takes hold of his T-shirt. His muscles flex as he puts it over his head.

All I want is to stand beneath a hot shower and scrub myself until I'm pink and raw. I collapse in the mouth of the cave, legs and feet warm in the sunshine, the rest of me cold where the shade from the cliff drapes over me. I draw my knees up and bring my legs into the shadow and enjoy the spreading chill as I bow my head. I'm aware of him then. He has moved near to me. Crouched. His hand rests against my lower back and rubs lightly.

'Hey, it's OK.' His tone is soft and silky like honey. 'Hannah, it's OK.'

He sits beside me and attempts to unfold me. My clothes are clutched in his hand. He places them beside him and picks out my shirt. He turns me a little and gently eases the shirt over my head, pulling my arms through each sleeve. The fabric is warm from where it's been lying in the sun.

'Listen,' he says, taking my hand in his. 'You don't need to thank me. Or say sorry. It's not your responsibility to put me back together. You don't have to repair me. And – *Jesus* – even if you did, you definitely don't need to do it with sex.' He pushes the wet tendrils of hair away from my face, then leans in and kisses my forehead. When he leans back I notice the scar in his hairline, a remnant of an injury he sustained on *The Annamae*'s fateful trip from which the crew were lucky to return, battered, shaken, their emotions spiralling wildly.

'How fucked up do you think we really are?' I whisper.

He laughs and entwines his fingers with mine. 'On the scale of fucked up? Pretty fucking fucked up.'

I laugh through my tears and he reaches up with his free hand to gently wipe beneath my eyes.

We sit like this for some time, our bodies warm where they touch, watching the incoming tide. The rhythm of the lapping waves and the imperceptible way they inch closer is calming. After a while, and without speaking, he leans to the side and takes hold of his jacket from which he produces two cans of Coke and a flapjack he must have bought at the café on Perranuthnoe. He unwraps the clingfilm and breaks off a piece which he passes me. It's delicious, soft and buttery, the syrupy sweetness exquisite after the seawater and the crying. I lie back, turn on my side to face away from him, and tuck my hands under my cheek. He lies down too and drapes his arm over me. He is close enough for me to feel the heat of his breath on the nape of my neck. It radiates outwards and warms me like a hot water bottle.

A round white pebble catches my eye and I reach for it. My fingers close around it and I run my thumb back and forth over its surface.

'After you left,' I say then, as I study the pebble from each angle, searching for an imperfection which I cannot find. 'I'd walk down your street and pretend we were meeting up to go out.' His body tenses a fraction, but he doesn't say anything. 'I'd walk all the way up to the Garnetts' door and lift my hand as if I was going to knock for you.' I discard the pebble with a flick of my wrist and it bounces a few times until it comes to rest and shines like an egg in a nest amid the greys and blacks of the other stones. 'One day Sheila was standing at the window, staring at me. She didn't move. Just stood there. Staring. But I don't think she even saw me.'

I recall how sad and lost she appeared, her pain mirroring mine. I never went back.

We lie like this until it's nearly dark and the water is at the highest tide, only a metre or so from our feet, and for the first time in years, my mind is still.

'I think we should find somewhere warmer for the night.' His voice is hard against the quiet.

I push myself up to sitting. The moon is full and round and trails a corridor of light over the black water in front of us like a torchlit pathway.

He sits up too. I turn to look at him, and then, well, I'm not sure how it happens, which of us it is who makes that first tentative move, but we kiss. It's slow and soft and silent. We take our time. Stroke and smile and touch. The waves break and the shingle sings softly as the water runs up and down it. Everything feels right. My body tingles as he kisses my breasts. I kiss and lick his skin, the salt sharp on my tongue, his smell so distant and familiar. When he attempts to enter me, I tense, my body instinctively bracing. I try and relax, but I can feel everything, body and mind, tightening. Fifteen years I've fantasised about making love to him but now it's happening, now it's real, I'm frozen up.

The concern on his face is lit by the moon. 'I'm sorry,' he whispers.

'You didn't do anything wrong. Please. Don't stop. I want

to.' Do I though? My stomach clenches and I bite down on my lip.

'Another time.' He smiles and strokes my face.

Another time.

No. This is the only time we have. I suspect Cam knows it too. This brief snapshot of how things might have been is our time. Everything I said to him in the woods still stands. I rest my head on his chest and thread my fingers through his.

'Hannah?'

'Yes?'

I tilt my head and see him staring up at the sky, the moon and stars, a billion miles away. 'He deserved it.'

My blood chills.

'He fucking deserved it and the guilt I live with isn't because he's dead or because I dumped him at sea or because we kept the truth to ourselves, but because I'm *pleased*. I'm pleased the bastard's dead.'

CHAPTER THIRTY-THREE

Hannah

I wake stiff and cold with his jacket covering me.

'Bloody hell.' His voice is groggy with sleep as he stretches his back. 'I'm too old to be sleeping rough again.' He smiles and rubs his face. 'And I'm famished. Breakfast? I fancy a full English.'

I retie my hair in a ponytail, trying as best I can to neaten it. I'm aware I must look horrible and wish I could shower, clean my teeth, and change into fresh clothes. I stand and wait for him to put on his trainers.

He gets to his feet and smiles again. 'Last night was—' he hesitates, 'special.'

'It was.'

The sea is still calm, flat and polished, the early morning sunlight colouring it a buttery yellow. I don't say any more. I don't want to ruin the moment by addressing the harsh reality which prowls like a cat beyond this hidey-hole of ours.

We climb the overgrown footpath which wends its way upwards, and when we emerge from the gorse and blackthorn tangle, a handful of herring gulls who'd been sitting on the pasture fence take flight with screeches of complaint. As we walk back along the coast path I search the sea, desperate for a glimpse of a basking shark or passing pod of dolphins. It's not dolphins which grab my attention, but my phone. It springs to life as we come into reception in a frenzy of possessed beeping. I pull it out of the pocket of my jacket.

'Shit,' I breathe, as I fumble to unlock the screen.

A sickening dread congeals inside me as I digest what's on my screen. Three texts from Alex. One text from Vicky. Twenty-eight missed calls from Nathan.

'Everything OK?' Cam calls over his shoulder.

I don't answer. He stops and walks back to me. His hand grips my arm. 'Hannah?'

I stare at my phone as I open the texts.

Alex: *Mum? Where r u?*

Alex: *Please call*

Alex: *MUM???!?*

Vicky: *Call me when you get this.*

Fingers of icy cold coil through me.

'Hannah?' Cam says again. 'What's wrong?'

'Nathan knows.'

CHAPTER THIRTY-FOUR

Hannah

Vicky's voice has become high-pitched and I can hear Phil moaning in the background. I picture him turning over and shoving his head beneath the pillow to block out his hysterical wife this early in the morning.

'Where the hell are you? Christ. I've been mad with worry.'

A cloying fear hardens in the pit of my stomach.

'What on earth are you doing and why didn't you tell me? Why did you lie? To me? Of all people? Is Nathan right? Are you with,' she hesitates, her confusion obvious, 'Cameron Stewart?'

I can't find any words. Images of Cam kissing my shoulder and the curve of my neck battle with the thought of her sitting in bed, sheets pulled up to her chin, aching with exhaustion having been up half the night wondering where I was.

She growls with frustration. 'Why didn't you tell me? If you had I wouldn't have called him.' The hurt in her voice is replaced by defensiveness.

'You called him?'

'Your landline.'

'But you never call the landline?'

'Well, last night I did. Your mobile went to voicemail.' She pauses and swears under her breath. 'I was drunk. Hammered, actually. And you said he wouldn't be there. You *said* he was in London with some man from Dubai. I missed you and felt bad you weren't with me. So I called you to tell you. And he answered. I asked him why he was there. I was cross. I was ready to tear strips off him for ruining our night away for no reason. Then he asked to speak to you and I had no idea what he was talking about. I said you weren't with me. I didn't think. Like I said, I was hammered. And he started yelling at me. I mean, he *really* went for it. He was shouting about Cameron Stewart. Saying you were having an affair. Are you? I said there was no way because you hate his guts. I was so drunk I nearly told him why. About Cam walking out on you when you told him about the baby. God, Hannah, why the hell did you lie to me?'

My head is swimming.

Cam furrows his brow and mouths, 'What's going on?'

I shake my head and flap my hand, indicating I'll tell him in a minute, then turn my back.

'So then I start telling him how much I hate him and how he doesn't deserve you.'

It goes from bad to worse and I swear quietly.

'And that it's criminal how he treats you, and then he says, *for God's sake what's she been telling you*, like he's shocked or something. Then he launches in and says I'm a bitch for encouraging you to go away with Cameron *flipping* Stewart?' She pauses. Sighs. 'He said you've never stopped seeing him and called me an interfering cow for covering for you. Then he mentioned the money I gave Alex and said it was because of me he was able to run away and Alex could have been killed and it would have been my fault.' She pauses as she tries to gather herself. 'I told him again you'd no way be with Cam because you hate him and he laughed. Told me I know nothing about you. He said you don't even like me; you just can't think of a way to get rid of me. I said that wasn't true then he said well, if you're really friends why the hell did you lie to me.' Quiet sobbing interrupts her flow. Vicky doesn't cry. The sound kicks me in the gut. 'Is that true? Do you wish we weren't friends?'

I can hear him saying those things to her. Twisting and shaping his words. Smiling to himself when he hears her faltering and allowing the self-doubt creep in. All these years she's managed to keep him at bay and he's finally got to her.

'Of course not.'

'But if it's not true why didn't you tell me the truth? Don't you trust me?'

Then I hear Phil in the background again. Now he is angry and frustrated, and makes no effort to lower his voice. He wants me to hear. 'For fuck's sake. Put the phone down, Vic. You don't need Hannah's shit in your life anymore. Just put the phone down and come back to bed.'

'Jesus, Phil.'

Their voices become muffled and I assume she's covered the phone with her hand, but it's not enough to disguise what he's saying.

'She doesn't deserve you. We've had years of their crap. I've had enough of it. You bend over backwards for her and all she does is take, take, take.'

A door closes. Then her voice, clear and loud, echoing slightly, as if she's moved into the bathroom. 'I've got to go.'

'I'm sorry,' I whisper. 'I'll explain. I'll—'

'If you don't trust me, what's the point of being friends? Did you think I'd tell Nathan? Or judge you? If you did, you don't know me.'

'It wasn't like that.'

'It's not like our friendship is that great anyway. An hour on a Tuesday morning to eat cold toast and deal fags?' She pauses. 'You made me feel like crap, Hannah.'

'This isn't about you.' The words have slithered out before I can hook them back in.

'*Excuse* me?'

I swallow. My chest has tightened. 'Please don't make this about you.'

'Are you *joking*? This is *all* about you. Everything is always about *you*.' Another pause. Another breath. 'You know what? Phil's right. I've had enough of this. Just leave me the fuck alone and sort your life out.'

'Vicky, don't, please. I—' But she's gone.

I stare at the phone for a moment or two and will her to call back. It stays quiet and I look up at Cam. 'Nathan guessed I'm with you. He thinks we've been having an affair all this time.'

Cam doesn't reply.

'He'll go to the police, I know he will.' I screw my face up hard. 'We should have told the truth back then. Gone to the police and told them what happened.' I bang the heel of my hand against my forehead. 'I need to get home. I need to make sure Alex is OK.'

I dial my son's mobile, but it goes straight to voicemail. I wait a few seconds and dial again. Straight to voicemail.

'His phone's off.'

'Call the home phone.'

I hesitate. Adrenalin fizzes through me. My hands are trembling when I dial the number.

But, of course, it's not Alex who answers.

'You depraved little *tramp*.'

My voice sticks in my throat as if he's rammed a fist down it. 'Nathan, I—'

'Where are you?'

'Can I speak to Alex?'

'Answer *me*!'

'Is Alex OK?'

'Of course he is,' Nathan snaps. 'It's the dog you should be worrying about.'

The line goes dead.

CHAPTER THIRTY-FIVE

Hannah

I can't stop shaking. Alex's phone is still going straight to voicemail and there's no answer from the landline. Cam drives too quickly and we swing about like a fairground ride as the bends come thick and fast. I glance at my phone every few minutes. I try Alex again. No answer. Just his voice.

Alex here. Well, I'm not. Do the message thing.

'Fuck,' I whisper. 'Fuck, fuck, *fuck*.'

'He won't have done anything.'

My irritation flares with an explosive mix of panic and lack of sleep. 'Why would you say that? You don't know him and you didn't hear him. He was so angry. Shit. What was I thinking? I should never have lied to Vicky. *Never* have met up with you. Of course he'd find out.' My hand moves to my mouth and I chew nervously on the side of my nail. 'What was I thinking?' I whisper to myself.

Cam places his hand on my knee but I shove it away. Unfair. But I don't care. I don't want affection or compassion. Instead, I have an overwhelming urge to provoke him until he gets angry and turns on me, metes out the punishment I deserve.

We turn on to the road which heads up to Gulval and slow up for a tractor, which is waiting to turn into a field. The farmer is taking his time. He opens the gate then walks back to the tractor and clambers into the cab. My fingers tap my thigh rhythmically as if I'm punching out a mayday. The farmer raises a hand to thank us. Cam nods. My head fills with pictures of Vicky hurling drunken slurs at Nathan. Nathan hitting the roof. Taking it out on Alex. My dog. God. What did he mean by that? It makes me sick to think of him knowing, whilst I was oblivious, lying on a beach kissing like a horny teen until my skin grew raw with stubble rash.

'Do you want me to come in with you? If you're worried? Or shall I wait in the car?'

I ignore him. Ask myself again what the hell I was thinking? Why am I incapable of making normal decisions? Nathan is right. I'm hopeless. I should never be left to my own devices. Because when I am, I fuck everything up. Again and again and again.

'Hannah? Did you hear me? Do you want me to come in with you?'

'No. No, it'll make things worse.' Still I chew on the side of my finger, biting repeatedly at a small tag of skin which is now hanging free. I need to calm down before I go in. I'm all over the place, a punctured kite, careening through the air.

We pass the track that leads down to Trevaylor Woods and I hear my voice telling Cam to leave me alone.

You and I don't get to live happily ever after.

The mist in my head clears and any lurking thoughts of ending my sham marriage dissolve. All I care about is my son and my dog. I know – as I've always known – that I'll say anything, and do anything, to keep them safe.

'Stop here,' I say.

'Sorry?'

'Stop the car!'

He breaks abruptly and we lurch forward in our seats. I unclip my seatbelt. Cam does the same then reaches for his door handle.

'No. Just go.'

'What if he hurts you?'

'Not his style.'

'But it's his style to threaten your dog?' He grabs hold of my wrist.

I flinch, take a deep breath, and firmly pull my arm away. 'He won't have hurt her.'

Am I telling Cam or myself?

I glance nervously up the lane, half expecting to see my husband thundering down towards us. 'You need to go. I promise you he isn't going to hurt me.' These words come out assured, hard as iron, but underneath I'm fighting a sliver of doubt. It's always been there, that question mark over whether or not he'll one day flip. 'Honestly, it'll be fine. I just need to talk to him.'

I pull back my wrist, but he holds firm.

'Cam,' I whisper. 'Let go of me.'

At last he nods reluctantly and his fingers release me.

I jog up to the house, heart hammering, legs shaky, and pull open the back door. Her basket is empty and there's no sign of her in the kitchen. I run through to the hallway and check the utility room.

Nothing.

'*Cass!*'

My voice echoes in the silence. The house is unlit and the light from the windows does little to ease the dullness. There's a single lamp on in Nathan's study. My blood chills instantly as I think of Nathan's father.

'Don't be stupid,' I whisper, and force myself to walk towards the study. I push the door open quickly and check the floor for dead fathers-in-law. He's not there and I wrap my arms around my body and walk into the room, drawn to the picture on the wall, at the hunters staring at me with pitying looks on their stylised faces.

'Oh, you silly girl,' I hear them say in unison.

'If you're looking for the dog it's not here.'

His voice makes me jump and I spin around. He's standing in the doorway, hands hanging limp at his sides, rage simmering.

I take a breath and try keeping my voice light, though it's almost impossible. 'Where is she?'

'Idiot animal got into the wheelie bin and found the poisoned voles. She knocked the damn thing over. Rubbish everywhere. Ran off with the bag and hasn't come back.'

'What? What do you mean?'

'I mean, your dog pulled over the bin and I spent an hour picking up rubbish strewn over the driveway.'

Panic digs sharpened claws into me. God. Cass. My poor girl. Picturing her out there, collapsed, poisoned, dying or already dead, leaves me weak with nausea.

'Where's Alex?'

'In his room,' Nathan says darkly. 'Locked himself in there. I thought he might look for the dog – I actually thought he cared about the flea-ridden creature – but evidently, like his mother, he doesn't seem to care about anything but himself.'

I can't speak. I want Cass back. I want her safe and not lying in agony somewhere, wondering why I'm not there to help her.

Christ. My stomach seizes as if I've got cramps. I push past him and run up the stairs taking them two at a time.

'Alex!' I call. 'Alex, are you OK?'

When I reach the landing, he flings open the door and falls into my arms. His face is flushed and sweaty, eyes puffy, cheeks marked with dried-up tear tracks.

'What happened?' I say, smoothing his hair away from where it's stuck to his hot, damp skin.

'Cass is gone. She ate poison. He said she pulled the bin over but she wouldn't do that. She never does that. He said it was her own stupid fault if she died. He said she ran away, but she wouldn't, would she? She never runs away. Why would she run away? He took my phone. He smashed it. He went mental. I've never seen him like that before. I ran up here and locked the door and he was banging on it. What's he done to Cass?' The words pour out of him in a torrent.

I pull him close and hold him tight as I try to think straight.

'He knows you were with Cam.'

'I know.'

'Why didn't you tell me?'

I don't reply.

'He's killed Cass, Mum.'

CHAPTER THIRTY-SIX

Cam, 1998

The Annamae drew back to Newlyn like a wounded soldier limping home from the trenches. The waves had eased, as if the storm was replete and, though the rain continued to lash the boat with relentless resolve, the wind had lost its fury.

The four of them sat, numb and mute, with mugs of whisky in front of them. Cam glanced at Davy for the hundredth time. His mouth was set, eyes fixed grimly, white knuckles gripping his mug so hard Cam thought it might shatter in his salt-calloused hand. Cam wracked his brain in search of something – anything – he could say to console him. Banter on the boat was easy. The teasing, the roughness, the barbed comments and rugged jokes, it all gushed out of them like a winter stream. Words of comfort? Well, they came harder. And what could he say anyway? He had a better idea than most of what Davy was going through. They might not have got on that well, but Cam knew what it was like to lose a father to the sea.

'He'll be OK,' Lawrie said, as he tipped his whisky into Davy's empty mug. 'I know he will.'

Cam winced, waiting for Geren to snarl or Davy to tell him to fuck off, but neither did. Geren lowered his head and Davy nodded, eyes closed, and drank.

Geren put his mug down with a bang. 'Fuck this. Jesus. Fuck this job. It's my fucking fault, isn't it? Me who said not to turn back.' His face screwed up with pain.

'No.' Slim's voice firm. 'It's not your fault. The only person at fault here is me. I'm the skipper. This is my boat.'

'But I fucking told you to stay out,' Geren blazed.

'And I told you we wouldn't. That I was turning back. That we'd shoot the gear one last time. I could have steamed home. But I didn't, did I? We shot the gear one more time and that was my decision.'

'So if he dies it's on your head?' Geren spat the words out like they were broken teeth.

'Yes.'

Cam rested a hand on Geren's arm to quieten him. 'It was an accident.'

'We shouldn't have come out.'

'Well we did. And twenty-four hours ago, we were all doing fucking backflips with pound signs in our eyes.' Cam's voice was a growl. 'It's part of the job and you know it. We *all* know it.'

Davy pushed away from the table and walked out of the galley like a storm cloud.

'We need to calm—'

'Fuck off, Cam,' Geren cried. 'Jesus. You always have to be the fucking hero, don't you? The one to make everything better.' Geren's vitriol speared Cam. 'No wonder those slags in the village climb all over you. Cameron Stewart, fucking good-guy hero.'

Cam didn't speak. He stared down at his whisky and caught his distorted face in its reflection.

Geren pressed on. 'All of them, opening their legs for you, telling their friends what a gent you are, what a fucking *hero*. But don't be flattered. I hear this latest minge goes with anyone. A wink and a Babycham and she's open-mouthed and on her knees—'

Before Cam had the chance to think, he'd thrown himself across the table and had Geren by the throat, rammed up against the wall, free hand drawn back.

'Go on then,' growled Geren, teeth bared.

'*Don't!*'

It was Lawrie. Cam glanced at him; he looked like a scared child.

Cam turned back to Geren, stared at him, crazed eyeball to crazed eyeball, panting heavily.

'Go on,' Geren hissed. 'Fucking hit me.'

Cam hesitated, then lowered his hand a fraction, and a look of disappointment slid over Geren's face. 'You pussy,' he rasped.

'Enough!' Slim said then. He stood up from the table and moved towards the door. When he reached it, he stopped and turned. 'Both of you calm yourselves down. We're all emotional – every one of us – but if you don't rein it in, you won't find yourself on *The Annamae* again.' Then he walked out of the galley and down into the bunk room where they heard him talking – low and indiscernible – to Davy.

Cam grabbed his tobacco from the table and headed out of the galley. It was too wet to smoke on deck, so he hovered in the doorway and rolled a cigarette. Who the hell did Geren think he was? How dare he talk about Hannah like that? And in front of Slim? And Lawrie too? Within earshot of Davy? He drew on the cigarette and smacked his hand against the doorframe. What worried him more than Geren being a dick was how out of control he'd felt. A thick fog had obscured all rational thought. Nothing Geren said about her was true, but hearing it, just thinking about her with anyone else, sent him into an intense rage which terrified him.

Martin didn't die, but they did take his arm from just below the shoulder. Sheila phoned the harbour office from the hospital and spoke to Davy who nodded and grunted in one-syllables whilst tapping a grubby finger against the desk.

'He was lucky to make it,' Davy said as he came out to join the others who were huddled tight, smoking in the rain which now spat gently in the wake of the storm. 'She thought we'd lost him.' Davy lowered his head and took a cigarette out of the pack Geren proffered. 'He won't fish again. Doubt he'll work again.'

Slim rubbed his face hard and he cleared his throat.

Geren slipped another cigarette between his lips. 'Fuck this job,' he breathed.

As they waited, weary and shell-shocked, not talking to each other or anyone else, Slim took the haul to market. It was surreal to Cam that Newlyn carried on as normal. He was detached from it all, as if he'd prefer to be out at sea, not around people for whom the accident on *The Annamae* was merely a shocking story with the salacious detail of Martin's taken arm to enjoy passing on.

The catch was big and the prices high, and the envelopes of money Slim had for them were heavy. *The Annamae* was one of only a few of the fleet which had risked the weather, and as they knew, this meant rewards were high. But the mood was sombre as he handed their money over. Usually it was the part of a trip which made everything worthwhile. But not that day. That day there was no joyful whoops and exaggerated kissing of folded notes.

Cam slipped his envelope into his back pocket. All he wanted was to be with Hannah. He closed his eyes for a moment to block out the image of Martin's arm, of the splinters of bone pressed into his flesh, his face growing paler and paler, ghostly in the lights which illuminated the deck in the raging storm. He tried to replace the image with her face. Her smile. Her hand flat against his cheek. The smell of her, perfumed and creamy, the washing powder which clung to her clothes.

'I sometimes wonder, why the hell do we do it?' Slim's voice dragged him back to the rainy pier.

Cam looked at him and saw a man aged ten years.

'Because of what we're holding.' Geren's face was dark. 'Because of the money. And because we don't know anything but the sea. We risk our lives every day we're out there. But, hey,' he said as he waved the money in his hand, 'got to earn a living.' He looked round at them all as he slipped the envelope into his jacket pocket. 'Sitting here crying like little girls isn't going to bring Martin's arm back, but you know what? Martin's alive and that's something to be thankful for. That was a mighty gale and we're all back and we're all alive. And I for one am going take this cash and celebrate being alive. I'm not going to mope because a man got unlucky with some rigging. I'm going to go for a fucking lash-up, drink enough booze to ground an army, then I'm going home to fuck my wife, because if we don't celebrate being alive – if we don't drink and fuck – then what's the goddamned point of any of it?'

CHAPTER THIRTY-SEVEN

Hannah

I am aware of Nathan behind us and I feel Alex tense. I turn and push my son behind me as if to protect him.

'Well? Are you going to tell me where you've been?'

'No. I'm going to take Alex and we're going to find our dog.' I take my son's hand and pause in front of Nathan so he can step aside.

'Horrible, isn't it?' he says as we pass him. 'To lose something you love.'

'You're an *arsehole!*' Alex cries. 'You did it. If she's dead it's because of *you*. Why? *Why* would you do that?'

Nathan sucks on his teeth, mouth set hard, one corner of his upper lip is lifted in a cartoon snarl. 'I did nothing of the sort. The dog got into the bin where your mother put a bag of poisoned voles. Not me. Blame her. If she'd kept them where I put them the dog would be safe.'

'You pulled the bin over. You poisoned her. She wouldn't go through the bins.'

'It's a dog. It's a scavenging beast.'

'I hate you.'

Nathan snorts. 'Oh, please. It's not me you should hate, it's your lying cheating mother who ran off and—'

A shout from downstairs interrupts him.

A man's voice.

'Hannah?'

It's Cam.

Nathan laughs a short bitter noise like a gunshot. 'Oh my god. Are you serious? He's *here*? In my *home*?'

'Please, don't—'

'Shut up, Hannah. You have no right to tell me what to do, and you know what? I'm done with you. The murdering bastard can have you.'

My heart skips. I glance at Alex but he's panting hard, staring daggers at Nathan, and doesn't seem to have registered what Nathan said.

'Hannah? Alex? Are you up there?'

I swear. Why is he here? Why didn't he listen? He ignored me. I told him to stay away. A surge of anger swells inside me. Fuel on the fire is the last thing we need and I told him to stay away. Why did he ignore me?

'Go *away*, Cam! We're fine. *Please*.' I choke back my tears. 'Go.'

But still he doesn't listen. Footsteps on the stairs. Alex swipes at his tears and straightens his shoulders like a soldier standing to attention.

Cam appears beside me. I roll my eyes and glare. He shouldn't have come. I can handle this, but not if he's here.

'Is everything all right?' He looks at me and then at Alex.

'Excuse me?'

Cam ignores Nathan. 'Hannah? Alex?'

'Get out of my house. I'm calling the police. You hear me? I'm calling the police and I'm telling them everything.'

300

'Do it,' I say then, my voice calm and flat. 'I don't care any-more.' I pause. Stare at him. 'But if you do, you'll be arrested, too. They'll charge you with concealing a crime.'

His face doesn't flicker. He's ready for me. His face folds into a smug smile of victory. 'No, they won't, because I'll tell them how you blackmailed me. And how *he*,' Nathan points aggressively at Cam, 'threatened to kill me. I'll tell them I was terrified and I've lived in fear all these years.'

'Then we'll tell them you're lying. There's no body. You can't prove *anything*. It's your word against ours.'

'Mum?' Alex's voice cuts through me. 'What are you talking about?'

'It's OK, Alex,' Cam says.

'*Jesus Christ*, would you just get the hell out of my house!' Nathan's screech rips through the air. 'Get out of my house, you murderous bastard, and take the two of them with you,' he says through clenched teeth. 'Take your slut. And take your son and get the hell out of my house.'

Cam stares at him for a moment, then glances at Alex, and with his face full of regret says, 'He's not my son.'

The past is snapping at my heels like a rabid dog.

Nathan smiles nastily. 'Well he certainly isn't mine.'

Alex is looking between the three of us, bewildered and small, amid all this chaos and shouting. All I wanted was to protect him.

I'm so sorry.

I look back at Nathan and swallow, dredging up the strength I need to do this. 'Alex isn't Cam's son.'

Nathan's eyes narrow with unbridled contempt. 'Oh Hannah, didn't you work it out? He has to be. I can't have children.'

His words punch the air from me. A flash of that night rips through me. The smell of him. The sound of waves lapping in the darkness. I want to push it all away, but I can't.

My poor son. My poor boy.

'I got myself tested ten years ago. When we couldn't get pregnant. I knew it couldn't be you, because of Alex, so I went secretly. Had tests. It came back conclusive. I am not able to have children. Never was. So, we know, don't we, that Alex isn't mine.'

As I stare at him, my brain floods with questions. 'You didn't tell me.'

He looks at me with indignant bafflement. 'Why should I have to tell you anything? I owe you nothing. *Nothing*.'

'Hannah. I'm… I don't know what to say.' It's Cam, stuttering, struggling to get his own head around things. Stupid, really. It wasn't hard to work out. But here I am, with two men who convinced themselves of what they wanted to believe. Slowly, realisation dawns on Cam's face. His own understanding of the past shifts into position.

Not Nathan's child.

Not his child.

There was only one other person.

My knees buckle and all I can do is steady myself with a hand on the wall. I'm melting and it hurts so much. Ignoring Nathan's blustering and Alex's questions, Cam walks to me and wraps me tightly in his arms as he whispers into my hair.

CHAPTER THIRTY-EIGHT

Cam, 1998

Though Cam felt a little more human after a shower and a change of clothes, he couldn't wash the disquiet away. It lingered on his skin and in the marrow of his bones. It ran along his sinews. Part of him wanted nothing more than to climb into bed and hide from the images assaulting him. Pictures of Martin's arm, that indefinable mush of blood and bone and oilskin came again and again, mixed with his wailing mother drinking herself to oblivion the night his father drowned, and flashes of his own fist clutching Geren's throat as an uncontrollable rage surged through him. But he had to see Hannah. He ached for her. Ever since *The Annamae* had docked he'd been thinking about her and how much he loved her. He knew he wanted to spend the rest of his life with her and he didn't want her waiting at home not knowing if he was going to return. He thought of Sheila, sitting beside Martin in hospital, staring at the empty space where his arm used to be and worrying about how they were going to eat and pay the mortgage and keep warm. He didn't want that for Hannah. It was time to get off the trawlers. Time to get a job onshore with a regular wage, regular hours, and where the biggest problem was running out of milk in the tea room, and he had to tell her what she meant to him. So he would go to the pub as planned. Drink with Slim and Davy and Geren, raise a glass to Martin, and see Hannah.

He touched his fingers to the cut in his hairline to check it wasn't still bleeding. He probably should have got it stitched, it would scar, but he was glad, a reminder of how close he'd come to being lost. Then he straightened his collar and picked up Slim's unlucky knife, which he'd forgotten to return to him amid the chaos.

When he got to The Packhorse it was heaving with sweaty bodies crammed in like sardines, and the moment he pushed through the door, he realised he'd made a mistake coming. He would find Hannah, give Slim his knife back, and get out of there.

He scanned the crowd but couldn't see her. She said she'd be there as soon as she'd shut up the bakery for her dad. Where was she?

When he felt a hand on his lower back, he turned expecting it to be Hannah, but it was Maisie, a pretty girl he'd been out with a couple of times, nothing serious, a few drinks in the pub and a couple of end-of-the-evening snogs which tasted of Juicy Fruit chewing gum. 'Hey. How're you doing?'

He shrugged. 'You know.'

She sucked air through her teeth. 'Mum says Martin actually died and they had to use those electric shock things to wake him?' She shook her head. 'Must have been bad out there.'

'Not great.'

'I'm glad you're OK.' She smiled at him with affection and he smiled back, grateful for the sliver of softness.

Cam checked the door again and noticed young Lawrie Mould hovering nervously nearby. He looked shattered and far younger than his seventeen years. Cam raised a hand and got his attention. He pointed at the bar and mouthed 'Drink?' Lawrie smiled shyly and nodded.

Cam went to the bar and ordered three pints and Lawrie came up beside him and hung at his shoulder like a shadow.

'He the right age?' asked Cora behind the bar, hair piled high on her head, one button too many undone, pointing at Lawrie who seemed to be trying to make himself invisible behind Cam.

'Yup,' lied Cam. 'And this young man saved Martin from being crushed and killed by the rogue beam. Pushed him clear. Lad's a hero and going to make a fine fisherman.'

Cora nodded at the beers on the bar. 'On the house, then. Need to keep our heroes happy,' she said and winked at Lawrie over Cam's shoulder.

They located Davy and Geren at a table in the corner and squeezed through the gathered people to get to them. Cam placed one of the pints in front of Davy, who acknowledged the drink with a nod, picked it up, and downed half of it in one. He paused, seemed to consider the drink for a moment, then finished the rest.

By the time Hannah and her friend Vicky arrived around seven-thirty, both dressed in versions of the same – denim skirts, cropped tops revealing trim midriffs, knee-high boots and hoop earrings – the men had put away another three pints.

'Your bird's here,' Geren nudged Cam and pointed towards the door. Cam saw her searching the room and when she caught sight of him her face exploded into the widest smile.

He stood and watched her pushing through the crowd to get to him and when she reached him she jumped into his arms and kissed him all over. 'I'm sorry I'm late! Sorry, sorry. I didn't finish until nearly six and wanted to make myself pretty for you and, well, it took ages!'

She grinned and kissed him again. Geren and a few of the others jeered. Even Davy managed a lopsided smile, eyes wavering with drink and tiredness. The few hours kip the men had managed to grab between arriving back and going out weren't nearly enough to make up for a sleep-deprived week at sea.

'Anybody want a drink?' Hannah smiled at the table. 'I've been paid today so this round's on me.'

'How about a kiss instead?' Geren grinned at Cam. 'You don't mind do you, Cam? Something nice to start the weekend.' He winked at Hannah and drank some of his pint.

Hannah laughed. 'Cam doesn't mind. And, hey, it's Friday, you're back and there's fun to be had.' She bent down and kissed Geren on the cheek. 'Now, drinks?'

'First a kiss for Davy.'

Davy shook his head and made a face at Geren. Cam glared at Geren and took hold of Hannah's hand.

Geren shook Cam's shoulder. 'Lighten up, mate. It's not like I've asked her to sleep with me or anything.' He glanced at Hannah and raised his eyebrows. 'Though, of course, if you fancy it?'

Hannah laughed and shook her head with cheerful exasperation. 'Blimey, I forgot what idiots you lot can be when you're lathered.'

'Go on. One kiss. His dad lost an arm; it'll make him feel better.'

'No, it's fine—' Davy started.

'Just ignore him,' Cam said. 'Geren, maybe you need to go home?'

Geren laughed and pointed at Cam. 'That, my friend, is the exact opposite of what I need. What I need is more booze and a bit of marching powder.'

'Hey,' said Hannah then to Davy. 'I'm sorry about Martin.'

Davy looked up and nodded.

She smiled.

Cam saw Davy's stare linger on her breasts – the clingy material of her top leaving nothing to the imagination – and the now-familiar stab of jealousy got him in the gut.

Her friend appeared in a haze of giggling and breathless energy. 'Come on, Han. We need to catch up with this lot. Tequila?'

Hannah smiled and kissed Cam's cheek. 'Back in a sec,' she said, and whispered something he didn't catch.

Geren watched her go and whistled through his teeth. 'You need to keep an eye on that one.'

'Fuck off.' Cam drained his drink and pushed away from the table.

He lit a cigarette and smoked it on the way to the toilets. Why was he letting Geren get to him again? This is what they did. They fished. They drank hard. They talked crudely about women. Why was he so wound up? Hannah wasn't bothered by it. She'd taken the banter as it was meant. Lighthearted. He had to do the same. He trod his cigarette out on the floor and leant on the sink in the toilets, lifting his head to stare at himself in the mirror.

'You look like shit,' he breathed.

He ran his hand beneath the tap, rubbed his face, then dried it with a couple of paper towels from the dispenser. His cut had dripped a little, and he rubbed at the smear of blood with the balled-up towels before throwing them in the bin.

'And pull yourself the fuck together,' he told himself.

The atmosphere was charged with electric energy. People who'd finished work for the weekend had descended from all around on the infamous Packhorse for an evening of drink and drugs and dancing. He watched Geren laughing with Hannah and Vicky. Hannah turned her head in the direction of the toilets and caught sight of him. She smiled and patted the empty spot on the bench beside her. Vicky leant close to her and whispered something. Both glanced at Cam and giggled.

'Cameron Stewart,' slurred a voice. A heavy hand fell like a load on his shoulder. It was Slim, one eye half-closed, the other unable to focus. 'Heading home, lad.' He nodded and was unbalanced by the movement.

Cam caught his arm to steady him. 'You OK there, Slim?'

'Yeah. Sure. You know... ' He stumbled to his left and bumped into a man holding a drink who glared at him. Cam mouthed a sorry then led Slim through the people and out of the pub, gripping him around the waist and under the arm, taking most of his weight.

Outside, the icy cold raked Cam's skin like sandpaper. The rain had finally eased and the moon shone off the wet pavement, and drips of water fell from the guttering with a steady beat.

Slim crouched and leant back against the wall, head in his hands, moaning softly. 'Sorry,' he whispered. 'Drank too much. Jesus... ' He leant his head back and softly banged it against the wall. 'Really fucked up.'

Cam stared down towards the harbour and the snatch of dark water beyond. The white tops of the choppy waves like a dusting of snow. The streetlamps surrounding the harbour flickered over the black sea like party lights. He had a sudden flash of his father, the smell of him catching in the back of his throat, oil, unwashed clothes, the stench of drying fish guts, and the sound of his boots in the hallway as he returned from a trip with a twinkle in his eye and, in perfect imitation of his Scottish ancestors, would smile and say, 'Aye, son, tonight we'll be eatin' like kings 'n' drinkin' like fishies.'

Slim pushed himself off the wall and stood for a moment, swaying gently as he squinted to focus. 'Home to the missus,' he said. 'Should get yourselves home too. Everyone's wired. Geren. On the edge.' He started walking away, his voice fading to a drunken mutter. 'Davy needs his bed... '

Cam watched him weave up the road and pictured the face of the long-suffering, short-fused Betty when she opened the door to his drunken hammering. With a sudden flash he remembered the knife. 'Slim!' he called. But the man didn't stop his weave up the hill.

The girls were sitting at the table when Cam returned. Geren and Hannah were squashed tightly together, his arm around her shoulder, gesticulating wildly with his cigarette as he told them all about the storm and the accident. Everybody was rapt, Davy too, staring fixedly so it was obvious to anybody who knew these things he'd dropped a pill or taken a line.

Someone arrived at the table with a tray of shots.

'Cam!' Hannah cried, staring up at him gleefully.

He noticed her smile had loosened up with drink.

'Where have you been?' Her fingers closed around a shot glass, which she thrust out towards him, some of the liquid sloshing out and spilling on the table.

He shook his head, glaring at Geren who held the cigarette

in his lips and squinted against the smoke as he passed the drinks around the table.

'I'm done in. Let's split.'

'Noooo! It's too early!' Her voice rang with a slight whine like a child begging for sweets. 'Do a shot with me?' she said.

'I said no.'

Her face fell.

Geren picked up a shot. 'Ignore the prick. I'll do one with you.'

Her momentary sadness was replaced with a beaming smile as they clinked glasses and knocked back the clear liquid. She grimaced, lips and chin shining wet with spilled alcohol, as she stamped her feet and shook her head against the bite of the liquor.

Geren laughed and slammed his glass down on the table hard enough to break it. He handed one to Davy who did his shot obediently. Hannah laughed and leant playfully against Geren who clapped Davy on the back.

Cam tensed. He was about to ask her again to leave with him, but then noticed something had caught her eye. Her face fell and she raised her arm to try and obscure her face, whilst glancing again at whatever it was she'd spotted. Cam followed her gaze and saw a man standing at the entrance of the pub and scanning the room.

Was that Nathan Cardew?

He looked out of place, uptight, dressed in navy suit trousers and an open-necked shirt, like some ponce from London. Cam watched his face relax into a smile when he saw Hannah. He waved and walked through the drinkers towards her. Hannah muttered something under her breath and Geren's face fell into a dismissive sneer.

Nathan cleared his throat and attempted to speak to her, flapping at the cigarette smoke which hung horizontally like a layer of sea mist.

'What are you doing here?' said Hannah. Cam noticed she was making an effort not to sound drunk, finishing her words distinctively, her smile vanished.

'Oh.' He was clearly taken aback. 'You said to meet you here?'

Cam's body tensed.

Nathan squirmed under the hostile glares of the men in the pub, who sneered unkindly at his ridiculous clothes and posh-boy haircut. Cam might have felt sorry for him if he wasn't seething at the balls of the prick. Walking into The Packhorse of all places? On *his* patch, to meet *his* girlfriend.

'You invited me to come. Remember? You said when I got back from Paris.' He said the word 'Paris' with emphasis. Geren snorted with laughter and Nathan glanced at him, momentarily faltering, before continuing. 'I've been looking forward to seeing you. Counting the hours, if truth be told.'

His voice was polished, tainted with *notions*, as Sheila Garnett would say, and any Cornish accent he might have had growing up was now buried beneath his fancy education and affected manner.

Cam could see Hannah panicking as she searched for something to say. It reassured him.

'Maybe we could talk for a moment?' Nathan asked hesitantly. 'Outside?'

'Can we talk here?'

'It's a little— ' he hesitated and cast his eyes warily around the people at the table who all stared at him as if he were some sort of alien, '—noisy. Just a few minutes?'

Hannah nodded reluctantly and eased herself out from the table. Cam grabbed her wrist and pulled her to him as she walked passed him. 'What's going on?' he hissed.

She rolled her eyes. 'Nothing,' she said, keeping her voice low. 'It's fine. We had, like, one dinner out – and only because he kept hassling me – and now he thinks we're in love or something. It's sad. I thought he was OK, but he's weird and really creepy. I've had a letter every other day from him since he left.' She tapped the side of her head and made a face like Nathan was nuts. 'I'll send him on his way. Back in a bit.' She kissed him.

'Why didn't you tell me?'

'Tell you what?' She looked perplexed. 'That a guy likes me?'

Cam didn't reply.

'Look, it's my fault. I should have just told him I wasn't interested but he didn't want to listen. I knew he was going away and I thought he'd get bored and meet a French girl or whatever. I should have been clear. He's—' she hesitated, '—desperate, if I'm honest.' She paused. 'Can I ask you a favour? Can you not let on we're together? Not tonight. Let me get it sorted. I don't want to upset him more than I have to.'

Cam stared at her.

'Honestly. Don't look at me like that. It's fine. Nothing happened. We ate some food I didn't like which cost the earth in a restaurant you had to whisper in. I thought he was harmless when I met him, but he's strange and I've no idea why he's got such a thing for me.'

While she was gone, Cam drank his pint slowly, eyes glued to the door, and waited for her to return. When she finally came in, her face was pale, lips tight, arms crossed over her body protectively.

'You OK?' Cam asked as she neared him.

She grimaced. 'God,' she said, her voice lowered. 'He *cried*.'

Cam couldn't stop a small smile at the thought of that prick in his fancy shirt and stupid haircut crying like a baby outside a pub full of fishermen, but then a flash of doubt crossed his mind. Surely no man would be that cut up after only one meal out? Was she lying to him? Was there more to her and Nathan than she was letting on? 'What did he say?'

She drunkenly waved her hand and shook her head dismissively. 'You know what? I can't be bothered to talk about it. It's done now.' She reached across the table to grab one of the last remaining shots which were dotted among the empties and knocked it back. Then she glanced over towards the door, turned back quickly, and dropped her head. 'Jesus, he's back. Why won't he get the message?'

Nathan was looking around the pub, agitated, chewing the thumb of one hand, the other flapping manically against his thigh. The jukebox had gone on and people were starting to sing and dance, arms slung around shoulders, swaying and singing tunelessly to some eighties track Cam couldn't stand.

Hannah cast her eyes over at Nathan again. Cam leant over and tried to kiss her. She drew back sharply. 'Don't. Not now.'

Irritation bowled into him. 'I thought you didn't care about him?'

'What?' she said, putting her finger to her ear.

'Let's go,' he said, making sure she could hear him over the racket in the pub. 'This place is doing my head in tonight.'

'Stay for a bit?'

'I'm knackered.'

Hannah was distracted. Eyes on the door. Cam turned and saw Nathan pushing out of the pub.

'Right, he's gone. Let's leave.'

She took hold of his hand and squeezed it. 'One more drink. Please? I want to make sure he's gone. Seriously, if he's waiting outside and he sees us leaving together—'

'Then what? So he knows. Who cares?'

'Hey, lovebirds,' said Vicky, interrupting them as she piled over in a rush of drunken excitement. 'What's up?'

Hannah groaned. 'Nathan Cardew won't take no for an answer. He's hanging around trying to talk to me. I tried to get rid of him and he said he loves me.'

Cam bristled.

'Loves you? How could anyone love *you*?' Vicky grinned. 'He's gone anyway.'

Hannah stared at the door with a doubtful expression. 'He might be outside though. I don't want to see him. He might start up again. I seriously think he might be a bit mental,' she said.

'He's certainly a persistent little prick,' Vicky said with a laugh.

Hannah snorted and raised her empty glass in a toast. 'Here's to getting rid of persistent little pricks.'

Cam sat there, ears ringing, body exhausted, the cut on his head throbbing in time with the music, wishing he was able to rub away the sourness of the fishing trip. The sounds of the pub, the clamouring voices, the music, weighed down on top of him like a collapsed cliff. Hannah said something to

Geren. Geren nodded. Vicky laughed. Davy knocked another drink back. Geren leant close to Hannah and whispered. She laughed. The two of them got up. She winked at Cam as she stood. Geren held out his hand to her. She moved to take it but stumbled, too drunk, and he caught her fall. They started to dance. Davy joined them, swaying as if he was back at sea.

As Cam watched them dancing, he became aware of how people around them were looking at her. The men. Staring. Hungry. Wanting to do things to her only he was allowed to do.

He stood and went over to her. Put himself between her and Geren. Leant close to her. 'OK? You ready?' he shouted over the music.

'Ten minutes?' Hannah tapped her wrist to mime the time.

'Can't we just go?'

'What?' she shouted.

'I want to go!'

She spun away from him as Geren expertly twirled her then dipped her back. She laughed. Eyes half closed. Body gyrating like a belly dancer.

Blind jealousy swooped in on Cam again. He shoved Geren hard on the shoulder. 'Leave her the fuck alone.'

Geren laughed, exchanged amused looks with Davy.

'Hey,' Hannah said. 'Look, it's OK—'

Geren spoke. 'Relax, lad. We're only dancing.'

Was that a smirk on his face?

Cam pushed him again.

'Easy, mate.' He held his hands up.

Cam squared up to him. Blinked hard. The room was spinning. Hannah stepped between them.

'Fucking hell,' Cam breathed. 'I thought you were supposed to be home with your wife?'

Hannah opened her mouth, but Geren spoke first.

'What the fuck's up with you tonight?'

'What up with *me*? It's you two—'

Hannah made a face at him. 'What on earth have *I* done?'

Geren furrowed his brow. 'You know, you seem a little,' he paused and leant into Cam's face, 'uptight. Maybe you should go and have a drink with that twat over there.' Geren gestured towards the door. Cam turned and saw Nathan, back, staring at them, lip twitching. 'Because right now? You're kind of pissing on everybody's party.'

'You forgotten Martin? Lying in hospital with no fucking *arm*? Forgotten we nearly died last night?'

Geren gritted his teeth. 'Of course I haven't forgotten, but I'm sure as shit not going to mope around like a loose fart in church, because how the fuck would it help?'

'Go home to your *wife*.'

'She's pregnant. Tired. I was going to stay in but she told me to get out and blow off some steam.' Then he shook his head. 'Why the fuck am I explaining myself to you anyway? Piss off if you don't want to be here, but I want to enjoy myself so chill out.'

Geren walked off in the direction of the toilets, pushing aggressively past people to get there. Cam looked down at Hannah. 'I'm done here. Come with me or stay. Your choice.'

Hannah's hands went either side of his face. His vision blurred. He blinked hard to refocus. She turned his head and stroked his cheek to get him to look at her.

'Hey,' she said again, applying more pressure to turn his face. 'Look at me.'

Finally he yielded and she smiled. He expected her to say she was coming with him.

But she didn't.

'Don't give Geren a hard time. He's dealing with what happened in his own way.'

'Sorry?' Cam shook his head as if trying to clear it.

'Maybe he's right? Maybe you should try and relax? Have a dance. A laugh. You had a bad time out there, but you're all home and – *God* – that's something to celebrate, isn't it?'

'Hannah—' Cam grabbed her arm.

Distracted suddenly, Hannah looked over his shoulder and swore under her breath. 'Why won't he just leave?'

'Stop worrying about Nathan fucking Cardew!'

'Cam. You're *hurting* me!'

He hadn't even realised he was holding her and he let go immediately. 'I'm sorry. I—'

She rubbed at her wrist. 'Jesus, Cam. Enough, OK?' She walked away from him and he watched her grab Vicky, who was sitting on some guy's lap he didn't know and whispered something in her ear. Vicky glanced over at Cam before saying something to the man she was with, taking Hannah by the hand and dragging her through the crowd towards the toilets.

He sat at the table beside Davy. Slim's knife dug into him. He pulled it out of his pocket and studied the handle. Yellowed whalebone etched with delicate black lines describing a clipper ship on the waves. He tilted the knife and stared at his distorted reflection in its tarnished silver surface.

'Everything works out for you, doesn't it?' Davy said, his words slurred at the edges.

Cam looked at him then back at the knife he was turning in his hand. 'What?'

Davy looked at him. 'People loving you.'

'What the fuck are you talking about.'

'You know Dad would prefer you as his son. He's so fucking *proud* of you.' Davy leant forward and grabbed a drink with an unsteady hand. 'It was you he reached for on the boat. Not me.'

'I was the closest to him.'

'When they kicked me out of the army, the first thing he said was, why can't you be more like Cam Stewart?'

'Kicked out? I thought you left?'

Davy sniffed and drank his drink. When he put the glass down he tried to take hold of the knife, but Cam was too quick and pulled his arm back.

'Cam! *Jesus.*'

Hannah was behind him.

'You nearly took my bloody eye out. What the hell are you doing with that?'

'It's Slim's. His lucky charm. I have to give it back to him.'

'Well, put it away for God's sake. You'll hurt somebody.'

'Some lucky charm,' he whispered. He stared at the knife then, without warning, brought his hand down hard and drove the blade into the table. He shimmied the knife back and forth to release it and, when it was free, slammed it down again.

People were starting to look. Cam worked the knife free again, but Hannah stilled his hand. 'You know,' she said, 'maybe you should go outside for a smoke. Get a breath of fresh air and calm down. OK?'

Cam didn't need fresh air. All he needed was her to take

him away from the chaos and hold him somewhere quiet. But instead of telling her this, he nodded with a disdainful sneer said, 'Sure. Whatever.' As he walked away from her his stomach filled up with self-loathing. He was being a dick and he couldn't stop himself.

When he reached the door, he came face to face with Nathan. 'For fuck's sake,' he said. 'Just leave her alone!'

'Excuse me?'

'Hannah. She's my girlfriend. And she thinks you're a wanker. So leave her the fuck *alone*.'

Cam pushed past him, shoving him hard, shoulder to shoulder, and once outside, he rested his forehead on the rough wall. His cut throbbed. His head spun with alcohol and disorienting jealousy. He breathed deeply, trying to slow his heart which was racing unnaturally fast. Gradually the peace outside the pub, the wind and the roar of the sea beyond the harbour wall, diluted his anger. When his mind stilled, he remembered Slim's knife, and swore silently. He'd left it jammed into the table. He had to go back in and get it; Slim would kill him if he lost it. And he had to apologise to Hannah. He was an idiot to take his bad mood out on her. It was unfair. She'd done nothing wrong and he'd been a dickhead all night.

He was vaguely aware of the pub door opening. The voices and music inside The Packhorse filling the air for a moment or two before the door closed again and muffled the noise. Footsteps approached him. Please be Hannah, he thought. But it wasn't Hannah. It was Nathan.

He stood, silently, clearly agitated as he pulled at his shirt sleeve, eyes flicking left and right, unable to settle.

'What?' Cam said in a caustic voice.

'You're… ' Nathan hesitated. 'You're not good enough for her. She deserves better.' His voice was thin and weak. 'She deserves better than you. You can't look after her like I can.'

Cam pushed himself off the pub wall and stepped close to Nathan. 'What did you say?'

'She's too good for a no-hoper like you.' Nathan's voice trembled. 'She needs someone… like me.'

'Are you serious—'

'I studied at one of the top universities in the country. I'm a lawyer. I own a large and beautiful home. I can give her the very best life. And you? What can you give her? A fisherman with nothing. I bet you don't even own your own house?'

Cam baulked.

'I knew it, you see?' Nathan said with an unmistakeable note of victory. 'You have nothing to offer her.'

Every nerve in Cam's body was fizzing.

'Do the decent thing and step aside and let her be with someone worthy of her. There are plenty of women more suited to you. But Hannah? She's—'

Cam didn't wait to hear what Nathan Cardew had to say about Hannah. He drew his fist back and launched it at Nathan's face and caught him on the lower right-hand side of the jaw.

Nathan stumbled and fell into the wall of the pub. He lifted a hand to his mouth. Looked down to check it.

'Yeah, you're bleeding, you fucking arsehole.'

'You hit me?' There was a strength in Nathan's voice now, as if he were vindicated, as if Cam had proved he was no good.

Cam hadn't hit anybody – not properly – since school. Jesus. He'd let this little prick get to him? How? Why? Who gave a shit about Nathan Cardew? Cam swore and shook out his hand.

'I'm sure Hannah will be very interested to know what kind of man you are,' Nathan said.

'She'd have hit you too if she heard what you were saying. But, yeah, sure, grass me up. Let's see how impressed she is by some princess who gets his arse handed to him without even fighting back.'

Cam turned on his heel. Adrenalin pumped through him. He swore again and again as he went, one foot in front of the other, walking faster and faster until soon he was running, pounding the pavement down towards the harbour and along the road which headed out of town in the direction of Mousehole. As he left Newlyn behind him, the streetlamps ended and the road was plunged into darkness.

When he finally stopped, he leant over and caught his breath, his head spinning with the exercise and alcohol. The road ran parallel to the sea. He climbed off the narrow pavement and down on to the rocks, where he sat and stared out over the black water and the moon which bounced off it in shards of white.

'Fuck!' he screamed into the darkness. '*Fuck!*'

All he could think about was Nathan telling her. He could hear his reedy voice whining on about how Cam had gone for him with no provocation. What details would he add? A look of enjoyment in Cam's eyes? An extra punch? Would she feel sorry for Nathan? Would she go to the bar and ask for a cloth and gently clean up his blood?

The thought made him sick to his core. He was an idiot. That prick was right, he didn't deserve her.

CHAPTER THIRTY-NINE

Hannah, 1998

'He's been ages,' she said, her eyes on the door. 'I think I should check on him.'

'Leave him be,' said Davy, turning Slim's knife over and over in his hand.

Geren, now back at the table, smiled. 'Don't worry. Cam's fine. Honest. He'll be back in no time. It was bad out there on the water. We've all had it rough. He'll take a walk, blow off some steam, have a smoke, then come back for you. I know him like my own brother.' Geren patted her shoulder. 'He's mad about you. And, hey, if he doesn't come back, I'm always here?' He grinned.

Hannah wasn't sure how she was supposed to respond, but as Davy laughed she assumed it was no more than a joke, so gave an awkward smile. She was beginning to feel angry with herself. She'd missed Cam so much and had been desperate to see him. Why the hell had she let Nathan Cardew of all people ruin their evening? She should have ignored him like Cam told her to. She'd been selfish and not at all sensitive to what Cam needed; she'd been a terrible girlfriend.

'You know, I'm going to try and find him.' She held her hand out towards Davy. 'If you give me the knife, I'll take it back to him.'

'It's Slim's, not Cam's.'

'I know. I'd still like to give it back to him, a sort of peace offering. He can give it to Slim in the morning.'

Davy shrugged, unbothered, and handed it over. His eyes wavered with drink. Poor sod, she thought. Must have been awful to watch his father get injured like that. Sheila's sister told Vicky's mum his arm was like tenderised steak before the doctors took it off with a hack saw. She dropped the knife into her bag.

The pub door opened and caught her eye. She hoped it was Cam and dreaded it being Nathan, but it was just two girls. She checked her watch again. It was nearly half an hour since Cam left.

'Want me to come and look after you?' Geren asked, giving a flick of his eyebrows over the rim of his glass.

'No, I'll be fine, thanks. Safe on the sleepy streets of Newlyn.'

'Or maybe you don't trust yourself?' he laughed.

Hannah forced a smile. 'Well, yeah, there is that. I mean what woman could resist?'

He winked and rested his hand on her lower back. She shifted, moving herself away from his touch. 'Now, now. Hands to yourself. And, anyway,' she said, 'shouldn't you be getting home to Gemma?'

He winced and shook his head drunkenly. 'The last thing Gem wants is me piling in like this. She hates me drunk.'

She laughed.

'So if this is goodbye, a kiss before you go?' he reached out and grabbed her wrist.

He was drunk, that was all. Drunk. But also annoying. She was aware that if Cam walked in and saw him touching her he might kick off again. 'Let go, Geren.'

His smile verged on a leer.

'Please let go.'

He held on for a moment, but then released his grip and raised both hands in mock defence. 'Fair enough, but you're missing out. You won't find a better kisser this side of the Tamar Bridge.' He smiled. 'Hey, relax, girlie. I'm joking. Surely you can take a joke?'

She forced herself to laugh. It was so much easier to appease drunk men than take a stand. Getting annoyed never worked. It just wound them up. 'Give my love to Gemma,' she said.

Geren nodded drunkenly and lifted his pint in acknowledgement.

Davy was hunched over the table. He looked exhausted and sad. Her heart went out to him. 'Take care, Davy.' She rested a hand on his shoulder. 'And I'm sorry again about your dad.' She leant down and kissed his cheek. 'See you around.'

Vicky was at the next table kissing the guy she'd been dancing with. Hannah tapped her on the shoulder and she turned and grinned drunkenly. 'Sorry,' Hannah said, 'just to say, I'm off.'

'What? *No!* You *can't* go! What will I do?'

Hannah laughed and looked at the man who was busy concentrating on getting his hand underneath her top. 'I think you'll be OK.'

Vicky glanced over her shoulder as if surprised to see him and pushed his hand away, pretending she was appalled. 'He's called Phil, but he's not as fun as you.'

'Liar.'

Vicky laughed and turned to resettle in their clinch.

It was freezing outside. The rain had eased but the air was

damp and icy. She didn't have enough clothes on – stupid not to take a coat or wear tights – and rubbed her arms as she looked up and down the empty street. There was a figure standing in the shadows by the wall. It looked like a man. When the orange tip of a cigarette flared in the darkness she thought it might be him.

'Cam?' she called hopefully, but he didn't respond and when she drew a little closer she could see it wasn't him.

She tried to think where he'd have gone. Not back to Martin and Sheila's, not without her. They hadn't had that big a row. He'd just needed to cool down. No, she was convinced he was, as Geren said, walking it off. If it were her, she'd have walked to the beach. But then she thought about his boat, moored down at the harbour, no more than five minutes' walk away. That made sense. She could imagine him there and he would know she'd look there if she was going to try and find him. A thrill wriggled though her as she recalled his hands on her body, skin peppered with goosebumps, beneath that old tarpaulin. As she thought about it, it made more and more sense that he was there. Cooled down, waiting for her with a couple of beers and their makeshift bed.

Away from the pub, the street was quiet and eerie, like a ghost town, and her footsteps echoed on the concrete pavement, giving the illusion somebody was following her. She turned to check behind her, but there was nobody. Just her. The harbour was dark beyond the streetlamps. She walked quickly past the offices and the shadowy heaps of lobster pots, fish boxes, and discarded nets. She was careful not to slip on the wet wood of the jetty as she made her way down to his mooring. Her heart sank when she saw the boat bobbing dark and empty with no sign of Cam. She stepped on to the deck and sat down, angry at herself. She'd been such an idiot. She tried to work out what to do now. Where was he? Perhaps she should just head home and make it up to him in the morning.

Then, as she stood to leave, she heard footsteps.

'Cam?'

No answer.

The moonlight was obscured by thick cloud, but in the dimness she could see a figure walking towards the jetty.

'Hello?' she called. 'Cam? Is that you?'

The figure moved down the jetty and as he approached the boat she recognised him.

'Oh,' she said, unable to hide her disappointment. 'I'm looking for Cam. Have you seen him?'

Davy was silent, hands shoved deep into his pockets.

There was something unnerving about him. Something alarming about the way he was looking at her.

'Has he got beers down there?'

'Sorry?'

'Beer. He keeps some on board, doesn't he? Sure he wouldn't mind if we had one.' Davy stepped on to the edge of the boat and jumped down.

'I'm heading home, actually. I think Vicky's waiting for me.'

'Your friend? She went already.' His voice was raspy and faraway, not quite connected to his body. 'With that guy she was with.'

'Oh, then I should probably get going.'

Hannah stood and tried to move past Davy, but he grabbed her shoulder.

The rest? Well that happened in a blur.

A bang to her head when she was thrown downwards. Booze and stale breath. The weight of him. His hand clamped over her mouth. Too hard. Snatches of voice whispering. Telling her to relax. Telling her she was pretty. That Cam never needed to know. It was their secret. When she scratched his face he slapped her.

'Sssh,' he whispered. 'It doesn't need to be this way.'

CHAPTER FORTY

Hannah

Cam's face is torn in two by the sadness which pushes up inside him. He steps towards me but I'm not interested in his sadness, guilt, or pity. And I'm not interested in addressing Nathan's anger which crackles like a fire. All I care about is my son. I push Cam aside and go to Alex.

'Alex,' I say into Alex's hair. 'Listen to me. I'm sorry—'

Nathan erupts. 'You're sorry to him? What about *me*? Where's my sorry? You *lied* to me. You told me you were pregnant with my child.'

'No,' I say sharply. 'I told you I was pregnant and you assumed the rest.'

There's a sweetness to spinning history like this, sweet though perhaps not edifying. I'm not proud of what I did. I'm not proud of concealing the truth from him. But I'm not ashamed either. I wanted a home for my son and I wanted Cam safe, and that's what I got.

I think back to ten years ago to when Nathan must have worked out Alex wasn't his. Pieces of the jigsaw are slotting into place. The sharpness. The impatient snapping and the filthy moods. The start of his affairs. The hours he spent locked away in his study with the ghost of his *drog-polat* father. I should have guessed. But perhaps it was wilful ignorance. Not wanting to question anything. Not wanting to risk being thrown on to the streets or sending Nathan to the police. I'm shocked to discover how angry I am. I want to scream and shout. Punch walls. Smash windows. But because of Alex I hold it in. 'You should have told me you knew.'

Nathan scoffs and my fist balls. 'Why would I do that? Unlike you, I'm loyal to a fault. I'd taken you both on. I was stupid enough to be duped and I would live with the consequences of that. I am a good man. I've always been a good man. You were my wife and he is your son. So instead of doing what most men would have done and running away—' He glances at Cam here, one corner of his mouth raised in a sneer. '—I stayed and continued to provide for you, and, in spite of your malicious and heinous manipulation, love you.'

He's standing only a few paces from the top of the stairs and I have a vivid image of running at him and slamming my weight into his chest. I imagine his arms windmilling as he struggles to keep his balance. Falling backwards. The sound of him hitting the tiles below, his head cracking like a coconut and blood collecting in the channels of grout between the flagstones.

'Why did you lie to me? Both of you did.' Alex looks from me to Cam. 'I came to you,' he says to Cam. 'But you denied it. Why?'

Cam's face knots in anguish. 'I didn't lie. I wish – more than anything – I was your father, but I'm not.'

'Why are you still saying that?' Alex cries.

My heart bleeds that he still doesn't understand. That there is more for him to have to hear. I wish more than anything I could shield him from the truth, but my web of lies is unravelling and it's inevitable.

'He's lying,' Nathan spits. 'She was pregnant before we got together. Pregnant before she sent him away. But, like an idiot, I was blind to her mendacity. She is no more than a manipulative cuckoo.'

Alex is wide-eyed with bewilderment. He looks from me to Nathan to Cam and back to me, as if being threatened from every direction with no idea which way to run.

Tears spill down my cheeks. I should say something – anything – but words won't form.

'And while we're all being honest, there's something you should know about the man who fathered you—'

'Nathan!' The word comes out in a screech.

The look he gives me is a mixture of pleasure and triumph. This is his finale. The moment the audience has been waiting for. The moment he gets to deliver his lethal blow.

'He's a *murderer*. A cold-blooded killer. He killed a man and dumped his body, and then he ran away like the coward he is so he wouldn't get caught.'

Alex's face registers confusion and he turns to me for reassurance. Cam drops his head, his hands push through his hair, raking his scalp. My mind races, still desperate to find a way out of this, to keep the cotton wool casing I've wrapped him in all these years intact. But I know I can't.

The lies end here.

Cam raises his head and looks at my son with red-rimmed eyes, a film of tears across them, lips drawn tight. 'Alex, listen I—'

I interrupt him. 'He didn't kill anybody.' Cam starts to protest, but I silence him and repeat myself. 'He didn't kill anybody.'

'Stop lying!' Nathan's face is ablaze. 'I saw him. That man.' He jabs the air aggressively in Cam's direction. 'He attacked me the same night. He's a lunatic. I saw him with the body in his boat. I watched him take it out to sea and come back empty-handed. I *saw* him kill the man and dump the body. He's a murderer, Hannah, and you know it. You can't cover for him any longer. You know the truth. Cameron Stewart is a murderer.'

My eyes bore into his and I speak clearly and calmly. 'Cam didn't kill anybody. I did.'

CHAPTER FORTY-ONE

Hannah, 1998

The side of her head throbbed and there was a burning pain between her legs. Her skin stung where his stubble grated. The thick smell of him invaded her, so unfamiliar, catching in her nose and throat as the sea lapped at the sides of the boat.

He lifted off her. Stepped back. Pulled his trousers up and stumbled with the sway of the boat. 'Thank you,' he said.

She snatched at her skirt. Her heart banged violently against the bars of her chest. She noticed her underwear, ripped, on the deck beside her. She grabbed it and reached for her bag and pulled in on to her lap. She held it close, as if it might offer her some sort of protection, and tucked the offending slip of torn cotton inside. As she did, her fingers brushed against something cool and metallic in her bag. Slim's knife. Her fingers clasped the scrimshaw handle.

He was zipping his fly. Running a hand through his hair to smooth it. 'Maybe see you around?'

She tensed. Was he smiling? He was. He was fucking smiling. A rage she didn't know she was capable of feeling welled in the pit of her stomach.

'Fuck you,' she whispered. 'You're an animal.'

Another smile?

'Hey,' he said, and took a step towards her. 'Don't be like that.'

'Stay away from me.' Her hand tightened around the whalebone handle of the knife.

But he didn't stay away. He came closer. Bent down. Reached his hand out to touch her cheek as she drew herself back from him.

'You really are very pretty,' he said softly. 'Maybe we should do this again? I'm sure Cam won't mind.'

'Stay away.'

His face loomed near hers.

It happened in a flash. Her hand flexed around the knife. Jerked from the bag towards him.

'Get away from me,' she said. 'Get away!'

The knife made contact. There was a resistance. His eyes widened. He fell back and looked down. Touched his fingers to the inside of his thigh. When he pulled them away they were shining, wet and black like oil.

'What the fuck?'

'I said stay away from me.'

'I'm bleeding, you bitch.' He tried to press both his hands to his inner thigh. But even in the muted light she could see how much blood was coming out of him. 'My artery. You got my fucking artery.' He threw his head back and swore, his head circling slowly, eyes rolled back in their sockets. '*Jesus.*'

'What do I do?' she whispered.

'Put your hands on it for fuck's sake. Press.' His voice was fading. 'Press… hard.'

Hannah's body was rigid, as if all her muscles and fibres had been frozen solid, but she forced herself to kneel. Crept closer to him. Reached out and pressed against his thigh. She glanced down and in the scant light saw blood pumping through her fingers like a burst water main.

Davy Garnett fell back against the side of the boat. He tried to speak, but his voice was too quiet, no more than a guttural rasp, any words he was trying to say indefinable. His head swayed and tipped over to one side. There was a heavy thud as he hit the deck. Then stillness. She stayed rooted to the spot. Eyes on him. Hands pressed against the wetness of his leg.

'Davy?' she whispered. She held her breath and waited for him to answer.

But he didn't.

He lay there still and silent, and all she could hear were the waves breaking against the harbour wall and the distant sounds of laughter and music coming from inside the pub as she drew herself away and huddled, trembling, against the back of the boat.

CHAPTER FORTY-TWO

Cam, 1998

How long had he sat there? He had no idea. Half an hour? An hour? Maybe even longer. When he finally uncurled his back and stood, he felt better, lighter. The sea, its expanse and clocklike rhythm, had calmed him. His mind had some clarity now his heart rate had slowed and the fog of alcohol had faded. As he turned away from the water, he recalled the impact of his fist against the pasty cheek of Nathan Cardew and winced.

What was wrong with him?

It was as if he were walking a tightrope. Teetering on the edge with every step. People wouldn't describe him as a violent man. The opposite. Most people gave him credit for being steady and cool-headed. His moments of lost control in the last few days made him uneasy. Especially when it came to Nathan Cardew. Rational thought told him Hannah – the Hannah he knew and loved – could never love a man like Cardew. Cam had seen the look she'd given him in the pub. It bordered on repulsion. But still Cam had let him wheedle his way into his head. The guy was an idiot. Cam could have leant into his face and said 'boo' and the prick would have collapsed. He had no interest in hurting Nathan Cardew. So why had he? Was it his breathtaking sense of entitlement and superiority? Or the demeaning way he'd talked about Hannah as if he owned her? Maybe it was all down to the stress of the fishing trip and knowing they all could have died out there. Whatever the reasons, he'd been an idiot and he needed to say sorry to Hannah. Nathan was wrong. Cam was worthy of her. There was nothing he wouldn't do for her. He loved her and that was all that mattered.

He headed back down the road to Newlyn. His watch told him it was nearing one. The Packhorse would do a lock-in tonight. He prayed she'd still be there as he pushed forward down the hill. The wind blew in frozen gusts off the sea and he drew his coat tighter around himself and kept his head low as he picked up pace and began to jog. At the harbour car park, he came to a halt and paused for a few moments to catch his breath and, as he did, he heard a faint noise. A mewling cry from the direction of the pier. He held his breath and listened again.

Nothing.

Must have been the wind.

He started to cross the road, but then heard it again. A woman's voice. A small sob. Talking. One voice or two? He turned and followed the direction of the noise. He stopped and listened again. Then another noise. It was coming from the water, from the boats moored at the bottom of the jetty.

'Hello?' he called.

The noise stopped.

'Who's there?' he said as he stepped on to the jetty. 'Hello?'

'Cam?' The voice was faint but unmistakably Hannah's.

He hurried down the slippery jetty and went to his boat.

He could see the outline of her visible in the muted light from the distant streetlamps, huddled in a corner of the small deck.

'Hannah? What are you doing here?' He began to climb into the boat.

'You need to leave.' Her voice was cracked and broken.

'What's wrong?'

'You need to go. Just *go*!'

'What's happened? Is everything—' He stopped speaking when he caught sight of the dark shape lying in the shadows at the side of the deck.

He jumped down and realised the deck was wet, a pool of liquid surrounding the shadowy figure, which glinted in the snatches of moonlight.

CHAPTER FORTY-THREE

Hannah, 1998

A band grew tight around her chest. Her fingers and toes were numb and hot bile stung the back of her throat. Cam knelt down beside her. Hand on her upper arm. She flinched. She couldn't let him touch her. She was dirty. Unclean. That man's smell clung to her. Inside and out. Her lungs kept constricting until every molecule of air was squeezed out of her.

In the dim light she saw his face was deformed by panic. Her fear thickened and her breaths grew shorter, coming in taut snatches as she started to shake uncontrollably. Cam glanced back at the motionless figure of Davy Garnett, his eyes staring, unseeing, up towards the cloudy night sky, and pressed two fingers against his neck. When his fingers fell away, he dropped his head and groaned.

'What happened, Hannah? It's going to be OK. But you have to tell me.' His voice was soft and gentle and she wanted to wrap herself up in it.

'Tell me,' he said.

She hesitated. 'He… ' Her voice stuck in her throat. 'Hurt me.'

The words sounded faint and detached as if spoken by another person. Her body thrummed with the cold. The backs of her legs stung where they'd rubbed against the rough deck.

'What happened?'

'He came out of nowhere. He was hurting me. I... I didn't mean to. The knife. I... You left it in the pub... ' Her voice faded. It had started to rain again, light drops, which turned razor-sharp in the wind. The waves beyond the walls seemed to be crashing harder and louder, angry perhaps, with what she'd done, with what she'd let happen. Was this her fault? She had flashes of Davy in the pub. Her hand on his. Her lips against his cheek. Her smiling as he handed her a drink. Then a violent image of her torn underwear. She clutched her bag tight to her. Cam couldn't see. He couldn't know. She pulled on her hem to draw her skirt as low as possible and winced at the flash of pain between her legs. She didn't want him to see her like this. She wished the sea would suck her under and swallow her whole.

'He hit me.'

Cam touched her shoulder. She flinched again then looked down to see what he was reaching for and noticed her top was torn at the neck and her bra-strap exposed. She inhaled sharply and threw up her arm to cover herself.

'I'm sorry,' Cam whispered.

Had he guessed what Davy had done? She didn't want him to know. She didn't want to be tainted and ruined. She didn't want to be this new version of her. She wanted to turn back time and have it like it was before.

CHAPTER FORTY-FOUR

Cam, 1998

Cam rocked back on his heels, head in his hands, as the full implication of what he was looking at set in: the dead body of Davy Garnett lying on the deck of his boat in a swimming pool of blood. He leant forward. Looked closely. Checked the body with the flats of his hands until he found the tear in his trousers and a deep wound in his thigh. An artery, Cam guessed. It would have taken no more than a few minutes before he bled out.

Cam glanced again at Hannah. Her eyes were tightly closed and her body trembled uncontrollably as if a low electrical charge was pulsing through her. Cam took his sleeping bag from the chest and wrapped it around her shoulders. As he did he noticed her hands were glistening with what he knew to be blood.

He had to think.

'Hannah,' he said after a moment or two, the calm to his voice belying a mushrooming fear. 'I need you to listen to me.'

'I did it.'

'Hannah.'

'I killed him, didn't I?'

Cam looked back at Davy, half expecting him to sit up, for

Geren to appear and both of them to start laughing, point at Cam and call him a gullible twat. But Davy didn't move and there was no Geren. Cam's thoughts were jumbled. He had to get a grip of the situation. The moon came out from behind a cloud and in the faint light it threw out, he noticed a smear of blood on the soft white skin of her thigh and felt a thump to his solar plexus.

'The knife was in my bag,' she whispered. 'I didn't want him to touch me. I was looking for you.' She closed her eyes. 'I thought you might be here. On your boat. He... ' Her words came in sobs. 'He tried... I said no. I did... I promise you. But he was too strong. He kept on and on... He said I... I couldn't tell... you... '

Cam stared at Davy wishing he could kill him all over again.

'I didn't mean to. He came at me... again. He... ' Her voice trailed off and her eyes unfocused, and she began to rock gently as if soothing a baby. 'I tried to help. I didn't know what to do. I couldn't stop the bleeding. He—'

'Where's the knife?'

She didn't answer him.

He put his hand on her knee and squeezed gently. 'Hannah? Where's the knife?'

She shrugged vaguely, but offered nothing else.

Cam went back to Davy's body and searched the deck with the flats of his hands, desperation growing until at last he found it, lying in the corner of the deck, up against the side of the boat. He grabbed it and instinctively touched the blade. When his fingers came away they were dark with blood.

'We need to call the police,' she said faintly.

Think, Cam. Think.

344

The incongruous sound of muted merriment, music and laughter floated through the chilled air surrounding them. It sounded like a distant land.

'Cam? The police.'

Yes. The police. But was that the right thing to do? Should they call the police? His head felt fuzzy as if it was stuffed with fabric. There was an ache behind his eyes. If they called the police, then what? She'd say he attacked her. It was self-defence in an unprovoked assault. What else could she do?

But would they believe her?

Half the town had seen her drinking and dancing, flirting, doing shots with Davy and Geren, even kissing them. They saw Cam storm out of the pub. They would hear about how he punched Nathan Cardew? Would they think she went with Davy to punish Cam? Would they believe Martin Garnett's son attacked her? If they did, would she go to prison anyway? He was dead, after all. He had no idea how the law worked, but he couldn't take the risk. Then Cam thought of Martin, lying in hospital, arm gone and in its place a sewn-up stump. He saw a flash of bone and flesh ground into yellow oilskin. He thought of Sheila. Lovely, soft Sheila, floury from baking pasties with their initials etched into them, humming a song only vaguely recognisable. How would she cope? How would she deal with discovering her son was a monster? Sitting through a court trial where his name would be mud. A funeral soured by salacious whispers. What would it do to her? What would it do to Martin?

Who would the truth help?

Nobody.

The truth was no good to any of them. It wouldn't bring

Davy back and it would destroy all their lives. He glanced at Hannah, at the silhouette of her shivering and numb, damaged irreparably.

She looked at him and the look stuck in his gut like a fishbone. Was it anger? No. Maybe blame? He could see it in her eyes. This was his fault. He never should have left her. Never should have allowed his pathetic jealousy to take control of him. If he'd stayed with her none of this would have happened. It was all his fault.

Now he had to make it better.

'We need to call the police,' she breathed again.

His mind raced. He had to get rid of Davy. Hose the boat down. Wash away the blood. Clean Hannah's hands. What about her clothes? Get her somewhere safe. It had to look like an accident. Davy was drunk. Took his boat out. Fell in.

Stupid man.

'Cam? Please. Call the police.'

'We're not calling the police.'

'But I killed him.'

'Listen to me, Hannah. I want you to do exactly what I say. I'm going to deal with it. I'll take care of you. I promise. It'll be OK. But I need you to listen and do everything I say.'

A car engine started up not far from the harbour. More noise as a group of people emerged from the pub and their drunken voices carried over to them, fading as the merrymakers walked away towards Penzance.

They didn't have long before daybreak.

If he was going to make this OK, he had to hurry.

CHAPTER FORTY-FIVE

Nathan

Did he tell you he punched me in the face and split my lip?
Nothing which followed surprised me at all.

It was easy to walk away from him. I'm not the type to
resort to violence. If you can't win an argument with words and
intellect, if you have to use your fists, you've lost. Self-control,
Hannah. That's how you measure a man. Don't get me wrong,
I was angry. More angry than I'd ever been. But I am able to
handle myself with class.

I sat in my car for a long time, going over it all in my mind,
repeating everything you said to me. You were so confused.
On one hand telling me how lovely I was and that I'd make
the perfect boyfriend. You said I was funny. You said I was
interesting.

But then you told me there was someone else.

'Who?'

'It doesn't matter.'

'I don't understand.'

'I'm sorry, Nathan.'

I didn't mean to get emotional in front of you. I was embarrassed about it, if truth be told. But that's how much you
meant to me. It felt as if you'd dug into my chest and pulled

out my heart. And what type of man had you chosen over me? A violent thug. It didn't make any sense.

I remember studying myself in the rearview mirror. My lip was swollen. There was a bruise developing on my jaw and a streak of blood crusted my chin. I thought of my sister. She'd have liked you. And you, of course, would have adored her. You reminded me of her in many ways and as I thought about her, staring at my face reflected back at me, I had the sudden and overwhelming realisation that I wasn't going to give up on you. Certainly not for a man like that.

I loved you and I was going to fight for you.

I braced myself against the chill wind and rain which had started up again and walked back down the hill into the centre of Newlyn. The pub was still full. I scanned the room, but couldn't see you, only that friend of yours acting like the common slut that she is. But there was no sign of you and there was no sign of him. It could have been the stench in the place, thick with body odour and cigarettes, or maybe it was the thought of the two of you together somewhere, but a wave of sickness swept over me. I went outside and breathed in fresh air. I don't mind admitting I was nervous of Cameron Stewart reappearing. But I told myself to be brave.

You love her. She is meant to be yours, I kept saying. *She's meant to be yours.*

A movement caught my eye. Down the road. A man moving through the lamplight into the harbour car park. It was hard to make him out – he was a distance away – but by the size of him, the way he was carrying himself, I was certain it was Stewart.

Was he on his way to meet you?

I recall hesitating. My split lip had started to pulse angrily. The image of his twisted face as he hit me came at me again and again. Would he hurt you? What if you were down there, already hurt? I couldn't walk away. Not now I knew what Stewart was capable of. What kind of man would I be to turn my back without checking you were safe?

When I got to the harbour, I was careful to keep myself concealed in the shadows, tucking myself in behind the office buildings. It was then I heard low voices. His and yours. For a while I kept still and tried to listen. But it was too hard to make out what you were saying. I crept around the edge of the building, slowly and silently, careful to keep myself hidden.

I peered around the edge and, down on the jetty, I saw him – Cameron Stewart – on a boat. It was hard to make everything out. I crept as close as I could and then, when the moon came out from behind the cloud, I saw you in the boat and a dark mass between you. Cameron Stewart was agitated. Rocking. Looking up at the sky. Something was wrong. I crept back into the shadows and watched.

A few minutes later he helped you back to the car. I took a risk, but when you were gone, I ran quickly down the jetty and peered into the boat. There was a shadowy mass. It was a man. No. It was the body of a man. A motionless body of a man who stared up at the sky with unblinking eyes. I panicked then. My heart thumped. I ran back to my hiding place. I couldn't let him see me. I couldn't let him hear me. Who knew what he would do if he discovered me?

He walked past, head lowered, arms bare, just a T-shirt wet through with freezing rain. I watched him climb into the boat.

He started the engine. It moved slowly over to another tether. Was he untying a boat? A dinghy, maybe. It was hard to be certain in the snatches of muted light. Then his boat chugged out towards the harbour wall. The second boat was being dragged behind. He disappeared through the gap in the wall and the pitch blackness swallowed him up.

I waited.

When the boat returned. There was no dinghy. He washed the boat down. Spent time doing it. Bending and getting into every crack and crevice. Then he climbed off the boat and walked like a condemned man up the jetty. When he passed my hiding place, I saw how shaken he was. His hands fluttered at his sides. His knees seemed almost unable to support his weight. He paused. Didn't move for a while. Then started up again and went back to the small red car.

'Oh, Cameron Stewart,' I whispered. 'What have you done?'

It didn't take much to work it all out. I could see it all so clearly. I should have been a detective. After he assaulted me, Stewart went back into the pub. He saw you dancing with another man. Flew into a jealous rage. He lured him down to the harbour – somewhere quiet where he knew he wouldn't be seen – and beat him to a lifeless pulp. It didn't surprise me. I'd seen the violent red mist which overwhelmed him. I moved my hand to my chin and I rubbed my aching jaw.

Moments later the car drove off, out of the car park and up the hill, away from Newlyn towards Mousehole.

I leant back against the freezing brick wall and stared up at the sky, which was growing lighter as the dawn set in. I closed my eyes and listened to the incessant roar and crash of the open sea, the gulls, a truck on the road, the sound of a couple of drunks singing tunelessly as they wandered home to their beds. When I finally stepped out of the shadows, I couldn't help but smile, and there was a definite spring in my step as I walked.

Getting you back was going to be much easier with Cameron Stewart behind bars.

CHAPTER FORTY-SIX

Hannah

Nathan blinks rapidly. 'I don't understand.'

'I killed him.'

Nathan continues to stare at me. His eyes flicker as the conviction he's held unequivocally for all these years disintegrates like ash in the wind. Watching him wrangle with what I've told him gives me a strange sense of satisfaction.

Then I look at my son and his look of childlike bewilderment as he faces everything I've fought so long to shelter him from skewers my heart.

'Hannah. I don't think—' Cam starts to speak, but I interrupt him.

'No, Cam. No more lies.' I try to reassure Alex with a smile. 'A man died. Nearly sixteen years ago. He went missing and his dinghy was found on some rocks the next day. Everybody saw him drinking. They assumed he got drunk and took his boat out. That he fell overboard and was drowned.' I pause and take a breath. 'But that's not what happened. He didn't drown. He was killed. And... ' My voice trembles. 'It was me who killed him.' I pause to gather myself. Each of them seems about to speak so I force myself to continue. 'I didn't mean to.'

Sharp fragments of that night attack me. A recollection of

the creeping horror which seeped into me as I realised what was going to happen. My utter helplessness. A flash of pain as I tried to push him off me. A moan which sounded like pleasure. The billowing sickness when he thanked me and the eerie thud as he fell on the deck.

Then the worst bit of all.

The terrifying stillness.

'He… ' I hesitate, my voice no more than a whisper. 'He forced himself on me.'

Shame sweeps over me. I've fought this shame ever since he appeared out of the shadows on the jetty. Accusatory voices in my head hounding me constantly. Why did you wear such a short skirt? And your top left nothing to the imagination. You drank too much. Dancing and flirting like that? Well, what else did you expect? But now I'm able to push them away. It wasn't me. It was him. It's taken me years to realise that he was the monster. *What ifs* plague me. What if I'd stayed at home with Cam? What if I'd left when Cam wanted to leave?

What if Davy Garnett hadn't attacked me?

'I had a knife,' I continue. 'It wasn't mine but it was in my bag. He came at me again. I told him to keep away. But he didn't… '

Cam is agonised, as if each of my words is a dart. I hear his voice repeating the same thing over and over as we lay in numbed silence in his car at Lamorna.

I shouldn't have left you.

I'm so sorry.

I stare at Alex. I can see from the look on his face he has finally pieced it all together, and now, standing on the landing in this hateful house, he knows exactly who his father is.

I open my arms to him but his eyes well with tears and he shakes his head. 'The man,' he says flatly. 'Who is he? Does he have family here?'

I think of Martin and Sheila Garnett. Sheila – lovely, stoic, gentle Sheila – who passed away from breast cancer a few years ago. I heard the news from Vicky, whose mum was one of her closest friends.

'It's so sad,' Vicky had said to me. 'She never got over Davy's death.' Then she'd lowered her voice, preparing, I knew, to deliver syrupy gossip. 'You know, Mum told me a few days ago that he didn't quit the army at all. He was thrown out. Apparently he assaulted one of the girls who worked in the barracks kitchen. Sheila only told her quite recently and swore her to secrecy. They didn't want anybody to know. Well,' Vicky said, with a sad sigh of understanding, 'I suppose you wouldn't, would you? It's not exactly the type of thing you broadcast around a small town. To be honest, there was a look about him; I didn't trust him at all. Still, poor bugger, shouldn't talk ill of the dead.'

'His mum died a few years ago,' I say. 'His father is alive. He still lives in Newlyn. He was badly injured in an accident on a fishing boat.' I glance at Cam who looks at his feet. 'The community is kind to him.' I think about the times I've seen Martin Garnett. Thin and gaunt, moving trollies at the new supermarket, his one empty sleeve pinned up as if pledging allegiance to an American flag.

'Let me get this straight.' Nathan makes an exaggerated expression of trying to understand. 'While you were with me and carrying on with him,' he gestures in the direction of Cam, 'you screwed someone else?'

Cam takes a step forward and Nathan raises his eyebrows and shakes his head disdainfully. 'Oh, here we go, coming to beat me up again, defending the honour of a cheap slut.'

There is an deafening shriek as Alex runs at Nathan. I try and grab at his arm but he yanks it out of my grip. He hurls himself at Nathan, teeth gritted, one balled fist raised to hit him. 'Don't talk about her like that.' His voice rumbles like distant thunder. 'Never – *ever* – again.'

Nathan's features settle into an amused snarl. 'You're going to hit me? Perhaps you really are Cameron Stewart's son.'

Alex draws his arm back a little further, a fire blazing in his eyes.

'Alex, it's OK,' I say. 'We all need to calm down and talk about this.'

Alex hesitates and blinks hard. Then the tension leaves his body and his arm lowers.

'*All* of us. Together.' I look first at Nathan, then Alex. 'OK?'

Alex shakes his head. 'It's not OK though, is it? It's the opposite of OK.' His eyes are reddened and brimmed with tears. 'And no amount of talking can change that.'

Then he pulls away from me and tears down the stairs. I call his name and run after him. Beg him to stop. But he's out of the front door and away from me before I'm even off the staircase. From the doorway I watch him haring out of the gate, which bangs shut behind him and swings repeatedly against the catch. My stomach churns as I scream his name. I run down the path, lean over the gate, and see his lithe figure disappearing down the lane. I shout for him again, but he ducks to his right, jumps over the drystone wall into the field, and is gone like a dog from the traps.

CHAPTER FORTY-SEVEN

Hannah

'For God's sake, leave him.'

I don't say anything, but grab my phone and jacket from the hook inside the kitchen door.

'Hannah! What are you doing? Didn't you hear me? You're not going anywhere. He'll be back, but right now you and I need to talk.'

'I heard you.'

His eyes widen at the sharpness in my tone. He opens his mouth to reply, but I speak first.

'We'll talk when he's back.'

'And if I call the police in the meantime?'

'Then I guess they'll be paying me a visit.' I attempt to keep my impatience at bay but I'm unsuccessful; I have no time for this game of Nathan's. 'But right now, I'm going to find my son, who's just heard the most horrendous thing. There's no way I'm sitting here like a hopeless idiot waiting for him again.'

Cam follows me. 'I'll help.'

'Thanks, that's—'

'*Christ!*' cries Nathan, turning his glare on Cam. 'What are you even doing here? Just leave us alone. This is between me and my wife.' He turns back to me, 'Hannah, we need to talk—'

I fix Nathan with a hard, unbending stare. 'First, you are going to help me find him,' I say through gritted teeth.

'For God's sake, this is what he does. It's his *thing*. Running away for attention. He'll come back when he's blown off steam.'

'Nathan, he ran off in a dreadful state. He needs us. You are his father, the man who brought Alex up. Not Cam. Not Davy Garnett. *You*. Please help me find him. Stop thinking about your bruised pride and help me. When he's back we'll talk. God knows I want to talk about everything as much as you do, but not until I've got my son home safely.'

The tension is palpable. It's remarkable how much hatred is contained in this small area. The calm of last night on the hidden beach feels a million years ago. Here, now, is the culmination of years of lies and guilt and shame all stemming from what Davy Garnett did to me. I've agonised over what happened, tried to relive it, willed time to reverse so I could prevent the sequence unfolding. For so long I blamed myself, feeling pity, guilt, sorrow even, for what happened to him. But nobody made Davy Garnett do what he did, and the consequences changed the course of my life. Now I have an opportunity to reclaim whoever it is I am. Behind bars or not, one thing I know, things are going to change again. I'm going to reconstruct myself sinew by sinew until I'm as near to restored as possible.

'I'll follow him into the fields. Nathan, take your car and drive down to the station. Make sure he's not there. Can you head to Newlyn, Cam? There's a chance he'll go looking for Martin.'

I don't wait for them to answer before walking out of the

door. It crosses my mind briefly that perhaps they might fight, but frankly I don't care if they do or they don't. Right now they can tear each other limb from limb. All I want to do is find Alex.

As I climb the stile and follow the direction Alex headed in, my mind begins to whir. Things would have been so different if we'd called the police that night like I'd wanted to. That night is blurred in parts, some of the facts are hazy, some gone, others exaggerated, possibly beyond reality, but I'm not sure why I let Cam do what he did. Taking Davy and his dinghy out to sea, making it look like an accident, concealing the truth despite me asking him to call the police again and again.

As I stare down over the fields towards St Michael's Mount, the sea shimmering silver, so still, like a painting, I recall the words Cam spoke from beside the bloody body of Davy Garnett.

'I'll take care of you.'

The same words Nathan said to me when I sent Cam away, terrified, shell-shocked, my body still sore, days after, from where Davy Garnett forced himself on me.

I'll take care of you.

All those times I'd fantasised I was married to Cam Stewart. Pretending it was him I shared a house with, cooked for, made love to. Perhaps even in the cave on our hidden beach I had that thought in the back of my head, that I'd leave Nathan and end up with Cam. But as I follow the footpath across the fields in the direction of Penzance, it isn't a new life with Cam I'm craving: it's my freedom. I don't want to be taken care of anymore. I want to make my own choices and fix my own mistakes. I want to be the mother my son deserves and someone he can be proud of.

My phone rings. I look down at the screen and see Vicky's name. I blanch as Phil's wearied irritation snakes through me.

You don't need Hannah's shit in your life.

I turn the call off, unwilling to load her with yet more of my shit, more truths I should have told her, further admission that I'd cut her out of so much of my life. I've always wondered if I should have told her everything and I know what a mistake I made in not doing so. Having her understanding, advice and guidance would have been a lifeline, not to mention explaining why I live a life she cannot comprehend.

But at the time, as hard as it was, I couldn't do it.

Once Cam had disposed of the body I had no choice but to keep the truth hidden from everybody. How could I have expected her to keep my secret and not go to the police? I wouldn't have put that on her. To keep Cam – and myself – out of prison we had to stay quiet. Nobody could know but the two of us. Now the truth is out she is going to know about it. The thought makes me weak.

My phone buzzes in my hand. It's a text from her.

Alex called me. Was in real state. He wants to see your mum. I picked him up and we're heading to Treliske now. He made me promise not to tell you. What's happened? If you need a cab, I'll pay when you get to hospital. Hope all OK? Vx

My lungs burn with the exertion of running as I trip and stumble over tufts of grass on the way back across the fields.

Neither Nathan or Cam are at the house when I get there. I consider calling Cam and not Nathan, but Nathan deserves to see Alex; he is after all the only father he's had in his life. Panting heavily, I dial the number and he answers at the first ring.

'He's at the Treliske,' I say breathlessly.

'He's hurt?'

'No, he went to see Mum. Can you come back and drive me there?'

For a moment I think Nathan might tell me he's going straight there without me but he doesn't, and in a little over five minutes he's turning his car into the driveway.

He drives five miles an hour beneath the speed limit, hands at ten to two, feeding the steering wheel as he turns, and checking his mirrors continuously. I have to bite my tongue to stop myself yelling at him to drive faster. I can feel him waiting for me to talk, expecting, I'm sure, profuse apologies and desperate excuses. No doubt he'd like to see me break down and plead for forgiveness or beg him not to go to the police. But I do none of this. Instead, I sit in silence and I know it's killing him. A couple of times he draws breath as if to speak, but I keep my head turned resolutely away from him, tapping my finger rapidly against my lip, my stare fixed on the world beyond the confines of the car.

Finally, the silence is too much for him. 'So you have nothing to say?'

I don't reply.

'Why didn't you tell me what that man did to you?' His concern is contaminated with a hint of disgust, like a drop of poison in sweetened tea. 'If you had, then maybe... '

I close my eyes and block him out as I have done so many times. As his voice drifts away from me, I take myself to a windy clifftop. I'm walking Cass. As soon as she comes into my head, however, a vivid image of her lying dead in a ditch somewhere kicks the air from me. I flick my eyes open but can still see her, her eyes turned yellow and glassy by the rat poison, her lips retracted to reveal her teeth like the macabre masks on the voles left rotting in the bin.

'Are you even listening to me?'

'Yes,' I lie. 'Of course.'

'Tell me then, how are we going to move on from this? If I go to the police—'

'You won't.'

'Oh?' he says. 'And you're sure about that?'

'No,' I say after a moment or two. 'But why would you risk losing your job? Maybe even prison? Imagine the headlines in the newspapers. Imagine what the people at the council would think? Their award-winning citizen sent down for helping to conceal a murder.'

He answers with a stony glower. 'So, what? We're just going to carry on as normal?'

This word is so comical I can't help emitting a sharp explosive laugh. '*Normal?*' I turn in the seat so I'm looking directly at him. 'Are you joking? Nothing about any of this is – or ever has been – *normal*.'

His hands grip the steering wheel tightly. I can clearly see him trying to formulate a reply that will twist and manipulate what I've said. I wonder if whatever he's constructing has him painted as hero or victim.

I don't wait to find out. 'I don't love you, Nathan.'

He lets out a scoff, loud and dismissive.

'I never have.'

'That's not true.'

'Nathan, listen to me. It was all a lie. From that moment you sat on my bed – when my body was aching and sore from what Davy did to me, my mind clouded with guilt and confusion over what I did to him – and told me you'd seen Cam kill a man. I lied when I told you I loved you. I lied to keep Cam out of prison. He didn't deserve to be punished. I did. Everything up until this morning has been a lie. Every time we had sex. Every time I smiled. Every time I agreed with you. Our marriage is my punishment for what I did.'

He shakes his head as if trying to dislodge my words. His face moves through a range of emotions from surprise, to shock, to pain. Should I feel sympathy? Possibly. But I don't. Not a whisper of it. Perhaps this isn't fair. Perhaps Nathan did his best, a damaged man plagued by his own demons, who believed himself to be a good husband to a girl who needed saving. Perhaps it was me who manipulated him. After all, as I've said all along, I took his deal willingly.

My freedom for Cam's.

'You have a good life with me.' Nathan stares at the road ahead. 'I've provided for you and provided for your son who I treated as my own. Even when I found out he wasn't mine. I could have thrown you both out on the streets, but I didn't. And now you call our marriage a punishment?' He glances at me and I see his fight is returning. 'A beautiful house? Clothes and meals out? Presents. Flowers. A husband who treats you like a princess? You think that's a *punishment*? Do you know how many women would swap their life for yours?'

The face of the woman from the award ceremony sidles into my head, her eyes consuming my husband as she fiddles with her necklace, the flesh on her finger fattened around her dulled wedding ring.

'What about the money?' I'm appalled to hear my voice wavering as the force I'd mustered leaks out of me. 'You took my credit card.'

He furrows his brow. 'Do I need to tell you again how terrifying it was when you left in the middle of the night with your depression running ragged. You were nearing suicidal. I couldn't trust you to look after yourself. Without a credit card I knew you couldn't try and run again. All I wanted to do was keep you – and Alex – safe. What kind of a husband would have done nothing? Did I do the right thing? Maybe not. Perhaps it was an overreaction, but I was scared of losing you. Terrified you'd do something stupid and endanger yourself. I was at a loss. Watching you struggle like you did was agonising. Do you know what it's like to see somebody you love in that kind of state? Taking away your access to money was my way of reducing the risk you posed to yourself.'

I'm reminded of the paralysing postnatal depression which came after Alex was born. Days and nights lost in a fug. I was petrified in case I saw anything of Davy Garnett in this child. Paranoia set in. What if I walked past Sheila and she recognised him in Alex? What if she became suspicious? I was hounded by nightmares of Davy's waterlogged body, his fingers trying to grab me, his blood turning the whole sea scarlet. I was a mess, Nathan's right about that, and at the time I could barely dress myself let alone manage money.

My head pounds as I become confused.

Nathan slows and flicks the indictor on and waits to turn into the hospital. He circles the car park, looking for a space, and when he finds one he parks and switches the engine off.

'All I've ever wanted,' he says softly, turning in his seat, and taking hold of my hand, 'is to take care of you. You aren't strong enough to look after yourself. You *need* me to take care of you.'

His words act like a defibrillator and I feel a surge of energy. I recall all those times he thrust into me, my body dry and unresponsive, biting the pillow to keep myself quiet. I recall the time he demanded nine pence change back. How again and again he belittled me and twisted my words. I recall with an aching heart all the friends he drove away.

'I'm leaving you.'

'What?'

'You and me. This.' I gesture around us with my hands. 'Whatever this is. It's over.'

He swallows and needles his eyes into me. 'And your mother? How do you think you'll pay for the care she needs without a penny from me?'

The change from desperate, loving husband to vindictive manipulator happens in the blink of an eye. I marvel at how good he is at concealing himself. He is as good a liar as I am.

'I'll get a job.'

His burst of laughter is sharp and unkind. 'Good luck with that! Not too many jobs out there for a middle-aged woman with a couple of GCSEs and no A levels, who hasn't had a job for fifteen years and only ever worked in her daddy's bakery.'

The air was rancid with malicious victory.

'Thank you,' I say, as I open the car door and get out. 'You've made this easy for me.'

When I get to the hospital entrance, I glance backwards and see his car pulling out on to the main road and accelerating away, and as I push through the revolving door I am filled with an intoxicating sense of freedom.

CHAPTER FORTY-EIGHT

Hannah

The first person I see as I walk on to the ward is Vicky. She is sitting on the chairs near the reception holding a plastic cup, her hands clutched around it as if she is huddling for warmth. I falter. Last time I spoke to her she sounded so angry, so disappointed, and facing her now fills me with an ominous dread. What if she rejects me? What if she acknowledges me briefly then leaves? But before I have an opportunity to say her name, she's caught sight of me. She places her cup on the floor and gets up and runs to me with outstretched arms.

'I'm so sorry,' she says, squeezing me in a python-like embrace. 'I said awful things to you. I've been in pieces. I've been feeling sick with worry.' She lets go of me and smiles, kissing my cheek. 'I was just so cross with Nathan. And I couldn't stop thinking about how he'd ruined my weekend, and even though Phil kept telling me to forget about it, I couldn't. I was fuming. But then he told me he thought you were with me and I felt like such an idiot and, well, I was hurt.' She lowered her eyes. 'And I felt guilty too, because I knew you'd get it in the neck when he found out you'd lied to him.'

'You were right to be cross. It was a shitty thing I did and you have nothing to be sorry about. It's me who should be sorry. I should have told you and I never should have lied to you. There's a lot I should have told you.'

Even as I say the words, I know I won't tell her about Davy and what happened. I know Nathan won't. Nor will Cam. I can't be sure what Alex will want to do. It'll be up to him and I won't try to influence him, but I have a suspicion he'll stay quiet. Davy Garnett's bones will remain lost at sea and our secret will stay hidden with them. Too many years have passed and it helps nobody for Cam and I to end up in prison. Does this make me a bad person? I suspect it probably does. Perhaps, one day, when Alex is grown up and Martin has passed on and is safe from the distress and scandal, perhaps then it will be time.

Or perhaps not.

'Over a bottle of wine, I think,' Vicky says, rubbing my arm. 'Right now you need to be with Alex. He's so upset, but he wouldn't tell me why.'

'He had some difficult news.'

She waits for me to expand, but I don't. It's strange but I don't feel any guilt about not telling her. It's as if I'm at peace with it now. There was only one person who had to know the truth, only one person it's relevant to, and that's Alex. 'Something else to discuss over wine,' I say.

'You and your secrets.'

'How about being the first to know I'm leaving him?'

'Leaving who? *Nathan?*'

I nod and, though she does her best to mask it, her pleasure is palpable. But then her smile fades and she folds her arms and gives me a hard stare. 'Leaving him to be with Cam Stewart?'

Her question surprises me and I falter as I search for the words to answer her.

'Sorry,' she says. 'It's none of my business.'

'No. No, it's fine.' I hesitate. 'No. Not to be with Cam.' And it's true. I don't want to be with Cam. 'To be honest I'm looking forward to giving men a wide berth for a bit.'

She smiles, and I can see her holding her tongue, and realise there are lots of thoughts and feelings and opinions she's keeping from me in return. 'Look, if you and Alex need somewhere, you're welcome at ours for as long as you need. And if you need any money, a loan or something, just ask.'

We hug each other and when she steps away from me, she dries the corners of her eyes with her sleeve and laughs. 'God, look at us. Let's not argue ever again, OK?'

I laugh through my own tears and nod.

'Right, I'll be in the car park when you're ready to go.'

'Haven't you got to get back to the kids?'

'Phil's working from home. He can pick them up. They like that. He buys them sweets.'

As I walk away from Vicky and down the corridor thick with disinfectant and institutional food, my nerves jangle and grate. How can I face Alex? What if everything he's heard has turned him against me? I would understand if that was the case, but even so, if he rejects me, what on earth will I do?

My mother's privacy curtain is drawn around her cubicle. I approach quietly and peer though the gap in the tired, blue fabric. My heart splinters when I see them together. They are serene, connected, like two subjects in a painting called *Tenderness*. Alex has pulled a chair over and is sitting with her hand held in his. The oxygen mask has gone from her face and

369

her expression is peaceful; aware, I'm certain, that her grandson is with her. It's then I notice the storm glass, the delicate glass bird I took from her room at Heamoor, sitting on her bedside table beside a posy of flowers in a small vase.

As I step through the curtain I clear my throat. I'm surprised at how nervous I am and how terrified of rejection. When he looks at me my stomach clenches, his face is red and puffy, cheeks burning hot from crying, and clearly exhausted.

I sit at the foot of Mum's bed and he drops his head, resting it on top of her frail hand. I reach out and rub his shoulder, wondering at how difficult it is to speak.

'Are you OK?'

He turns his head, and tries to smile. His shoulders shrug imperceptibly and he sniffs.

I nod in the direction of the little glass bird, the crystals inside suspended like a moment in time. 'Did you bring this to her?'

He glances at the bird then nods. 'I saw it at home. I know how much she loves it and I thought it would make her happy. You can take it back if you want.'

I bite back tears. 'No. Let's keep it here with her.'

We are quiet for a while, until finally, he says, 'Mum?'

'Yes?'

'I need to ask you something and I need you to tell me the truth.'

There is a breathless quavering to his voice, as if the words hovering on his lips are so terrifying they're causing him actual physical harm, and it breaks me in two.

'Of course.' I'm trying my best to disguise my trembling nerves, but I know I'm not managing it. 'Ask me anything.'

He glances at my mother then back at me and I watch as he plucks up the courage to spit the toxic words from his mouth.

'I need to know… ' His voice is so quiet. 'Do you hate me? Because if you do, I'd understand.'

His words slam into me. '*Hate* you? How could I possibly hate you?'

'Because… ' Alex hesitates. I watch him squeeze my mother's hand for reassurance, and wonder how much of it he's told her peaceful sleeping figure, the perfect confidante. 'Because of *him*.'

'Oh, Alex, you must never think that, do you hear me? Never. *Hate* you?' I put my arms around him and pull him gently in towards me. 'There is nothing in this entire world I love, or have ever loved, more than you.'

He nods but the sadness seems to intensify rather than ease. He looks down at his hand and watches his fingers stroking Mum's paper skin. 'Do you,' he says so softly I can barely hear him, 'ever wish you'd got rid of me?' He hesitates, his eyes flicking briefly up to mine. 'When you found out you were pregnant. You must have thought about it. Do you ever wish you had?'

I don't answer him straight away. He wants the truth and the truth is I did consider it a few times at the beginning of the pregnancy. I think if I'd been less scared and felt less alone, then there's a possibility I might have. But it wasn't that easy. There was a part of me that thought if I just ignored it, pretended it wasn't happening, then perhaps the pregnancy would just go away. Of course it didn't, and as my stomach swelled it was hard to separate what was happening inside me from what

Davy Garnett did. But when Alex was born, things changed. Something kicked in. Perhaps the helplessness of this little tiny creature. There was nothing evil about him. And, though it surprised me, looking at my baby didn't remind me of anything bad, instead it dulled the pain. I had something – someone – to take my mind off it all. A greater purpose.

'No. I have never wished I got rid of you. As soon as you came into this world, the moment the midwife put you in my arms, I knew deep inside me you were supposed to be here. I believe you are my guardian angel and I believe it with my whole heart. You were given to me to give me something to live for,' I whisper. 'I'm not sure I'd still be here if it wasn't for you. You are the most important thing in my life.'

He wipes fresh tears from his cheeks. 'I was looking in the mirror earlier and wondering if I look like him. If I have his eyes or his nose? If we have the same colour hair?' His eyes are wide and limpid, black eyelashes dampened by tears. 'Do you remember it every time you see me? When you look at me do you see… *him*? You see? I don't know how you can't hate me. How can you not?'

Each word stings like a wasp and a lump of emotion lodges in my throat. 'Listen to me, Alex. After that hellish night, I thought my life was over. Literally over. I was like a zombie. I went through the motions of living. I ate and slept, washed and dressed and cooked. And on more than one occasion I thought about going down to the cliffs and ending it all. But then you came along and you were everything. For I while I was depressed, suffering mentally, but then slowly you brought light back into my life and for the first time in almost a year everything made a bit more sense. When you were born

I was no longer alone, and you were this beautiful, *beautiful* thing amongst all the ugliness.'

Tears fall like raindrops on to his lap.

'I didn't think about whose child you were. That became irrelevant. You were a gift and you saved me.'

I pull him close to me again and rest my chin on his head, then close my eyes and recall the softness of him when he was a baby. His smell. How helpless and vulnerable he was.

How pure.

'And now, fifteen years later, look at you,' I say as I lean back from him and brush his damp hair from his eyes. 'You've grown into the most wonderful young man, brave and loyal, and you make me so proud. So, no, when I look at you I don't see him. When I look at you all the trauma and pain and guilt which suffocates me disappears.'

I smile and lift his lowered chin with my finger so he's forced to look at me.

'But what if I'm like him? What if I'm bad?'

'You aren't bad. You're the opposite of bad. You're a good and kind and gentle person. You're the type of boy who thinks to find his grandmother photographs to make her happy and picks her flowers and brings her a little glass storm bird to watch over her. You are loved by everybody who meets you. You have nothing to worry about. Do you understand?'

He purses his lips and sighs, unconvinced, as he dries his eyes with his sleeve.

'I promise you, Alex. You aren't bad.'

'But… ' His voice has become strangled again. 'But… back there, I had these… these *thoughts*. When I went for him, I… I wanted to kill him.'

A laugh explodes from me. 'Oh, sweetheart,' I say softly. 'I've lost count of the times I've wanted to kill him. I've got close a few times. Once I fetched a carton of his rat poison from the greenhouse and tipped it all into a stew I was cooking. For about an hour I fantasised about him eating it, mouthful by mouthful, swallowing the lot, then keeling over, face first in what was left of it. Then I threw the whole lot away and started again. Made it exactly the same, but left out the poison.'

He regards me with a furrowed brow, trying to work out if I'm joking or not. I laugh as if I am and wink. At that moment, my phone starts vibrating in my pocket. When I look at the screen, it's a number I don't recognise. 'Am I allowed to answer it on the ward?'

Alex shrugs so I accept the call.

'Hello?' I say, keeping my voice down.

'Mrs Cardew?'

'Speaking.'

'It's Hayle Veterinary here.'

My heart skips a beat. 'Yes?'

'We have a dog here. Her chip is registered to you. Have you lost your dog?'

'Yes. Yes, we have. Cass. A collie cross with a wall eye. Is she hurt?'

'Somebody's brought her in. I'll be honest, she's not great, she's eaten some sort of poison, but she's in with the vet at the moment.'

'Oh my god,' I breathe. 'Will she be OK?'

For a heart-stopping moment I expect the woman on the end of the phone to tell me Cass won't make it, but then she says, 'Yes, we think so. But I don't want to get your hopes up. We'll know more once the vet's finished.'

'Do you know where she was found?'

'No, the man didn't say. Just that he'd been out walking and discovered her. He didn't stay long, just dropped her in at reception and left.'

CHAPTER FORTY-NINE

Cam

Cam walks down through the centre of Newlyn in the direction of the harbour. It's surreal to be back but at the same time more comforting than he could have imagined. The warmth of the sun on his back, the seagulls screeching, and the potent smell of fish mixed with engine oil is as familiar as his own reflection. He stops as he passes the bakery and stares in through the window. It's like a museum with nothing changed in fifteen years. The saffron buns, bright yellow and studded with blackcurrants, are lined up next to sugary doughnuts and golden pasties. It could be a photograph from the past. He pictures her standing behind the counter and catching sight of him. He sees her clearly, smiling at him, waving, gesturing she'll be out in five, before blowing him a kiss.

On the corner, a little further down the road, is The Packhorse. The sight of its sign, swaying in the breeze coming up off the sea, brings a mix of memories and emotions. So many evenings spent in that place sinking pints with his mates like there was no tomorrow. Dancing and singing tunelessly, words slurring, arms looped around the necks of other fishermen. He pauses outside the pub, and hears the sound of his fist making contact with Nathan Cardew's jaw and winces at the memory, wishing he could erase it. He remembers kissing Hannah there, her leaning against the wall, him resting both hands either side of her, forgotten cigarettes burning to nothing in their fingers.

He walks on and comes to the main road with the harbour and pier in front of him. The feelings inside him grow tight as he has a flash of himself, young and angry, high on the trauma of that ill-fated fishing trip and piercing jealousy, running up the hill, away from Newlyn. Away from Hannah. He shoves his hands into his pockets and anxiety floods him, the *if onlys* jostle for attention. If only he hadn't run off. If only he'd gone to his boat instead. If only he'd stayed at home, had a bath, and got some sleep.

If only…

The port is bustling with boats coming in, fishermen loading supplies in preparation for trips, hosing down decks, stacking crates laden with ice and fish on to trollies, some weary, some laughing and joshing.

Cam walks down the jetty where he used to keep his boat. He remembers that night in the freezing cold when he saw the body of wretched Davy Garnett slumped on the deck. When he knelt beside him and made the decision to dump him in the unlit waters. He recalls his frozen fingers struggling to undo the knot on the dinghy's tether, waves rolling high, then setting her free and watching as the tiny vessel faded into the blackness. Davy's body had been hard to manoeuvre, so heavy, his pockets stuffed with fishing leads, and he'd struggled to tip him over the edge of the boat, the splash barely audible against the roar of the furious sea. He'd stared at the scrimshaw knife in his hand, its delicate carvings, Davy's death smeared all over its shining blade. Cam had hurled it into the darkness and pictured it falling downwards like an autumn leaf to settle in the sand and seaweed not far from Davy's body. Slim would ask him a few days later where the knife was.

'I've been scared of telling you,' Cam had said, flushed red and jittery. 'I lost it. Had it in my pocket to give to you, but got drunk and it fell out. I'm sorry. I'm really sorry.'

Slim had shrugged. 'Didn't bring much luck, did it? No doubt it's best wherever it is.'

Cam turns back up the jetty and heads along the pier where the trawlers are tied. When he nears the first boat he sees a man beside it, on the shore, sitting on an upturned crate, sewing up a torn net.

'Have you seen a young lad?' Cam asks him. 'About fifteen. Skinny. Black jeans. T-shirt.'

'Sorry, mate,' the man says, not looking up from his work.

Cam walks on to the next trawler. It's shiny and well cared for, the freshly painted hull gleams in the sunshine and the windows are polished without a smear of salt scale. The boat's name, *The Octopus,* is written in immaculate black cursive. It crosses his mind this is an odd name for a boat, but he'd come across plenty stranger. The man up on deck has a spanner in hand, and is occupied with the hatch, repeatedly lifting it and lowering it, investigating, Cam imagines, a faulty hinge.

Cam halts beneath the boat and calls up. The man stops what he's doing and leans over the rail. 'Can I help you?'

'I'm looking for a boy. He's done a runner and his mum's worried. You seen him? He's wearing black jeans—'

'Jesus,' the man says, whistling through his teeth. 'Is that Cam Stewart?'

Cam does a double take and squints through the sunlight,

lifting a hand to shield his eyes. The man laughs, climbs the rail, and jumps down on to the dock, landing lightly on his feet.

'Fuck me, Cam Stewart!' He walks towards Cam and takes his cap off, stroking back his hair to smooth it. 'It's Lawrie? Lawrie Mould? *Fuck*. Cam Stewart.'

Cam smiles. 'Young Lawrence Mould?'

Lawrie laughs and steps close to Cam, then embraces him warmly, before stepping back and shaking his head in disbelief. 'Cam Stewart, as I live and breathe!'

'Lawrie Mould,' Cam says again. 'Well, I never.' Cam wouldn't have recognised Lawrie had he passed him in the street. He's tanned and fit, filled out, with longer hair which shows no signs of thinning. He's wearing jeans and a clean, ironed shirt. 'Blimey. Look at you. All grown up.'

'You sound like my grandma!' Lawrie says with a laugh. 'Jesus, Cam. It's good to see you. I heard they all lost touch with you when you left. I'd have liked to say goodbye, but I know how these things are. Geren was here for a few years, but he moved a while back now. Went to Wales, I think, and found work at a car plant in Bridgend.'

Cam smiles sadly. His friendship with Geren never recovered. Geren was too cut up about Davy for Cam to be anywhere near him. The guilt was too much. Remembering him now, the laughs they had, the years of friendship they shared, he realises how much he misses him.

'Did he have a boy or a girl?' Cam asks. Hearing it out loud, it's an odd question and Cam looks at his feet, his cheeks flushing.

'Boy. Then twin girls. You still fishing?'

'Me? No. Haven't fished since I left.' Cam gestures at the boat behind Lawrie. 'Guess you are though?'

Lawrie winks at Cam. 'You're looking at Newlyn's top grossing skipper for the last two years.' He smiles. 'Bet you wouldn't have put money on that?'

Cam laughs. 'I'd be lying if I said I would.' He tries to keep the smile on his face, but it's hard. He has a flash of the open seas, the sun and the seagulls chasing the boat, the waves flat and calm and stretching out for thousands of miles. 'I'm happy for you, Lawrie. You deserve it. And, you know, you look well.'

'I am,' Lawrie said. 'I got a great crew. Good men. Two kids at home. Boys. Little rascals. My wife doesn't want them to fish, but I've got other plans.' He stops himself and his face falls serious. 'Shit, it's good to see you.' He nods and sniffs, puts his cap back on and adjusts it. 'You know, it's all down to you, this. Some of it anyways.'

Cam isn't sure what he means. 'Me? How?'

'The advice you gave me.'

'I gave you advice? And you took it? Jesus, you fool.'

Lawrie Mould laughs. 'You were everything I wanted to be. That night of the accident? You were just, I don't know, so calm. You got on with it, knew what you had to do, didn't panic. I watched you and you never lost it once. Your head stayed clear and you looked out for all of us. And what you said to me, about making it as a fisherman, telling the barmaid I saved Martin's life. I don't know. I guess it struck a chord in me. You gave me purpose and made me realise I wasn't a loser and that I could do it. You and that bloody octopus. You changed my life.'

'I forgot about that octopus. In your bed, wasn't it?'

'It was a bit of a turning point, I suppose. The moment I grew up.' Lawrie smiles bashfully and his cheeks flush pink.

'Ah, listen to me going on. I sound like a proper twat.' He held his hand out and Cam shook it. 'Look, seriously, it's good to see you, and if you ever want to fish in Newlyn again, well, you've a place on my boat. Just say the word.'

'Those days are over, my friend.'

'Over or not, you know where I am. And the money's good at the moment.' He raises his eyebrows and nodded. 'All hail the hake.' He winks then climbs back on to his boat. 'I'll tell the lad you're looking for him if I see him.'

Cam raises a hand and the two exchange a look of mutual respect.

Hannah's text comes through as he walks back up to his car, which is parked in the small car park behind the pub.

Found him. Cass too. All good.

He smiles and reliefs floods him as he texts back.

Where are you? I'll come and get you.

He carries on walking, head down, eyes locked to his phone screen, waiting for a reply. But none comes. When he gets to the car, he opens the door, and climbs in. A moment later the phone rings. It's Hannah. He smiles and answers the call.

'Look, I'm at the hospital. I can't talk for long. Alex came to see Mum,' she says. 'Vicky's going to drive us to get Cass then take us home.'

'Can I see you later?'

There is a hesitation on the end of the phone. He rests his head back against the headrest and mouths silent swear words.

The hesitation, though only for a beat, tells him all he needs to know.

'You can't be staying with him,' he says softly.

'Cam,' she says, and he girds himself for her rejecting him all over again. 'I'm not staying. I'm leaving him, but I need some time on my own.'

'But there's still something there. I know you feel it too.'

'I'm not in that place. We can't go backwards and start from where we left off. We're different people now. First and foremost I'm a mother and I need to concentrate on Alex.' She pauses. 'On myself, too.'

He doesn't trust himself to speak.

'Cam? Do you understand?' she asks.

No, a voice inside him screams. I don't understand any of it. I love you and I never stopped loving you. I've loved you since the first time we met, since you brushed your finger against mine in the cinema.

But he can't put this on her. Words Martin Garnett used to say ring in his ears like a bell. 'Lad, if you love someone, set them free. If she comes back, she's yours; if she doesn't, she never was.'

'I understand,' he manages to say.

She is silent for a bit. Is she crying? Has she changed her mind? Is she having second thoughts?

'When are you leaving for Reading?'

He breathes in and rubs his face. 'I was thinking of hanging around for a bit. The flat in Reading's a shithole and the council are trying to evict me anyway. I've missed Cornwall and Newlyn. I thought I might see if there's any work going here.' He pauses. 'I mean, if that's OK with you?'

'Of course it is. We only have one life and we've wasted enough already. You should definitely stay here. This is where you belong,' she says. 'Cam?' she adds after a hesitation.

'Yes?'

'I hope things work out for you. Maybe see you around for a drink some time?'

'Maybe.'

'Take care of yourself.'

'And you.'

Then the phone goes dead.

He pulls out his wallet and retrieves the photo of them taken on the dock on that happy day, laughing and in love, free as birds without a care in the world.

He strokes his thumb over her face.

'*My a'th kar.*'

Then he slides the photograph back into his wallet and starts the engine.

CHAPTER FIFTY

Hannah

Cass runs along the beach ahead of us. It's March. Nine months have passed since I closed the door on Trevose House and its pervasive air of death and confinement. Though not without problems, and frequent bouts of self-doubt that leave me breathless, overall things have been easier than I, or Nathan, would have predicted.

Three days ago Alex told me he's never been happier. He used those exact words and hearing them made my heart sing. He's changed his plans – Nathan's plans – to study law and is set on becoming a vet. It's given him purpose. He's working hard at school and doing really well. In fact, he's flourishing. It was the vet who saved Cass who inspired him.

Cass was very poorly when she arrived at the vet's, weak and convulsing and struggling to breathe. They said it was lucky she got to them when she did. A few more hours and the poison would have killed her. I asked the receptionist if the man who brought her in had given her his name and phone number so I could thank him. But he left no contact details. When I asked what he looked like, she smiled, remembering, perhaps, a flirtation with the dashing, compassionate stranger who'd carried Cass in. Good-looking, she said, slim, around forty-years-old with dark hair, coloured ash at the edges. Very clean. Dressed nicely. Polite too. Oh, she said, and he drove a nice car. An Audi, she thought. Or maybe a BMW?

When she thanked him he'd smiled and said, 'Nothing that any decent member of the community wouldn't do.'

A shame, she said, that he hadn't left his number.

We are at the beach in Wherrytown for a picnic to mark my dad's birthday. The weather is fresh and cool, the sky blue, and the sun is bouncing off the pebbles and turning them from the drab brown I know they are to silver. Cass bounds in and out of the waves, snapping happily at the spray, and trying to find the stones which Alex is throwing for her.

Even after these few short months, I already feel more like my old self, more connected to my past, and freer. I've put some weight on and cut my hair. My skin is clear and healthy from daily walks by the sea, and I try to avoid routine as much as possible. I never eat lamb on a Tuesday.

I have a job. I'm working in a café overlooking the wide, golden beach at Praa Sands. It's easy to get to by bus. I haven't braved driving lessons yet, though when I've saved enough money, it's on my list. The work is straightforward enough, the pay isn't bad, and there are tips which are shared between the staff. The others tell me that tips are good over the summer. The people I work with are lovely and I'm beginning to make friends. Last week I even went for a drink with a few after work, and the owner of the café, a middle-aged hippie with a wide smile and tie-dyed trousers, has asked me to join her book club. They only serve vegan snacks, she told me. But there's wine, of course. When I imagine what Nathan would think of her, I smile.

Alex and I sit on the wall and I unpack the picnic we put together this morning. Chelsea buns from the bakery in Newlyn and pasties. Hopeful young seagulls with mottled feathers hop about near us, waiting and watching for carelessly discarded tidbits. I pass Alex a bottle of water. He drinks and passes it back.

'Happy birthday, Granddad,' Alex says, looking up at the gulls who are wheeling above us.

When I left Nathan, we stayed with Vicky and Phil for a month or so. Phil was kind and welcoming, but was quick to offer to drive our stuff to the flat on the outskirts of Camborne when it was time to go. The flat was pretty grotty when we got the keys, but it's ours and I loved it from the first night we spent there. Vicky helped us give it a lick of cream paint and I made curtains with some material she picked up from a discount fabric sale in Falmouth. Cass sleeps in with Alex, supposedly in a basket in the corner of his room, but as soon as he thinks I've turned in, he pats the bed and she jumps up beside him. Some nights, when I can't sleep, I stare at them from the doorway. The sight of the two of them warms me to my bones.

According to my solicitor I am entitled to half of everything Nathan owns. It's complicated because he doesn't own the house. It's still in his mother's name. The solicitor seemed concerned about that, but I don't care. If it was up to me I'd take no money at all. It feels like blood money. Vicky has told be to stop being an idiot.

'Think of it as back pay.'

I will put anything I get into savings for Alex. My mother is happy. The home the council put her into isn't as bad as I'd feared. The view out of her window isn't as lovely as the rose garden at Heamoor as it looks out over the car park, but there's a tree right outside. I hung a bird-feeder filled with peanuts and lard in the branches and she sits in her chair and watches them for hours. I visit every day and help out when I'm there: empty the bins, freshen the place up, take her soups and casseroles I've made for her. She struggles with speech and can become frustrated, but mostly she seems content. The little bird, my storm glass, sits on her window ledge and keeps her company when I'm not there.

Two weeks ago, Nathan sat outside the flat at night for four hours. It's not the first time. He parks across the road. He has a different car now, a navy Range Rover, but it was him without a doubt. I concealed myself behind the curtain and watched him. He didn't move a muscle. Eyes bolted to the front door. Hand tapping the steering wheel non-stop. Last week I found a bunch of flowers on the doorstep. No note. Roses – pink and white – tied with a purple ribbon. I unceremoniously dumped them straight in the wheelie bin.

Alex found them and asked who gave them to me and why I'd chucked them away. My instinct was to lie and tell him they were nothing to do with me, that someone had shoved them into our bin, maybe a disgruntled girlfriend not interested in the empty gestures of her cheating boyfriend. But I don't lie to my son anymore. I vowed I wouldn't in the hospital that day. He is worth more than that. It's worrying how often I have to stop myself lying. It's as if, after years and years of dishonesty, it became my default. It seems to be getting easier and certainly the truth is becoming less intimidating.

'No note,' I'd said to him. 'But I'm pretty sure they're from Nathan.'

Alex nodded. 'Right place for them then.'

Cass barks on the shingle below us. With a pasty in one hand, Alex jumps off the wall and, as he eats, he searches for a piece of driftwood. When he finds what he's looking for he draws his arm back and throws it as far along the beach as he can. Cass bounds after it, scoops it up in her mouth and runs a huge circle around him. I laugh and watch them tear off down to the water's edge.

There is a shout. My name. I turn and he waves at me and walks down the steps from the road. Alex spots him and waves at him. Cass spots him and bounds over to greet him, jumping around him, barking excitedly. He bends and ruffles her fur with both hands, kissing the top of her head. Alex jogs up to him and they exchange a few words. Alex runs off with Cass nipping at his heels and Cam shoves his hands in his pockets and walks towards me. I shield my eyes from the sun and smile up at him.

'You ate without me?'

'You're late and we were hungry.'

I plucked up the courage to call him around Christmas time. It – *we* – felt unfinished. I needed, as the Americans call it, some sort of closure. We met for a drink and talked until they started clearing up around us. Cam and I had been together for seven weeks in 1998. Is seven weeks enough time to fall in love? I do believe so. We were lovers derailed by tragedy. I don't know if I knew how much I loved him at the time. I think it was only when I watched him walk away that day fifteen years ago, traumatised and broken, that I realised.

We aren't together. Not officially. We've kissed but not slept together. I'm not ready. Maybe I never will be. But I love his company. He makes me feel at ease. Safe. He listens to me. Listens properly, as if he's interested in what I'm saying, in what I think. He laughs at my jokes as well. In fact, we spend a lot of time laughing. It's nice to have someone to curl up with on the sofa. Someone to make me a cup of tea. Someone who notices what kind of mood I'm in.

Cam sits on the wall beside me and grins. His hair is tousled from the wind and his eyes are glinting as if somebody's lit a fire inside him.

'You look like you had a good morning?' I say.

'Yep.'

'And?'

'Lawrie Mould offered me full-time.'

'As deckhand?'

Cam beamed. 'No. Not on the boat. On shore. His fish agent resigned and he reckons I can handle it. It's a great job. Decent money, holidays, regular hours. He thinks it'll be right up my street.'

'That's great and of course you can handle it. I'm really pleased for you.'

He puts his hand inside his jacket pocket and takes out his cigarettes. He doesn't offer me one. I don't smoke anymore. I haven't since the day I left Nathan.

Cam smiles then looks out over the sea. We sit there for a while and watch Alex and Cass playing on the beach as the seagulls screech. I'm aware of him next to me, the heat of him, his hand resting on the concrete between us. We are nearly touching. I inch my own hand a little closer. My finger brushes his skin and his thumb almost imperceptibly rubs against me.

CHAPTER FIFTY-ONE

Nathan

'Everybody leaves in the end.'

My mother said these words to me twice.

The first time was soon after my father killed himself. That day will haunt me for the rest of my life. The air in my bedroom rang with the echo of the gunshot. Kerensa started screaming. Glass-shattering shrieks which tore up the house. I ran out on to the landing and took the stairs two at a time, heart hammering.

She was in the doorway of his study.

'What is it?' I said, my voice breathless with adrenalin.

She turned, her face white, eyes wide. When she saw me she thrust open her arms as if tied to a crucifix, blocking my view. I craned my neck, ducked and dived, to try and see past her, desperate to know what she was trying to hide.

'No!' Her sharp cry was strangled by tears. 'No, Nate. *No!* Go back to your room. Do you hear me? Now!'

'But I want to see—'

She was sobbing. Begging me not to look. Then Mother appeared, looming over both of us. She pushed Kerensa to one side and I saw him lying there, crumpled on the floor, a gaping bloody hole where the right side of his face should have been.

That's quite a sight for a child to see and the image etched into my mind hasn't dulled one fraction over time.

Kerensa grabbed me and pressed my face into her chest. Her arms wrapped around me and held me to her. I struggled and pulled against her but she held on, whispering words I couldn't hear into my hair.

'Upstairs both of you.' Our mother's voice was cast iron. '*Now!*'

We ran, Kerensa pulling me after her, our feet hammering the stairs, across the landing, into her room. She pulled the door shut and we sat on her bed, holding each other, neither of us speaking for what felt like years.

Everything else is snatched memories. The police arriving. The ambulance. The sounds of people in the house. Mother's shrill voice barking orders at people. We knelt up on the bed. Looked out of the window and down at the people moving about in semi-darkness. There was a stretcher. On it was a huge black bag. There was no sign of my mother and I remember wondering if I'd still get to open my birthday presents. She appeared around midnight. Her silhouette filled the doorway. 'Go to sleep,' she said, her voice dry and flat. 'Everybody leaves in the end.'

A few nights later, I can't remember how many, Kerensa crept into my room. She lifted my bedcovers and climbed in beside me. She was crying. She hadn't stopped. The day after my birthday, I found her sitting under the apple tree, sobbing so hard her body shook like she was having a fit. I worried she might actually cry herself to death. She was a sensitive soul. Gentle and pure.

'Aren't you sad?' she asked through her shuddering sobs.

'Of course,' I said, then pinched myself hard until tears came. 'See?'

But rather than sad I felt angry, angry he didn't care enough about us to stay alive, and angry he was so weak. In the hours which followed his death I grew to despise him.

'Coward,' my mother had said, her voice edged with hatred and disrespect. 'A weak-willed coward.'

Even at thirteen, I knew there was no glory in weakness and cowardice. The only things he left behind, other than his mutilated body and a ruined rug, was a hidden stash of empty bottles and a debt which threatened to bankrupt us. What kind of a husband and father would do that?

I lay in bed with Kerensa, my manufactured tears long dried up, and stared at her beautiful, devastated face in the blue-white moonlight which spilled in through the window.

'Nate,' she whispered, when her sobbing finally stopped.

'Yes?'

'I want you to promise me you'll be different to them. Promise me you'll be happy. You need to find love. You *have* to be happy. Do you understand?'

I'm not sure I did. Not then. Not aged thirteen.

'Whatever you do, make sure you find love, and when you do – are you listening? – when you do find it, do *everything* you can to hold on to it. We aren't going to be like them. Do you hear me? We are going to find love and we're going to hold on to it. We're going to be *happy*.'

'But how will I know?'

'Know what?'

'When I find love?'

She thought for a moment or two. 'You'll know because it

will hit you. Maybe out of the blue. That's what they say, don't they? They say, when you know, you just *know*.'

'Who says it?'

'The people who know about love.' Then her hands squeezed mine. 'Promise me you'll find love and, when you do, you'll never, *ever*, let it go. Promise me.'

I nodded.

'Say it.'

'I promise you.'

She smiled, but it was fleeting. 'Nate?'

'Yes?'

She hesitated. 'I have to go away for a while.'

'What?' Horror hit me full on. 'No! *No*. You can't—'

She put her fingers against my lips. 'I have to. Mother and I are fighting all the time. I hate her. I hate it here. I can't get the image of him out of my head. I need to get away.'

'But what about me?'

Her face twitched, as if some sort of pain had grabbed her, and she was quiet for a few moments. 'I'm sorry,' she said finally. 'It won't be forever. I'll be back, I promise.'

I idolised my sister. She was a mother and father wrapped up in one person. It was Kerensa who read to me when I was small, who kissed me goodnight, who made me laugh behind Mother's back and rolled her eyes when our father came back so drunk he couldn't walk. It was Kernesa who snuck into my room when the shouting and screaming got too loud and covered my ears with her hands. She was the only joy I knew and when she died all the lights went out.

You asked me, Hannah, why I didn't tell you I knew Alex wasn't mine. I thought your question was strange. Because if you knew me at all you'd know. My family was destroyed by scandal. It was destroyed by a weak man, a coward, who allowed his family name to be dragged through the dirt. I vowed at thirteen I'd be nothing like him. The Cardew name would never again be associated with scandal and immorality. How would it look if word got out that I wasn't Alex's father? That I was the type of man who'd take on a philandering wife? That I was a man unable to father my own children? Most men wouldn't have forgiven their wives for what you did, for the lies and the deception. But I'm not most men. You brought a cuckoo into the nest. I could have thrown you both out. But I didn't. And now, looking back, knowing what I know about Alex's father, I understand you so much more. I know what it's like to be damaged and how the darkest things can erode us from within.

I still love you, Hannah.

When you left, I remember thinking how sad you looked. How full of regret. You moved heavily, laboriously, not with the energy of somebody doing something they want to do. I watched you heave your two suitcases to the front door and tried not to picture the empty cupboards upstairs, your creams gone from the bathroom, my dressing gown hanging alone on the hook on our door.

'Where will you go?'

You didn't answer me. Perhaps you didn't trust yourself to speak. Perhaps you knew if you did your resolve would falter.

'With him?'

A flicker of doubt crossed your face. You shook your head. Told me, again, there was nothing between you and Cameron Stewart. But I saw the lie in your eyes. He'd got to you, wheedled his way inside your head, poisoned you against me. Blood pumped faster around my veins. Were you really going through with it? The pain I felt when you opened the door was intense.

'Don't leave me.' Desperation strangled my voice.

For a moment I thought you might stop, turn back, kiss me, and tell me how sorry you were.

But you didn't.

'Goodbye, Nathan.'

The door closed and I was left alone with nothing but my mother's voice ringing around the bricks and flagstones like a tolling bell.

Everybody leaves in the end.

The second time she said those words was when I found her sitting in my father's study with a photograph of my sister in a silver frame on the desk in front of her. She turned and looked at me. No tears. Mouth set with what appeared to be hatred.

'Your sister is dead.' Her clipped words like slivers of ice.

'I don't understand.'

'What's to understand? I told you, didn't I? Everybody leaves in the end.'

And now, here I am, parked in the car park overlooking the beach. You are sitting on the wall, your hair taken by the wind, and you are smiling. I recall the first time I saw you through the bakery window. Your skin clear and fresh, your eyes bright with an innocent joy, reminding me, in that split second, of my sister.

Kerensa was right.

When you know, you just know.

You laugh and I can hear the noise in my head. Then you catch sight of something and wave. And that's when I see him walking across the shingle towards you. Alex runs to him. You smile and when he sits beside you it's all I can do to stop myself screaming. His face is smug and triumphant. He thinks he's won. But he hasn't.

I won't give up, Hannah. I'll bide my time and I'll get you back.

It's not the end. Not yet.

I'll get you back if it's the last thing I do.

ACKNOWLEDGEMENTS

Thank you to my wonderful editor, Kate Mills. You give me the space to breathe and, with your insightful direction and guidance, help make my stories better. Thank you also to the entire HQ team. Without exception, your combined enthusiasm, talent, professionalism and dedication make this journey a pleasure. Thank you to my agent Broo, as always a tower of strength, encouragement and friendship.

Thanks to Dieter Newell for donating to CLIC Sargent and naming 'Young Lawrence Mould'. Generous as ever.

Heartfelt thanks to author and friend Quentin Bates who helped me sort the gunwales from the winches, and provided me with such fabulous anecdotes from his time on the Newlyn trawlers 'back in the day'. Any fishing-related errors are my own. To my early readers – Cos, Sara, Melissa and Charlie – thank you for your kind words, positivity and suggestions. Siany, thank you for your superb observations and constant cheerleading. You are always there for me, even when facing tough times. What a friend you are. Dearest Lucy, thank you for forensically reading such a horrendous early draft of this book and not telling me to burn it forthwith. From patiently discussing initial thoughts, through to brainstorming final drafts, I can't thank you enough. To Hannah, thank you for lending me your name and for offering excellent input at the eleventh hour. Thank you to my 'local crew' who are always there to cheer me on. You know who you are.

I'd like to thank my readers – you, in fact – who make it all worthwhile. Thank you for sharing the ride with me. To the reviewers, bookshops, librarians, festival organisers, and bloggers who help spread the love of books far and wide. You are incredible. Thank you for your unending support.

A massive thank you goes to my writer friends. Numerous and heavenly. You keep me laughing. You keep me company. You keep me sane.

And, lastly, thank you to my family. To Saffie, for making sure my feet are always warm beneath my desk. To the rest of the menagerie, how I love your furry, feathery cuddles. To my three beautiful and brilliant girls, who I love so very, very much. To my parents and sister for your love and support always. And to Chris, to whom this book is dedicated, you make me a better writer and I love you, still and forever. And with who, like Hannah and Cam, I share such perfect memories of the mad late nineties. (But thankfully no body in a boat...)

ONE PLACE. MANY STORIES

Bold, Innovative and
empowering publishing.

FOLLOW US ON:

@HQStories